Acclaim for Kelly Irvin

"*Peace in the Valley* is a beautiful and heart-wrenching exploration of faith, loyalty, and the ties that bind a family and a community together. Kelly Irvin's masterful storytelling pulled me breathlessly into Nora's world, her deep desire to do good, and her struggle to be true to herself and to the man she loves. Full of both sweet and stark details of Amish life, *Peace in the Valley* is realistic and poignant, profound and heartfelt. I highly recommend it!"

—Jennifer Beckstrand, author of *Andrew*

"With a lovely setting, this is a story of hope in the face of trouble and has an endearing heroine and other relatable characters that readers will empathize with."

—*Parkersburg News & Sentinel* on *Mountains of Grace*

"Irvin (*Beneath the Summer Sun*) puts a new spin on the age-old problem of bad things happening to good people in this excellent Amish inspirational . . . Fans of both Amish and inspirational Christian fiction will enjoy this heart-pounding tale of the pain of loss and the joys of love."

—*Publishers Weekly* on *Mountains of Grace*

"Kelly Irvin's *Mountains of Grace* offers a beautiful and emotional journey into the Amish community. Readers will be captivated by a heartwarming tale of forgiveness and finding a renewed faith in God. The story will capture the hearts of those who love the Plain culture and an endearing romance. Once you open this book, you'll be hooked until the last page."

—Amy Clipston, bestselling author of *The Farm Stand*

"Irvin's fun story is simple (like Mary Katherine, who finds 'every day is a blessing and an adventure') but very satisfying."

—*Publishers Weekly* on *Through the Autumn Air*

"Kelly Irvin's *Through the Autumn Air* is a poignant journey of friendship and second chances that will illustrate for readers that God blesses us with a true love for all seasons."

—Amy Clipston, bestselling author of *Room on the Porch Swing*

"This second entry (after *Upon a Spring Breeze*) in Irvin's seasonal series diverges from the typical Amish coming-of-age tale with its focus on more mature protagonists who acutely feel their sense of loss. Fans of the genre seeking a broader variety of stories may find this new offering from [Irvin] more relatable than the usual fare."

—*Library Journal* on *Beneath the Summer Sun*

"Jennie's story will speak to any woman who has dealt with the horror of abuse and the emotional aftermath it carries, as well as readers who have questioned how God can allow such terrible things to happen. The choice Jennie makes to take a chance on love again and to open her heart to God after all she has suffered is brave and hopeful, leaving readers on an uplifting note."

—*RT Book Reviews*, 4-star review of *Beneath the Summer Sun*

"A moving and compelling tale about the power of grace and forgiveness that reminds us how we become strongest in our most broken moments."

—*Library Journal* on *Upon a Spring Breeze*

"Irvin's novel is an engaging story about despair, postnatal depression, God's grace, and second chances."

—*CBA Christian Market* on *Upon a Spring Breeze*

"A warm-hearted novel that is more than a romance, with lovable characters, including two innocent children caught in the red tape of government, and two people willing to risk breaking both the *Englisch* and Amish laws to help in whatever way they can. There are subplots that focus on the struggles of undocumented immigrants."

—*RT Book Reviews*, 4-star review of *The Saddle Maker's Son*

"Irvin has given her audience a continuation of *The Beekeeper's Son* with complicated young characters who must define themselves."

—*RT Book Reviews*, 4-star review of *The Bishop's Son*

"Once I started reading *The Bishop's Son*, it was difficult for me to put it down! This story of struggle, faith, and hope will draw you in to the final page . . . I have read countless stories of Amish men or women doubting their faith. I have never read a storyline quite like this one though. It was narrated with such heart. I was fully invested in Jesse's struggle. No doubt, what Jesse felt is often what modern-day Amish men and women must feel when they are at a crossroads in their faith. The story was brilliantly told and the struggle felt very real."

—Destination Amish

"Something new and delightful in the Amish fiction genre, this story is set in the barren, dusty landscape of Bee County, TX . . . Irvin writes with great insight into the range and depth of human emotion. Her characters are believable and well developed, and her storytelling skills are superb. Recommend to readers who are looking for something a little different in Amish fiction."

—*CBA Retailers + Resources* on *The Beekeeper's Son*

"*The Beekeeper's Son* is so well crafted. Each character is richly layered. I found myself deeply invested in the lives of both the King and Lantz families. I struggled as they struggled, laughed as they laughed—and even cried as they cried . . . This is one of the best novels I have read in the last six months. It's a refreshing read and worth every penny. *The Beekeeper's Son* is a keeper for your bookshelf!"

—Destination Amish

"Kelly Irvin's *The Beekeeper's Son* is a beautiful story of faith, hope, and second chances. Her characters are so real that they feel like old friends. Once you open the book, you won't put it down until you've reached the last page."

—Amy Clipston, bestselling author of *A Gift of Grace*

"*The Beekeeper's Son* is a perfect depiction of how God makes all things beautiful in His way. Rich with vivid descriptions and characters you can immediately relate to, Kelly Irvin's book is a must-read for Amish fans."

—Ruth Reid, bestselling author of *A Miracle of Hope*

"Kelly Irvin writes a moving tale that is sure to delight all fans of Amish fiction. Highly recommended."

—Kathleen Fuller, author of the Hearts of Middlefield and Middlefield Family novels

PEACE
in the
VALLEY

Other Books by Kelly Irvin

Amish of Big Sky Country Novels

Mountains of Grace

A Long Bridge Home

Every Amish Season Novels

Upon a Spring Breeze

Beneath the Summer Sun

Through the Autumn Air

With Winter's First Frost

The Amish of Bee County Novels

The Beekeeper's Son

The Bishop's Son

The Saddle Maker's Son

Stories

A Christmas Visitor in *An Amish Christmas Gift*

Sweeter than Honey in *An Amish Market*

One Sweet Kiss in *An Amish Summer*

Snow Angels in *An Amish Christmas Love*

The Midwife's Dream in *An Amish Heirloom*

Mended Hearts in *An Amish Reunion*

Cakes and Kisses in *An Amish Christmas Bakery*

Candlelight Sweethearts in *An Amish Picnic*

Romantic Suspense

Tell Her No Lies

Over the Line

Closer Than She Knows

Her Every Move (available February 2021)

PEACE

—*in the*—

VALLEY

Amish of Big Sky Country

KELLY IRVIN

ZONDERVAN®

ZONDERVAN

Peace in the Valley

This title is also available as a Zondervan ebook.

This title is also available as a Zondervan audio book.

Requests for information should be addressed to:

Zondervan, *3900 Sparks Dr. SE, Grand Rapids, Michigan 49546*

ISBN 978-0-310-35679-0 (downloadable audio)

Library of Congress Cataloging-in-Publication Data
Names: Irvin, Kelly, author.
Title: Peace in the valley : Amish of big sky country / Kelly Irvin.
Description: Grand Rapids, Michigan : Zondervan, [2020] | Series: Amish of big sky country | Summary: "After a devastating wildfire sweeps through her town, one young Amish woman is shown a different way to practice her faith . . . but will it cost her everything she holds dear?"-- Provided by publisher.
Identifiers: LCCN 2020008303 (print) | LCCN 2020008304 (ebook) | ISBN 9780310356769 (trade paperback) | ISBN 9780310356776 (epub) | ISBN 9780310356790
Subjects: GSAFD: Christian fiction.
Classification: LCC PS3609.R82 P43 2020 (print) | LCC PS3609.R82 (ebook) | DDC 813/.6--dc23
LC record available at https://lccn.loc.gov/2020008303
LC ebook record available at https://lccn.loc.gov/2020008304

Printed in the United States of America

20 21 22 23 24 LSC 10 9 8 7 6 5 4 3

For my Northwest Hills United Methodist Church family.
Thank you for helping me cling to what I
believe and understand why I believe it.

Therefore let us stop passing judgment on one another. Instead, make up your mind not to put any stumbling block or obstacle in the way of a brother or sister.

—Romans 14:13

Deutsch Vocabulary*

ach: *oh*
aenti: *aunt*
Ausband, the: *songbook*
bopli(n): *baby*
bruder: *brother*
daadi: *grandpa*
daed: *father*
danki: *thank you*
dawdy haus: *grandparents' house*
dochder: *daughter*
Englischer: *English or non-Amish*
fehlas: *literally failures, either biblical sin or violations of the Ordnung*
fraa: *wife*
Gmay: *church district*
Gott: God
groossdaadi: *grandpa*
groossmammi: *grandma*
guder mariye: *good morning*
gut: *good*
gut nacht: *good night*
hund: *dog*
jah: *yes*

kaffi: *coffee*
kapp: *prayer cap*
kind: *child*
kinner: *children*
kossin: *cousin*
mammi: *grandma*
mann: *husband*
Meidung: *shunning, excommunication*
mudder: *mother*
nee: *no*
onkel: *uncle*
Ordnung: *written and unwritten rules in an Amish district*
rumspringa: *period of running around*
schweschder: *sister*
suh: *son*
vorsinger: *leader of the choir*
wunderbarr: *wonderful*

* The German dialect spoken by the Amish is not a written language and varies depending on the location and origin of the settlement. These spellings are approximations. Most Amish children learn English after they start school. They also learn High German, which is used in their Sunday services.

Featured Families

Harley and Wilma Beachy

Jeannie (married) · Nora · Amelia (deceased) · James · Atlee · Menno · Seth · Solomon

Grandparents: Jacob and Esther Beachy

Ike and Roseanna Beachy

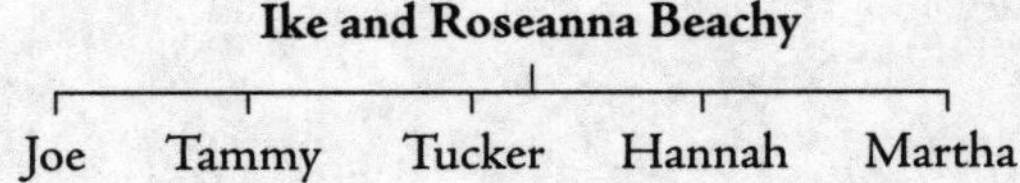

Joe · Tammy · Tucker · Hannah · Martha

Pastor George Brubacher (widower)

Wyatt

Daryl and Jeannie Coblenz

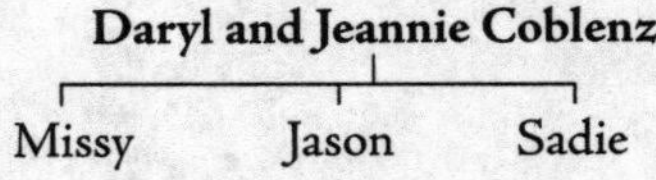

Missy · Jason · Sadie

Jack and Beatrice (Raber) Moser

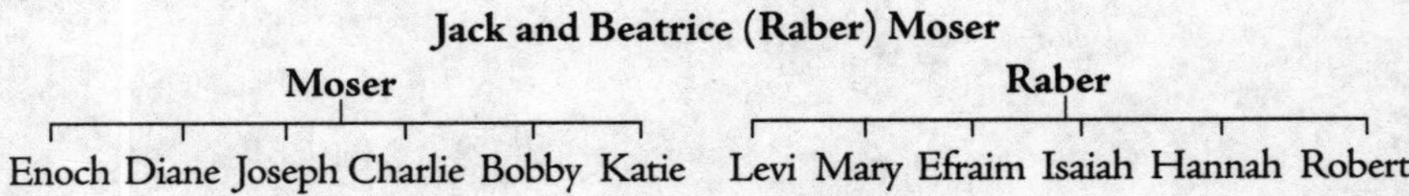

Moser

Enoch · Diane · Joseph · Charlie · Bobby · Katie

Raber

Levi · Mary · Efraim · Isaiah · Hannah · Robert

1

West Kootenai, Montana

A cotton nightgown and a wispy lock of pale-blonde baby hair wouldn't take up much room in the box. Nora Beachy's hand hovered over the only keepsakes that remained to mark the birth of her sister who passed away a few hours after her birth. The wildfire racing through Montana's Kootenai National Forest this Friday before Labor Day weekend might destroy everything in its path—including the home Nora had lived in her whole life. It couldn't, however, take the memory of humming a lullaby to that tiny, strangely silent bundle of sweetness for a few brief moments before returning her to Mother.

Wiping at her face with her sleeve, Nora took a long breath. Her dry throat ached and her lungs burned. The stench of acrid smoke hung in the air. She coughed and gagged. The fire must be getting closer. Moving faster, she laid the nightgown aside and tucked the lock of hair back in its yellowed envelope. She tried to hum her favorite English hymn, "How Great Thou Art." Music usually calmed her. Not today. The biscuits with apple butter she'd eaten for breakfast sloshed in the coffee she'd drank to force them down.

"What are you doing?"

Nora whirled. "You scared me."

Mother stood in the doorway to the bedroom she shared with Father.

"You're supposed to be packing the kitchen."

"We can buy more sponges, clothes soap, and towels." Nora picked up the faded green-and-blue patchwork quilt Grandma Rachel had made as a wedding gift for Mother and Father. She brushed it against her cheek. It smelled like the cedar chest. "Some things can't be replaced."

"Cleaning supplies cost money." Mother crossed the room and took the quilt. She glanced down at the cotton nightgown yellowed with time and tears. "We only have so much room in the wagons and the buggy. Go finish packing the kitchen."

Grandma Rachel's tinkling laughter in the middle of one of her stories about Grandpa's youthful shenanigans sounded in Nora's ears even though Grandma had been gone five years. A picture bobbed in her mind's eye of the way Grandma worried her lower lip as she threaded the needle for another crib quilt for one of the great-grandchildren. "*Jah, Mudder.* I just—"

"Don't be crying over material things. It's not as if we can take them with us when we pass from this life." Mother's wan smile took the edge from her words. Behind silver wire-rimmed glasses, her eyes were bright and teary. "*Gott* will provide everything we truly need."

Nora lifted her chin and straightened her shoulders. Her faith was strong. God could use the fire for her good and the good of every person in its path. That didn't mean she had to like the way lightning had started a fire in the forest, tinderbox dry after a long, hot summer. In a mere twenty-four hours, that fire had consumed stands of magnificent ponderosa pine, Douglas fir, and the homes of the wildlife who lived on fourteen thousand acres of forest north of Lake Koocanusa. "I'm not crying. The smoke is burning my eyes."

It's not my place to ask, I know, but I was just wondering, what is Your plan, Gott?

God's mighty eyebrows surely bumped the highest star in the sky at the temerity of her question.

Don't mind me, Gott.

"It's hard to think we might not have anything to come home to, but people make homes, not furniture." Mother gently tucked the keepsakes into the box and handed it to Nora. "We'll make room on the wagon for these and for your *groossdaadi*'s Bible."

Her dishwater-chapped fingers grazed Nora's hand. "You have a soft heart, *Dochder*. Never change."

Mother could read her mind. Comforted by the thought, Nora trotted into the front room, where she added the Bible, along with Father's German-English one, to the box. As an afterthought she snatched the box of checkers that kept her brothers busy on many icy winter nights. In the kitchen she added the lighter box to one filled with canned goods from the cellar. She glanced around the room. Canning pickles, baking bread, making gingerbread men and popcorn balls for Christmas. The smell of bacon, elk sausage, and pancakes on a snow-blanketed winter morning. Those were the memories that made a house a home.

A fire couldn't take those memories.

But it could take future ones. For two years she and Levi Raber had been saving their money to buy a small plot of land near his parents' property. Then they could get married. Two years of scrimping and saving her checks from the Kootenai General Store. Two years of stolen kisses, sweet hugs, and a growing hunger for more.

If the fire took the house . . . No, she wouldn't think about that.

Straining under the weight of the boxes, she tramped down the hall and out the front door into a frantic beehive of activity as her father and five brothers set up sprinklers and soaked the house, wood shop, and barn in hopes of staving off fire damage.

Smoke hung like fog in the air. The boys had donned respirators. They looked like strange aliens invading the farm with soaker hoses as weapons. Another thought she wouldn't share with her parents. They found her flights of fancy a bit too fanciful at times.

Father slid his respirator back and let it rest on his silver curls. His brown eyes were bloodshot and his lined face wet with dirty sweat. "Get your mudder. It's time for you to leave for Rexford."

The Dublins, owners of the store in Rexford, had offered them use of an RV on the other side of Lake Koocanusa. But first they had to travel nearly twenty miles from West Kootenai across the longest, highest span bridge in the state and north on Highway 37 to Rexford.

It would be a long drive with an overloaded wagon, two small boys, and a dog. They'd driven that road hundreds of times. Now the path seemed murky with smoke and uncertainty.

"Not without you and the boys." The words were out before she could test them for impertinence. "I mean, shouldn't we stick together?"

"We need to soak everything for as long as possible." Father tugged the boxes from Nora. "Take the little ones and go."

He turned and called to Solomon and Seth, nine and five years old respectively. After Amelia passed, God had blessed Mother and Father with five more boys, but Jeannie, now married and the mother of her own daughters, and Nora were their only girls.

Dust kicked up on the road. A truck or a car headed their way. Coming fast. Nora's stomach clenched. Not more bad news?

A siren screamed, a foreign sound in this part of God's country. Father whirled and headed toward the road. Nora followed. A filthy Lincoln County sheriff's SUV roared into the driveway and halted within inches of the first wagon. Sheriff Emmett Brody left the engine running and hauled his bulky body from the truck the second it came to a full stop.

His usual hearty smile was missing. "You folks have to go now." His chest heaving as if he'd been running in the thin air of high altitudes, he pointed at the mountains behind them. "It's coming fast. We're telling everyone to get out now."

"You said we had four or five hours." Father clutched the hose. The look on his face was foreign, as if rooted in his own despair but clinging to hope. "It hasn't been two hours yet."

"The wind picked up." Emmett pulled a can of spray paint from the SUV's front seat. "It's moving faster than we figured it would, and it didn't slow down in the meadows. Time to go."

"What about the others? Is everyone else out?" Nora edged closer to the sheriff. "All the Plain families, I mean."

Not that she didn't care about the English families. They were good neighbors and good friends, but coming right out and asking about Levi specifically would raise eyebrows—especially those thick bushy ones above her father's eyes.

"She wants to know about Levi." James, brother number one, elbowed her with a silly grin that came and went. Leave it to him to make light in the midst of an impending inferno. "Is her special friend safe?"

"Hush, *Suh*." Father frowned. "This isn't the time."

"The other families are all on the road." His fair skin ruddy with heat, Emmett removed his white cowboy hat and slicked down sparse carrot-orange hair with an impatient gesture. "You're my last stop."

Levi was on the road. To where? Some families would go to Rexford, others to Eureka, or even farther if they had family in Libby or St. Ignatius.

Libby. Her parents would never go there. Even though they had more family in the Eagle Valley Amish Ministries district than they did in Kootenai.

Mother tottered through the front door with two bulging suitcases. "What is it, Harley? What's happened?"

"We have to go." The words sounded stuck in Father's throat.

"Is there anyone else in the house?" Emmett shook the can of spray paint. "Get everyone out."

"We're out. What are you doing with the paint?"

"That's how we know who's gone and who's staying."

"We can stay?" Father's gaze went to the house. "I could stay and keep the water going."

"No, I didn't mean that." Emmett clapped Father on the shoulder. "I know everything in your gut is telling you to hang on. But you gotta go. Think of your kids. Do you want to leave them fatherless over a bunch of buildings that can be rebuilt? We have a few idiot folks who refused to leave, but they had to sign a form saying they stay at their own risk. No one will rescue them. Just take a good look and tell me it isn't time to go."

In unison they turned. Nora's breath caught in her throat. Her hands came up to her face. A raging vortex of angry flames hurled themselves down the mountain, decimating everything in their path. They headed straight for Kootenai.

Straight for their home.

"*Fraa,* go. Suhs, in the buggy." Father tucked Solomon onto the back of the wagon. Seth scrambled in next to him. Stinker, the no-good, lazy dog loved by all, planted himself between them.

Emmett spray painted a big fat zero on the sidewalk. "Godspeed."

2

The head count refused to come out right. Stifling a cough, Levi Raber shoved his straw hat back and tried again. The Lincoln County deputy had stopped only long enough to say they had to evacuate immediately. The fire roared down the mountainside, devouring every living thing in its path, and somehow Levi couldn't keep track of his siblings. All eleven of them.

Ignoring the billowing smoke that burned his eyes and throat, he counted again. Five boys ripped off respirators, dropped hoses, and ran to the first wagon. Three girls shoved last-minute items into a second wagon and climbed aboard. Bobby played in the mud. Of course, what Bobby did, Katie did as well. At three and two, they were inseparable. Mudder scooped them up, mud pies and all, and handed them to Mary and Diane. Levi lifted his finger and counted again.

Still one missing.

Charlie.

At five, Levi's brother already had a reputation for being a wanderer. Now was not the time to take a hike to the pond to go fishing or try to catch tadpoles to put in a jar. Levi surveyed the yard. No sign of the little squirt. "Mudder, where's Charlie?"

Her dark-rimmed glasses perched in the midst of beads of sweat on her long nose, Mother looked around. Her placid expression disappeared. She raised her index finger and began to count. "*Ach*, that child. He was packing the little ones' clothes—at least he was supposed to be." Barely contained desperation drenched her words. "We need to find him right now."

"I'll get him."

"He fussed about Gussy when I told him to pack." She whirled toward the house. "I'll check the bedrooms one more time."

"We can all look." Diane started to hand Katie to Mary. "It'll be faster."

"*Nee*. Everybody stay where you are. We'll end up searching for you too."

Gussy would not be in the house. The dog had showed up one day and invited herself to stay—to the kids' delight. Mother only saw another mouth to feed. Gussy liked to eat—a lot. The mutt was as round as she was tall. Mother had stopped complaining when she scared off a bear one day the previous winter when the kids were playing in the yard. Now she occasionally patted Gussy's head and said, "*Gut hund*," when she thought no one would notice.

In the time after his father died—before Jack entered the picture—Levi had become accustomed to riding herd on his five younger siblings. He had been fourteen and old enough to be the man of the house. Then Jack showed up and brought his three with him, and now he and Mother had added three to the family.

Knowing Charlie, he was hiding in the barn. He'd made it clear he didn't want to leave Kootenai. He was sure he would be fine. Charlie had that kind of confidence. His sweet optimism appealed to Levi. His little brother had the right attitude—light in the dark.

Levi slid the doors open. "Come on, Charlie, we have to go. Deputy Trudeau says the fire is coming. I know you want to stay, but the stuff here doesn't matter. As long as we stay together, we'll be fine."

"I can't. I have to stay." Charlie's high voice floated from the dark interior.

Can't was different from *won't*. "What do you mean you can't?"

"Come see."

Levi strode through the barn to the last stall where Charlie knelt in the straw, his back to the door. "This is no time for argument. Get up before I throw you over my shoulder and cart you out of here."

"I can't."

"Charlie—"

"Look." Charlie scooted back. "Puppies."

Gussy hadn't been fat. She'd been in a family way. Five tiny, roly-poly puppies squirmed and mewled next to her. They looked nothing like their butterscotch-colored mom. Dad must've been dark brown and black. Levi dropped to his knees. "They're beautiful."

"Aren't they?" Charlie grinned and reached for the closest one. Gussy growled. "Oops, it's okay. I won't hurt them."

Not great timing, but it was fortuitous that Charlie found them. They would get mama dog and five newborn puppies into one of the wagons. And do it quickly. *"Where there's a will, there's a way,"* Father would say. They couldn't be left behind. "Hurry. Get a box. Now." Levi patted Gussy's head. "Gut job, hund, but it would've been nice if you'd picked a better time."

"Did you find him?" Jack's gravelly voice boomed. "We have to move."

"Gussy had puppies." Charlie jumped up and ran to his father. His arms wrapped around his dad's middle. "Five of them. We have puppies, *Daed*."

"We'll have to move them. We can't leave them in the path of the fire."

"We don't have time or room for puppies." Jack scooped up Charlie and did an about-face. "The fire's on top of us."

"Get everyone out of here." Levi raced after him. "I'll use my buggy to bring the dogs."

"Nee, it's not worth the risk." His voice hoarse—whether from smoke or emotion—Jack picked up his pace. "I won't risk your lives for some stray dogs."

Gussy hadn't been a stray for a long time. She was a full-fledged member of the family.

"We can't leave Gussy." Sobbing, Charlie struggled in his father's arms. "I'm not going. I'm not going. I'm not leaving the puppies."

Jack tightened his grip on the boy. "I'm sorry, *kind*. There's no time." He tossed him into his brother's arms in the first wagon. "Hang on to him. Do not let him get down."

Charlie was old enough to know better than to argue with his father, but his sobs grew. "Levi, don't let the puppies die. Don't let Gussy die."

"I'm right behind you." Levi dashed past his stepfather. There had to be one big box left somewhere in the house. "Go, just go!"

"Levi, get in the buggy." Mother already had her wagon turned around, facing the road. Jack climbed in the second one and took the lead. Efraim, brother number two, had charge of the family buggy. "I don't want to be separated."

"I'll catch up. Go, go!"

By the time Levi came out of the house with a ragged blanket found under the kitchen sink and the biggest empty box he could find, they were gone. Chester, his Haflinger, stomped his hooves, tossed his flaxen tail, and whinnied. The whites of his eyes flashed. Levi ran past him without stopping. "I know, I know, I'm coming."

He refused to look back. It would do no good to see how fast the fire traveled. It ate up terrain like an insatiable monster.

He raced into the barn and laid the box next to Gussy. The dog raised her head and whined. "Jah, well, it doesn't make me happy either. You can trust me, friend. I promise."

By the time he had convinced Gussy to trust him with her new babies, smoke filled the barn. Every breath hurt. He hurtled through the doors into a sea of fog. The smell had changed. It was no longer simply burnt wood and a forest floor of decomposing leaves and plants. The fire had moved on to consume houses.

Coughing, his chest tight, his eyes burning, Levi shoved the box into the buggy's backseat and hauled himself aboard. "Go, Chester, go."

Only then did he look back.

The hungry monster had arrived.

3

Rexford, Montana

RVs appeared enormous when they passed a buggy on the road, but crowd an Amish family of eight, including five growing boys, into one and claustrophobia set in. Nora squeezed past James and Atlee, who were hooting over the miniature stove, and bumped her hip on a Formica-topped table that might comfortably seat four. Seth and Solomon were busy arguing over who would sleep in the top bunk bed, while Menno tried to figure out how to turn the sofa into a double bed. Bedlam reigned.

The smile Mother had managed to hang on to through the long drive to Rexford, the stop at the Dublins' store, and their first view of the RV disappeared. The deepening wrinkles on her forehead suggested a stern rebuke was in the works.

"Maybe we should cook burgers for supper outside. There's a campfire ban, but we can set up the Coleman stove." Nora motioned toward the boxes of groceries that covered the table. "There's really not room to cook in here. It'll cool off when the sun goes down. We can make fry pies. It'll be like camping. We love camping. We could even go fishing tomorrow."

Camping, fishing, hiking, hunting—the stuff of which Montana summers were made. Why would anyone live anywhere else?

"You're right." Mother mustered a semblance of her old smile. "It was nice of Terry and his fraa to offer us this place. We'll make the best of it. First things first—the boys can set up tents outside. They can sleep out there."

"Aww—"

"No discussion." Father stood in the driver's compartment, a giant who didn't know quite where to put his enormous hands or his size fourteen steel-toed work boots. "Nora's right. It's all about attitude. We're safe. We have a roof over our heads. We have food to eat."

Father agreed with her. Nora couldn't contain her own smile. "I'll set up the stove on the picnic table and start unpacking."

"Hello, hello." Jeannie stuck her head through the door and started up the stairs into the RV. "Do you have room for a few more folks?"

A few more, as in Jeannie, baby Sadie, two-year-old Jason, three-year-old Missy, and Jeannie's six-foot-four beanstalk husband, Daryl.

The more the merrier.

"You made it." Mother scooched past Nora, James, Atlee, Menno, Seth, and Solomon before she finally reached her oldest daughter. "Is everyone all right?"

Jeannie, once a slender teenager—the exact opposite of Nora, who had always been the plump one—still had the roundness of childbearing about her. Plus the exhaustion that went with having a preemie born at a Missoula hospital and coming home to two toddlers in various stages of potty training. Her face was peaked, her blue eyes bloodshot, and her dress wrinkled. She seemed older than twenty-four.

"We're doing fine." Jeannie attempted a smile, but it didn't amount to much. "But Sadie isn't breathing so good. It worries me. All the smoke in the air has to be hard on her lungs."

"All the boys out. Out, everyone, out." Mother shooed the majority of the RV's occupants into the great outdoors. "Get busy out there while the womenfolk talk."

His expression relieved, Daryl ducked his head as if fearful of hitting it on the ceiling. He scooped up Jason and led the charge from the RV.

Nora took her sister's precious burden. Sadie's breathing sounded labored, but her eyes were bright and curious as she stared up at her aunt. At three months she was still a tiny mite who tucked easily into the crook of Nora's arm. Nora inhaled baby smells of spit-up and diaper rash cream. Heavenly scents. "Aren't you the sweetest niece a girl could have?"

Sadie crowed and shook her fists in apparent agreement. A second later, she sneezed and croaked a halfhearted cry. "Ach, you poor thing. It's okay, sweet pea. This nasty smoke makes all of us cranky."

What would it be like to have her own baby? Levi's baby. The thought sent heat through her. Not thinking about the how of getting a baby was impossible. If only she could ask Jeannie about it. She had six years of marriage behind her and three children. She was an expert. Plain folks didn't talk about these things. Yet nothing could be sweeter than to hold a baby created in love by a husband and wife.

Someday, God willing, she would know. Until then she could sow the joy by being the best aunt ever. She settled on the undersized couch and made room for her sister. "Have you taken her to the clinic?"

"Yesterday. The doctor recommended we head south, away from the smoke. But how could I do that with the other *boplin*?" Jeannie rubbed her eyes. Her bun of blonde hair was lopsided and peeking out from under her crooked *kapp*. Her hands and lips were chapped. "Daryl has to keep working. By November he won't have a lot of work. We only have September and October left."

The demand for cabin kits and building construction tapered

off when summer ended, along with lumber production and sawmill operations. Everything died completely during the long, snowy winter months. They all knew what a struggle finances could be during Montana winters. Families had to stretch their savings and their canned goods for months.

"You can stay here with us." Mother smoothed her apron with restless fingers. "We're putting the boys in tents. Your little ones can share a bunk bed."

"I talked to *Mammi*."

Nora stopped tickling Sadie's peaches-and-cream cheeks. "You called *Groossmammi* Esther?"

Phone calls were rare in their district, but calls to the Libby folks were nonexistent.

"She left a message at the phone shack. I called her back." Jeannie responded before Mother could. "She wanted to know when they would get to see the bopli. Sadie's three months old, and they haven't held her yet."

"They could've come to the hospital when she was born." Mother's scowl grew. "They wouldn't even need a driver."

The fact that Grandpa Beachy had applied for and received a driver's license at a mere sixty-four years of age had been a topic of conversation chewed up one side and down the other for weeks. Now almost seventy, he occasionally visited his grandkids in Kootenai, driving a beat-up tan minivan missing part of its bumper. He refused to say how or when the bumper went missing, but theories abounded. His thick, black-rimmed glasses might be a hint.

"*Daadi* and Mammi are getting old." Sadness pinched Jeannie's cheeks. As if sensing her distress, Missy crawled into her lap and patted her face. Jeannie wrapped her arms around her daughter and squeezed in a mommy-size hug. "We don't know when Gott will take them home. I can't see how it would hurt to spend some time with them."

"You know why it would hurt." Father's voice trumpeted from the door where he stood, his broad shoulders filling its frame. "They've fallen away from their Plain beliefs. They can hardly call themselves Plain anymore."

"But it's not contagious." Seeing defeat on her sister's face, Nora jumped in. She'd spent many hours gnawing on this thorny issue as she hiked, hunted, baked, cleaned house, and stocked shelves at the store. Her grandparents, her aunt and uncle, her cousins—they all lived a different life only sixty-four miles away in a district on the outskirts of Libby. "If we know what we believe, we shouldn't worry about being swayed by the way they think."

Exactly how the way they thought differed remained a mystery to Nora. No one really said. The difference in the way they lived was more obvious. For the last fifteen years they'd shed almost every aspect of their Amish faith. They drove cars and trucks. Some of them wore English clothes. Some had electricity in their houses. They had a church building. Yet they still called themselves Amish.

If they believed in the same God and His Son, Jesus Christ, they believed the same as the Kootenai Plain folks. Didn't they?

"We're to keep ourselves apart from the world." His brown eyes dark with disapproval, Father clomped to the sacks on the slim strip of cabinet between the sink and stove. "I need a bandage for Seth. He caught his finger in the tent poles."

The conversation was over as quickly as it had begun—to Father's way of thinking.

"The doctor says Sadie's lungs are still weak. She came a month early, and they were underdeveloped." Her forehead wrinkled with worry, Jeannie absently straightened Missy's tiny kapp. "Then she had the RSV. Now there's all this smoke."

"I know it's been an uphill battle, but she's gaining." The lines fell away from Father's face. He leaned down and planted a kiss on

Sadie's forehead. "She's a strong girl, made of sturdy stock. She'll be fine."

Sadie gurgled. Her tiny lips formed an O, as if she wanted to return her grandpa's kiss. Instead, she coughed and gasped for air. "It's okay, bopli, you're fine." Nora rubbed her back until the coughing subsided. "You're fine."

"The doctor wants her away from the smoke." Jeannie tugged the strings of her kapp from Missy's plump fingers. "Mammi offered for us to stay with them until the fire is contained and we're able to get back into Kootenai."

Silence ensued for several beats. Mother and Father exchanged glances. Mother opened her mouth. Father shook his head. She leaned back in her chair.

Father picked up Missy. "Let me take this little whippersnapper outside. Solomon will play with her and Jason. You can put Sadie down for a nap while we eat burgers."

"Daed?"

"You are a married woman. It's not for me to say what you'll do. That is between you and your *mann*."

"But your opinion matters to Daryl and me."

"I understand it would be best for the bopli's health." His gaze bounced to Nora and Sadie, then back to Jeannie. "But I worry more about your soul than your body. Hers too."

"Let me go with them. To help her take care of the boplin." The words flew from Nora's mouth before her thoughts were fully formed. The fire had created a chance for her to visit Grandma, Grandpa, and her cousins, and a chance to spread her wings. She'd never gone anywhere without her parents in her whole life. The fire might offer one small silver lining—an adventure. From the mountains to the valley. The idea took root and sprouted. "The RV is too small for all of us. Going to Libby means fewer bodies and fewer mouths to feed. Jeannie needs our help. She's a mess."

"Danki, Schweschder." Her smile rueful, Jeannie smoothed her wrinkled apron to no effect. "Mudder needs you. You're the only dochder she has to help with the cooking and the wash and the cleaning."

"I'm capable of taking care of my family." Mother's eyebrows sprang up. "But that's not our concern—"

"No, indeed, it is not." His weather-beaten face stony, Father crossed his arms. His gaze bore into his oldest child. "Nothing is more important than the living hope of eternal salvation. Not even life itself. I'd rather we burn in this earthly fire than in the fires of hell."

No one replied. How could they?

A chill raced through Nora. Not even the stuffy, airless heat of the RV could stifle it. Her father rarely spoke of faith. The *Ordnung* forbade Sunday school or small group Bible study. He led the Lord's Prayer at the beginning and end of each day. Sometimes when they gathered before bed, he recited prayers from *The Prayer Book for Earnest Christians*. Prayer at mealtime was silent.

What Nora knew about their faith she learned in the long sermons at church and in baptism classes where they'd studied the Dordrecht Confession of Faith's eighteen articles—many of which she didn't understand. The bottom line, according to Levi, who was baptized with her, was to follow Jesus' teachings and do what He did. Be humble, obedient, patient, uncomplaining, and self-sacrificing. Die to self. Whatever that meant.

Her sister's consternation bowed her shoulders. *It's okay.* Nora tried to telegraph her support. Sadie would have her fresh air, and Nora would have her adventure. "Is it possible we can have an effect on them, instead of the other way around?" She ventured the words softly, with no challenge. "Has there been any thought of that?"

"It's not our place to judge. We offer a witness by the way we live. Do you think the elders of our district haven't prayed for the will of Gott in these fifteen years since your *onkel* and *aenti* left us and my daed and mudder followed them? They chose this new way of worship and living. They're barely recognizable as Plain."

"But they're still family."

"They're family who are no longer allowed to worship with us. That we're allowed to visit back and forth is more than some Plain *Gmays* would allow."

"If Nora could go with us to help with the boplin, I would feel better." Jeannie's imploring gaze went to Mother. "We have to go. I can't risk staying here with Sadie. Nora and I will keep each other on the straight and narrow. Daryl too. With my sister at my side, I know we'll be fine. Nora's faith is unsinkable."

A warm wave of affection flowed over Nora. Jeannie never said much, but being the only two girls in a herd of boys had drawn them together in a tight bundle. The loss of baby Amelia had brought them closer, especially when no other girls followed. Jeannie and Nora tag-teamed household chores, including cooking, baking, mending, sewing new clothes, washing dishes, washing clothes, cleaning the house, planting their gardens, and mowing the yard. When Jeannie married at eighteen, everything had changed. Nora had her friends Christine Mast and Mercy Yoder, but it wasn't the same as having someone to curl up with on the bed and share secrets after everyone else was asleep. She smiled at her sister. Jeannie smiled back.

I missed you, too, the smile said.

With three babies in six years, she surely didn't have time to miss Nora, but now Nora could help her. "It's only until the fire is contained. The smoke will clear." Nora tilted Sadie so Father could see her angelic face. She responded, as if on cue, with a huge yawn followed by a sleepy sigh. "We can't take a chance with her poor lungs, can we?"

Father snatched a bandage and a tube of B & W ointment from

the first aid kit. It seemed he wouldn't respond. At the door he looked back. "Your mudder and I will talk some more about it."

That surely meant the answer was yes. If it was no, he would say so flat out. Father lived in a black-and-white world. His world had no room for Amish folks who weren't quite Amish anymore. No room for Plain girls who wore lime-green T-shirts and jeans or Plain boys who played guitar and sang English rock songs by groups with names like the Beatles and Rolling Stones.

Nora handed Sadie to Mother, who immediately cooed and clucked over her youngest grandchild. Jeannie pulled Nora into a hug. "I think that means jah," she whispered. "I hope it does. I've been sick with worry."

"I can hear you." Mother lifted Sadie up and sniffed. "Whew, you need a diaper change, little one."

"Do you think the answer is jah?"

Her knees cracking, Mother stood and rummaged through Jeannie's bags with her free hand until she found the diapers. "I think your daed will pray hard and long. Then he'll say jah, because he will be thinking of Sadie first. You can think of Sadie first, too, but you must also think of every soul who will be touched by what you see and hear in Libby. You must not be swayed."

"We've both been baptized," Nora pointed out. "We're committed to our faith."

"So had your onkel Ike and aenti Roseanna. Yet they chose to go another direction and take Daadi and Mammi with them." Worry lines joined the sun-kissed crow's feet around Mother's eyes. Her full lips thinned into a frown. "Don't be fooled by their talk of freedom. Their kind of freedom isn't really free."

Nora exchanged glances with Jeannie. Her sister's raised eyebrows indicated she had no idea what Mother meant either. Nora summoned a placating smile. "Don't worry, Mudder. We'll be fine."

Mother didn't return the smile. Nor did she look convinced.

4

The bullfrogs and crickets took turns serenading the breathless, still night. The noise, the stuffy air, and the lumpy ground under Nora's sleeping bag conspired to keep her wide awake. She rolled over for the third time and stared into the darkness.

Growing up, she loved sleeping in a tent. When Mother had offered the beds to Daryl, Jeannie, and their children, Nora had been happy to give up her bunk bed for the little ones. She loved camping. But this wasn't camping. No, they'd fled for their lives, leaving behind most of their worldly possessions. They could do without them. She couldn't do without her family.

Or her friends. Mercy and Christine were somewhere in the park. But where? They needed a meeting ASAP. That's what they called it when they needed to talk, mostly about the men in their lives. Now would be a good time for a cell phone. They could call or text. Wouldn't technology bring them closer together in this case? When they all lived within rock-throwing distance in Kootenai, it didn't matter. Now it mattered.

Mother and Father would surely have some way to debunk such outlandish thinking.

And Levi. Where was Levi?

She sat up and wiped her hair from her face. It was no use. Sleep would not come. Not with the unknown, a tunnel from which no light shone, facing her come morning. Her parents had agreed. She would accompany Jeannie and her family to Libby, but only until the smoke subsided.

Somehow she had to get word to Levi. Their plan had been for her to be in Rexford. He could visit from Eureka. They would be separated for the first time since they began courting. He wouldn't be happy. She would miss him, but it was an opportunity to be on her own—maybe for the last time before she married and bowed to her husband's wishes.

The chance to visit at length with Grandma and Grandpa for the first time in years was a gift even if it came courtesy of a destructive wildfire. It had been at least a year since she'd seen either of them. Grandpa drove up to the house in his minivan. Seth and Solomon went running. The boys crowded him. He produced Tootsie Pops and lemon drops, his favorite candies.

"I can't believe how much you've grown. You're the spitting image of Mammi at that age." He never held back on the hugs. Her ribs hurt afterward. "You have her dark-blue eyes and her perky nose."

How could he be bad? He liked to fish for salmon at Lake Koocanusa and take them for walks on the HooDoo Trail. He told stories about Father when he was their age. He did all the things grandpas did. Except worship like Father thought he should.

The same old question floated to the top. Did God care what they wore or whether a car was parked in the driveway?

Better to keep those thoughts to herself. She'd learned that the hard way. As deacon and their baptism teacher, Noah Duncan had been horrified when she'd asked what would happen if they decided to use electricity like the Eagle Valley Amish in Libby.

"They're not Plain. Not anymore."

And that had been that. Noah's expression had told her to zip her lips and mind her elders.

So she had. Now she would learn firsthand what bogeyman

lurked behind her estranged family's wayward worship. Or was it Beelzebub?

Nora tried humming again. Filling her head with music blocked out all the ifs, ands, and buts that kept her from sleeping. "Amazing Grace" was a good one or "How Great Thou Art," her favorite.

Humming, she lay down and wiggled onto her side.

"*Pssst, pssst*. Nora. Nora?"

The whisper boomed like a shout in the night.

Nora sat straight up. "Levi?"

If it was Levi, he had the wrong tent.

"What are you doing here?" James's deep bass, so like Father's, carried across the campground. "It's the middle of the night."

"It's only ten." It would take a lot more than skinny James to intimidate Levi. They were the same height, but Levi's barrel-chested body would be an immovable object in an avalanche. "I didn't mean to wake you."

Her fingers all thumbs, Nora hurriedly wrapped her hair in a bun and slapped her kapp on top in a haphazard mess. She unzipped the pup tent and crawled out. "Hush, you'll wake the *kinner*. It's only Levi, James."

A flashlight directed at Levi, James stood outside the tent he shared with the other boys. Levi had one hand to his forehead to shield his eyes.

The dark, starless, smoke-filled night hid her brother's expression. Surely he understood. He had his own special friend out there somewhere. Eureka. St. Ignatius. Lewistown. Nora had no idea where Lilly Shrock's family would go, but the feeling in the pit of his stomach in this topsy-turvy world would be the same. "We just want to talk for a minute or two."

James grunted. After a second, he lowered the flashlight. Its beam bounced across the cement parking pad. "Don't go far." His begrudging tone didn't match the words. "I'll be right here."

And Father is right here. The unspoken words resounded more loudly than those he chose to express.

Levi didn't speak. He turned and shone a flashlight on the path that led from the RV pad to the parking lot and beyond.

Together they crossed the asphalt, ducked between two trucks, and picked up the hard-packed dirt trail that led to the lake. He glanced back, but the dark hid his expression.

"I should've waited, but I wasn't sure if you were staying here or moving on to Eureka tomorrow." His hand came out. Nora took it. They moved forward together. "I know it's wrong to worry, but when I couldn't come by your house, all I could think about was where you were. I stopped at the store, and Terry told me he loaned the RV to your family. I was so relieved."

"I was lying in my tent thinking about you, and now you're here." The words sounded awkward when spoken aloud, but they were true. "None of this seems real. The fire, being here at the lake, you appearing when I needed you. It seems like a dream."

Levi stopped so abruptly she bumped into him. "You needed me?"

"I did."

His fingers squeezed hers.

Nora leaned closer. Levi smelled of long days and hard work. She wanted to bottle the scent and keep it with her when he was far away.

"It's not a dream. I'm here." He leaned in and caught her in a hard kiss. His lips moved from her mouth to her cheek and her neck. She ceased to breathe. His hands cupped her face. "It does my heart gut to know you need me."

"Always." She staggered back a step. Her legs seemed to melt under her. The fire on the mountains must feel like the one on her skin. Levi always had that effect. From their first kiss the first time he gave her a ride home from a singing when they were both sixteen. Did other girls kiss so early in courting? Mercy and Christine didn't, but her best friends since toddlerhood had egged her on when she told them about Levi's freely given kisses and hugs. "Where are we going?"

"There's a spot close to the water. No one will be there at this hour." His arm tight around her shoulders, Levi guided her toward the spot. "There are no stars tonight, but the frogs will provide music for us."

Just as they had on their horseback rides and hikes taken during their *rumspringa*. Levi claimed they were both part mountain goat. Nora preferred bobcat.

They wove between picnic tables, grills, and campfire circles until they reached the lake's shore. The sound of the water lapping against the rocky outlet calmed Nora's sore spirit. The smell of wet moss, fish, and rotting leaves brought waves of memories with it. Family camping trips smelled like that. Carefree childhood smelled like that.

Levi brushed off a boulder just the right size for two and plopped down. "Have a seat."

With pleasure. Was it wrong to be so happy to see a mere man? She didn't need a light to know what he looked like. She had memorized him head to toe. He felt solid when she hugged him. Their bodies fit together perfectly when she let herself relax against him. His tightly curled brown hair hung below his straw hat when he needed a haircut, which was often.

His brown eyes turned darker in his tanned face when someone irritated him—like his many younger brothers and sisters—and warm as a summer sky when his face hovered over hers, ready to deliver another sweet kiss. Nora eased onto the rock and wiggled closer. His hand took up residence with hers again. She rubbed her fingers over familiar calluses. "I'm so glad to see you. I was afraid we'd miss each other and I wouldn't know where you were."

"We're camping nearby."

"All fourteen of you?"

"We're packed like sardines into the tents." Levi punctuated the words with a half snort, half grunt. "But it's only until tomorrow. Jack has *Englischer* friends in Eureka. They have a rental house they're letting us use. Gott provides for our needs."

That he managed to say Jack's name without a hint of sarcasm reflected how hard Levi had worked to accept his stepfather's place in the family he'd inherited when he married Levi's mother a year after Levi's dad died in a buggy accident.

"We got caught up in a long line of buggies and wagons. It took us forever to get here. Did you have any trouble?"

"It took a while, but I was farther back. I had precious cargo."

Precious cargo? "You took the little ones, then?"

"Nee. Gussy had puppies."

"I'm glad they're okay and you're okay."

"Me too. Jack wanted me to leave the hunds, but I couldn't."

"Of course not."

"I understand why he felt we should hurry, but Gussy having brand-new puppies seemed like a sign from God." Levi smiled and shrugged. "New life comes even amid destruction. Life goes on."

"You always see the best in every situation. Even with Jack."

"Not really. I try, but some days I'd like to tell him what I really think of him. I just don't want to hurt my mudder."

"He knows what's in your heart. No one is perfect."

They were silent for a few moments. The lapping of the water and the soft breeze humming through the tree branches soothed. Nora closed her eyes. She had to ask. "Do you think our house will still be there?"

They thought of the house on three acres of land on the edge of Kootenai as their house because they'd spent two years saving for it. The owner was in no hurry to sell it. He'd retired and moved into Eureka because of his health. An English couple rented it.

They could decide at any time to buy it.

"Gott has a plan for us. The plan will unfold. His will be done. If it's not that house, it will be another one. I have no doubt of that." Levi dropped a kiss on her forehead. "Whatever happens, we'll be together—eventually."

Levi's faith never faltered. Another quality to be treasured. The part about being together no matter what sounded good. The *eventually,* not so much. "Even if that plan separates us?"

Levi leaned back and studied her. Even in the darkness, his assurance glowed. He believed, and so should she. His fingers brushed her cheek. The simple touch sent tingling heat through her entire body. She snuggled closer. He laid his head on hers. "Your hair's falling down." His voice dropped to a whisper. "It's so blonde and soft. I like it."

A hot flush replaced the tingling. Nora squeezed her eyes shut. The light weight of the kapp disappeared. His hands ran through her long hair, freeing it to tumble down her back to her waist. Small, feathery kisses touched her forehead and then her nose as he tipped her head back. His mouth covered hers. She slid her arms around his neck. She could die without complaint at this moment of sheer happiness.

His hands ran down her back to her waist. She took them in her own and leaned back. "Levi."

"I know." He scooted away. "You are my temptation."

"We could marry now. We don't have to wait."

"And live with your family? Or better yet, mine?"

"Daed likes you."

"I like him, and I'm honored that he likes me." Levi's sigh spoke of his desire for patience in trying circumstances. "I'm twenty years old. I don't want to start out married life like a child still living under his parents' roof. Our house will survive. Another year and we'll have enough money to pay for the property outright. Don't you think that's the best route for us to take?" His thumb rubbed across her knuckles. "Even if it's hard to wait?"

They'd discussed this path numerous times. Try for a bank loan and make payments. But they had no collateral, and the English world of finance offered a slippery slope. What happened if he lost his job at the furniture shop? They could lose their home too.

"You're more practical than I am—we both know that." Nora could admit her flaws. Levi didn't seem to mind her desire for adventure around every bend. "I don't want to wait, but I'm a grown-up woman. I'll make the best of it because you're setting the example."

"Inside, I'm still a kid who wants what I want when I want it." He chuckled. "Patience is the bedrock of our faith. God in His infinite wisdom knows what we need and when we need it."

He was right. They would wait for God's timing. He had a plan for them.

Levi landed a kiss on her neck and nuzzled her cheek. To be able to have that touch all the time and without the need for restraint would be a joy and a relief. Each time it became that much harder to resist. "I'm trying to be patient. I really am." Giggling, she tugged away from his touch. "You're not making it any easier."

"Don't get me wrong. I'm just as eager as you are to marry. To make boplin." His laugh was low and warm. "To be with you all the time. But for now, we wait. Gott will do what's best for us. Dwelling on the delay doesn't help. Let's talk about something else."

Good idea, but no amount of talking would take Nora's mind off the feel of his lips on hers. "Did you see Mercy or Christine? Did everyone get out okay? What about Juliette and her family?"

Her closest friends scattered to the winds. They'd talked about this when the preevacuation notices came, but it still felt odd and empty. Nora, Christine, and Mercy had grown up never being more than a bicycle ride apart. Juliette, their closest English friend, showed up in their lives like a raucous English birthday party whenever she was in Kootenai.

"All out. They're around here somewhere—I think at Rexford Bench campground. Juliette's folks went into Eureka." Levi rubbed his eyes and yawned. "What a day. It looks like you have a full RV. I saw Daryl's horse next to yours. Are they staying here too?"

Nora launched into an explanation of why Jeannie and Daryl had come to the RV.

"Whoa, whoa. Hold your horses." Levi's voice rose, drowning out the frogs. He swiveled on the boulder and leaned in closer as if trying to see her face. "Your daed is letting you go to Libby? And you want to go?"

"I have to go. Jeannie needs me." It was the truth. Maybe she did want to go, but more than anything, she wanted to spend time with her sister and take care of Sadie. She didn't have her own sweet baby to hold yet. So much waiting, and now they might have to wait even longer. "It's only until the fire is contained. And it gives us a chance to visit with Daadi and Mammi. We hardly ever get to do that. Only when they come to Kootenai."

"There's a reason for that." His smile gone, Levi stood and crossed his arms. "They're not like us. They've been banned from worshipping with us."

"Even so, they're my family. You know that. You've met them." Nora scrambled to her feet and went to tuck her arm under his. She leaned against his shoulder and stared at the water. Somewhere an owl hooted. A coyote howled. Sad, lonely sounds. "Surely you aren't worried about my faith. It will stand the test."

"I like them, but I've heard stories of their worship services." His gaze on the murky darkness, he shuffled his feet. "People are overcome and fall to their knees in extravagant shows of religiosity. It's their way, and I pass no judgment. But it's not ours. Not the one we chose when we were baptized. I wonder if sometimes folks are influenced by the others around them in the chaos of the moment."

Plain services were quiet and reverent and three hours long. They also sang, but one song could go on for twenty minutes in low, slow chants in German. If someone jumped to his feet and shouted, "Hallelujah!" the bishop would surely faint. "It hasn't been so long that I've forgotten my baptismal vows."

"You have a soft heart and too much curiosity for your own gut." His arm slid around her and tucked her against his chest. She could feel his heart beating under her cheek. His voice dropped to a whisper again. "I love both those things about you. But it also means you tend to jump before you think. You want to help with no thought of consequences."

"Not true—"

His lips covered hers again for a quick beat. He drew away before she could respond. "Promise me you'll remember what you vowed in your baptism."

The memory washed over Nora. Grateful tears of joy that she couldn't begin to explain had trickled down her cheeks as the water ran onto her head from the bishop's cupped hands.

"Yes, I believe that Jesus is the Son of God.

"Yes, I renounce the world, the devil with all his subtle ways, as well as my own flesh and blood, and desire to serve Jesus Christ alone who died on the cross for me.

"Yes, I will uphold the teachings and Ordnung of this church, faithfully attend services, and work in it and not forsake it, whether it leads to life or to death."

Vows that couldn't be taken back. Or if failed, led to the *Meidung.* Separation from her parents, the boys, from all her family. Her heart would stop beating without them. "How could I forget?"

Another kiss, this one deeper and longer.

She pulled away. "You don't think I can stand strong?"

"I think folks stronger than we are have fallen."

"I won't be one of them." She whirled and trotted away. "You can count on that."

"I mean no disrespect." His footsteps clattered behind her. "Don't be mad."

"I'm not mad."

"I'll come visit you as soon as I can."

"You don't have to check up on me." They were having their first argument. So this was how it felt. Not good. "But if you do, you'll see that they're gut people still."

"I know they're gut people. I've visited with them when they come here. We took the horses and went hunting. Your *kossin* Tucker bagged a deer. So did you." Levi sounded as if he was trying to convince himself of his own words. "Just don't let your grooss-daadi teach you to drive."

He knew how much she wanted to try driving during their rumspringa. He forbade it as if they were already married. He was afraid she would get hurt. So his intentions were good, but Levi had his share of faults. Bossiness being one. But Nora had hers too. Like leaping before looking. A wife was to bow to her husband's wishes. If Levi got under her skin sometimes, it was good practice for when they married. The opportunity to drive never presented itself, so the bridge never had to be crossed. Would she have done it over his objection? They would never know. "He won't want to. He won't want to make Daed mad."

"But would you be tempted if he offered?"

Levi knew her better than anyone in the world—even better than Mercy and Christine. "I don't think so. The vows we took included following the Ordnung. I do my best to live up to it."

"I know you do, but you can act on a whim sometimes."

Nora bit her lip to keep her mouth shut. Again, good practice for when she became Levi's wife. No point in arguing a scenario that might never materialize. They walked in silence through the quiet park. Occasionally a dog lifted its head and huffed. A cat streaked across the path, but it didn't slow her down.

Did Levi really think she was that weak? They'd both been baptized at eighteen. Her rumspringa was uneventful—most of it spent with Levi. Their rides into the countryside had lasted longer and longer and later into the night. He only wanted to spend time with her, and that suited her fine. That and an occasional foray into Eureka with her friends for a movie, but that was it.

She hadn't even tried alcohol or English clothes. Neither interested her. Not when she had Levi to fill the hours with her hunting, fishing, and hiking.

"Nora, please."

The tents, arranged from smallest to largest, came into view against the outline of the Winnebago that glowed white in the overhead RV pad light. Their home away from home.

"Stop, will you?" Levi caught her arm and whirled her around so she smacked against his chest. "I didn't mean to hurt your feelings."

"I may jump into life with both feet, but that doesn't mean I don't know where to draw the line."

"I would never think that. My brain is all cattywampus with the fire and leaving our house and not knowing when we'll see each other again." Levi's voice went hoarse. "I don't want anything to happen to you."

"And I don't want anything to happen to you. We're in agreement, so let's not argue."

"Who's arguing?" He kicked at gravel with his dirty work boot. "Maybe I should talk to your daed about it."

"Please don't do that. Daed is older and wiser. If he thinks it's all right, then surely it is."

Levi growled, a sound she'd never heard from him before. "When will you go?"

"I don't know. It depends on what happens with the fire. If Gott hears our prayers and spares our homes, maybe we won't have to go at all."

"Jack wants to head to Eureka by the end of the day tomorrow. He doesn't want to spend more than one night in the RV."

"Maybe we'll move into Eureka. At least for a day or two until we hear more from the sheriff. There's less smoke there."

Nora wound her arms around his waist and kissed him first this time. He needed assurance. She would give him assurance. His response was quick. His hands cupped her face and slid down her neck to her shoulders. His heat burned through her dress's thin cotton material.

Time stood still. Worries fled. Uncertainty fell away.

Nothing felt like this. Nothing felt like Levi did.

Harrumph-harrumph.

The sound of a throat clearing shattered the quiet night like a shotgun blast.

Nora staggered back, stumbled over a parking block, righted herself, and turned. A Ball canning jar filled with cold tea in one hand, Father stood at the RV door. He stepped outside and let it close behind him. "Go inside, Dochder. You can sleep with Missy."

His tone forbade offering an explanation. As if one was needed. "*Gut nacht.*"

Neither man responded to her murmured good night. Neither did they move.

Her heart thumping, chest heaving, Nora slipped inside, closed the door, and leaned against it. No way she could hear the words exchanged. She put her hands to cheeks, hot with embarrassment. She didn't need to hear. The look on Father's face said it all.

5

That's what Levi got for talking big. Now that the opportunity to speak to Nora's dad about letting her go to Libby had presented itself, he couldn't find the words. The sentences didn't want to form. When was the last time he was at a loss for words? When Mother had announced to him and his five brothers and sisters that she planned to marry a man she'd met only months earlier and had courted a number of times that could be counted on fewer than ten fingers.

"He needs a fraa. I need a mann. You need a daed. His kinner need a mudder."

Simple enough reasoning.

Despite heat that singed his face and neck, Levi threaded his way through the tents in front of the Beachys' RV toward Harley. They would speak man to man. "It's late. It's been a long, hard day. I'm surprised you're not sleeping."

"I could say the same for you." Faint sarcasm dusted Harley's deep voice, made hoarse by smoke and exhaustion. "These are unusual times, but not so unusual that decorum doesn't still apply."

"Courting is private." Levi inhaled the calming scent of decaying leaves, dirt, and fir trees. *"Choose words with care."* His father's voice—clear as the Montana sky in spring even after six years—chided him. No good time existed for aggravating his future father-in-law. "We didn't realize you were there. We were saying gut nacht."

"I know what you were saying." Harley took a sip of his tea and meandered toward the picnic table. He was barefoot, which oddly made him seem less intimidating. "I'm not so old that I don't remember."

Levi eyed the table. He edged that direction. One day they would be family. Time to start acting like it. "We won't get ahead of ourselves. Nora is a gut girl."

"And you?" Harley wasn't one to beat around the bush. "You've been up to the house many times over the past few years. You were baptized with our dochder. Your buggy passes our way on a regular basis. It's between you and Nora, but I can't help wonder . . ."

The struggle on his weathered face obvious, Harley paused. Plain parents weren't supposed to interfere. Rumspringa gave Plain youngies the opportunity to decide whether to join the church and to whom they would marry. Parents turned their backs and pretended not to notice the hikes off the path their children took. As long as they came back.

"It's not because I don't want to ask. I have asked . . . sort of." Levi rushed to explain. "We're saving for the old Sutton place. We want to be able to have our own home when we marry."

Harley scrubbed at his face with both hands. Embarrassment colored his craggy face. "I would help with that if I could, but money's tight—"

"We can make our own way." As much as he longed to be married and settled, Levi couldn't take money from Harley when it surely meant taking food from his table or clothes from his children's backs. "Waiting is gut for us."

"As long as you don't wait too long."

That same embarrassment burned through Levi. "We're almost there. If the house still stands after the fire and the family living there doesn't decide to buy it."

"Gott willing, you mean. Would it be so bad to live with family?"

"Your home is bursting at the seams. So is mine." Every day it became harder to live under his stepfather's dominion. Jack didn't mean to be bossy. It was just his way. He didn't mean to favor his sons or the children he'd made with Mother. It was just his way. "We'll keep ourselves according to Gott's will until such time as we can marry."

"Maybe it's a gut thing Nora will go to Libby with her sister." Harley drummed his thumbs on the table, but his hard gaze connected with Levi's. "You'll have time to think and make certain of your feelings."

"My feelings are certain."

"Yet you let material things stand in the way."

"Is it wrong to want to be able to provide a roof over my fraa's head?"

"Nee, not wrong."

"I don't believe letting Nora go to Libby is a gut idea." Levi hesitated. His opinion had not been solicited. "They've made it clear what they think of our way of worship. They think we're lost. You know they'll try to convince her to see the error of our ways."

"If you were married, you would have a say in it." Harley's grim smile did nothing to soften his words. "Jeannie needs Nora's help, and the bopli needs to be clear of this smoke."

"There's smoke in Libby."

"Not like here."

Would they agree on nothing?

"It wasn't an easy decision." Harley eased from the picnic table bench and stretched to his full height. "I've spoken with Jeannie's mann. He'll keep an eye on them. He'll make sure they don't wander into dangerous territory."

Harley didn't sound any more convinced than Levi felt.

After all, who would keep an eye on Daryl? "You'll not reconsider then?"

"Nee. It's my decision."

To say more would be to disrespect the man's authority and his decision. Levi gritted his teeth and counted to five. "Gut nacht."

Harley dipped his head but said nothing. His posture left no doubt that he would stand guard until Levi left his RV pad.

Levi let the breeze cool his burning face as he walked back to the lot where his family slumbered for the night. The only time peace would reign in such small quarters. Like the Beachys, they'd set up tents to give everyone more room to spread out.

He squeezed past the first tent that housed the girls and headed toward the larger one, filled with his brothers.

"It's late to be gallivanting about, especially in a crowded park. All that puppy sitting didn't wear you out?"

Two fathers back to back. The bishop said God had a sense of humor. He was right. Levi bowed his head and chuckled.

Jack stepped from the shadows cast by the RV in the lot's single overhead light. "What's so funny? I could use a joke about now."

"Nothing." Levi kept his tone carefully neutral. He was too tired for jousting. "I just needed to stretch."

"Me too."

Levi put his hand on the tent flap. He had nothing to say at this hour or to this man.

"Just one thing before you turn in." Jack moved his coffee mug to his lips but then let it drop without taking a drink. "Don't do it again."

"Do what?"

"Go against my wishes."

He couldn't be talking about Gussy and the puppies. "That wasn't my intent. I just couldn't leave those dogs to die. It would be wrong and a terrible lesson for Charlie."

"A life lesson, to be sure. Charlie and the others need to understand that their daed's word prevails in our house."

"They know that."

Jack had made it clear from the first day he'd moved into their home and made it his.

"I'm not sure you do."

Levi would not argue this subject with his stepfather. His own father had taught him to respect his elders, to respect authority, and to be obedient. "I only wanted to save the hunds. It was the humane thing to do."

"I have no wish to be cruel." A tendril of regret wound its way around the words. The ice in Jack's tone melted. "In the moment I made what I believed to be the right decision."

"I know."

"I only want to keep everyone safe. That includes you. Sometimes you must make hard decisions."

Jack included Levi in the number of people for whom he was responsible. As much as Levi didn't want or need his protection, the thought warmed the cold place in his own heart. Could it be they were two of a kind? "This time we were able to do both. For Charlie's sake, I'm glad I was able to bring the puppies out."

"This time everything turned out for the best. How would Charlie have felt if you didn't make it out after he had asked you to get the puppies? Would you like for him to have that on his conscience growing up?"

"Nee, I wouldn't."

"Something to think about when you say your prayers." Jack turned his back and stomped up the steps to the RV's door. "Gut nacht, Suh."

Suh. The single syllable held so much pain. Did Jack know that? Could he be that oblivious to Levi's hurt? Or was this another lesson to be learned?

Levi had learned all the lessons: That his father's death was God's will. That Father's days on earth were numbered. That he was only passing through. God's will be done. In this world there would be trouble, but Christ had overcome the world.

No doubt there were more. For tonight these were enough. Levi slipped into the stuffy tent and bedded down next to his snoring brother.

He closed his eyes, prayed for the ability to love his stepfather, and went to sleep still waiting.

6

West Kootenai, Montana

Given the massive swatches of blackened forest that stained the mountainside around Kootenai, the devastation within their tiny community should come as no surprise. Inhaling the stench of smoke, burnt wood, melted rubber, and singed metal, Levi willed his emotions to stay behind the massive wall he'd built brick by brick on the ride into town with Deputy Kimberly LaFortune. They were given an hour, maybe less, to check on their homes and grab any needed items before they had to retreat again. The fire could change directions any second and make another run at Kootenai.

As if it hadn't done enough damage in the twenty-four hours since they'd been forced to evacuate. Mangled metal curled up in strange shapes, and thick piles of ashes lay where the house of his dreams had stood only twenty-four hours earlier. The Adirondack chairs on the front porch were gone. So was the porch. The gangly sunflowers, gone. The festive red-and-blue curtains blowing in open windows that belonged to the front room, gone. The four-bedroom, two-bath, two-story house reduced to rubble.

His and Nora's dream, gone.

With a deep breath Levi removed his straw hat and fanned his damp face. He had no time for a pity party. His family home still stood. No one had been hurt. Others had been less fortunate. The Yoders' home had been destroyed, as had the Knowleses'—along with all of their outbuildings. Three cabins that housed some of Kootenai's Plain bachelors were gone.

He closed his eyes and bowed his head. *It's just a house. Sheetrock and siding. Wood and brick. Inconsequential in the bigger scheme of things in this world. I'm sorry, Gott, for my weakness. Please forgive me.*

"I can't believe it's gone. All gone."

Levi opened his eyes. Vince Collier, current occupant of the dream house, stood at his side. He removed his black cowboy hat and held it over his heart.

"I'm sorry." The puny words didn't begin to express Levi's shared sense of disbelief and sorrow. "Were you able to get your furniture out?"

"Not much. I ran home from the shop and picked up Charlotte and the kids." Vince slicked back straw-colored hair with fingers that had grease ingrained around all five fingernails. A person wouldn't have trouble guessing his occupation as a mechanic. "We grabbed what we could and threw it in the back of the truck, but it wasn't much. We left behind the crib, the high chair, the kids' toys, most of their clothes, and most of the furniture. We just finished building a play set for the boys."

Vince and his wife had a six-month-old girl and two older boys who had to be four or five.

"It happened so fast."

"We did all the right things too." Vince's jaw worked and his eyes reddened. "I took out those two pines that were too close to the house. I kept all the leaves and needles raked up. The kids even helped. We built a lean-to for the firewood to keep it away from the house. I even cleaned the roof to get rid of any debris after storms. We did everything the Forest Service said we needed to do."

"They also said no guarantees. This is what happens when folks build so close to the mountains where lightning strikes causing fires are common." Levi had been to those same meetings with the U.S. Forest Service ranger. He chewed his lower lip, trying to think of a way to soften the words. "It was such a dry summer, too, so we shouldn't be surprised, I guess."

"Yeah, I just feel bad for Chet." Vince squatted down and traced one long finger through the ashes. "He was a good landlord. He always came right away when the dishwasher stopped working or the AC went on the blink."

Two problems that would not occur if his tenants were Plain. "He'll want to rebuild. You could work together on that."

"Naw, we'd already given our notice." Vince eased to his feet and brushed his hands together. "I guess you didn't hear. I took a job at a car dealership in Bonners Ferry. It's more money. We were planning to move next week."

"I didn't know." Levi swallowed against the ache in his throat. A better man would be more concerned for his neighbor and less focused on his own selfish wants. The house would have been Nora's and his new home. Rent to own. That's what his English friends called it. No matter. This was not about him or Nora. "A fresh start then."

"We can always look at the bright side—moving will be easy." Vince's laugh was halfhearted. "No furniture to lug into a moving truck and drive to Idaho. And we have renter's insurance, so we'll get to buy new furniture for our rental house. Maybe someday we can afford to buy."

Me too. Levi and Nora would buy someday—God willing. Right now they would be thankful that no one had been hurt and would help the others rebuild. Their needs would come later. "I wish you and your family the best in your new life in Bonners Ferry."

"Thank you. You and yours have been good—"

A horn shattered the silence. They both turned. Brakes screeching, Deputy LaFortune rolled to a stop in her Lincoln County SUV on the gravel driveway. She rolled down the window. "Sorry, guys. Time's up." She shoved her Ray-Bans on top of her auburn hair with a touch of impatience. "Sheriff Brody and the others are at the school, loading the desks into somebody's pickup truck. After that, everyone is out of here."

"Do they need help?" Levi trotted to the SUV. "Do we have time to swing by and give them a hand?"

"They've got it covered, but we can follow them into Eureka to Grandma Knowles's house to help with the unloading if you want."

The children staying in Eureka would still have school. That was good. Maybe he should let Nora's parents know. They might consider moving the RV to a park in town so their boys could keep up. He jerked open the door to the backseat and slid in next to his younger stepbrothers, Joseph and Enoch. Beyond them sat Jack, his straw hat on his lap, his hands black with soot. His stepdad glanced at Levi and then turned to look out the window. The truck's cabin smelled of sweat and smoke. Ash darkened their shirts.

Not about to apologize for his jaunt to Chet's house, Levi leaned into the cool air that blew from the AC vents. "Once we get situated in Eureka, it sounds like the kids can get back to school with Mercy."

"Nee, that's okay." Enoch, who was thirteen and almost done with school, rolled his eyes and grimaced. "A wildfire is a gut reason to be done with school. We have work to do rebuilding. Who needs composition and spelling for that?"

"You go where you're told to go." Jack fanned his face with his sweat-stained hat. In its battered state, it looked a hundred years old. "Levi, I was surprised you came out here instead of helping us load up the table and chairs and your mudder's things at the house."

At the house Levi lived in long before Jack came along. "I needed to see . . . if this house . . . still stood." Mother would understand.

She and Father had married at eighteen and had Levi at nineteen. The memory of them singing *"Das Loblied"* as they worked in the vegetable garden together flooded him. The Praise Song was sung at every Sunday service, twenty-six times a year, without fail.

"Ha, ha." Enoch elbowed Joseph, who giggled with his older brother. "Levi has a special friend. They were going to live in that house."

That Enoch knew of his courting didn't surprise Levi. The grapevine wound itself around every road, every house, and every nook and cranny in tiny Kootenai.

"That's none of your business, Suh." At least Jack recognized this fact.

"You had my bruders to help. We can help with moving the school desks now."

Jack's forehead furrowed. He squinted behind black-framed glasses. "You're not going to tell me why you're mooning over a house that's not yours?"

Jack was like that. He would worry the subject until defenses crumbled. Levi took a long breath and let it out. "I've been saving to buy it."

"Planning to move out then?"

"Eventually."

"That's what a man does."

His tone suggested Levi didn't measure up to the standard. "Like I said, that was the plan. Now we'll—I'll have to see what Chet plans to do with the property. If he sells the land, I'm not sure I'll have enough savings left to rebuild too."

"There are other properties."

"Land isn't cheap here."

"I'm aware." Jack leaned back on the seat and pulled his hat down on his tanned forehead. "Can't help you there."

"I'm not asking for your help" teetered on Levi's lips. He corralled the words before they crashed into the chasm that gaped between his stepfather and him. "I'm aware."

"In the meantime your help will be needed to rebuild the barn and the shed on our property. The house is still standing but not much else."

"Understood."

So were the words not spoken. Jack expected Levi to put his life and dreams on hold for as long as necessary. Levi would do so with willing obedience.

But he would never relinquish them.

7

Eureka, Montana

Not knowing when they would see one another again made saying goodbye to her best friends even harder. Nora plopped in her seat in the Eureka High School auditorium and watched as Christine threaded her way through the crowd that had attended the community meeting about the fire and the now three-day-old evacuation. Mercy would stay in Eureka and teach her scholars in Grandma Knowles's garage. Christine would go to St. Ignatius. Juliette's family would stay in Eureka. They had no way of knowing for how long. The dejected set of Christine's shoulders said she hurt from the news that her special friend, Andy Lambright, had left for Lewistown without saying goodbye. Surely Levi wouldn't do that to Nora.

He had to be here somewhere. Unless he was so angry over her trip to Libby that he didn't plan to speak to her.

Father's description of Kootenai had been terse after his trip Thursday to gather belongings for them. He unbent enough to say that Levi had been there. Other than that, he simply reiterated that their home still stood—unlike the homes of Mercy and Juliette. Two of her best friends were now homeless.

Mercy no longer had a special friend and Juliette's deputy

couldn't date her because of her lack of faith. Their problems were so much greater than Nora's. She should stop worrying about herself and start thinking of ways to encourage them.

"There you are."

The low voice that made her heart careen off course came from above. Nora looked up. Levi squeezed into the row and plopped down two seats from her.

"Here I am." She glanced around. Their backs to the auditorium seats, Father and Mother were talking to Juliette's parents. Jeannie and Daryl stood with them. The boys had gone outside to mess around with their friends. "I reckon Daed won't be too happy to see us talking in front of everyone."

"I think we're okay. We talked after . . . you went inside. He understands."

"I don't know about that. Mudder's been following me around with a worried look on her face like she thinks I might do something sinful in front of Solomon, Seth, and Stinker."

"They're not so old that they don't remember what it's like." Levi had the audacity to chuckle. It didn't seem all that funny in the light of day. "Come on, he saw us kissing. It's not the end of the world. People in love kiss."

"Are we still in love then?"

"What kind of question is that?" Levi's smile turned into a scowl. "If you mean am I still unhappy about you going to Libby, the answer is yes, but I spoke with your daed about it—"

"You tried to convince him otherwise?"

"I did, but he refused to budge."

"Gut."

"You are a stubborn woman."

"You are a bossy man."

Plain women didn't talk to men like this. Or did they? How much experience did she really have with this aside from her parents?

Who knew what went on between her parents behind closed doors after twenty-seven years of marriage and eight children?

Levi elicited the best and worst of Nora, that she knew for sure. Maybe changing the subject would help. It couldn't hurt. "Sheriff Brody did a good job calming the waters, I thought. People listen to him better than the Forest Service rangers. They trust him to get us back into our homes as soon as possible."

"There's something I need to tell you." The irritation disappeared from Levi's voice. He studied his hands in his lap, then stared at the empty stage. "Or did you already hear?"

"I heard. Mercy's house burned down. So did Juliette's. Christine's family is moving to Kansas, so she's staying with her aenti and onkel in St. Ignatius. Everyone is leaving. Nothing will be the same when we finally do get back in."

"There's more."

"What is it?" Nora studied his profile. He seemed sad. Levi rarely let his emotions show. He even did a good job of hiding his angst over his mother's decision to marry Jack. "What's wrong? Daed said your family's home still stands."

"But ours doesn't." He ran the words together as if anxious to have them out of his mouth. "It burned to the ground. Everything is gone."

The crowd that filled the auditorium shrank and disappeared. The noisy conversations became muffled squawking somewhere faraway. Nora stared at the flags on the stage, but she saw the pale-blue one-story house with darker blue shutters and Adirondack chairs crowding the front porch. A tinkling wind chime played its tune in a soft summer breeze. Dahlias, strawflowers, lilacs, and amaranth bloomed in the front yard and in flower boxes under the windows. Flowered curtains fluttered in the open windows.

"All gone?" she whispered.

"I'm sorry." Levi's hand slid across the chairs that separated them.

She didn't dare reciprocate. Not with her parents a few yards away. His sweet brown eyes filled with shared pain. They said he wanted to hug her and hold her and make her feel better. "Vince was there. I felt bad for him and his fraa. They lost everything."

"I'm so selfish. My first thought is of me. Of us."

"You're not selfish. Only human." He wiggled in his seat. His expression said there was more to come. How could there be more? "They were about to move to Bonners Ferry. He got a job there. The house would've been—"

"Available for rent or sale."

"Jah."

Her fingers hurt. They seemed to belong to someone else. The joints, white with the force of her grip, ached. She breathed and loosened them. "It's hard to understand, isn't it? How can this be Gott's plan for us? Is it awful of me to think of that when we still have homes to return to?"

"Like I said, human. But we have to do better." He leaned forward and grabbed the chair in front of him with both tanned, calloused hands. "It's hard, but Gott never promised us an easy life."

"What do we do now?"

"I'll talk to Chet to see if he plans to rebuild. I reckon he will. I can help. The other men will want to help."

Just as they would help with rebuilding the other English homes. The English families would help them in return. Religion didn't serve as a barrier in their small community. They were united by their love of the land and the mountains. "What if he doesn't? What if he decides to sell the land instead?"

"We have savings." His hands smoothed the chair back in front of him. "Just promise me you won't change."

"Change? I'm not going to change—"

His head came up. His eyes blazed with light. "Your family in Libby will have a phone. Call me if you need me."

He reached over, grabbed her hand, and placed a small scrap of notebook paper in it. Then he gently folded her fingers around it. His strong carpenter hands were warm. "It's the number at Kevin's house. The rental house is across the street. Call me—"

"Time to go." Father loomed over Levi's chair. Mother hovered behind him. "You best get moving or get left behind."

That would never happen. Father's expression assured Nora of that. He appeared as unhappy as he had in Rexford. Levi stood. Father took a step back, and Levi strode past him. In the aisle he turned and looked back. "We're staying here in Eureka now, but I plan to visit Libby later, depending on how long the evacuation lasts."

If Levi cast a challenge in those words, Father didn't seem to notice. He nodded. Mother's hands fluttered. She cocked her head toward the doors. "Let's go, Dochder. We've decided to drive the RV into town tomorrow morning. The rental house is close enough for the boys to go to Mercy's school at Grandma Knowles's. You'll leave for Libby in the morning. Your daed just talked to the driver."

They had work to do. Stow the tents and camping equipment. Clean up the RV pad. Moving like nomads. Her entire life, Nora had never lived anywhere but Kootenai. Now her friends were spread across this corner of the world.

Nora stood. Levi's determined stride took him farther and farther away. What did the future hold for all of them?

8

Libby, Montana

Mountains and valleys. Nora studied the wide-open spaces of Eagle Valley as the van approached the outskirts of Libby. September was an in-between month in this valley. The previous hot, dry summer had turned the pastures brown. Yet the valley had still held on to its charm with its wooden fences, horses nibbling at the grass, and reddish-brown log cabins dotting the landscape alongside the dirt road. Not as beautiful as living in the mountains on the edge of Kootenai National Forest, but the mountains in the distance created a pleasing vista everywhere she looked.

Not even Sadie's fretful squalling or Jason and Missy's bickering could spoil Nora's determination to make this a family visit as much as it was an escape from the fire. They would spend precious time with Grandpa and Grandma Beachy, with Aunt Roseanna and Uncle Ike, and with her cousins.

Their driver pulled up in front of Grandma and Grandpa's two-story homestead constructed from hand-peeled rustic pine logs. It was big compared to Nora's house back home, which was good. Her grandparents wouldn't be tripping over three extra adults and three children, two of whom liked to run wild.

Arms flapping, Grandma pushed through the screen door and scurried down the steps. She had to be in her late sixties, but she still moved like a young mother. "You're here, you're here." She tugged the van's sliding door open before Nora had a chance to push it from the inside. "Nora, you've grown into the spitting image of your mudder. You are the picture of health and youth."

That was a compliment indeed. Nora didn't look like her mother. Jeannie did. Much more pleasing to the eye. No one said that, of course. Nor did it matter. But the kind words touched Nora. "Danki. You look gut too."

"I eat too much and sit too much." Grandma patted her generous belly. In her long blue dress, apron, and kapp, she didn't appear any different from the grandmothers in Kootenai. Maybe Mother and Father's concerns were overblown. Grandma was 100 percent Plain. "I like my own cooking too much, I reckon."

If memory served, Grandma's pies had flaky crusts, and her bread melted in a girl's mouth. She also made a mighty savory elk chili.

"Come, come, everyone out. I want to see that new bopli. And where is little Missy? Hiding behind her mudder? I see you, Jason. Get out here and say howdy."

A wide smile on her wrinkled, sun-leathered face, Grandma clapped and helped the little ones from the van. She dispensed hugs and kisses as if her supply was endless. After a swift once-over of Jeannie, she shook her finger at Nora's sister. "You need help, kind, and rest. You're run-down. We'll get you feeling better in no time."

"She's doing fine, just tired." Daryl slammed the front passenger door. "She's capable of taking care of her own kinner."

"I'm sure she is." Grandma didn't seem at all fazed that he'd taken offense at her observation. "But a groossmammi likes to feel useful."

Jeannie's face crumpled. "Mammi, it's so gut to see you."

The two shared a long hug, Sadie between them. When Jeannie stepped back, tears wet her face.

Nora's sister needed help more than anyone realized. Certainly more than Daryl wanted to admit. Nora scooped up Missy and tucked her on her hip. She took Jason's hand. "Lead the way."

Grandma took Sadie from Jeannie's arms and led the procession up the steps and into the house. The scent of chocolate cake or brownies greeted them like an old, much-loved friend. The foyer opened up into a huge space, with the kitchen on the right and an enormous living room with a vaulted ceiling on the left. Both rooms had pine floors partially covered by colorful piece rugs. A long pine table with benches on either side separated the two spaces. A hallway on the other side led to other first-floor rooms. "I've made up the beds and spruced up the bedrooms upstairs." Grandma headed for the stairs. "Let me show them to you, and then I'll get lunch on the table."

"I can help." Nora glanced around. The kitchen didn't seem different from the one she'd grown up with. No dishwasher or newfangled appliances. A wood-burning stove, a propane stove, and a refrigerator took up one long wall. A counter on the far wall included a double sink and at least a dozen cabinets, top and bottom. Shelves full of canned goods, dry goods, and baking pans, bowls, and utensils filled the front wall, along with two floor-to-ceiling windows covered with white cotton curtains.

A massive stone fireplace with a wood mantel served as the centerpiece of the living room. Grandma's crocheted lap blankets in reds, blues, and purples covered the back of a sagging brown couch and two hickory rocking chairs. Again, sweetly familiar. In the bright morning sun no lights were turned on. Did they use propane lamps, or did they have electricity? "Where's Daadi?"

"He's working at the shop making the log cabin kits." Puffing, Grandma grabbed the stair railing and started up the stairs. "He's old, but not that old. He likes to feel useful. When they don't need him at the shop, he goes to the sawmill. He's even stocked shelves at the store."

The Eagle Valley Amish community had a thriving economy, according to Nora's father. They'd bought eight hundred acres of pristine land where they built the Farm-to-Market Store, frequented by local Englischers and tourists, a sawmill, and a log cabin assembly kit shop. The three endeavors employed most of the men in the district. They also built a church and a school. The thought of the church sent a slight chill through Nora. She'd never attended a service in a church building. Was it any different?

"Where two or more are gathered." That's what Father said. No special building needed.

She shifted Missy to her other hip and tightened her grip on Jason's hand. One thing at a time. They followed the others up the stairs and down the hallway. Jeannie and Daryl had the room next to Grandpa and Grandma. Grandma had placed a crib she borrowed from a friend in the next bedroom, along with two bunk beds side by side for the kids.

"I think the bopli needs to be in with me." Uncertainty flared in Jeannie's face. "She's so small, and her breathing—"

"My friend gave me a baby monitor—"

"Nee," Daryl intervened. "We'll not be using any of your newfangled English machines."

"It's not a machine." Mammi's expression didn't change, nor her tone. "It runs on batteries. It lets you hear the baby cry during the night. That's all. Jeannie will get more sleep with the bopli in another room, but she'll have the assurance she'll hear Sadie when she cries or coughs."

"It doesn't sound so bad." Jeannie appealed to her husband with a touch to his arm. Daryl's frown softened. She smiled at him. "You'll sleep better, too, if Sadie's cry doesn't keep waking you."

"Let me have the monitor." Nora could be useful. Jeannie did appear run-down. Having a job to do would pass the time. "I'll take care of Sadie during the night while we're here so you can get caught up on your sleep. When she needs to eat, I'll bring her to you, and then you can put her back to bed. If it's coughing or congestion, I know what to do."

"Oh, I don't know—"

"Perfect." Grandma snatched a small rectangular object from the dresser and handed it to Nora. "All you have to do is flip this switch and it's on. Turn it off when you aren't using it so you don't run down the battery. Easy-peasy."

"Easy-peasy."

They all turned to stare at Daryl.

"I suppose if it's not electric, it's not so bad." Daryl edged toward the door. "I'll leave you women to chatter like a bunch of mother hens while I get the bags."

Jeannie grinned at Mammi. "That's a jah."

Mammi turned to Nora and winked. "Your room's the last one on the other side. I'll have Daryl bring the rocking chair up and put it in there in case you want to rock that sweet bopli."

Nora shooed her small charges onto their beds. They immediately began to giggle and wrestle. She followed Mammi to her room. It was big and held a double bed, a desk, two straight-back chairs, and a bookshelf filled with paperbacks. "Martha and Hannah shared it before they married. It'll be nice to have you here."

"They haven't been back to Kootenai in forever. How are they doing?"

"Martha is in a family way again. Number four. They're in St. Ignatius still. Her mann is the assistant foreman at the dairy now." Grandma smiled at the thought. "Hannah has her hands full with her five. They've moved from St. Ignatius to Moore so her mann can work at the leather shop there. He makes some beautiful saddles."

Both Nora's aunts had married traditional Plain men. Only Uncle Ike and his wife chose this life. "Do they visit often?"

"Not as often as I'd like."

Nora spied the propane lamp. The room had no overhead light fixtures.

Grandma chuckled. "Don't look so disappointed. I'm like Daryl. I cling to the old ways I grew up with. I took vows, just like you did."

"So, no electricity."

"Nee, no vacuum. No dishwasher—except me. No electric refrigerator with an ice maker and a water dispenser. Just a simple Plain house. Your groossdaadi is my mann, and he has the last say on most things, but I'm the one who takes care of the house. It was my choice."

Was it disappointment she felt? Nora smoothed the Bear's Paw quilt on the bed. No, it couldn't be. "And you chose the old way?"

"Some would say the right way."

"Do you regret moving to Libby?"

"I go where Jacob goes. He is my mann."

Not an answer, but Nora understood. One day she would be the same with Levi. "Are you happy here?"

As a girl she would never have thought to ask such a question, but now as she stood on the cusp of marrying and starting a life as a wife who would bow to her husband's wishes, she wanted to know. Could a woman be happy when her husband wanted something she did not?

"I choose to be happy in my circumstances. That's what is expected of a fraa. By her mann and by her Gott." Mammi's huge brown eyes—Father's eyes—were sharp. She saw much. "If you're thinking of yoking yourself to a young man, be sure your feelings are such that you can do that."

Of course Nora could. That's what wives did.

"Where is everyone? Fraa?"

Daadi's bass filtered up the stairs.

"He's here." Grandma's huge grin made her look like an elfin girl, old and young at the same time. "He likes his meal on the table when he walks through the door. We better skedaddle."

So they skedaddled. Nora and Jeannie shepherded the children down the stairs where Grandpa waited, arms wide. Jason hid behind Jeannie's skirts while Missy began to wail. They weren't old enough to remember this tall, rotund man with a long, white beard, wire-rimmed glasses, and hands the size of bushel baskets. His black felt hat hid his silver hair. He wore a faded blue shirt, suspenders, and dark-blue denim pants. His gray eyes were as sharp as ever. "You two women can't be my girls. You're too old and too grown-up."

"It's us." Jeannie stepped forward first for a quick embrace. Grandpa had never been one for physical affection like Grandma. "I'm the mudder of three boplin now. Can you believe it?"

"And you?" Grandpa surveyed Nora. "No young man has scooped you up?"

As if she would marry without inviting Grandma and Grandpa. They could attend the reception, if not the church service. "I'm working on it."

Grandpa roared with laughter. He had a belly laugh. The one Father had when they told him knock-knock jokes as children. He and Grandpa were alike. Yet Grandpa had been the one to break away with Ike, not Father.

Trying to understand family made Nora's head hurt. Instead, she helped Grandma serve cold chicken salad sandwiches, fried potatoes, macaroni salad, and sliced tomatoes, followed by thick slabs of frosted brownies.

They settled around the table, prayed, and ate. Excitement mixed with apprehension had kept Nora from eating breakfast. Now her stomach clamored for food. She shoveled in a big bite of macaroni salad and smiled at Grandpa's attempts to entice Jason into taking a bite of chicken salad. The child was a picky eater.

A ringing sound ripped the air. Nora dropped her fork. Jeannie jumped. Frowning, Daryl lowered his sandwich to his plate.

"Jah, we have a phone in the house." Grandpa wiped his face with his napkin. "So far Gott hasn't smote me with a bolt of lightning over it."

"No one ever said He would." Daryl's frown deepened. He pushed his plate away. "It's a matter of not being pulled into the world."

"It's not the world calling. It's probably Ike. He probably wants to know if you're here. He and his fraa are coming for supper."

The phone continued to ring, a strident sound that irritated Nora's ears. A phone in the house wasn't such a big thing. Some of the Plain businesses had phones. They needed to keep in touch with their customers.

Father said giving in on little things led to bigger ones, a slow erosion of family life until it was no longer the same. Family became second or third in line in a person's priorities. Faith, family, and community—those were the most important pillars in a Plain person's life.

Grandpa dropped his napkin on the table, stood, scooted from the bench, and went to the hall, where he picked up the receiver.

Nora glanced at Grandma. Her face pensive, she picked at her potatoes with her fork. She caught Nora's stare and shrugged.

God might not have smote Grandpa, but the phone had already caused a crack in the Beachy family's life.

9

In Amish households visiting means food and lots of it. Nora and Jeannie barely had the table cleared and the dishes done when Grandma started on the feast they would serve for supper. She sent Jeannie upstairs for a nap, but she allowed Nora to sit at the prep table and chop vegetables while she did the heavy lifting. The celebratory meal would include moose steaks for the adults, hot dogs and hamburgers for the children, baked beans, coleslaw, potato salad, chips and ranch dip, and apple pie or brownies with homemade vanilla ice cream.

Within the hour company arrived. If Grandma and Grandpa still dressed the part of Plain folks, Uncle Ike and Aunt Roseanna's children made up for it. The kids stampeded through the house, shrieking with laughter and jockeying for position so they could tell Grandma about their latest escapades at school. Uncle Ike had Father's massive build, silver hair, and brown eyes. In fact, they could have been twins. His choice of a green polo shirt and tan work pants told the real story. At faith's fork in the road, they'd set out in opposite directions.

With a terse greeting Uncle Ike settled onto the couch and began discussing the fires with Grandpa. Aunt Roseanna, on the other hand, had much to say. Mostly advice to Jeannie, who had rejoined them after their first blast of noise, on how to take care of

Sadie. She cooed over the baby as she peeked under her dress and examined her from her wispy blonde hair to her ten toes. As the mother of eight, including premature twins, she had plenty of wisdom to share. She, too, eschewed traditional garb, but she did wear a floral print dress that reached below her knees, black tennis shoes, and a white scarf over her wheat-colored hair. She at least looked Mennonite, if not Plain.

Her children were another matter. At nineteen, Tammy was the second oldest of the unmarried children and the one Nora knew the best. She wore blue jeans with sequins on the pockets, a red tank top, and leather sandals that revealed toenails painted purple. Her honey-blonde hair hung uncovered to her waist. She had Aunt Roseanna's toothy grin. Tucker, who was sixteen, had a solid build, brown eyes, and the jet-black hair that reminded Nora of her daed before silver overtook his thick hair. He was well on his way to having Father's height as well. In other words, he was a younger, more worldly version of Father in his jeans, green T-shirt, and Nike tennis shoes.

"Nora, I'm so excited you're here. We always visited you, and now you get to see how the other half lives." Tammy tossed her hair over her shoulder and started up the stairs. "Let's go to your room. Tucker brought his guitar. We're practicing songs for Sunday's service. You can learn them too."

What a treat that would be. Music would take Nora's mind off the fire, leaving home, and missing her family. Music was the best medicine. "We need to help Mammi get supper on the table."

"I reckon the food's been ready for at least an hour." Despite her words Tammy backed down the stairs. "That's the way Mammi is. She loves to cook for her kinner."

"True, it's ready." As much as Nora wanted to pick Tammy's brains about life in Libby, she couldn't let Grandma bear the brunt of so many visitors. In Kootenai Grandma and Grandpa would be living in a *dawdy haus* by now. "Let's carry the food to the table and fill the water glasses."

"You're right. Mammi shouldn't be on her feet so much." Tammy tromped back down the stairs and followed Nora to the kitchen. The conversation in the living room grew louder. Libby residents were receiving their own pre-evacuation notices due to a fire started by lightning northwest of town. So far it didn't include the Eagle Valley Amish community.

"The Westfork Fire will never reach this far south of town. The preevacuation notices went out to folks north of Quartz Creek Road." Grandpa leaned back in the rocking chair and sipped his lemonade. "The worst we'll get is smoke."

"Figures. That's why we came down here. To get away from the smoke." Daryl rocked harder in his matching chair. "Pretty soon we'll have to rent a hotel room in Missoula."

"Not a bad idea," Uncle Ike said. "The Forest Service ranger at our community meeting said there are twenty-one fires now. Something like five hundred thousand acres have burned. Smoke is blowing through half of Montana. That's what happens when so much of the state is in a drought."

"No need to worry yet. Let's see how things go. You just arrived, and my fraa wants a gut visit with the kinner." Grandpa tugged off his glasses and cleaned them on his shirt. "Lightning started fires that cleared the forest and allowed fresh, new growth. It was part of the plan. Then humans decided to build houses on the mountains close to the forests."

"You think we were wrong to build in Kootenai?" Nora settled a bowl of coleslaw on the table and peeked at the group of men. The scowl on Daryl's face indicated what he thought of a woman horning in on the conversation. "I never thought of it that way is all. We love the land and the forest and all the wildlife. I thought we were gut neighbors."

"You are. We are." Uncle Ike didn't seem perturbed by her interruption. He smoothed an unruly beard that reached to his lower ribs. "It's impossible to touch nature and not have an effect on it. Since Adam and Eve's fall in the garden, we've turned the earth to ashes. We're a fallen race."

"Not everything humans do is bad." Tammy frowned. "We make music and sing and dance and grow flowers and paint and write poetry—"

"Jah, jah, Dochder." Ike laughed that same belly laugh as Grandpa and Father. "You are my optimistic music maker. Gott made you that way, and I rejoice in it."

Tucker's guitar case leaned against the wall in the living room. What would it be like to pluck the strings and have a song emerge? If the songs were hymns or songs that praised God, how could it be bad?

The thoughts tiptoed into Nora's brain with no warning. *Shoo, shoo.* She brushed them away with an imaginary broom. Nora offered a smile to her uncle. His grin widened. "Gott has given us the means to make this world a happier place, and it's gut that we use it. Music lightens our load."

They'd strayed far from the topic at hand—fires. But Nora didn't mind. The fire had draped its smothering smoke over them for more than a week now, and it made the world a dreary place. She missed the old world. She wanted it back. "Supper's ready."

Between Ike and Roseanna's bunch and the visitors, they filled the table. Nora waited for Grandpa to bow his head. A blessed moment of quiet ensued when everyone was seated.

Instead, Ike bowed his head and said, "Let us pray."

He proceeded to ask for blessings on the food and on the visiting family—aloud. His deep voice boomed in the silence. Nora sneaked a look at Jeannie. She shrugged and clasped her hands in front of her. Nora did the same.

The more things seemed the same, the more they were different.

Did it matter? God heard their prayers, whether silent or spoken. What would be the problem with Ike praying aloud? Did it seem grandiose? Did it draw attention to him instead of God? Did it put words in the mouths of those who surrounded him?

Father would have an answer. This might be trickier to navigate than a trail high in the mountains. Nora breathed a sigh of relief when Ike said, "amen." Less than a day and she already missed Mother. Being able to ask her questions had been the saving grace during the baptism classes. Mother never chided her for not understanding, and she never laughed at stupid questions. Like why they didn't pray aloud at mealtimes.

The Beachys' supper was a festive affair with much good-natured bickering over who would get the last roll and who would refill the water glasses and whether potato salad was better than coleslaw.

After they cleaned the kitchen and put away the last of the pots and pans, Tammy motioned for Nora to follow her outside. Tucker sat on the porch swing, strumming his guitar and singing an English country song Nora had heard on the radio at the café in Eureka. He nodded and kept singing.

Tammy plopped on the steps and patted the spot next to her. Nora joined her, leaned against the post, and watched Tucker. He had a nice voice, and his fingers were nimble on the guitar strings. He made it seem easy.

He smiled and stopped. "Hey, cuz, did you want to learn to play the guitar?"

Was Tucker challenging Nora's beliefs or simply offering her a chance to learn something she might never have otherwise? How could he know how her fingers itched to pluck those strings? Less than twenty-four hours and her defenses needed reinforcements. She straightened. "I don't think so."

"Afraid of hellfire and damnation?"

Definitely a challenge. "I promised to live by the Ordnung. We don't play musical instruments." Amazed she still remembered some of the deacon's lessons from her classes, Nora picked her words as carefully as she would roses from a thorny bush. "It's not that we think playing an instrument will make us go to hell. We don't want to draw attention to ourselves. We want to be humble and keep all the attention on Gott. We don't want to be prideful because we know how to do something others don't."

"Playing music on the guitar gives people who hear it joy." Tucker sounded sure of himself. Sixteen-year-old boys usually did. "They're not thinking about me. They're thinking about the music and how it makes them feel."

"They should be thinking about Gott, not themselves." The deacon's familiar words came easily to Nora. Did she parrot him, or did she believe in the sentiment? She wanted to believe. It would also be fun to play the guitar. "It's not about feelings. It's about worshipping Gott."

"It's praise and worship music. That's exactly what they're doing with the music—worshipping Gott. They sing and play instruments in the Bible."

How easily he blew holes in her arguments. Nora clung to what she knew for certain. "I just know what the Ordnung says. No instruments."

"Which is the point." Tucker strummed three cords that sounded like the beginning of a German song sung a cappella at most Plain services. "You are taught to follow the rules without questioning them. You don't understand them. The elders prefer it that way."

"Who told you that?" Nora managed to keep her voice level. Tucker had been brought up differently than she had. *Don't judge us, and we won't judge you.* "We have classes where we study the articles of faith. We know what we're agreeing to when we're baptized."

"What does electricity have to do with believing Jesus Christ is your Savior?"

"Tucker, stop it. Seriously. Stick a sock in it." Tammy put both hands in the air, palms up. "Nora just got here. She shouldn't have to explain herself or justify her beliefs. Remember what Daed said."

"Yeah, yeah, yeah." Tucker chortled. "Hey, I know that song." He belted out the lyrics of a song that started with "She loves you, yeah, yeah, yeah."

Not very creative. Nora kept her mouth shut.

Tammy rolled her eyes. "Don't worry about him. He just likes to hear himself talk."

"What did he mean? What did your daed say?"

"Nothing. He just didn't want us doing what Tucker is doing—baiting you." She turned her back to her brother, who rolled his eyes in return. "He says it's better to wait and let you spend some time with us and observe our lives before we approach you gently about what we believe."

"Don't you believe the same thing we do?"

"Not exactly." Tammy stuck her elbows on her knees and her chin on the palm of one hand. "I'd rather let you hear it from Daed. We mean no offense. We just want you to know there's so much more to our faith than what you have now."

Not possible. The Plain people in her district lived and breathed their faith. Faith, family, community, in that order.

"Let's not worry about that your first night here. Come on, spill it all. Are you still going out with Levi? Are you getting married anytime soon?"

Chewing her lip, Nora turned with her back to Tucker and scooted closer to her cousin. "Levi and I are still together, but he's mad about me coming here. He made a huge deal about it, more than Daed did, and he *hated* the idea. I know he'll be the head of the family when we get married, but sometimes his bossiness is hard to take. But then he was so upset when our house burned down, all I wanted to do was hug him and make it better. Loving someone is really hard."

"You had a house before you got married?" Tammy's freckled nose wrinkled, and lines appeared on her fair-skinned forehead. "And you think *we're* too liberal?"

"Nee, not like that." Nora explained the fate of her dream home. Unexpected tears clogged her throat. She sniffed and pretended to stare up at the sky, searching for hidden stars. "Now we're starting over, and we can't even do that until we can get back into Kootenai. We don't even know if Chet will want to rebuild."

"The will of Gott be done."

At least they both believed that.

"Now tell me about Levi. How's the kissing?"

"Tammy!"

"Come on. Don't you just love kissing? I used to think it was gross. My first boyfriend was a terrible kisser. It was all slobbery and nasty. He tasted like Cheetos and smelled like hairspray. He broke up with me because he said I always had my nose stuck in a book. The books were more interesting than him."

"You? A bookworm?" Nora stuck out her arm to fend off Tammy's mock pummeling. "Truly, I think you're well rid of someone who doesn't love you for who you are."

"Danki, Kossin. You're sweet." Tammy's pretend punches turned into a one-armed hug. "It's okay. I think you should be able to have both—a person who kisses like a dream and likes you for who you are." Her fair cheeks turned delicious apple red. She ducked her head.

Something was up.

Nora leaned closer and whispered, "You have a special friend too. That's *wunderbarr*. Tell me everything."

They jumped up and skipped down the sidewalk, arm in arm, like third graders.

"Are you going to tell me who he is or what?"

Tammy slowed and let go of Nora's arm. "I think I'd rather talk about kissing right now."

"Hmm, I'll pry it out of you sooner or later, Kossin." Nora parked the question on the stove's back burner for now. "Kissing is wunderbarr, isn't it?" The feel of Levi's scruffy chin rubbing on her cheek assailed Nora. His soft, full lips warm on hers. The soapy scent of his clothes and the peppermint on his breath.

She glanced around as if he might be nearby. "You're right there in the middle of it, and everything else disappears. You can't think about anything else except the way it feels. Even though you kiss with your lips, your whole body feels his whole body. You could do it forever if you didn't run out of breath, because who wants to stop feeling like you're the most loved girl on the face of the earth?"

"How do you know it's the real thing?" The frown on Tammy's face said this was no idle question. Who was this guy she'd kissed? "How do you know it's love and not just the way he kisses?"

"It's like getting run over by a moose. And you're so discombobulated, you stutter and you can't think of words and you say silly stuff. You forget how to count and what your mudder's name is."

"Boy, howdy, I can relate to that."

"I was hooked after one ride home from a singing. Levi says it was the same for him." Nora stopped at the fence that separated the road from the pasture. The ears on three horses grazing on the other side pricked up. One beautiful roan ambled their direction. "I love riding horses. Levi and I rode our horses in the mountains when we first started courting."

They'd ridden hard, fast, and long. By the time they slowed, Nora's kapp hung from her neck, and her hair lay on her shoulders.

"We can ride horses while you're here." Tammy pointed toward a black gelding that stayed out in the pasture. "See Sable out there? He doesn't like to be ridden. He's a tough ride."

"Perfect for me." Nora loved a challenge. "Let's do it now."

"We can't. Not without asking Grandpa, and he'll say no. It's too dark and Sable is too skittish."

Disappointed, Nora kissed the soft nose of the butterscotch mare. Love was like riding a half-tamed horse, up and down, too fast, impossible to control. "Maybe later. I wonder if we're supposed to enjoy kissing so much."

Tammy patted the roan and whispered sweet nothings to him. "I know. It almost makes a girl feel guilty."

"It's not like we can ask our mudders." Nora had felt shame that first night, certain they'd moved too quickly into the physical territory of their relationship. Mercy and Christine had no more experience than she did. Juliette recommended Nora "jump his bones." Her friends had shouted her down, and Juliette had admitted that Tim, the man in her life, didn't allow any bone jumping. He wouldn't even officially date her. "Levi put his arm around me, and I felt a tingle from my toes to my nose. He hugged me, and I didn't want to let go."

"And one thing leads to another." Tammy shot Nora a sly grin. "That's what our mudders would say."

"Not with us."

"Gut. That's gut."

"I like to think I only enjoy it so much because it's Levi." Nora had already revealed more to her cousin than she had to her best friends. Maybe it was because Tammy lived in Libby. When Nora returned to Kootenai, she wouldn't see her cousin for many months, maybe longer. Plus, she was family. "It wouldn't feel that way if I didn't love him and trust him with my feelings. I thought he felt the same way. But last night it almost seemed as if he didn't trust me. He didn't think I could stand on my own two feet."

"About your faith, you mean?"

"Exactly. He's worried about the pressure that will be exerted by everyone here."

"He doesn't want you to change without him." Tammy's expression turned serious. "You have to invite him to come here. That way he can see you're in no danger of losing your faith. In fact, you'll have a stronger faith. He can too."

"His faith is strong now. So is mine."

Tammy climbed up on the fence's top rung and wrapped her legs around the lower one. Nora stayed where she was. Climbing fences in a dress had its challenges. Tammy's face turned serious. "My guy's name is Wyatt. I think he's an angel."

She couldn't keep her secret to herself, after all. Nora grinned. "You think he's too perfect and nice—too godly—for a girl like you? You'd have to clean up your act?"

"Nee, I mean I think he's an angel. My kind of angel."

10

The mysterious man and potential angel named Wyatt didn't live in Libby. Nora didn't get a chance to ask how courting would be possible if he lived in faraway Missoula. Tammy volunteered that he was the son of an evangelist who regularly visited the Eagle Valley Amish community and preached at their services. The rest of the time his father held tent revivals all over the country, and Wyatt traveled with him.

"It's perfect timing." Tammy hopped from the fence and dusted off her hands. "You'll get to attend your first service and meet Wyatt."

"I can attend your services?"

"Of course you can." Tammy's nose wrinkled, and her pale, almost white eyebrows lifted. "Why wouldn't you? Our church and our community are open to anyone who would join us in worship."

"I thought because your parents were banned from our services—"

"We'd do the same thing to you, tit for tat." Tammy rolled her eyes and threw her hands in the air as if appealing to God Himself. "We're not like that. We embrace people, welcome them, and encourage them to join us in worship. It's the only way there's a chance they'll change their way of thinking when it comes to having a personal relationship with our Lord Jesus Christ."

Once again they skittered far too close to the subject they'd both been avoiding all evening—differences in their faith.

"Then I'll look forward to the service on Sunday."

"No you won't. I can see the nervousness in the way your neck is getting all red and blotchy."

Nora groaned. Her neck gave her away every time. At her baptism everyone thought she had hives or a terrible sunburn. "I'm not nervous. Just too warm. Let's go back to the house and get more ice cream. I wonder if Mammi has chocolate syrup."

"I bet she does. She keeps all the ice cream toppings, including sprinkles and nuts, so we can make fudge sundaes."

They strode past Tucker double-time, but that didn't keep him from singing a song with lyrics that started with "Here comes the bride."

The blotches on Nora's neck were probably redder than radishes at that point. She ignored him. After they had their ice cream in large soup bowls, they went upstairs to her room. It was strange not to be working on something. Her evenings were usually filled with mending clothes or piecing rugs or creating blocks for a quilt. Sometimes she played checkers with Father or read Westerns aloud to the boys. Here everyone had gone in different directions after supper.

"You have beautiful hair." Tammy took Nora's kapp from her head and undid her bun. "It's such a nice color. Not dishwater blonde like mine."

"It's average, really. Yours is prettier."

"I bet Levi likes it."

The memory of how Levi's hands felt tangled in her hair only two nights earlier in Rexford sent a tingling sensation racing through Nora. He had liked her hair. A lot.

"We're not supposed to wear our hair down. It's unseemly." She grabbed the long strands and wound them in a knot so they sat under her kapp again. "Modesty is so important for women."

"But not men?"

"Men, too, but we don't want to give them something to think about that might get them in trouble with Gott." Too late. The wonder in Levi's voice as he touched her hair had spoken volumes. "I don't want to do anything that causes Levi to falter."

"It's just hair, for goodness' sake." Tammy threw herself back on the bed and stretched her long, slim arms over her head. She popped back up like a jack-in-the-box. "I know what we can do. Let's call Levi."

"What? Nee, we can't call him. Calls should be reserved for important information." Her folks didn't use a phone for a casual chat. It had to be something important. Definitely not to find out what time to come to supper. Or to ask, *Are you still mad? Do you still love me? Do you miss me?* All the things Nora wanted to say to Levi. *Did you talk to Chet? Is he rebuilding? When can we go home?* "I should write him a letter."

"A letter? *Phfffst!*" Tammy rolled off the bed and paced the small strip of rug between it and the matching dresser. "I wish Daed would let us have cell phones. He says one phone in the house is enough. He's not as wild and woolly as Onkel Harley thinks. I just wish he wouldn't draw the line on cell phones. Then I could talk to my friend whenever I want. And text. And send pictures."

Wyatt, in other words. Nora had played with Juliette's cell phone a few times, but she didn't need to call anyone. Her family and friends lived within a bicycle's ride. Face-to-face talks were much more satisfying. "Onkel Ike and I agree on this one."

"That makes you a fuddy-duddy, but I still love you." Tammy went to the door and opened it. "Come on. Let's use Grandpa's phone. He won't mind. No one will."

The desire to talk to Levi sparred with the certainty that someone, somewhere, would mind. Making sure he didn't hold a grudge would allow her to sleep later. Surely the fire created a situation where people needed to call each other. This wasn't a call to chat. It was a call to make sure he was okay. Levi was a stickler for the rules, so how wrong could it be? "Levi gave me a number to call. I could let him know we are fine and make sure he is too. It's not like we'll be chatting about stupid little stuff."

"Exactly my thought." Tammy clapped and did a funny little jig. "That's known as a Snoopy dance. Can you Snoopy dance?"

Making a phone call was enough for one day. Dancing was definitely against the rules. Nora followed Tammy down the stairs. Tammy halted, hand in the air, as she peered around the corner. "Quick, they're busy talking."

If they weren't technically breaking the rules, why did it matter if the men saw them? No point in examining that question too closely.

The men were discussing something about pricing on the log cabin kits. The women were at the kitchen table, eating snickerdoodles and drinking iced tea. Nora picked up her pace behind Tammy and scurried into the hallway, where the cordless phone sat on its base on the small half-circle table.

Tammy grabbed the phone and pushed through the door to the only bedroom on the first floor. "It's for when Daadi and Mammi can't make it up the stairs anymore," she whispered. "Shut the door."

If they had to sneak around and whisper, it couldn't be good.

Nora did as she was told. The room smelled like roses. Grandma kept it ready for company at a moment's notice, it seemed. Nora sat on the pieced rug, her back against the double bed. Better not to muss up the Log Cabin quilt. "Now what?"

"Go on, do it. It's easy as pie. Just punch in the number, and voilà, you're talking to someone in Eureka. Is that where he is? Eureka?"

"Jah, but who says he'll be in the house with the folks who loaned his family the rental house?"

"It's worth a shot."

Indeed it was. Nora unfolded the scrap of paper on which Levi had scrawled the phone number. *"Call me if you need me. I'll come get you. I'll be right there to get you, I promise."*

She swallowed hard and punched in the number. Her fingers shook. *Don't be a silly goose. It's only a phone call.*

The number rang once, twice, three times. "No one's answering. No one's there." Nora held out the phone so Tammy could hear. "He's not there."

"Just give it a minute." Tammy pushed the receiver back at Nora. "Don't be so impatient."

She wasn't impatient, just nervous. Nora held the phone to her ear. A man's voice boomed, "Hello, hello? Hello! Who's there?"

"It's Nora Beachy." Her voice quivered. She took a breath. *Don't be a wuss.* "I wanted to see if I could talk to Levi Raber, please."

Shuffling noises filled the crackling line.

"See, that wasn't so hard." Tammy's whisper was so loud the man probably heard it on the other end of the line. "You're a pro at this."

Not a pro. Sweat from her hand made the receiver slick. "Hello, are you still there?"

"Who's this?" A different voice, this one deeper and with that clipped English that came from learning Pennsylvania Dutch first and English not until school. "Levi's not here. This is his father, Jack."

Dare she say who she was? Jack might not appreciate Nora's use of the phone to call his stepson. He might even tell her father. "It's Nora Beachy."

"Ah." A distinct pause followed.

The bedroom door swung open. Daryl loomed over them, legs apart, arms crossed, glaring. "What are you doing?"

The one person who would care. Nora's dress felt damp between her shoulders. A trickle of sweat rolled down her temple. She pressed the receiver to her chest. "I wanted to make sure . . . I mean, I'm calling . . . It's just that—"

"She's calling her boyfriend to let him know she's okay and see how he's doing. She also wants to ask him what the guy said about the property they want to buy." Tammy hopped to her feet and stepped between them with the fearlessness of someone who had no idea what she was up against. "They were planning to move into a house that burned down."

"None of that is anyone's business." Daryl's tone stopped just short of a growl. "They won't get married until after the banns are made public, and that hasn't happened."

He brushed past Tammy and jerked the phone from Nora's hand. "Nora has to go."

He hung up the phone and turned back to Nora. "You know better. You've been here less than a day, and you're already sliding down their slippery slope." He didn't seem to know or care that Tammy still stood behind him, hearing every word.

She stuck her tongue out and put her thumbs in her ears so she could waggle her fingers. Childish, but it felt good to know Tammy wouldn't let Daryl's tirade hurt her feelings.

"These are difficult times, but we still need to obey the Ordnung. That's why I'm here, to make sure you stay on the path of righteousness. Is that clear?"

"Jah." Nora managed to utter one syllable. Her lungs were constricted with shame and doubt. Daryl would take the most conservative posture on this subject. Mother and Father would allow wiggle room on this subject, but not their son-in-law. "I'm sorry. I just wanted—"

"I know what you wanted." Daryl's voice softened. He shook his shaggy hair. "I know what it's like. I courted your sister."

"It won't happen again."

"Levi talked to your daed. He said he would come here when his family is settled in Eureka. I know it's hard to be patient, so in the meantime, write him a letter."

Good advice from a man who had patiently courted Jeannie for two years. Her sister had been less sure of marriage than Nora. She had taught school before Mercy, and she liked it. But once Daryl convinced her to take the plunge, she'd gone after it wholeheartedly. No one made a better wife and mother. And Daryl was a good father. A stickler for rules, but that was as it should be.

"I will write him a letter. I don't know what I was thinking."

Daryl turned to stare at Tammy. "I do. Don't forget what happened to Adam and Eve when they listened to the serpent."

"What's all the commotion about?" Uncle Ike stuck his head through the doorway. "It's time we get home, Tammy."

"No commotion. Just a conversation." Daryl handled the phone to Tammy. "We may be in Libby, but we're still Plain folks from Kootenai."

If he heard any challenge in that statement, Uncle Ike didn't react. "I haven't forgotten what the Ordnung says, but Tammy isn't as familiar."

"Nora is."

"We have to go. We hope you'll join us for worship on Sunday."

Daryl shuffled his feet. His shoulders hunched. "We'll see."

"We don't bite. Everyone is welcome at our services." Uncle Ike put one arm around Tammy's shoulders and squeezed. "I'm doing the preaching. I'm not so awful, am I, Dochder?"

Tammy leaned into his big body. "You're the best, Daed."

"What she means is, I'm not as boring as the other ministers we've had."

"Daed!"

"Anyway, come for the service and stay for lunch."

They were barely out the door before Daryl turned back to Nora. "No phone." He tromped out.

"No phone," Nora whispered as she drew her knees up and wrapped her arms around them. She laid her head on top of them and sighed. "What a day."

Whether Jack would tell Levi she'd called was anyone's guess, but she wouldn't bank on it.

11

The unassuming log cabin didn't look like a den of iniquity. Still, Nora fought the urge to turn and flee. Her first three days in Libby had been quiet, mostly filled with helping Grandma with chores and entertaining the children, who weren't sleeping well in this new place. The Eagle Valley Amish congregation met in a church complete with a steeple and a bell. Rows of chairs crowded the single room with a high ceiling and windows clothed with white curtains on either long side. Neither Tammy's gleeful smile nor Jeannie's nervous titter helped.

Stifling a yawn, Nora slid into a folding chair between Tammy and Tucker—Tammy had informed her on the walk over that they could sit wherever they wanted. It didn't have to be with family. Jeannie and Daryl sat on the other side of Tammy, a child in each lap. Grandma had charge of Sadie. Grandpa had charge of himself.

One sweeping glance told the story. This was no Plain service. Men and women were not separated. Nor did the elders take the front rows with the youngies in the back. The range of garb ran from traditional Plain dresses to jeans and T-shirts. Many of the women, like Tammy, didn't cover their hair, although some wore white scarves. At the front of the room, a piano filled the space next to a microphone on a stand. A banjo and a guitar had been placed on racks next to the piano.

An early morning soft breeze lifted the curtains in open windows, heralding the start of autumn. If it were any warmer, she'd have trouble staying awake. Sadie's cries had awakened her three times during the night. The third time, Jeannie stumbled into the hall to take the baby from Nora. She hadn't argued.

If only the cooler weather meant rain and snow were in the forecast. The fires would subside, and Nora could go home to services held in her friends' homes every other Sunday. Life would get back to normal. She and Levi would be together again.

That would be her prayer this morning.

Tammy elbowed her. "That's him."

"Him who?"

"Wyatt." Her whisper barely reached Nora's ear. "The angel. They got into town last night."

Nora followed Tammy's gaze. Wyatt did indeed have an angelic facade—if an angel wore a gray suit with a white shirt and had blond curls that fell on his pale forehead. And kissed a girl like Tammy. His eyes were blue and his cheeks dimpled. He was slender and short for a man. A strong wind might blow him away. He didn't look as if he'd done a hard day's labor in his life. Plain people didn't talk much about angels, but they were mentioned in the Bible more than a few times. He smiled at the folks around him. Everyone smiled in return. How could they not? Nora took a breath.

"See what I mean?"

"He's only a man."

"I know. I was kidding. He just looks like an angel. But he kisses like a man." A bemused expression on her face, Tammy twisted a lock of her hair. "He's so handsome, and he doesn't even know it. He's so filled with the Holy Spirit it flows out of him and all over everyone around him."

Despite the warmth of so many bodies crammed into one room, Nora shivered. It didn't seem right to link the physical with the spiritual. Had Jesus been a handsome man? She'd seen one or two artists' depictions, but the bishop said they were flawed human perceptions of what He might have looked like. Sometimes Jesus had blond hair, and Noah pointed out that Jesus lived in the Middle East, so His complexion was likely brown and swarthy. He was a carpenter who worked hard with His hands. Mostly His physical appearance didn't matter, only what He did and who He was.

Wyatt hugged a preschooler who grinned and skipped away. He turned. Their gazes connected. His blue eyes were lighter than a March sky after a long winter. His gaze dove past the exterior—her pale-lilac dress and white apron—to her heart of hearts in less than a second. He knew her. He smiled, all dimples and pearly white teeth. The urge to cover herself overwhelmed her as if she'd been stripped bare. She swallowed and managed a courteous smile in return.

"He's coming over," Tammy murmured. "He's coming right to us."

"Try not to slobber on his jacket," Nora whispered. The feelings he elicited with a simple glance were the product of Tammy's description of Wyatt, nothing more. No angels walked the earth in human form. They were busy doing God's bidding in heaven. "He'll know you have a crush on him."

"It's not a crush. I like him. He likes me."

"You have a crush on an angel."

He was upon them. "Hey, Tammy." He leaned over and hugged her. She lifted her arms to return the favor, but her gaze went to Nora. Her eyelids fluttered. *He's so cute.* Wyatt's hand lingered on Tammy's shiny hair. He straightened and turned to Nora. "Who's this with you?"

Tammy seemed dazed. She didn't answer.

"I'm Nora, Tammy's kossin from Kootenai."

Wyatt held out his hand. She had no choice but to shake it. His grip was strong and tight. His other hand slid over the top and held on a second longer, but not too long. He squeezed again and let go. "I'm pleased to meet you. Is it your first time to a truly God-serving church service?"

Jeannie shifted in her seat. Nora glanced at her sister. Her questioning frown matched Nora's own disbelief at the question. She squashed it and introduced her family. "We've attended church in West Kootenai our entire lives."

"Gut. You have a strong foundation. Here, we can build on it. To God be the glory."

He winked, did an about-face, and went to the small upright piano, where he sat down. A few seconds later Uncle Ike broke away from a circle of men and joined Wyatt at the front. A broad smile on his face, he welcomed the crowd. "We're honored to have with us once again our good friends the Reverend George Brubacher and his son Wyatt. George says he's only visiting today and not prepared to preach. He'll have announcements later about the next tent revival. If you have any questions, be sure to collar him afterward. Let's give them a mighty welcome."

The congregation broke into a rousing round of applause with much hooting, hollering, "Amen," "Welcome, brothers," and "Hallelujah." Nora and Jeannie exchanged glances again. Her eyebrows raised, Jeannie chewed her lower lip. Daryl shifted in his chair.

Wyatt began to play, softly at first, then more fiercely as his voice grew and deepened. The music filled the small building and escaped through the open windows. No one moved. No one spoke. "I can only imagine." He came back to those words again and again as his voice, the words, and the notes urged Nora to imagine. What would it be like when she met Jesus face-to-face? What would she do?

Her pulse skipped a beat. It seemed to race ahead with every keystroke on the piano. Wyatt played with his eyes closed and his head raised to the heavens. Nora closed her eyes. Her hands went to her throat. The sound of Wyatt's sweet baritone transported her someplace she'd never been before—so close to heaven, she wanted to drop to her knees and praise God.

An elbow jabbed her arm. She forced her eyes open. Jeannie frowned at her, her expression a big question mark. Daryl's sour face joined in. Beyond them, Grandpa beamed but Grandma sat stony-faced, staring at her hands.

Nora shrugged. Didn't everyone feel it? How could they not? Maybe she shouldn't feel this way. Was this the temptation of which Mother and Father spoke? It couldn't be. Something that brought a person within inches of heaven could only be God-given.

Ignoring her sister's raised eyebrows, Nora sought Wyatt's face again. His beatific smile encompassed the room. The music faded away.

The congregation rose to its collective feet and clapped. The applause bounced from the rafters. Shouts of "Hallelujah!" and "Amen!" joined forces.

Wyatt simply nodded and let his hands drop into his lap.

A man seated on the front row began to sing with no accompaniment. The Eagle Valley Amish Ministry had not abandoned the *vorsinger* tradition, it seemed. Everyone joined in, singing the familiar German song from the *Ausband*, "Das Loblied." The Praise Song. Every Plain child learned all twenty-eight lines with 140 German words before any other song.

Everyone remained seated and joined in. The song went on and on, one long note held after another. Nora peeked at Jeannie and Daryl. They had relaxed. Grandma and Grandpa joined in.

The song lasted fifteen minutes, but no one seemed to tire of it. Their voices were united. No single person stood out. No one had a special talent. It didn't matter if someone sang off-key or moved to the next note too soon.

Nora closed her eyes and listened. God moved in a different, slower, more solemn way through the congregation. Still, He moved.

The song ended. Uncle Ike stood. He picked up a microphone and began to talk.

His somber bass filled the room. At first it was familiar Scripture from Acts and then Paul's letters to Corinth. He spoke of a closer walk with Jesus, of the need to spend time in Scripture, to read the Bible and ponder its meaning. He urged everyone in the room to seek a personal relationship with their Savior.

Everyone hung on his words. They didn't seem puzzled at his meaning. Nora glanced at Jeannie. Her sister's eyebrows rose and fell. Daryl shifted his feet under the chair in front of him. He studied his fingernails. Her brother-in-law looked as if he'd rather be chased up a Douglas fir by a grizzly bear than sit in his chair.

Uncle Ike was just getting warmed up. "Have you been born again? Do you feel the fire of the Holy Spirit burning in your heart? If you don't, ask God to come into your heart right here, right now. If you believe Jesus Christ is your personal Savior, you will have eternal salvation." His face, so like Father's, was transformed. The lines around his mouth and eyes deepened. His voice went hoarse. He raised one fist, then jabbed at the sky. "No more sorrow, no more pain, only the joy of the Lord is yours for the asking for all eternity. You are born again into the family of Christ. You will be free forever and ever."

The fire had been lit in this one-room church. Almost everyone stood. They didn't simply stand. They hopped. They jumped. They danced. Their hands were raised high. Laughing little girls danced in the aisles with one another. Their long dresses whipped behind them in their exuberance.

With every sentence from Uncle Ike's mouth, the shouts rang out. "Amen!" "Yes, Lord!" "Hallelujah!" "Praise the Lord!"

A warm and sweaty bedlam descended on the building. It was

as if the Holy Spirit had turned the occupants into jumping beans. Either that or they drank too much coffee with breakfast.

Did she stand? Nora couldn't yell or jump or hop. Not in church. She sought Grandma and Grandpa. Grandpa stood and clapped. Grandma didn't. She sat silently, arms cradling Sadie, her face set in neutral lines. Nora clung to the sides of her chair. Her body wanted to stand. Her mind said, *nee, nee, nee*. Sweat trickled down the back of her neck. As the air grew warmer, her entire body began to perspire. She wiped slick hands on her apron.

"Come on!" Tammy popped from her chair and joined the little girls in the aisle. She twirled them around and laughed, her face alight with joy and enthusiasm. "Come on, Nora. Dance. The Lord won't strike you down if you dance for Him. He loves you and wants to hold you close."

Embarrassment ran rampant through Nora. She couldn't. She shouldn't. Her legs shook and her arms quivered. *Gott, are You there?*

"God doesn't care what you wear or if you drive a car. He doesn't care if you cover your head or have buttons on your clothes." Uncle Ike held up the leather-bound Bible toward the sky. "God loves His children. He wants to walk with you and talk with you every day. He wants the relationship of a Father and son, a Father and daughter. How do I know? The Bible tells me so.

"Today, Lord, shake the chains of religion that have bound our brothers and sisters and kept them from a personal walk with Jesus. Without criticism or judgment, we ask for Your freedom, love, and grace for them. We ask for a mighty outpouring of the Holy Spirit on the whole state of Pennsylvania. Pour Your Spirit out on the whole state of Ohio. Do what man cannot do. The traditions of men have rendered Your Word ineffective in those regions. We ask that You ignite our brethren with a desire to know You more deeply and more personally.

"Let sovereign signs, wonders, visions, and encounters with the supernatural visit upon the church elders in these regions. Let the Holy Spirit fill up Amish churches across this country from east to west and north to south."

Jason on one hip, Daryl stood and walked out.

Her cheeks pink and her face damp with perspiration, Jeannie wrapped her arms around Missy, who covered her ears and sobbed, and followed her husband.

Stay or go?

Making sense of Ike's words was hard in the midst of so much noise. How could any of them absorb his meaning when they were carrying on like a bunch of people possessed by demons? Or was it supposed to be the Holy Spirit? Did the Holy Spirit make people act crazy in church?

How could Uncle Ike claim not to judge and yet condemn his Amish family? How could he suggest that Mother and Father and the entire Gmay in West Kootenai somehow didn't measure on God's yardstick? Chains of religion? What chains?

Her head aching, Nora squeezed into the aisle. Tammy whirled and grabbed both of Nora's hands. "Hallelujah, Kossin. Praise the Lord." She danced around Nora in a frenzy of twirling and bowing. Her glowing face became ethereal. *She* looked like an angel. Nora tugged free. She scurried from the church.

Outside, a fall breeze, only faintly tainted with smoke, cooled her hot cheeks. The noise trumpeted from the open windows, but the birds still sang and the sun still shone.

"I've heard about churches like this one. They make it all about them. They're egotistical. They dare to assume they know Gott's will." His face fierce with anger, Daryl paced while Jeannie tried to comfort Missy and Jason, who both cried now. "Don't you understand? He trashed our traditions from the pulpit. Our way of dressing. Our choice to live apart from the world. That, too, is in the Bible. Didn't you hear him say it?"

"I'm not sure." Jeannie's voice faltered. She nuzzled Missy's hair with her chin. "Everybody was talking at once. It was confusing. I thought he was talking about Jesus being our Savior. We believe that, don't we?"

"We don't presume to have an assurance of anything." Daryl would wear a bald spot in the grass with his pacing. He snorted and sped up. "Do we know the future? Can we read an omniscient Gott's mind?"

No they couldn't.

But Daryl wasn't done venting. "We have a living hope. Gott is just and merciful. We humbly await His decision when we face eternity."

"Would it be such a bad thing to study Scripture and to have Bible studies so we can better understand the things Onkel Ike said in there?" Nora took Missy from her sister. The little girl blinked against the sun, hiccuped a sob, and laid her head on Nora's shoulder. "Wouldn't it be nice to be so sure of what the Bible says?"

"The Bible says what it says. It's not up to a man—any man—to interpret it for us. Next he'll say God spoke to him and told him what to say and what these people should do. He's forgotten his Plain roots. He truly isn't Plain anymore."

Uncle Ike and Aunt Roseanna had been banned from the Kootenai district's services more than fifteen years ago. No sense in arguing with Daryl. It wasn't Nora's place, and she didn't have enough understanding of the divisions between the two churches to begin to talk about them.

"He said he wasn't judging us, though." Yet the words felt like a judgment that Plain folks all across the country were somehow in need of the Holy Spirit. Chained to their traditions about clothing and not driving cars. "Maybe we left too soon. Maybe he went on to say more that would help us understand what he's getting at."

"I heard enough." Daryl scooped up Jason and plopped the boy on his shoulders. "I'm going back to the house. You should stay here, Jeannie, until your groossdaadi can drive you home. It's too far for you to walk with the bopli."

Fury in every elongated stride, he soon disappeared from sight.

Nora settled onto a picnic table bench and gave Missy her faceless doll to play with. "What do you think, Jeannie? Do our traditions keep us from a closer walk with Gott?"

Jeannie sighed and shrugged. "I've never felt a lacking. Have you?"

"Nee. Not that I noticed."

They sat in silence for several moments. It felt good, cool, clean, and fresh. Missy trotted around them, picking up rocks and sticks and piling them on the bench like special treasures. Jeannie hummed a few notes of an old German hymn. A person could have a closer walk with the Lord without making a lot of noise. In fact, not talking at all seemed to invite His presence.

"I miss Mudder." The realization hit Nora only after she spoke the words. "I even miss James and the boys."

"I even miss Stinker."

They both laughed.

"It's only for a little while." Nora flicked away a piece of grass Missy had deposited on her apron. "Soon we'll be home, helping the Yoders and the Knowleses rebuild their houses."

The others would help Chet rebuild his house—if that's what he wanted. Levi and Nora would have their chance at a long and happy life.

"You miss Levi, don't you?"

"You're not allowed to read my mind."

"I felt the same way about Daryl when he was working with his dad in Lewistown."

Nora kept quiet.

Jeannie laughed. "I know you don't like him much."

"That's not true."

"He wants to do the right thing. He promised Daed he would make sure we stay out of trouble. He takes that promise seriously."

"He saw me making a phone call."

"I know. He told me." Jeannie patted Nora's knee. "When you decide to do something here, ask yourself if it's something you'd do at home. If it's not, then you shouldn't do it."

"Is that what you're doing?"

"Daryl and I talk it over, but jah. You can always ask me if you're not sure."

"Danki." Having an older sister who had her head on straight had many benefits. "It's harder than I thought it would be."

The church doors opened. People streamed out laughing and talking. They didn't appear much different from how Nora's friends and family looked when a three-hour service ended in Kootenai. Tammy made a beeline for Nora. She stood. Jeannie grabbed her arm. "One other thing, Schweschder."

"What?"

"Be careful with that man Wyatt."

"You don't even know him. What makes you say that?"

"Something about him bothers me." Jeannie's grip tightened. "Just promise me."

"Tammy jokes that he's an angel."

"Remember what Noah said about angels?"

Nora wracked her brains. Noah said a lot of things about angels, most of them good. "Gott sends them as messengers. Like the angel who told Mary about the baby Jesus."

"He also said Satan comes masquerading as an angel."

An angel of light. The sermon came back to Nora. They shouldn't listen to the Englishers' music. It would fill their heads with garbage, and there'd be no room for the good stuff.

Was Wyatt garbage or good stuff?

12

A man with dimples and a cherubic smile who invited a person to be his friend couldn't be all bad. Nora settled onto a picnic table bench with her ham sandwich, potato chips, ranch dip, and spicy dill pickle. Wyatt slid in on one side of her and Tammy on the other. Tucker and his friends took up the bench on the other side. They shoved and elbowed each other, bellowing and hooting like all the Plain teenage boys in Kootenai. Except they looked anything but Plain.

"What did you think of the service?" Sheer contentment on his face, Wyatt loaded a chip with dip and stuck it in his mouth whole. He smelled like sandalwood aftershave even though his pale, baby-smooth skin couldn't possibly need shaving. "You left before it was over."

"It was interesting." Nora picked up her sandwich, then put it down. How did she respond to his question without being rude or judgmental? She had no right to criticize how others worshipped. "Very . . . enthusiastic."

"You didn't like it, did you?" Wyatt dusted his fingers on a paper napkin and applied himself to a fruit and whipped cream salad in a Styrofoam bowl. "But that's because you don't understand it. Give it time. Keep an open mind. You're a believer, so you're halfway there."

Grandma would call that a left-handed compliment. Nora called it judgmental. She didn't judge Wyatt. He should offer her the same latitude. "Only halfway?"

"We shouldn't bug her about religion over lunch." Tammy peeled an orange. The sweet tangy citrus scent floated on the air like perfume. "It'll give her indigestion. Daed says it takes time to win over the hearts of the lost."

Anger mixed with bewilderment burned through Nora. More judgment. If the Libby folks were still Plain, they wouldn't be so judgmental or so sure they had God's ear. "I'm not lost. I'm not chained by religion." Whatever that meant.

"I didn't mean you specifically."

But she did. Nora's sandwich turned to cement in her mouth. She took a long drink of sweetened iced tea. What had seemed a strong foundation the day of the evacuation now seemed diminished. Only half listening to Tucker and his friends compete to see who could eat sandwiches the fastest, she chewed mechanically and stared at her plate.

"Don't be sad." Wyatt moved closer. His soft, gentle words warmed her. "We don't mean to offend you or scare you. We care about you."

Nora eased away. "You just met me."

"Yet I can see you have a beautiful soul and a caring heart. Plus I know what Tammy has told me. She's a good judge of character." He offered her a chocolate chip cookie from his plate. "None of that really matters. We're called to win the lost and make disciples. While you're not lost in the same way that those who've never heard the good news are, you could have so much more. I want that for you."

Goose bumps prickled on Nora's arms. A thin, brilliant heat like a Fourth of July sparkler sizzled up and down her spine. She accepted the cookie. How could she not when it was offered with such caring words that stirred something warm and sweet inside her? "Danki."

He smiled. His face lit up with that same glow that had been in Tammy's face as she danced and twirled in the church aisle. "You have crumbs on your face."

Nora grabbed her napkin. "Thanks. I don't want to go around like a piglet."

"Your piano playing was great today, Wyatt. I love that MercyMe song." Tammy hopped up and spun around to Tucker's side across from Wyatt, where she plopped down. "Will you teach me to play it? I've been practicing the hymn you gave me all week."

"One thing at a time." Wyatt's good-natured smile encompassed them both. "With music and with faith."

"Have you seen the movie they made about Bart Millard, the lead singer of MercyMe? It's about how his dad treated him when he was a kid. Dennis Quaid plays his dad." Tammy leaned forward until Nora could see her face. Her cheeks were pink and her expression determined. Of course Nora had no idea who Bart Millard or Dennis Quaid were. Nor had she seen the movie. Tammy knew that. "Wyatt's teaching me to play the piano."

Tammy, being her closest cousin-friend, also knew how Nora secretly pined for the chance to play a musical instrument. She'd never admitted it to anyone else. "I thought you played the violin."

"I do, and the flute. I love all musical instruments." Tammy stood again. "In fact, come on, this would be a good time for band practice."

"You have a band?"

Tammy dumped her plate in a nearby trash can. "Yep. Wyatt's an honorary member since he can't be here all the time. Come on, you guys, let's practice. Practices are usually closed, but you can come, too, Nora, since you're visiting."

A chance to play a few chords on Tucker's guitar. Or maybe even the piano. At the very least, Nora could sing with the instruments. Maybe Tucker was right. The Bible had instruments. David sang and danced to the Lord. His wife made fun of him, but he did it anyway.

The tables still held stragglers, but they weren't paying attention to the older teens. The church crowd had thinned. Jeannie sat talking with a woman about her age, wearing a white scarf around carrot-orange hair in a bun. Both held sleeping babies. Missy played nearby on a wooden playscape and fort. Grandma and Grandpa visited with an elderly couple Nora didn't recognize.

"Let me tell Grandpa."

"We practice right here at the church." Tammy pointed at the building. "They won't care." She started toward it. "I'm glad you're coming. I brought you a surprise."

Nora took her plate to the trash can. Wyatt did the same. "We could take a walk after, if you're interested." He waved away a determined bee that proceeded to buzz Nora next. "We could talk about today's service. I'm happy to answer any questions."

His smile held her there, hand still poised over the overflowing trash can. Butterflies caught in a net must feel this way. She could walk away, couldn't she? "I don't know. It depends on how long the practice lasts. I need to get back to help Mammi with supper and take care of the bopli for my schweschder."

"We'll see." He brushed away flies that wanted their portion of the leftovers. "If not today, some other day. I promise you, it'll be nice."

Nice? How did he define nice?

What would Tammy think of her angel taking a walk with Nora?

"Come on, you guys!" Tucker's belch punctuated his impatience. "Time's a'wasting."

One thing at a time. Music practice. Tammy's surprise. What could be more surprising than the service that morning? Uneasiness tackled pleasure and left it sucking dust. Surprises were nice, but coming from her cousin, the word held many possibilities.

Inside the church Wyatt, Tucker, and the others went straight for their instruments. Tammy led Nora to a corner in the back where she unzipped a faded green backpack. "These are for you." She held up a pair of denim jeans and a short-sleeved purple blouse made of a soft, filmy material. "My friend Mona is your size. At least she was. She's put on a few pounds. She was going to give these away, so I grabbed them for you."

"That's nice of you, but I don't think so." A mirror presented itself in Nora's mind's eye. A tall, gold-framed mirror long enough to capture her from head to toe. Would she still be Nora Beachy? Would Levi like what he saw? The delight on his face when her hair cascaded down her back reflected in the mirror. He would like it. If only he were here. "I can't."

"You can. Just try it so you know how it feels. You'll see. You won't get struck by lightning. Your faith won't be diminished one iota. Nothing will change." Tammy took Nora's hand and laid the jeans in it. "Make it like an experiment. If you listen to Daed's messages and you think about what's being said, followed by trying a different way of living, you might learn something about yourself."

"How did you get this way?"

"Get what way?" Tammy added the blouse and a pair of leather sandals with a strap that went between the toes to the pile. "I'm me."

"You are so sure of your faith, and you talk about it to people. We don't do that."

"No judgment. No criticism. That's what Daed says." Tammy's voice deepened in a spot-on imitation of Uncle Ike. "I get it from him. We are called to win the lost. Everywhere we go we're in the mission field."

She not only sounded like him, she used his words. Did she really understand the meaning, or was she parroting? "You don't think it's like you're taking over God's place in the world? He didn't put you in charge."

Or Uncle Ike.

"No, but he gave us an instruction manual—the *Holy Bible*." She propelled Nora toward the bathroom. "I gave you a gift. Now you can give me one. Try them on. You don't have to leave them on. Just wear them for the practice. You'll hurt my feelings if you don't."

Hurting Tammy's feelings when she was being so kind was the last thing Nora wanted. "It's nice of you to give me a gift, but you know I can't wear them."

"Just try them on then. Maybe you'll change your mind when you see that Gott doesn't smote you with lightning. Practice is closed. I always put a sign on the door."

Nora started toward the bathroom.

"Nora, wait."

She turned. Tammy's face flushed. She edged closer. "Wyatt's the one. He wants to keep it low-key because of who his daed is. People talk about the preacher's kid." Her voice dropped to a whisper. "Just so you know."

"I already knew."

"You're not interested, are you?"

"Nee, my heart is promised to another."

Even if he might be having second thoughts.

Tammy nodded, but her face turned a deeper shade of crimson. "He's hard to read. He never says anything like . . . you know . . . he likes me."

Nora glanced toward the front of the church. Wyatt sat at the piano, his hands running up and down the keys in a saucy rendition of "Amazing Grace." "I haven't been around him enough to know, but I'll be watching."

"Thanks. Now go on." Tammy's smile held relief. "I can't wait to see the new you."

Nora would not be new because of jeans and a shirt. Or sandals.

Jesus wore sandals, didn't He? Or did artists make up that detail too?

Her heart pounding in her chest as if she were pursued by a mountain lion, Nora trudged into the small bathroom that smelled of canned lilacs and bleach. Despite the dank humidity of the dingy two-stall room, she shivered.

Would God care? Maybe Tammy was right. Maybe clothes had nothing to do with it. Adam and Eve had gone from nakedness to fig leaves to animal skins. Juliette's family went to church every Sunday, and they wore regular clothes. Juliette said Tim was the most devout Christian she'd ever met. He wore jeans, a western shirt, cowboy boots, and his cowboy hat to church. The rest of the time he wore a Lincoln County sheriff's deputy uniform. Either way, he was still Tim, a follower of Jesus.

What difference did it make? What did it mean to have a closer walk with Jesus? Did He answer questions like this one? Women in foreign countries covered themselves from head to toe. Only their eyes showed. Did that make them more religious?

Nora gazed at herself in the mirror over the sink—something she never would have done at home. Her cheeks were red and her neck blotchy. She swallowed against the knot of uncertainty in her throat, but that did nothing for the rock sitting in her stomach.

"Just try it. Just this once." She smiled at the nervous Nora in the mirror. "Millions of people all over the country wear clothes like these. They still believe."

She couldn't. She hadn't done it during her rumspringa, when most girls did. She couldn't do it now. She had no desire to be English. Plain woman dressed modestly so as not to draw attention to themselves.

"Nora, come out. I want to see you."

Nora opened the door. She held out the pile of clothing. "I can't. I'm sorry."

Tammy didn't try to hide her disappointment. Nor did she take the clothes. "It's okay. Keep them. Try them on later. At Mammi's."

"Are you sure you don't want to keep them?"

"They don't fit me." Tammy patted her shoulder. "Don't throw up. We'll try them another day."

In the sanctuary the boys were already set up to start playing.

"Do you sing, Nora?" Tucker cocked his head toward the microphone. "Come sing with us."

"I couldn't." She sang with her mother all the time while doing housework or gardening. In church they sang together but without instruments or amplification. Their voices mingled. No one voice stood out. "I don't know the song."

"You don't know 'I'll Fly Away'?"

She did know it. Mother loved that song. She nodded.

Tammy sat with Wyatt. He scooted closer to her and began instructing her. After a few seconds, he placed his hands over hers. The loopy grin on her face said Tammy was in her own earthly heaven.

Her blood pulsing in her ears, Nora trudged to the front. She hesitated. "I'll sing, but I really don't need the microphone."

"Whatever. Just stand there and sing to your heart's content."

Singing did make her heart content. It had since Mother sang her lullabies. It had since she sang lullabies to the boys. Church songs, English songs, silly songs, sweet ballads—they all spoke to her. The boys began to play. Tucker and Wyatt sang, too, while Tammy played the piano.

Nora didn't touch the microphone. She didn't get close. She opened her mouth. The words came. They were so loud they reverberated in the small church. Was that really her singing? The sound grew and entwined with the notes of the guitar, the banjo, and the piano. Note after note rising and falling in a way she'd never heard before.

Together they made a joyful noise to the Lord.

She closed her eyes and let her voice come from deep in her chest. The notes rose from her belly. If only Mother could hear how beautiful it sounded.

She opened her eyes. Her voice faltered. She stopped and put her hands to her mouth.

The music died.

"What's the matter?" Wyatt rose and came to her. "You have a beautiful voice."

"It's not supposed to be about me. All the glory should be to Gott."

"It is. Who do you think gave us the gift of music? Who gave you the gift of a beautiful singing voice?"

"No one person should stand out from the others."

"The band members play together. You sing with me and Tucker and Tammy. Together we're standing on sacred ground. God gave us these gifts, and He expects us to use them to His glory. This is our ministry. Didn't you like the way it sounded, the way it made you feel?"

"I did." But that wasn't the point, was it? What she wanted or liked or felt? "But it's not right that people stare at us instead of focusing on the Lord."

"Our songs lead people to a deeper relationship with the Lord. That is what this is all about." Wyatt turned toward Tucker. "Let's do 'Blessed Be the Name.' You don't know this one, Nora, but you'll catch on. It's a beautiful song. I'll sing with you. So will Tammy."

They gathered around the microphone with Nora in a tight circle. Tammy took Nora's hand. The music began. Wyatt was right. The words were easy to learn and powerful. Watching Tammy's smiling face and seeing the exuberant way Wyatt lifted his hands high and bounced around as he sang made Nora smile.

How could this be bad? How could such enthusiasm for worship be wrong?

Finally, the song ended. Tammy and Wyatt clapped and laughed, the same glow on both their faces.

"Come sit with me at the piano." Wyatt touched her arm. "You have musical talent. You can learn to play the piano in a snap."

Nora glanced at Tammy. Her smile froze. Her imploring eyes said no. Wyatt's piano instruction was reserved for her. "I've always wanted to learn to play the guitar. We would never have a piano in our homes. How would a Plain person practice?"

Tucker strummed his guitar and hooted. "I win, Wyatt, you lose."

He was such a boy. He zipped over to stand next to her. "Do you read music?"

"Nee."

"I can teach you the chords. It's easy." He surveyed her with a critical eye. "Your hands are small. It'll be hard for you to reach some of the notes." He began to play a popular song she'd heard on the radio in town. A song about two people in love, but one stepped out with someone new. "Do you know this one?"

"I thought we were playing church music."

"This song is easy. It only has three chords."

The deacon's words knocked on her memory. *"Satan writes popular music. It fills people up with lust and greed. People fill their minds up with garbage from TV programs, movies, and music. Pretty soon there's no room for God's Word."*

"Let's try something easier."

"Okay, how about 'This Little Light of Mine.'"

"Perfect." Relief rolled through her. She clapped like a child who would love this song. "I know the words and the tune."

Tucker slid the guitar strap from his neck and placed it over hers. She let her fingers brush across the strings. A thrilling low *thrum-mm-mm-mm* resulted. The wires were hard and almost sharp. To press firmly would cut into her tender fingertips. She strummed again, harder.

"You're playing the guitar." Tucker clapped and crowed. "You go, girl."

"Woo-hoo," Wyatt yelled from his spot on the piano bench next to Tammy.

Tammy smiled and blew kisses. "Rock on, Kossin."

"That's some beautiful music you're making." Grandpa strode down the aisle. He studied Nora and smiled. "This church is truly a place of transformation."

Nora's cheeks burned. If only she could hide behind Tucker. Or melt between the pine floorboards. "I really can't play the guitar either. I just wanted to . . . hold it."

"Jeannie is searching for you. She's ready to go home." His smile broadened. "You might want to return the guitar to its rightful owner."

If it wasn't something she'd do at home, she shouldn't do it here. She'd already broken that rule, and she'd only been in Libby two days. Nora handed the guitar to Tucker and scurried past Grandpa. Her face alight with a grin far too wide to have anything to do with music, Tammy met Nora at the door. "Wyatt says he'll walk me home. You can go on ahead with Jeannie."

"Gut for you. No wonder you're smiling."

"He's so sweet, cute, and smart. God is smiling on me."

Nora knew that feeling. Would Levi feel the same about her if he knew what she'd been doing today?

Levi wouldn't understand.

She didn't understand it herself.

13

Eureka, Montana

The hardest part of the evacuation was waiting for word. Would the fire take more Kootenai homes, or would it race in another direction? Worrying about it did no good and had the added liability of being a sin.

Levi left his horse and buggy on the far edge of the First Church of God parking lot so Chester could nibble at grass on the adjacent field, and he strode toward the narrow, L-shaped building.

The American Red Cross had set up an information center in the church, known for its enormous sign spelling out the Ten Commandments big enough for drivers passing by to see them—if not read them. He shoved through the double doors into a large meeting room with a laminate wood floor and a stage at one end. This had become a meeting place and lifeline for Kootenai residents. Everyone ended up here because the second hardest part of the evacuation was finding something to do. Plain folks were used to working sunup to sundown. Doing nothing wasn't an option.

Maybe the Forest Service ranger or one of the Lincoln County deputies would have word on which direction the fire had taken—in other words, which direction the wind blew.

"Hey, Levi, how are you? Is there anything I can do for you?"

Church secretary and jill-of-all-trades Angie Rockford waved from the table she manned near the double doors. Angie, with her purple-rimmed glasses and magenta hair, was hard to miss in her tie-dyed shirt and pink skirt. How she remembered his name after one meeting and in the mass of people who came and went hourly through her church boggled the mind. "The grocery store in Kalispell sent a big shipment of food earlier today. Help yourself."

"We're gut—good." Levi's mother had stockpiled her canned goods, including meat, since the first hint of an evacuation. She'd also made a dozen loaves of bread, rolls, cookies, and pies for her massive brood. "Have you seen Tim Trudeau or somebody from the Forest Service?"

Angie scooped up her youngest baby, a boy still in diapers, and stuck him on her wide hip. She pointed toward the far wall, covered with maps of Kootenai National Forest, where half a dozen men stood sipping coffee from Styrofoam cups. "They've been jawing for at least twenty minutes. I don't know how many ways you can say it's a booger of a fire and nothing the firefighters and hotshot teams and smoke jumpers do seems to stop it."

Her astute observations couched in the simple language of a Montana girl amused Levi despite the overall gloomy state of affairs. He tickled the baby's bare feet. He wiggled and chortled. So sweet. What would it be like to have a baby? A son with Nora? *Not now.* "Thanks, Angie."

"God bless you."

Levi squeezed past volunteers sorting and arranging donated clothes at a long row of tables. A Red Cross rep helped an English family with paperwork for hotel and food vouchers. Donated canned goods were arranged by content on more tables. The outpouring from communities across the state reflected an oft overlooked segment of the country—good people who still helped each other out in times of trouble, no questions asked, nothing needed in return.

Not so gloomy a state of affairs after all.

The boulder on his shoulders suddenly weighed less.

"Hello, stranger." Juliette Knowles planted herself in his path.

With loaded tables on either side of her, Levi had no choice but to stop. Juliette tended to discombobulate him. He never knew where to look. This evening's outfit featured a tight-fitting, plunging, blue tank top, cut-off denim shorts, and purple cowboy boots. She'd pulled her long blonde curls into a ponytail that swung below her shoulder blades.

"Hey, Juliette."

"Just the man I wanted to see." She pulled a Tootsie Pop from her mouth and waved it at him. "Have you heard from Nora?"

"No." Levi studied the boots. They seemed the safest bet. "How would I? She's in Libby."

"From what she told me, they're pretty progressive. I bet they have phones. I bet you could call her grandpa's house."

"She's only been gone four days. What makes you think we need to talk so soon?"

"I saw her at the community meeting. She didn't say much—we were all more focused on our houses burning down—but she seemed nervous. Worried." Juliette might embrace the part of a loose English girl, but she'd been friends with Nora, Mercy, and Christine since they were toddlers and met at a volunteer firefighters' fund-raiser. According to all three girls, she had a heart of gold under all that glitter. "Nora is a sweet girl. She's innocent. She believes the best of everyone, and she's never been away from Kootenai before."

Also a good judge of character. The image of Nora's round face, pink with sun, floated in Levi's mind's eye. Anytime he said something critical of a member of their district, she defended that person. She always gave people the benefit of the doubt. "I was hoping the evacuation would be lifted now that the fire has gone beyond Kootenai. Then she could come home."

And they could start over on their dream of owning a home.

Dread trickled down his spine. Nora insisted she would not be moved. But Juliette was right. Nora never met a person in whom she couldn't find redeeming qualities. "I will go there as soon as my . . . family gives me leave."

Why Jack was so insistent he stay in Eureka was unfathomable. He wasn't earning any money with the shop shut down in Kootenai. None of them were.

"When you get leave? Seriously? Do you love Nora?"

These girls told each other everything. Levi had learned to live with that. "That's between Nora and me."

"I can tell by that hangdog look on your face you do." Juliette twirled the Tootsie Pop between her fingers. "If you're not going there now, at least call her tonight."

"If she needs me, she'll call. I gave her the number at Kevin's house."

"Good for you. That's something." She patted his hand like a maternal grandmother—which she definitely was not. "Just don't wait too long. Go. You're what, twenty-one, twenty-two? Old enough to know what you want and go after it. Don't be a wuss."

A pep talk–slash–scolding from a former cheerleader in the middle of an English church. Could his life get any weirder? Levi nodded. "I'm twenty. I want to talk to Tim about the fire's status."

Juliette stepped between two tables to allow Levi to pass. "Good luck with that. Trudeau is picky about who he talks to these days."

Which meant he was peeved at Juliette again. Everyone knew the two of them were courting, even though the deputy tried his hardest not to date a woman with questionable religious beliefs. Or maybe it was none at all. Nora told Levi not to judge. That Juliette believed in God. She was mad at God about something. Nora didn't know what, but she recognized a hurting heart.

Nora was like that. She gave everyone a pass, but especially her friends.

Deputy Tim Trudeau, half a foot taller than the men who surrounded him, was the first to acknowledge Levi's approach. "How are you doing, Levi? There's coffee on the table. I hear it's nasty, but help yourself if that's your poison."

He pointed to an industrial-size pot on a nearby table. At nine thirty at night the last thing Levi needed was more caffeine. He shook his head. "What's the latest?"

"The wind shifted." Jack answered before Tim could. "They're afraid it's going to make another run at Kootenai. What are you doing out so late?"

As if he needed Jack's permission to leave Kevin's rental house. "I couldn't sleep."

Not doing a hard day's work saw to that. Plus the uncertainty. And the uncomfortable bedroll on the floor. Two of his brothers shared the double bed.

Chet stood at the coffee table pouring himself a cup. Levi excused himself and went to join him. The older man dumped a heaping portion of sugar followed by three packets of nondairy creamer into a small cup of coffee. He glanced up. "I guess you heard what happened to my rental?"

"I did. I'm sorry."

Chet sipped the coffee and made a face. He proceeded to add more sugar and stir with more vigor than necessary. The man had a belly the size of a watermelon popping out over a large silver belt buckle and pressed blue jeans with a white seam down the middle of each skinny leg. Juliette would call it a beer belly. Whatever it was, the guy didn't need more sugar or caffeine. "It's frustrating. That rental property helps me and the missus make ends meet. Her disability and my paycheck at the hardware store just don't seem to do it these days."

"It's hard, I reckon, for everyone." Even though he didn't much want it, Levi poured some coffee. "I was wondering, do you plan to rebuild?"

"You and your lady friend are still interested, I take it."

"We are, definitely, but we aren't sure if we can afford to build if you decide to sell the property without rebuilding first."

"It would be a heck of a lot easier to just sell the property." Chet rubbed the salt-and-pepper stubble on his chin. "But I wouldn't get as much for it, that's for sure. I have insurance. I don't know if it'll be enough to cover the cost of building a house like the one that burned."

Insurance was good. Rebuilding was good. "The Plain community, me included, will help you with the rebuilding. You know that. You'll get more for your money with us helping—more than you can imagine."

"I've seen your folks in action with a barn raising." Chet didn't sip his coffee. He gulped it, hot or not. "I believe you. The fact is, I won't know anything until the insurance adjuster gets in there and inspects the place. It would be like them to say it was an act of God and therefore not covered by my insurance. You never know what they'll come up with to avoid paying out. All those years of paying expensive premiums could go up in smoke."

Literally. "Just let me know."

"I will. But you're not the only one who's expressed an interest in that place."

Of course not. Properties were hard to come by in Kootenai. "Please don't sell it without giving me a chance to make an offer."

"I wouldn't do that to you."

"I appreciate that."

"Levi, it's getting late. Are you headed home?" Jack soaked the words in fatherly concern, but there was no hiding his meddling in an adult man's business.

Levi thanked Chet for his time and turned to his stepfather. "Did you need a ride?"

"Nee, I came with Kevin. He'll cart me home."

He kept saying home. A rental ranch-style house built in the eighties was not home. "Then I'll see you back there."

"Jah, you might want to call the Beachys in Libby once you get there."

Levi froze. "Why? Did something happen? Is Nora all right?" He blurted the questions before considering the consequences. Jack didn't need to know more about Levi's love life.

"I think she's fine."

"You think?"

"She called last night—"

"And you're just telling me?"

"You're skating on thin ice, Suh."

Every muscle in Levi's body screamed, *I'm not your suh,* but he managed to muzzle them. "I'm sorry. I don't mean to be disrespectful. If things were different, she would be my fraa now and we wouldn't be separated."

"You best mind the way you talk to your elders, all the same. I haven't seen you today. You were up and out early, and then I went to the Walmart with your mudder." He wound his fingers around his suspenders, his chest puffed out like a rooster ready to wake the entire farm. "She didn't get a chance to say much before she was cut off."

"Cut off? The line went dead?"

"Nee, Daryl came on the line and said she needed to go."

Daryl would take the most conservative approach to phone calls. Phone calls were for important matters like deaths, births, and family emergencies. To be made from phone shacks. Messages left. The words *important matters* were open to interpretation in Levi's way of thinking. Being evacuated because of wildfires elevated everything to a crisis level, didn't it? "I don't have a number for Jacob Beachy."

"I do. I went by Harley's place this afternoon and asked him for it."

"Why would you do that?"

"Because I knew you needed it and wouldn't want to ask Harley for it." Jack removed his straw hat and pulled a folded piece of paper from the band. "I didn't tell him Nora called for you. I said you were chomping at the bit to make sure she and the rest of his family had settled in. I said you would talk to his daed, Jacob, because you know Harley doesn't want his dochder making unnecessary phone calls."

"I-I-I'm, I mean, I—"

"I know you've always thought I wanted to act like your daed, when I'm not, but really I just wanted to give your mudder what she wanted—peace in her own home. Don't you think she deserves that? We don't abide much with expecting happiness in this fallen world, but peace in our own homes surely isn't too much to ask." He walked away.

Levi managed to shut his mouth. He watched as Jack stopped to chat with an English family from Kootenai at a food table, then with the American Red Cross rep, and finally with Angie at the check-in table. He was like that. He talked to everyone.

Was Jack right? Had the fissure between them always been Levi's fault? His mind traveled back to the wedding five years ago at the same home where his mother had married his father. To Jack's huge grin and mother's shy smile. So many well-wishers from Jack's family had packed the service. Had the sour feeling in the pit of Levi's stomach overtaken any possible joy at his mother's happiness? Was Levi that selfish that he didn't want to share his family with a man he barely knew? Who barely knew his mother?

He stared down at the crumpled notebook paper in his hand. Figuring out the situation with Jack—fixing their relationship—

would have to take a backseat to talking to Nora for the moment. No jumping to conclusions that something was wrong. Nora just missed him. Like he missed her.

The clock on the wall over the check-in table read nine forty-five. It would be after ten before he arrived at Kevin's. Nora would be asleep. Jack's words clamored for attention. Talk to Grandpa Beachy. That wouldn't put Nora in conflict with Daryl.

Levi forced himself to walk through the crowded room and out to the parking lot. Then he broke into a run.

14

No lights shone in Kevin's house, but the TV screen flickered through the open windows. Levi squeezed the front door shut with a gentle nudge and tiptoed through the foyer. Kevin waved from the living room couch, where he sat with a huge plastic bowl of popcorn on his lap and a can of beer in one hand. The noise coming from the TV suggested he was watching a shoot-'em-up action movie.

"No need to be quiet." For a small man of no more than five feet nine inches and 170 pounds, Kevin had only one notch on the voice volume button: loud. "A stampeding herd of cattle couldn't wake that bunch."

Kevin Beck and his wife, Shirley, had five kids ranging in age from three to sixteen. They were a noisy, friendly bunch who didn't seem to mind sharing their house or their backyard swing set and aboveground pool with the Raber family.

"Would you mind if I used your telephone?"

"Why would I mind?" Kevin saluted Levi. "Help yourself, and then come back. I'll save a brew for you. This is a good movie. You'll like it."

The good news about Kevin was that he treated his Plain friends no differently than any other friends. By the same token, he seemed blissfully unaware of what they did and didn't do because of their faith.

With a murmured thanks Levi rushed down the hallway to the kitchen, where the family's landline phone sat on the kitchen counter. Only the youngest members of the Beck family didn't have their own cell phones, but internet and Wi-Fi could be spotty in this part of the country, so they hung on to the landline. Kevin claimed that the only calls that came in on it were spam, but it served as a good backup.

He examined the number Jack had given him. Levi had some experience placing phone calls, but it still felt weird. No one would see him. Word would not magically be whispered in Noah's ear. Only Jack and Kevin would know. And Jacob Beachy. None of them cared.

Jacob was probably asleep. Levi didn't want to make this call in the morning when everyone would be awake, both here and at the Beachy house. He gritted his teeth and punched in the number.

To his surprise, two rings later someone picked up. "Hello."

Despite the sparse salutation, Levi recognized the gruff voice. "Jacob, this is Levi Raber. You probably don't remember me—"

"Sure I do. I ain't gone senile yet. You work at the furniture shop. You're Jack and Beatrice's suh."

Not exactly, but close enough. "That's right. Jack said Nora called last night."

"So I heard. Daryl gave me a piece of his mind this morning." Jacob didn't sound the least bit perturbed. "The man could use some work on his respect for his elders, but I reckon I understand his concerns. I'm not so old I don't remember how we used to wear ourselves out running to the phone shack for calls, like having a phone in the house would rip a family apart."

Not the time for this theological discussion. The intrusion of the outside world into family life began with small forays, like talking on the phone when it rang at mealtime instead of talking with your children about the day's events or plans for the next or why they had a bad day at school. "What was wrong that Nora needed to talk to me? Do you know?"

"Nora wouldn't bare her soul to an old coot like me. Tammy probably talked her into calling you. That girl loves to meddle in other folks' business."

"So you don't think anything is wrong?"

"What could be wrong? She's in my house with my fraa. We're her groossdaadi and groossmammi. Her schweschder is here. Daryl is here. We'll take gut care of her. Don't you worry."

"I don't mean any disrespect."

"Why don't you talk to her?"

"You said she's asleep."

"She's in her room. I suspect she'll be beside herself if she finds out you called and she didn't get to talk to you."

"If it's no trouble, I'd like that too. I figure what with the fire and the evacuation, we have reason to check up on each other by phone."

"Young love can be fairly urgent, from what I remember." Jacob chuckled. "Just hang on. It takes me a while to get up and down those stairs. I'm not as young as I used to be."

Levi leaned back in his chair and studied the rooster salt and pepper shakers. Jacob had no shortage of opinions. That had to be where Harley got it. And Ike. Two brothers at odds over faith. That's what happened when people started interpreting the Bible on their own. Divisions occurred. Families were ripped apart. Couples who loved each other faltered and fell away.

That wouldn't happen to Nora and him. He wouldn't let it.

✦✦✦

At least Nora's temporary bedroom had no mirror. It made trying on the clothes easier.

By the time she donned the outfit, sweat made her underarms

damp. The blouse and the jeans fit perfectly. The sandals were too tight. Barefoot, she stood in the middle of the room and closed her eyes. Did she feel different? Less Plain?

Nee, it's an experiment. Nothing more. Nothing has changed.

Was that God talking to her? Or the devil?

So this was temptation talking.

Fingering the buttons on the blouse, she sat on the edge of the bed. It was a pretty color. It didn't seem outrageous. She had purple dresses.

Not sleeveless dresses. At least her legs were covered. The jeans felt stiff and tight. Pants were for boys. She didn't feel different. Okay, maybe more comfortable. She tried sitting in the jeans. They stretched with her body. She crossed her legs at the ankles. Those were her legs in denim. Those were her bare arms, cool and goose pimply in the evening air.

She crossed her arms. Uncrossed them. Rubbed them.

What would Levi think? Would he like to see her arms?

Nora! Such thoughts were exactly the reason Plain women wore long sleeves. That's what Mother would say. Nora's lungs hurt. She couldn't seem to get a deep breath. The jeans' waistband bit into her hip bones. *What am I doing?* "Grrrr."

A sharp rap on the bedroom door brought her to her feet.

Nee, not now. Not like this. "Who is it?" Did she sound as guilty as she felt? "I'm sleeping."

"Levi is calling for you," Grandpa called. "Get dressed quickly. You can't come downstairs in your nightgown."

Her fingers all thumbs, Nora shucked off the jeans and resorted to pulling the blouse over her head after the last few buttons refused to budge. The sense of unreality made her pinch her arm. It hurt. She wasn't dreaming.

"Hurry, child, he's waiting." Grandpa's loud whisper probably echoed all the way down the hall. "I'm old. I may die soon."

Grandpa had a shortage of patience, not Levi. But who knew what phone Levi might be using. He might have to hang up before she managed to get to the phone. She stumbled over the hem of her dress. Nora's fingers still refused to cooperate when she tried to corral her hair into a quick bun. She stumbled over a shoe as she ran to the door.

"You go first." Grandpa moved away from the door. "I'll only slow you down."

"Wait." She scurried back to the dresser and snatched the baby monitor. "Ready."

Nora rushed down the stairs and grabbed the receiver from the half-circle table. "Levi?" Breathless, she made a mess of the two syllables. She drew a long breath and tried again. "Levi, are you there?"

"I'm here." He sounded a thousand miles away instead of just over sixty. "Sorry to wake you."

"I couldn't sleep."

"Me neither."

Neither of them spoke for a few beats.

"Jack said you—"

"I tried to call you—"

Silence again. Nora took a breath. *He's the man—let him go first.* "You go first."

Her back against the wall, Nora slid down on the floor and tugged her dress over her bent knees. She laid the monitor on the pine planks. She'd be happy to simply sit here and listen to Levi's voice.

What would he say if he knew what she'd been doing—and thinking—only moments ago? No wonder he didn't trust her. She couldn't trust herself.

"Jack said you called last night but Daryl took the phone from you."

Yet here she sat, talking on the phone in Grandpa's house for no good reason than she missed Levi. "He made me feel sneaky and guilty."

"Is that how you feel now?"

"I feel like I want to talk to you. Is that how temptation is? It grabs you and won't let you go?"

"I've thought a lot about this. These are unusual circumstances, with the wildfires. I think Noah would agree." Levi ran the words together as if to show her he could do it. "Why did you call? Is something wrong?"

"Not exactly. I'm homesick. I can't call my mudder and daed. I'm a grown woman. I should be able to handle staying here with family, especially with Jeannie here."

"Does that mean you miss me?" He sounded hopeful and doubtful simultaneously.

"It does."

More silence. Neither of them would broach the subject, then. Nora waited. *Let the man go first.* That's what Mother would say. *Be an obedient, loving wife.*

Someday, if she managed not to alienate Levi.

She never thought he needed that. He usually invited her opinion. His concern over her trip to Libby had produced their first fight. Was that because she didn't argue with him or because she agreed with him? This time in Libby might be a time of contemplation and delving deeper into that question. It might not feel like it, but it could be a way of growing together, not apart.

"I do have some news for you." His voice deepened as if he'd taken a breath and sat up straighter. "I talked to Chet. He says he can make more money off the land if he rebuilds the house, but he has to wait for an insurance adjuster to get in there and inspect it before he'll make a decision. He needs the insurance money to rebuild."

"But that's gut, isn't it?" Good that Levi still wanted to build a home with her. "If he rebuilds, it gives us time to keep saving. Plus we don't have to rebuild on our own if we are able to buy the land."

"Exactly. He said he'd give me first dibs when he puts it up for sale." The more Levi talked, the louder his voice grew. He must be somewhere where no one cared. Kevin's family would be asleep by now. Maybe their phone was downstairs too. Did they have a two-story house? She couldn't remember. Levi's excitement calmed her fears. He was as determined as ever. "I told him all the Plain folk would want to help him rebuild. Including us."

"He knows we will. He's lived in Kootenai as long as we have. He shouldn't doubt it."

"He's a half-empty-glass sort of man."

"Not like you. You've always been optimistic about our future." If only she could dive through the phone line and kiss him. The softness of his lips, the way he pressed her against the wall, his hands on her hips, the feel of his solid body against hers—she needed that the way she needed water to slake her thirst. "I miss you."

"I miss you too."

The sound of his breathing filled the line, its gentle rise and fall a balm to her sore heart. Neither spoke, but the thought of hanging up was too hard to contemplate.

"I had hoped to come soon."

"But you can't?"

"Jack said something tonight, something unexpected."

He'd been talking with his stepfather. That was progress. "The fire has upended his world too."

"And Mudder's."

"Something happened with your mudder?"

"He says she would never admit to worrying, but she needs her kinner where she can see them. That's the way he put it." A faint quiver in his voice reverberated in Nora's ears. He cleared his throat. "He says I'm the hardheaded one, the one who makes things difficult between us."

"And you think he's right?"

"Maybe. I always think of him as being bossy, but maybe I've picked some of that up from him in the last five years. Do you think I'm bossy?"

Nora stared at the high wire that suddenly appeared before her.

"Nora, are you still there?"

"It's hard for me to say. Sometimes I feel like you're bossy, but I also know you're learning to be a man and to take charge. That's your job." She took a breath and weighed her words. "I don't want to be full of myself. I want to be a gut fraa one day."

"You will be. My mudder tries to be a gut mudder and fraa. I haven't given her much credit for that."

"Maybe this is your chance to bridge the gap between you and him while easing your mudder's burden."

"Maybe."

His tone was tentative, but Nora knew him. The gauntlet had been thrown down. Levi had a soft heart, too, and the idea that he caused pain for his mother would haunt him. "So you must stay in Eureka."

"Are you sure?"

"I'm fine." She didn't feel fine, but she was made of sturdy stock. That certainly applied to the man she would marry. "Family comes first. Take care of your mudder."

"You sound funny, not like yourself."

"It's different here."

"You know what the Ordnung says. Follow it."

What if the Ordnung was wrong? Then their community was built on sinking sand. Even the suggestion of such a possibility could be grounds for excommunication. Levi's faith had never been tested like this. By grief, yes, at his father's death, but not by a way of worship that promised a deeper relationship with their Lord and Savior.

He thought following the Ordnung was easy, but he hadn't experienced the Eagle Valley Amish Ministry in its overwhelming glory. "The service was interesting. Onkel Ike talked about the Amish being chained by religion and rituals, by traditions not even we understand."

"Ike has fallen away from his faith. We all know that."

Parroting what the church elders said.

"He did make me think about some of our rules." She hesitated. Levi loved her. He'd told her that many times. He wanted to marry her. That kind of love would stand up to a conversation such as this. At least it should. Better to know now rather than later if the ties that bound them were made with a lasting love. He might even have answers that would still the doubts that suddenly welled within her. Like why they couldn't play musical instruments.

"Tammy has a band. She plays the violin and the flute. Tucker has a guitar. He showed me how to play 'This Little Light of Mine.'"

A hiss of air greeted her admission. "You played the guitar?" Levi's voice lost its soft, sweet tone. "What else did you do?"

A simple small thing like playing the guitar opened a chasm between them. Nora gripped the phone tighter. *Don't let me down, Levi.* "I sang with them. 'I'll Fly Away.' And 'Blessed Be Your Name.'"

"Singing is fine. Singing hymns is gut."

"I didn't touch it or stand close to it, but there was a microphone with a sound system."

Silence.

"Levi?"

"Why would you do that?"

"No one was there. Just the band." She didn't dare tell him about the clothes she shed only moments ago. He would hang up on her. "Besides, they sing and play instruments in the Bible. David danced and leapt for joy."

"Now you use the Bible to justify your sin."

"Is it a sin? Singing for the joy of the Lord? How could it be?"

"You've only been gone a few days, and already you've been sucked in by those who would tempt you into abandoning everything that's important."

"I haven't been sucked in by anyone. They're family. I have a strong faith, but they say it could be stronger and deeper. Don't you want that for me? For yourself?"

"Do you hear yourself?" Levi's voice sank to a whisper. "I can't believe what I'm hearing. I'm coming to get you."

"Nee. Don't you dare." Anger fought with disappointment. So much for love conquering differences. "I'm here to help Jeannie take care of the kinner. As long as she stays, I stay. Besides, you have your own family issues to attend to."

"I thought you knew your place as a woman and future fraa."

"I'm not your fraa yet." Nora swallowed tears. She never would be at this rate. "I thought we would talk through things and then decisions would be made."

"You just talked about the mann being the head of the household and the fraa following his lead."

"And we just talked about you being bossy."

"This isn't me being bossy. It's me being concerned for your eternal salvation. You need to come home."

"That's for Daed to decide."

"I'll talk to him."

"Nee, please don't. I have done nothing wrong. It'll go no further than this."

"I didn't think it would go this far."

A few songs. A single lesson on the guitar. Was that so far? Far enough to destroy a relationship that took two years to build? Surely not. "Nothing about my feelings for you has changed."

More silence. The sound of his breathing filled the line. "Levi? I hoped you would trust me and that I would be able to trust you. Isn't that what a relationship between a mann and his fraa should be?"

"I'll call you in a few days."

"You won't tell Daed?"

"I have to think. I need to think. We should hang up."

Nora tightened her grip on the receiver. *Please, Gott, let it be a short while.* "I love you."

His familiar response didn't come. *Say it, Levi. Say it. "I love you more."*

A game they liked to play on nights when he dropped her off after a ride through the countryside around Kootenai. *"I love you." "I love you more." "I love you even more."* Silly but sweet.

"Gut nacht." He hung up.

He didn't want to play anymore.

◆◆◆

The urge to slam the receiver on the table flooded Levi. He didn't dare judge Nora when he was so full of self-righteous anger that he wanted to resort to violence. Only a few days ago Nora had assured him nothing could go wrong in Libby. She would not be led astray. She sounded so sure of herself. Then temptation had hit her right between the eyes. Boom, down she went.

She should never have gone to Libby. Her curiosity and soft heart—usually good traits—worked against her there. Harley should have listened to Levi. Add pride to Levi's list of sins. Harley was a mature middle-aged man with seven children. He knew far more about parenting than Levi did.

He scrambled to his feet, laid the receiver gently on its base, and backed away.

How could Nora be so naive? She'd even tried to justify breaking the rules by citing examples from Scripture. She'd broken rules she vowed to follow when she was baptized. If the bishop found out, she would be disciplined.

Levi should tell Noah. They were expected to hold each other accountable. But if he did, his and Nora's relationship would never be the same. How could she forgive him?

He paced the kitchen floor between the island and the counter. The small room hemmed him in. He needed a wide-open space to hike and think. The wildfire had taken his refuge from him.

Maybe he should go for a walk. Or run like the English folks did. He'd never understood running for the sake of exercise. Working hard wasn't enough? Now that his days were empty, he could see the necessity. He grabbed his hat and darted down the hallway past the living room.

"Whoa, where are you going in such a hurry?" Kevin pointed a remote at the TV, and the *rat-a-tat-tat* of gunfire ceased. "Is a grizzly chasing you?"

"No. I need to take a walk."

"It's late. Why don't you watch this movie with me?"

"Thank you for the offer, but we don't watch TV."

"Sorry. I knew that." Kevin held out the enormous plastic bowl half filled with popcorn. "You eat popcorn, don't you? My eyes are bigger than my stomach."

His eyes must frequently be big, considering the way his gut bulged over that belt buckle.

Levi accepted the bowl, mostly because he didn't want to say no to Kevin a second time. The guy wanted to be nice. "Thank you."

"You got girl problems, I take it." Kevin guzzled beer from a silver can and then set it aside. "I know how that goes."

Kevin was married to the woman he loved. What did he know about girl problems? "I'm fine."

"That's why you came running through here like a bat out of h-e-double-hockey-sticks." Kevin snickered. "Is that why you needed to use a phone at ten o'clock at night? You guys never use a phone unless you absolutely have to. 'Course with this wildfire, everything is cattywampus."

"Okay, so it's girl problems. Talking about it won't make it better."

"You'd be surprised. Try me."

Talking about his love life with an Englisch man was as appealing as eating fried squid for breakfast. Levi dropped two pieces of popcorn in his mouth and chewed. It tasted too salty. "It's not something Englisch folks would understand. It's about our faith."

"I've never seen folks with more faith." Kevin burped behind his chunky hand. "'Scuse me. She's Amish, ain't she?"

She had been when she left for Libby. "I'm worried that she might change."

"How old are you, son?"

"Twenty."

"I know you Amish folks like to think of yourselves as all grown up by the time you turn twenty, but science says it ain't true. I just read a story in *Reader's Digest* about it. Your brains don't become grown up until twenty-seven or twenty-eight. It's true. I wouldn't make that up."

"What's your point?"

"If you're still changing physically, that noggin of yours is still growing too. Your girlfriend is younger than you?"

"Twenty."

"Still a girl. She's bound to change."

Kevin needed to work on his pep talks. "She's a grown woman. She's been baptized in our faith."

"Sometimes people do what's expected of them without really understanding it. They want to please."

That did sound like Nora. She agreed to spend her rumspringa with him, doing what he wanted to do. Which was spending time together. She did go to the movies with Juliette and once to Missoula, but that was it.

It wasn't wrong for a woman to want to please the man she planned to marry. In fact, it was a good thing.

Wasn't it?

"Whether my brain is full grown or not, I don't think I'll ever understand women."

"You and me both, buddy, you and me both." Kevin chortled so hard he spit. "Seriously, why do we need all those pillows on the bed? And why are there towels in the bathroom that are for looks only? These are things I ponder when I'm not perusing my *Reader's Digest*. It's there next to the stool if you want to borrow it."

"Maybe later. I better hit the hay." Levi set the bowl on the coffee table. "Thanks for letting me bend your ear."

"You said less than a dozen words, my friend." Kevin held up his beer can in a salute. "Good luck with your honey."

Plain people didn't believe in luck. All the same, Levi welcomed Kevin's sentiments. He'd take all the help he could get.

If he didn't handle this right, he stood to lose the woman he loved.

15

Libby, Montana

Nora hugged the phone to her chest. She couldn't seem to let go. Even the annoying *beep-beep* didn't force her to hang up the receiver. Here she sat, contemplating her future as a spinster aunt. Maybe when Mercy married Caleb, Nora would take over her duties as teacher. Or maybe she'd manage the store one day. So much for love conquering all. So much for talking things through and then coming to a compromise.

Levi couldn't step down from his high-and-mighty perch as a righteous man to explore the possibility there could be more to faith than waiting like church mice for the Lord to take them home.

This had to be what Meidung felt like. People who were supposed to love a person instead ostracized him.

For his own good, according to the bishop.

"I find your mammi's brownies and a glass of milk help me sleep when I have a lot on my mind." Daadi stood over her. She hadn't noticed his arrival. How much had he heard? "Or a bowl of ice cream. Ice cream is gut too."

He held out his hand. Nora placed the receiver on its base and let him pull her to her feet. Her stomach, still full from the earlier chocolate fudge sundae, balked at the thought of more ice cream. Not even she could eat it three times a day. Nor would she be able to sleep anytime soon. Maybe Grandpa would have answers. He'd been through the catastrophic division of a family and lived to tell the story. "I could eat a brownie."

More sugar. Maybe it would sweeten her angry, bitter disposition.

She followed Grandpa to the kitchen. The silence as she served him two frosted brownies and a large glass of milk before cutting a small brownie for herself didn't feel awkward.

"Hits the spot, doesn't it?" Grandpa licked frosting from his upper lip. He smiled blissfully. "My fraa makes a mighty fine brownie."

"Levi is upset because I played the guitar and sang with the band. Even though there was no audience."

Blurting it out was best, like ripping off the bandage. It didn't hurt quite so much. That didn't even include the clothes. Silently, she'd added a lie of omission to her sins.

"He's upset because he's afraid."

"Levi is never afraid. He's a very brave man."

"Everyone is afraid of something." Grandpa's sage words were no less wise for the milk mustache on his upper lip. "Right now Levi is afraid you'll change and you won't love him anymore."

"That would never happen."

"You're already changing."

"That's what he said."

"I don't know why people are so afraid of change." Grandpa took a slug of milk. The mustache grew. "You're growing. You're exploring. You're learning. Your faith is growing. That is a gut thing. Plain folks across this country are afraid of it. I'm proud of you for not being afraid."

But Nora was afraid. "How can you still consider yourself Plain?"

The question reeked of judgment. How could she judge Grandpa when she couldn't be sure of her own faith right now? Nora wiped drops of milk from the table with her napkin. "I'm sorry. I don't mean any disrespect."

"No need to be sorry. I could see that question bursting to get out ever since the service this morning. I thought Daryl might have a stroke." Grandpa started on his second brownie. "Clothes and cars do not take my ancestry away from me. I was born Amish and that's my history. I was baptized into my Amish faith when I was nineteen."

"But you're not Amish anymore."

"My faith has changed and evolved. I realized having a closer walk with Jesus made my faith more meaningful."

"What does that mean—a closer walk with Jesus?"

"I can talk with Him directly. I can listen for His response." Grandpa put one wrinkled hand to his ear and cocked his head as if demonstrating. "I'm not being too big for my britches. He offers that closeness to all of us. What we wear or drive or don't drive makes no difference to Him."

A chill rolled down Nora's spine. Goose bumps popped up on her arms. "But that's not what we are taught."

"I know. It's confusing. But we—the Amish—hold on to custom because tradition is safe. It keeps everyone on the straight and narrow. You submit to tradition because it makes you humble." Grandpa brushed crumbs from his silver beard. "Why do you think you aren't allowed to change your dress to short sleeves and shorter skirt—maybe above the knee? Why not make your *kapp* blue instead of white? What does not driving a car have to do with the love of Jesus?"

The questions bombarded Nora. She picked at the crumbs on her plate. "Because that's what the *Ordnung* says."

"Why?"

"The *Gmay* meets and discusses changes. They're voted on. Like allowing phones in our businesses."

"But not cars."

"I don't know why our ancestors decided no cars, but they did." Nora threw her hands up in despair. She fought to bring her voice down to its normal range. "The rules have been handed down for generations. There must've been a gut reason."

"I'm not trying to trip you up. I only want you to think." Grandpa shook his finger at her. "Your church elders don't want that—"

"There you are." Jeannie stood at the bottom of the stairs. She held Sadie in her arms. "Didn't you hear the bopli cry?"

Startled, Nora stood. The monitor. She'd left it on the floor in the hallway. "I'm sorry. I'm—"

"It doesn't matter." Jeannie's tone was stiff. "She needs to eat. I'll feed her."

"I'm sorry, Schweschder."

"It's okay." It didn't sound okay. "You should get some sleep. Morning light will come before you know it." She tromped up the stairs.

"She's right." Nora picked up her saucer and glass. "I should get to bed."

"If you could do one thing you didn't do during your rumspringa, what would it be?" Grandpa didn't get up. He licked frosting from his fingers. "You have a get-out-of-jail-free card."

"A what?"

"No strings attached. No worries. You'll not do it again when you return to Kootenai."

Nora carried her saucer and glass to the sink and washed them. "There was something." Something only Grandpa could help with. The words stuck in Nora's throat. Levi was already angry with her. "Nee, it's wrong."

"Knowing you, it's not something wrong, only something you've been taught is wrong. What you wear or what you drive is not Gott's concern. It's what's in your heart."

Nora's heart wanted to believe that. To be able to talk to God like a friend who cared and loved her, who saw her and heard her, that would be a whole new world.

"I've always wondered what it would be like to drive a car." There, she'd said it. They were so big and so powerful. How did a person harness that power? How did they keep it on the road? What kept it from going faster and faster until it flew? "Is that so terrible?"

Grandpa grinned. "Not terrible at all."

It would be terrible if Daryl and Jeannie found out.

Or Levi.

If it had to be hidden from the people she loved, it must be wrong.

Gott, help me to make gut choices. How do I know? None of this feels wrong. The rules of the Ordnung don't feel wrong either. So which is it?

Still no answer. What did it take to make this a two-way conversation? Or did Grandpa delude himself? Why would God speak directly to a simple man like him?

Or an even simpler woman like Nora?

"I want to know what it feels like to drive a car. That doesn't mean I want to own a car or even drive one again. It's an experience I want to have. I should've done it during my rumspringa, but I didn't." Because Levi didn't want to do it. Nora hadn't lived her own rumspringa. She'd lived his. "Do you think Gott will mind?"

"I don't."

No lightning struck her. Instead, a warm feeling like a hug descended over Nora.

Grandpa stood and went to the half-circle table in the hallway. He returned with a set of keys in his hands. He jingled them. "You shall have your wish."

"When?"

"When the right time presents itself, I'll let you know."

"If it's not something you would do at home, don't do it." Jeannie's words pestered Nora's tired brain.

She'd do it once and set the desire to rest.

Wasn't that what everyone said about temptation?

16

Nora sat on the fence, not sure which way to jump.

The next few days passed with the usual housekeeping chores and getting to know the other women in the district. They weren't that different from the women at home. The Eagle Valley Amish men went to work at the sawmill or the cabin-kit building shop or logging. The women cleaned, baked, cooked, and did laundry. Nora didn't feel that different. She was a turnip in a field of potatoes. Close but not quite the same.

Aunt Roseanna put Nora to work with Tammy in the Farm-to-Market Store, stocking shelves and making salads in the deli. Grandpa didn't say any more about driving, so apparently the time wasn't right yet. Levi didn't call. The desire to call him whispered in Nora's ear morning, noon, and night. Yet she didn't. If he wanted to talk to her, he would call. He was the one who'd hung up without saying goodbye. He was the one who was angry, not her.

The invitation to a frolic extended by Jeannie's new friend Samantha after their second church service was another example of their similarities. They had frolics. They worked together. Working took Nora's mind off another Sunday filled with singing and dancing—by everyone around her except Jeannie and Grandma—and band practice. The more time she spent with Tammy's friends, the more they became her friends. Wyatt hadn't been there, but he would be back in the next few days. Much to Tammy's delight.

Glad to have something to do, Nora hauled herself into the buggy and let Grandma do the driving to the frolic. Jeannie and the kids took up the backseat.

"What cobwebs have you been spinning, Nora?" Grandma snapped the reins, and the horse took off. "You've been awful quiet today."

"I was just thinking this is my first buggy trip since I got here."

"You don't see many buggies here. I put my foot down with your daadi. If he wanted a car, fine, but I still wanted a buggy."

"It feels gut."

"We have a fresh breeze on our face. We can hear the birds singing. The *clip-clop* of the horse's hooves is like music. The sun is shining. We go slow enough to enjoy it all."

The reason behind the rules. Buggy rides were nice. Nora relaxed and listened to Jeannie teach Missy and Jason a simple song. They giggled and bickered back and forth. Twenty minutes later the buggy pulled into the driveway that circled in front of a one-story log cabin–style house complete with a carport that currently housed an ancient station wagon. A pony-size dog, its tail whipping back and forth, barked its welcome from a pen on the other side of the house.

The door opened, and Samantha bounded down the porch steps. A skinny woman, she looked more Mennonite than Amish in her simple flowered dress. Her lime-green sneakers marred the effect, however. "You're here, you're here. We've already started. Come on in."

She helped Jeannie with the baby so she could wake Jason and Missy. Three children under the age of ten materialized before Grandma and Nora made it to the door. They took charge of the two toddlers and carried them off to parts unknown in the interior of the house.

"Are you getting settled in?" Samantha patted Nora's shoulder as she swept past with Sadie firmly tucked in her other arm. "Do you hear anything from home? Is the fire out yet? Jeannie, I set a cradle in the kitchen for the bopli. Esther, did you bring the rhubarb?"

They didn't have time to answer. Chattering about the price of apples and sundry other topics, Samantha trotted ahead down the hallway toward their destination. From the sweet, mouthwatering aroma of cinnamon, cooking apples, and cherries, it was the kitchen.

Half a dozen women crowded the room, peeling apples, pitting cherries, washing jars, and stirring the contents of large pans on the stove. Organized chaos. So like home that Nora expected to see her mother washing apples in the sink or supervising the making of apple butter. A lump grew in her throat. She slipped over to the open screen door to gaze at the familiar Cabinet Mountains to the southwest of the valley.

As if she sensed Nora's mood, Grandma squeezed between her and Samantha and held up her huge pot. "The rhubarb sat for three hours in the sugar, so it's ready to boil."

At least Grandma and Jeannie were here, and there was plenty of work to be done. Nora swiped at her face and turned to join in the fun.

"I'll make room on the stove." Samantha wiped her hands on her apron and took the pot. "Nora, we have enough cherries pitted if you want to start a batch of the jam. The directions are on the counter."

Mother taught Nora how to make jams when she was six. She didn't need directions, but she smiled and nodded. This felt like home. She poured the cherries and water into the pan, added sugar, brought it to a boil, and stirred until the sugar dissolved.

Heat singed her cheeks. Sweat rolled down her temples. The women's chatter filled the air. Jeannie hummed a song as she peeled apples. It was almost perfect.

"What did you think of Ike's sermon on Sunday?" Samantha added more jars to the hot-water bath on the gas stove's back burner.

"Did our style of worship seem more natural to you the second time?"

The bubble burst. Nora used her apron to wipe the sweat from her face. Never had she met so many people so eager to talk about their religion. The elders were right. Living it was better than talking about it. "It was interesting."

"We don't mean any disrespect by not standing." Jeannie grabbed another bushel of apples from the floor and set it on the table between Grandma and her. She picked up her paring knife. "It's just not our way."

"Do you understand why we do it?"

"Not really." Nora added two pouches of liquid pectin to the fruit and waited for it to come to a rolling boil again. "It makes it hard to hear sometimes and hard to concentrate on what Onkel Ike is saying."

"We're filled with the Holy Spirit."

A murmur of agreement from the other women seated at the prep table filled the air. "Amen." "Hallelujah." "Praise Gott." Their words laid like a wet blanket on Nora's shoulders. Her response would be reviewed. They were ganging up on her.

"The deacon told us the Holy Spirit dwells in everyone who believes." Those months in baptism class had paid off. Having Levi explain difficult concepts to her had been a godsend. God had given Levi smarts and then given him to Nora. "That's where the fruit of the Spirit comes from."

Which gave her the ability to be patient and exercise self-control with Samantha now. Nora gritted her teeth and managed to smile.

"David leaped and danced for joy."

"Not in the middle of a sermon." *Gently, gently*. Dissension came from people having their own interpretation of Scripture. Father wouldn't like this discussion. Nor would the bishop. "These cherries are ready. Are the jars?"

"Jah, they are." Samantha used a hot pad to line up the half-pint jars on the counter next to the stove. "Be sure to leave a quarter inch of headspace."

Nora bit her lip to keep from responding. Not only did Samantha know all about religion, she was an expert in jam making. *Patience, self-control, love, gentleness . . .*

Silence reigned while Nora concentrated on filling the jars with the hot concoction. She added the lids and gently lowered each one into the boiling water canner for their ten-minute bath.

"I don't mean to be a pest." Samantha grabbed a sponge and wiped down the counter where Nora had been working, even though Nora's twenty-twenty vision saw nary a drop of spilled fruit. "I'm not judging. My family in Indiana is Old Order. They don't think any more of our style of worship than you do."

"You're not a pest." Grandma slathered apple butter on a thick slab of white bread and handed it to Samantha. "Just enthusiastic."

"We're supposed to win the lost and make disciples."

That did it. Nora didn't bother to breathe or count to ten. "I'm not lost. We're no more lost than you are."

"She doesn't mean anything by it, Schweschder," Jeannie interceded. "Like Mammi says, she's just enthusiastic."

"I can speak for myself." Samantha's earnest face creased with concern. "The Plain people all over this country are lost. They're lost in a forest of rules so thick they can't see the skies or heaven anymore. That's what Reverend Brubacher says. It's what your onkel says. You're bound by the chains of your own religion."

Her words made no sense whatsoever. How could religion bind a person? Religion allowed Plain people to walk through this world unscathed. Nora grasped for an answer. Grandma's hand landed on her shoulder and tightened. "How are those cherries coming? I'm ready to jar the rhubarb and get it into the water bath."

The peacemaker. Nora took a breath. "I don't—"

"Hey, I'm here. I'm here." Her flip-flops slapping on the pine floorboards, Tammy pranced into the kitchen wearing a neon orange T-shirt and jeans sporting holes in both knees. "Let the frolic begin."

"You're late." Grandma handed her a bowl of cherries. "Start pitting."

"Ach, no, I'm in the pits." Tammy accepted her chores. "I don't mind. I eat as many as I pit."

Instead of joining the other women at the table, she settled the bowl on the counter and turned to Nora. "But first I have to talk to my kossin." She grabbed Nora's arm and propelled her toward the door. "We'll be right back, I promise. Nobody touch those cherries. They're all mine. And save me some apple butter."

Delighted to put space between Samantha and herself, Nora went willingly. Away from the dank, billowing heat, she could breathe again. She followed Tammy down the hallway and through the front door. A crisp fall breeze greeted her. She lifted her face and let the ire of the last few minutes float away. "Where have you been?"

"Wyatt is back."

Wyatt would pour more gasoline on the desire to lure Nora and her family into the church here. From the rapturous gaze on Tammy's face, he also fanned the flames of another fire. Nora leaned against the porch railing and crossed her arms. "They sure spend a lot of time here."

"They're planning the tent revival. We'll have it here on the community property, close to the church. Folks from all over Libby will come." Tammy plopped into a rocker and examined her fingernails. She picked one, chewed on it, and spit. "Daed and the reverend are like bruders."

"That would make you, Wyatt, and me cousins."

"I said *like* bruders." Tammy hooted. "I'm so glad they're not actually bruders."

"Do you think your parents would approve of the two of you courting?"

"I don't know. They like him. He's special and they know it."

"He's not Plain."

"Nee, but he's on fire for Jesus. That's what counts in my daed's book."

On fire for Jesus. What did that feel like? More importantly, what did it mean? Nora turned and raised her face to the sun. Did it feel like the sun's warmth? Did it dissolve old hurts and new pain? Was it like snuggling up in a blanket, drinking hot cocoa on a winter night next to the fireplace? Or did it feel more like grazing a hand against the wood-burning stove. Hot, searing, painful?

The desire to know swelled and grew. Nora touched her warm cheeks with both hands and sighed.

"Why so sad, Kossin?" Tammy stood next to her. Nora hadn't heard her approach. She didn't dare look at her cousin. Tammy nudged her with her elbow. "I get how confusing all this must be. I grew up this way, and sometimes I feel hemmed in. Daed says the Amish worry about rules more than salvation. He doesn't seem to notice how we have to live a certain way too. It's just a different set of rules."

"Levi still hasn't called." Nora studied the mountains in the distance. Tammy knew all about the phone call and the argument. Of course she couldn't understand Levi's reaction. She, too, thought love should conquer all. It always did in the romance books she devoured. Nora's reading tastes were more limited, but mail-order brides and prairie romance novels were much the same. "He might never call."

"Then you call him."

"He might hang up on me."

"True."

"I don't understand why what I did was so wrong. What's so

wrong with playing an instrument?" They'd already hashed and rehashed this subject. Tammy obviously agreed. "Some of these rules just don't make sense."

"Tell me about it." Tammy stuck both hands on the railing and stretched her legs. "We want to make new rules. We want to make our own rules. Leastwise, I do."

"What rules would you make?"

"We all stay up as late as we want to and get up late. We have cell phones and iPads. We eat dessert first and never, ever, have to eat okra. I would move to a bigger town and get a job in a bookstore or a library. What about you?"

The idea that Nora could make the rules boggled the mind. All church members, men and women, voted on changes in the Ordnung, but women didn't participate in the discussion. They only voted. Some rules would never change. They were the bedrock of the way her community lived. No one would ever ask her opinion. "I don't know. It has never occurred to me to think about it. We follow the rules because they *are* the rules."

"Do you like playing the guitar and the piano?"

"Jah."

"So start there."

"Rule number one, everyone is required to learn to play an instrument." Nora plucked the words from a bushel basket of possibilities. "Members of the district will take turns playing at services so no one gets a big head about it."

"See there." Tammy grinned and held up her hand for a high five. Nora did the same. Tammy's satisfied smile faded quickly. "It's a start. But not everyone wants to play an instrument. Not everyone is gut at music. Have you heard my mudder sing? Nee? Let me demonstrate."

She sang a few lines of "Amazing Grace" off-key and so loud Nora had to clap her hands over her ears. "Stop, stop!"

"Maybe you want to amend the rule to say people who want to learn instruments can and those who do will take turns so no one gets a big head."

"So amended."

Tammy laughed and Nora joined in. How could this freedom of choice be bad? Before they knew it, they'd have a sound system to amplify it and then electricity instead of a generator. The hole in the dike would become a gushing river that would flood and destroy their efforts to live a godly life. Or would it? That's what the bishop wanted them to believe. That's what Mother and Father believed.

That's what Levi believed. Nora had believed it, too, until she heard Uncle Ike speak and talked to Grandpa and watched Tammy sing and dance with the joy of the Lord in her heart.

Even though Tammy no longer sang, the noise in Nora's head still made her want to cover her ears. She turned around and leaned her behind against the railing. "Speaking of rules, when will you see Wyatt again?"

"When will we see him again, you mean?" Tammy chewed on a cuticle. The skin around her fingernails was red and puffy. "He's invited us to go for pizza in town tonight."

"Us? You and me?" Nobody enjoyed feeling like a third wheel. "Nee, I don't think so. You don't want company."

"It won't be just us. He's inviting some other friends. We'll hang out, eat, and talk. It's no big deal."

"Why?"

"Why what?"

"Why is it better than staying here? We can eat and play music and talk here."

"It's not the same with a bunch of adults watching over us." Tammy tucked her blonde hair behind her ears. "We're grown-ups now. This isn't a singing. Guys and girls get together to have fun and get to know each other better."

"I have a guy." At least she thought she did. Levi couldn't be so angry he'd give up on them. "Even if he gives up on me, I'm not giving up on him."

"You're not going to marry one of them. It'll be fun."

"I don't know—"

"There's no reason to be a fraidy cat, Kossin." Tammy pranced toward the screen door. "I need you to be my wingman. Or wing-woman in this case. It'll be fun. You'll see."

"You don't need me to have fun."

Tammy paused with the screen door ajar. "Please, pretty please, with sugar on it." Her expression reminded Nora of the little girl who used to beg Nora to go first when they jumped from the rocks into the lake. "I want to spend time with Wyatt. This was his idea. He asked me to invite you. I want to knock his socks off with my knowledge of theology, but I can't. I'm not that smart. If I can't think of something to say, you can jump in."

Tammy didn't give herself enough credit, and she gave Nora too much credit.

Still, the entreaty on her face couldn't be ignored. They were cousins and they were women. They had to stick together.

Fun. There was nothing wrong with having fun.

Levi's solemn face when he said goodbye at the community meeting drifted through Nora's mind. *"Don't have too much fun,"* his voice whispered in her head.

How much fun was too much?

And was this what Tammy meant by free will?

17

Eureka, Montana

No work and all play made Levi antsy. Chopping wood seemed the only solution. It might only be September, but winter would come soon enough. At least that's what Levi told himself as he chopped wood in Kevin's backyard in the warmest part of a fall day. The sun insisted on shining despite his desire for a dark and gloomy day to match his mood. How could Nora be so naive to think no one would mind—including him or especially him—when she broke Ordnung rules? She could face censure from the Gmay.

He raised the ax and slammed it down on the wood. Two more logs fell to the ground. He added them to the growing woodpile next to Kevin's deck. Under other circumstances, he would go to Libby and bring her home. But it wasn't his place. The fact that she didn't want him to tell Harley made it obvious she knew what she was doing was wrong.

"You'll break your back swinging that ax so hard." Mother traipsed across the yard, carrying two glasses of cold tea. "Kevin said you were back here chopping wood. I thought he was seeing things."

"I figured it was something nice I could do for Kevin to thank him for letting us stay in his rental property free of charge."

"That's nice of you." She held out one of the glasses. "I figured you might be working up a powerful thirst."

Levi accepted her offering and took a long draught. "Hits the spot. Danki."

"It seems to me like you're working out some frustration." Mother settled onto the deck and sipped her tea. "Is it helping?"

"What makes you think I'm frustrated?" Levi held the glass to his forehead. The ice cooled his skin. "I'm just keeping busy."

"You can always help the girls with the laundry and the cooking." She laughed at her own joke. In a family of fourteen laundry was never done. Or cooking. She was blessed to have the girls to help. "I'm hiding out for a few minutes before I have to hang more clothes on the line. Diane has a shepherd's pie in the oven for supper. Mary is sewing new pants for the boys. Every one of them is growing so fast their pants are high waders."

"That's gut. I saw Caleb Hostetler at the church this morning. He says someone from Eureka is loaning Montana Furniture warehouse space. By tomorrow they should have operations set up to fill all those holiday orders backing up as we speak."

"That'll help you keep your mind off of Nora, I reckon."

"Nora's fine. She's in Libby."

Probably doing something she shouldn't be doing at this very moment.

"Jack told me you got a call from her."

"Jack sure is chatty." Levi set the glass on the deck railing and went back to chopping wood. "Especially about something that is of no concern to him."

"Stop chopping for a minute and sit with me." Mother patted the space next to her on the steps. "You're swinging that ax so hard I'm afraid chips will fly off and take out my glasses."

She had a point. He leaned the ax against the house's foundation and picked up his tea glass. "What's this about?"

"Jack is concerned because he's your stepfather and he cares for you."

"He doesn't want the family shamed."

"As well he shouldn't. He also doesn't want Nora leading you down the wrong path."

"Nobody is leading me anywhere."

"Something's bothering you. I want to know what it is."

She usually left well enough alone. Twelve children from ages twenty to two saw to that. She shouldn't have to worry about her oldest son, now an adult. Levi mopped his face with an old bandanna. "I'm trying to avoid worrying."

"Worrying sucks the joy out of a day."

From life itself. "I know. That's why I'm chopping wood."

"Maybe I can help."

Telling his mother about Nora's transgressions would put her in an awkward position. As a member of the Gmay, she had an obligation to tell the deacon. "Can I ask you a question without getting into specifics?"

"Of course you can." Her expression somber, she swiveled so she faced him. "I won't stick my nose where it doesn't belong."

In a small Gmay everyone's noses fit into the nooks and crannies where they didn't belong. "Say a person has been baptized. Say he or she decides to learn to play a guitar and sing in a band. Say he or she—"

"Just say she, this will go a lot faster."

"She is being influenced by family members who've abandoned our ways. Her special friend may have added to the situation by calling to check on her. Just say her family keeps a phone in the house. Say she's doing other things she doesn't admit to. She sounded mighty guilty."

"And you want to know what you should do?"

"I should've married her sooner." He filled Mother in on their plans. "Now the house has burned to the ground, and it may be months and months before it gets rebuilt."

"No wonder you're in such a state."

"Are you making fun of me?"

"Suh, I buried the father of my children. I've seen a lot of heartache in my life." Her voice softened. "So it takes a lot to get me in a dither. But that doesn't mean your angst is for no reason. She's treading on thin ice. Better to find out now what she's made of rather than later."

"Could she be brought before the Gmay?"

"It's likely, if she keeps it up. Or she could go to Tobias, Lucas, or Noah, confess her sins, and receive counseling. If she takes it seriously, all can be forgiven."

"I feel like I should do something. I should go to Libby, talk some sense into her, and drag her home."

"What's stopping you?"

"She's not my fraa. Harley made the decision to send her with her schweschder." He picked up the ax and thumbed its blade. Anything to keep from meeting his mother's gaze. She must wonder what he saw in a woman who would stray so quickly. "Arthur wants me back at work. He's depending on his employees to keep Montana Furniture in business. The orders are backing up every day the business is closed. And anyway, I'm needed here. With my family."

"You're a gut suh, but a little on the proud side." Her deep-brown eyes twinkled behind the dark-rimmed glasses she'd worn as long as Levi could remember. "I have eleven other kinner, a mann, and I'm not senile yet. We'll do fine without you."

"Jack said you didn't want your kinner leaving the area."

"He did, did he?" She giggled. His mother giggled. What was this world coming to? "He's a sweet man."

Ach. Her feelings for Jack were not on the list of topics Levi cared to discuss with Mother. "That's not the point. The point is that fire has devastated Kootenai. You're living in a rental house in town. Everything is upside down. Jack's right—"

"How I wish he could've heard you say that." Mother crowed and clapped. "It's been my heart's desire for you and Jack to become closer. Maybe this fire is a way for that to happen. Our suffering always leads to something more. Something good. Gott has a plan. Don't ever lose sight of that."

"We didn't need Jack. Me and the others could've taken care of you." The words spilled out, furious and naked, after all these years. "You didn't have to marry him."

"Ach, Suh, I didn't marry him because I had to." She patted his thigh. Her hand was an old woman's hand, wrinkled with sunspots and chapped from washing dishes and clothes. A hand that had worked hard. "I married him because I wanted to."

How could she love Jack so soon after losing Father? That was the real question. It died in his throat. "It felt wrong."

"I know. To you it felt wrong because you missed your daed. Don't ever think I've forgotten him. I will always love him. But Gott blessed me with room in my heart for two gut men who loved me back. My heart is so full with family I feel as if I could burst sometimes. I hope you can find your way to feel the same."

Already the wildfires and the evacuation had given him much to think about. *"Our suffering always leads to something more. Something good. Gott has a plan."*

"I think what really bothers you is that you and Jack are so alike."

"We are not." Nora had said he was bossy, and the trait that bothered Levi the most about Jack was his bossiness. "Ach. Say it isn't so."

"He's doing what a man who takes his role as head of the household seriously does. He has a huge job with twelve children to wrangle every day. Jah, that includes you no matter how grown up you are. He wants to do good by all of you."

The realization that Jack's shoes were too big and uncomfortable for Levi struck him right between the eyes. He'd never tried to see the world through his stepfather's eyes. "He has gut intentions, no doubt."

"So stop judging him and fighting him every step of the way. You're such a gut man. This seems to be your only blind spot. What happened to us was Gott's plan. Jack was part of His plan. Accept that, and you'll feel so much better."

What was God's plan for Levi and Nora? Maybe God intended for this separation to test the true mettle of their relationship. "Libby's only an hour's drive."

"True. Have you talked to Harley about it? Does he know about her transgressions?"

"She asked me not to."

"Another sure sign she knows what she's doing is wrong. So do you."

"I honestly don't know what is right."

"Try talking to Tobias. He's the deacon. Wayward members are his bailiwick."

"Tattle on her?"

"We're to hold each other accountable."

That would be as much fun as chopping off a finger with the ax. Would Nora ever forgive him?

"I'd rather try to help her myself first."

"I understand why you feel that way. Just be careful of your arrogance. This may not be something you can fix, as much as you would like to." She leaned in and kissed his forehead. "See that you don't get snared in the same trap, my suh."

Warmth flooded Levi. He swallowed a sudden lump in his throat. Her show of affection was so rare he wanted to capture it and hold it in his heart. He cleared his throat. "I won't do that."

Knees creaking, she stood. "See that you don't. I may not need you to stick around, but I always want you here. You're my firstborn." Her smile turned bittersweet. "You favor your daed so much,

I'll never forget how handsome he was. I have you to remind me. Now go find Caleb and get some work done. Work comes first right now. While you're doing that, think about talking to Tobias. He'll be fair."

Mother had always been a fount of advice. The older she grew, the better the advice became. Levi laid the ax over his shoulder and strode after her.

He had work to do.

18

Libby, Montana

The belligerent *beep-beep* of a car horn penetrating the silence in Grandpa's house startled Nora. Wyatt and his gang had arrived. The fun was about to begin. She took another sip of cold tea in hopes it would wet her dry throat. Maybe she could tell Tammy she didn't feel well. Or that Daryl and Jeannie wouldn't let her go. That would be lying. Besides, Tammy needed her.

"Don't be a wuss, Kossin."

Free will.

What exactly did a wingman or wingwoman do?

The horn blasted again.

"That's for you, I reckon." Jeannie scowled from the rocking chair in the living room. "Hurry up and tell them to stop honking. Sadie's asleep. She's been so fussy lately I'd like twenty minutes of peace."

"Sorry." Nora smoothed her dress and trotted to the front door, where she grabbed her jacket. "I won't be gone long."

"It's okay to have fun." Jeannie's scowl dissipated. Envy tinged her words. "Enjoy this time. When you have a mann and boplin, your life will be different. It's a bit of freedom you wouldn't have had otherwise."

Free will. Make the rules.

Where did free will end and temptation begin?

Jeannie's tune had certainly changed in the days since they arrived in Libby. If, as a mother and a wife, she saw this opportunity as a good thing, maybe Nora should too.

"I'll do my best." Smiling, Nora donned her coat. She waved goodbye and pushed through the door to the porch. "I'll be back early, though."

A silver four-door car bigger than a boat sat in the driveway. Wyatt sprawled in the driver's seat, Tammy next to him. A lone man with a thick black beard and matching curly hair took up a lot of space in the backseat.

Nora halted at the bottom of the steps and glanced up and down the driveway. No other cars. No other friends. Wyatt lowered his window. "Hey, Nora. Get in. We're starving."

"Where is everyone?"

"This is it. Everybody else had plans." His sly grin suggested Wyatt had the plans. "It's okay, though. Come on, get in. Brandon doesn't bite. I promise."

"Where did you get the car?"

"It's sweet, isn't it?" Wyatt smoothed his hands around the wheel. "It belongs to your cousin Joe."

Joe was Tammy's older brother. Nice of him to loan Wyatt a car. Her palms suddenly sweaty, Nora tugged the door open and slid onto the seat next to Brandon, who was so tall he had to hunch a little to keep from hitting his head on the car's ceiling. "Hi."

"Hi." He ran his hand through his long, thick curls. "I'm Brandon. A friend of Tammy's."

Brandon wore blue jeans, a long-sleeved western-style shirt, and cowboy boots. A white cowboy hat sat on the seat next to him. He had the biggest feet she had ever seen. "I'm Nora."

Conversation petered out, and Nora stared ahead. How long

would it take to drive into Libby? Ten minutes tops. She could handle this for that long. She cast about for something to say. Nothing came to her.

Did Tammy know there would be only one other person in this "gang"? Had she lied, or had Wyatt deceived her?

Breathe. Just breathe.

"Brandon's a cowboy. He works on a ranch down by Yellowstone." Tammy slid around on her seat. Her cheeks were pink and her eyes were made up with mauve and pale-purple colors that matched her lipstick. Tiny gold hoop earrings sparkled on her ears. "Tell her, Brandon, how you rope cattle and how you won the rodeo two years ago."

"I ride broncs. I didn't win the whole rodeo, but I do all right." He sounded surer of himself now. "I busted my leg last time around, so I'm sitting out the circuit this year."

"That's nice."

What a silly thing to say. Bronc riding might be exciting or dangerous or adventuresome, but nice?

"You should show her your belt buckles sometime." Tammy tossed her hair over her shoulder with more dramatic flair than necessary. "They're as big as Mammi's pancakes, and they have rhinestones on them."

"Very nice." Apparently nice was the only word left in Nora's vocabulary.

"What do you do?" Brandon sat so close she could smell his spicy aftershave and see the acne scars on his cheeks. "Tammy didn't tell me anything about you."

Not even that she was Plain and that she had a special friend?

"I work in the store in West Kootenai. Just until I get married."

There. She'd put it out there. He would get the hint. So would Tammy.

"I'd like to make enough money so my wife doesn't have to work."

Brandon infused the words with enthusiasm. "Kids need their moms at home. Day cares can't bring them up right."

What did a twentysomething cowboy know about raising children? Nora kept that thought to herself.

"It's scriptural." Wyatt nodded. "Women should be at home."

No one was arguing with that. At least Nora wasn't. Tammy wiggled in her seat. "What about the band? A lot of performers tour in buses and take their kids with them."

"That's true, but it's a tough gig." Wyatt's tone turned somber. "Take it from a guy who's traveled around the country his whole life. It's hard to make friends, and when you do you never see them. Plus it makes school hard. It wasn't homeschooling so much as bus schooling."

It sounded exciting to a woman who'd spent her whole life in one place. Nora glanced at the rearview mirror. Wyatt's baby-blue eyes stared back at her. He winked, but he didn't smile. Nora redirected her gaze to the passenger window. "That sounds hard."

"You learn to be independent and meet new people. I can make conversation with a stump if I have to." He laughed. The somber note dissipated.

A minute later he turned into a parking lot and rolled into a space that faced the restaurant. The sign read Red Dog Pizza Parlor and Saloon.

A long, lean building with a log cabin facade faced an even longer half-full parking lot. Cracks marred the asphalt, and weeds had muscled their way through the humped cracks. The name filtered through Nora's brain. "It's a saloon?"

"Restaurant and saloon," Wyatt clarified. "They have great pizza, pool tables, and Foosball. You can't beat that."

Perspiration dampened Nora's palms once again. Tammy glanced back and shot Nora an imploring *go-with-it* smile. Nora responded with a fierce scowl.

Tammy shrugged and mouthed, *Sorry*. "I'm first at Foosball."

That feeling of being a spoilsport didn't set well. Nora followed her cousin into the restaurant. *It's a restaurant. They serve food. It's not a bar. Not a bar.*

She'd keep telling herself that.

Inside, the aroma of pizza baking wafted in the air, rich with oregano, basil, onion, and garlic. Nora's stomach rumbled. Families crowded tables on one side while pool tables filled the other. Tiffany lamps strung from the ceiling provided low lighting over rectangular wooden tables that held candles flickering in red globes. A country western tune played in the background. A baby fussed on his mother's lap.

The saloon didn't seem like such a bad place.

Wyatt and Tammy made a mad dash for the only open Foosball table, leaving Nora and Brandon at a table for four nearby.

"Do you play pool?" Brandon sounded hopeful.

"No, sorry. I never have."

"I could teach you."

"Do you think we should order food first?" The sooner they ate, the sooner they could leave. Nora tried to catch Tammy's gaze, but her cousin was too busy slamming the ball back and forth with Wyatt. From the sound of her whoops, she was winning. "What do you think they want to eat?"

"You didn't know it was just gonna be us and them, did you?"

Nora rearranged the Parmesan cheese, chili pepper flakes, and napkin holder in the center of the table. "Tammy said a group of people were going to hang out together."

"Sorry about that." Brandon sounded truly contrite. "Wyatt told me the same thing. Nothing like getting set up for a blind date and not even having time to prepare mentally for it."

"I don't understand why Wyatt would want company on a date with Tammy."

"I got the impression it was more about showing you a good

time." Brandon added a toothpick holder to Tammy's arrangement. He had a nice smile and pretty emerald eyes. Not as nice as Levi's brown eyes, but still. "I'm not an expert on this stuff. I don't go to his dad's meetings or the church there at Eagle Valley, but it seems like they want you to see how much fun they're having."

At least he didn't want to talk religion. Tammy's giggles mixed with Wyatt's deeper guffaws. "They may be having too much fun."

"That's not possible for two PKs."

"What is a PK?"

Brandon waited while a waitress placed four glasses of ice water on the table, along with a stack of red plates and silverware wrapped in red paper napkins. She fixed them with a polite look of inquiry on her chubby face. "What'll be?"

"A large meat lover's deep-dish and a veggie supreme on a thin crust." Brandon had done this before. Did he often double date with Wyatt? Did they have a system worked out? "A pitcher of beer and two glasses of iced tea for the ladies."

The waitress didn't even write it down. "We'll get that right out to you, sir."

As soon as she walked away, Brandon turned back to Nora. "Preacher's kid. Tammy and Wyatt are preachers' kids. They're not really kids anymore, but sometimes they still act like they have something to prove."

"Like drinking beer in a saloon?"

"Like that. Wyatt toes the line most of the time, but sometimes he wants to blow off steam."

At the Foosball table, Tammy did a victory dance around Wyatt, who laughed and shook his finger at her. He held up a handful of change, and they went at it again. Wyatt wasn't the only one blowing off steam. "We have a time when we do that."

"The rumspringa. I've heard of it. Did you do anything exciting?"

She hadn't. Now Tammy wanted to give her another opportunity.

Nora's cousin didn't understand the time for such exploration had come and gone.

"Not like this. There was already somebody special in my life—"

"You have a boyfriend?" Brandon's face went red. He scooted his chair back. "Seriously? I'm not the kind of guy who horns in on another man's girl. Wyatt knows that."

"Sorry."

"Don't be sorry." He sighed gustily and took a long drink of water.

The conversation faltered, then became nonexistent.

Eventually the pizzas came, Wyatt and Tammy joined them at the table, and Brandon's mood seemed to lighten. Wyatt urged him to share stories about life on a ranch and the rodeo. He also teased Tammy about her refusal to try the beer. She said it stank and tasted like skunk pee.

"When did you taste skunk pee?" Wyatt pretended to smell his beer. "It smells like hops and barley."

Tammy picked up Brandon's glass—which he hadn't touched—and held it so close to Nora's face she was in danger of ending up with foam on the end of her nose. "Smell it and tell me what you think."

"It smells like Sadie's wet diapers." Or worse.

"There you have it. A neutral third-party judge."

Wyatt shrugged. "It's an acquired taste."

Or maybe beer tasted like freedom to Wyatt. And temptation to Tammy. "I'm surprised you drink."

"I don't much." Wyatt gulped another swallow. "The Bible says to avoid drunkenness, for drunkenness leads to debauchery. One glass of beer will not lead me unto temptation."

"Jesus turned water into wine for the wedding because His mother asked Him to." Tammy added Parmesan to a thin slice of pizza loaded with mushrooms, green pepper, black olives, and sliced tomato, but she didn't pick it up. "Daddy says we have to make good decisions, and we can't do that if we have addled brains. Personally, I don't see why it's such a big deal. It's nasty and it makes you feel bad in the morning if you drink too much."

Said the voice of experience.

Nora squeezed lemon into her iced tea and took a long sip. She breathed in the clean scent of citrus. A flash of memory caught her mind's eye. Mother made fresh lemonade on a hot July evening. They all sat in the front yard, drank the tart-yet-sweet drink, and delighted in the slightest breeze.

Gott, I want to go home. I need to go home.

Not yet.

As clearly as if God leaned down and spoke in her ear, she heard His words. Her breath caught. Blood pulsed through her veins. Her heart beat.

The tinny music coming from bad speakers and murmured conversations faded with a fussing baby and a whining child.

God spoke to me.

What would the bishop say about such an audacious statement? What would Mother and Father say? They would insist she was deluded, that she'd been drinking, that she'd spent too much time with the likes of Wyatt Brubacher.

She caught Brandon watching her. He smiled. She smiled back. "The pizza's good." She nibbled at another piece of the meat lover's pizza with its sausage, bacon, Canadian bacon, and hamburger. The sauce was tangy and the crust thick and chewy. "I reckon we can all agree on that."

"I reckon you have pizza sauce on your lip."

His gaze focused on her mouth. Nora grabbed her napkin and dabbed. "Thanks for telling me." She slid her plate away. "I couldn't eat another bite."

"I'll ask for a to-go box." Tammy craned her head and searched for the waitress. "You can take it home, Nora. Daadi loves cold pizza for breakfast."

"Hey, don't act like the night's all over." Wyatt's hand covered Tammy's. "There's a band playing at Memorial Park tonight."

"I heard they're not bad." The blush on Tammy's face crept down her neck toward the gathered neckline of her peasant blouse that exposed her collarbone. "I'm just glad it's not Shakespeare in the Park."

"No kidding. If you need help sleeping, that'll do the trick." Wyatt laughed. "I wonder if they'll still have the chain saw carving championship next week."

Shakespeare was not taught in Kootenai's Plain school, but plenty of men in Nora's community could win a chain saw competition. No one was thinking of competition right now, not when they weren't sure if they would have houses to which they could go home. Chain saws would be needed for real work once that day came.

Wyatt paid the check with a bank card as if it were nothing. Nora offered to pay her share, but he gaped at her as if she'd grown horns. He dropped a cash tip on the table and stood. "Let's check out the band. Maybe the ice-cream truck will be parked close by."

"Wait, wait, I have to go to the restroom." Tammy pushed back her chair and stood. "Come with me, Kossin."

Gladly. Nora waited until they were in the bathroom to call her out. "You set me up on a date with a complete stranger, when you know I have Levi waiting for me."

"We have gut intentions." Her gaze fixed on her own image in the mirror, Tammy offered the statement in only a slightly apologetic tone. "You need to see that there's more to the world than what has been offered to you in Kootenai. Did you even date anyone besides Levi?"

"That's beside the point—"

"That is the point. Brandon is a great guy." Tammy pinched her cheeks and reapplied mauve lipstick. "He's sweet and kind and cute, and he won't fall over in a faint if you drive a car."

"He doesn't worship the way you and Wyatt do." Ignoring her reflection in the mirror, Nora washed her hands and dried them. "How can you square that with working so hard to convert me? Then you try to set me up with someone who's not religious."

"He's religious, just not evangelical. But Wyatt's working on it. Have you heard of friend evangelism?" Tammy pulled a pack of Doublemint gum from her purse and offered it to Nora. She declined. Tammy proceeded to stuff two pieces in her mouth. "Wyatt cares about Brandon, and he cares about you. So do I."

So this was all about conversion. Every frolic, every meal, every event designed to help people like Nora see the light.

Instead, it made her angry. "Promise me you'll never do this to me again."

"I can't." Tammy pinched Nora's cheeks. "Your summer tan is fading. I love you, Kossin, and I want you to be next to me kneeling at the throne someday."

How could Nora argue with such noble intentions?

Tammy's smile faded. "Do I look all right?"

"You always look nice."

"Do you think Wyatt likes the way I look?"

"He has eyes for you only."

"I said something to him I shouldn't have, and he's been weird ever since."

"What did you say?"

"I told him I thought I was falling in love with him." Tammy hiccuped a small laugh. "Isn't that stupid? You're never supposed to say it first."

"It should make him feel gut to know someone as nice and sweet as you feels that way about him. What did he say?"

"He said I was sweet."

"Ah." Nora wracked her brains for a suitable response. "You know how men are. They have a terrible time talking about their feelings. Give him time."

"I hope so." Tammy grabbed the door. "I felt so stupid."

"You're not stupid to tell someone you care for them. That's a gift. Just remember that."

"You're the one who's sweet." Tammy blew Nora a kiss and held the door so Nora could go first. "I want to be you when I grow up."

Very funny.

The men waited in the foyer. Brandon held the door open with one hand. "After you, ladies."

The keys jangled in his other hand. At Nora's curious gaze, he shrugged. "Designated driver."

The term meant nothing to her, but she understood when Brandon opened the car door for her as well. Tammy and Wyatt piled into the backseat.

Brandon started the car. Even over its purr, the sounds coming from the backseat were unmistakable. Wyatt might not say much about his feelings, but he apparently knew how to show them.

Don't think about it. How could she not think about it when the kissing didn't seem to end?

Bright red on both cheeks, Brandon rolled his eyes and turned up the radio. A country song about sitting on a truck tailgate drinking played. He switched channels. A guy wanted to know why his girl left him. Brandon backed out and drove from the parking lot. "Come on, you guys, give it a rest," he grumbled. "You're not exactly alone in the car."

"Sorry, dude." Wyatt didn't sound sorry at all. "We'll be good."

A blessed five minutes later they pulled into a parking space in the lot next to the park's bandstand. Nora flew from the car and sucked in fresh air. Never again would she go with Tammy and Wyatt anywhere.

"Young love." Brandon fell into step next to her. "It's so gross."

"That's a good word for it." The man's exaggerated gagging noises made Nora laugh. "I never thought about it, but I guess it would be the same if someone had to be around when Levi and I . . ."

Stupid, stupid thing to say.

Brandon shrugged. "It's okay. It's what people do. No need to be embarrassed."

"It's private."

"We can agree on that. At least we can keep our distance here."

A country music band, complete with a fiddle, keyboard, two guitars, and drums, played in the covered bandstand. Folks sat in folding lawn chairs, on blankets, and on the grass, listening.

Wyatt pulled Tammy into a grassy area where couples slow-danced to a dreamy ballad about love lost and found. The lead singer had a deep, bluesy voice that soared over the music.

Brandon stuck his hands in his pockets and studied his shiny boots. Nora tightened her sweater around her shoulders and tried to focus on the music. The band was good.

"It's a beautiful night," Bandon called over the music. "Perfect for dancing in the park."

"If it weren't for the smoke, it would be a starry night." *Where there's smoke, there's fire.* Why did that saying come to mind at this very moment? Wyatt held Tammy close. She laid her head on his shoulder. He whispered something in her ear. Tammy beamed. Nora focused on the guitar player instead. How many years did it take to learn to play like that? "The band is good, isn't it?"

"Yeah, especially for a little Podunk town like Libby." Brandon lifted his cowboy hat and resettled it. "I don't suppose you dance, do you?"

"No. I'm sorry." At least a dozen couples swayed to the music out in the wide-open space where everyone could see. What was so wrong about dancing? Shame fueled heat that burned its way across her cheeks and down her neck. "This was supposed to be a fun night for you too. They shouldn't have done this to you."

"It's okay. I don't mind." He pointed to a bench several yards from the crowd. "Let's sit and listen to the music. You're allowed to do that, aren't you?"

Sort of. Not exactly.

Nora joined him. She clasped her hands in her lap. A new, faster song started. Her toes tapped. *Stop it.* They didn't obey. Next she'd be snapping her fingers. It was only a hop, skip, and a jump from there to line dancing. Worse yet, Brandon wanted to dance. His boots were tapping too. "I know this is awful. It's awkward. I don't drink. I don't play pool. I don't dance."

"It's not the end of the world. I've done my share of dancing." He swiped a long piece of grass from the ground and began to twist it into knots. "Can you keep a secret?"

"I'm good at keeping secrets."

"I'm not a very good dancer."

"It doesn't seem like there'd be much to it." Nora studied the dancers two-stepping on the makeshift dance floor. "I'm sure there's a girl over there who'd dance with you if you asked."

"And leave you by yourself? That would be totally rude."

"I wouldn't blame you. You're stuck between a rock and a hard place."

"Yeah, poor me, stuck with the prettiest girl on the block. And you smell nice. You can make conversation." Brandon let out a low, mellow laugh. "Believe me, I've been on a lot of first dates, and you can't count on any of those things. Not that this is a first date."

Not something a woman who had a special friend could talk about. She scrambled for another topic. "Why didn't you drink the beer?"

"Because I could see it made you uncomfortable." He gave an exaggerated shudder. "And I've seen Tammy drive."

Nora laughed at the feigned fear on his face.

He leaned back and laid his arm across the bench behind her. Nora scooted farther away. "I'm taken."

"I can see why. Your guy is a lucky man."

"We don't believe in luck."

"I can understand that. I don't seem to have any—not that's any good, anyway."

"You've had hard times?"

"My parents split up when I was a teenager. My dad left town. My mom has a lot of boyfriends, so I've taken care of my little brother and sister." No self-pity echoed in the words. "I don't mind. They're good kids. I have had two real girlfriends. Both of them broke up with me because of the rodeoing."

"What's wrong with being in the rodeo?"

"If you ride the circuit, you're gone a lot, and bronco riding is dangerous."

"Why don't you stop?"

"Because I love it."

"More than you loved either one of them?"

"Now you sound like them." He snorted, but his grin was good-natured. "Life is short. You should live your dreams. Go for the gusto. I never feel more alive than when I slide onto the back of that horse and all that power is wound up underneath me. It's a high like nothing I've ever felt. Not even love feels that good."

It was a sentiment alien to Nora's way of thinking. A Plain woman did not go for the gusto. Or anything close. But love? Love was something different. "Maybe you just haven't met the right woman yet."

He pushed his hat back and leaned closer. "I don't know about that."

He smelled like the peppermint he'd taken from the bowl on the counter in the restaurant. He smelled better than beer, but it was still the scent of temptation.

"You're right. Life *is* short." Nora popped up from the bench. "I'm telling them to take me home. There's still time for you to do something fun with someone fun if we go now."

"It's okay—"

"No, it's not." Nora marched onto the grassy dance floor. The band had moved on from the slow ballad to something faster. The dancers dipped their partners and swung them around to the great delight of the crowd. People clapped and cheered. Nora gritted her teeth and kept moving.

Tammy's back was to her, but Wyatt saw her coming. He stopped in midswing. "What's up?" He had to yell to be heard over the music. "Where's Brandon?"

"I need to go home." Nora tapped on Tammy's shoulder. Her cousin turned. Her face was flushed. She grinned so wide her cheeks must hurt. Nora tugged her closer so she could talk in her cousin's ear. "Please take me home."

Tammy's smile melted into a pained expression. Her feet kept moving, but she ducked and talked over the music. "Come on, cuz—"

"Don't *cuz* me, Tammy Beachy." The music kept playing. Couples kept dancing. No one seemed to notice their little drama. Nora kept her gaze on Tammy. "Take me home now."

"I'll ask Brandon to take you home as soon as you do one thing for me." Wyatt stepped away from Tammy. "Let's pretend you cut in. You don't mind, Tammy, do you?"

Wyatt might be smart, a good preacher, a better pianist and singer, but he couldn't read faces very well. Tammy's smile disappeared. "Seriously?"

"Just give us a few minutes." Wyatt raised her hand to his lips and kissed the back of it. "We're right behind you."

Tammy trudged away.

What just happened here?

Wyatt took her hands and placed them on his shoulders. "Okay, here we go." He pulled her closer and began to sway. "Close your eyes and let your body respond to the music."

"I'm not dancing." Nora leaned into him to be heard over the music. "I told Brandon I don't dance, and I don't."

"No, you're not. You're letting the music move you like you did as a little girl before they started telling you it was wrong." He clasped her closer. "Close your eyes and imagine that little girl. Imagine how she twirled about. Then think of how King David leaped and danced to celebrate before the Lord."

A new song started. The vocalist's rich baritone rose and soared over the crowd into the dusky sky. He sang a mournful ballad about a man who left the woman he loved to ride one last horse in a rodeo. She didn't want him to leave. But he went anyway and died doing what he loved. The melody and the story, like all good songs, captured the listener and wouldn't let her go. Nora's body began to sway. Her mind's eye pictured the woman as she screamed her dead lover's name.

How she ran into the ocean, calling his name.

Held captive by the song and the feel of Wyatt's hand on her waist, Nora couldn't stop. Didn't want to stop.

How easily he reached for Scripture to make his point.

The thought broke the spell. She halted. "No. No."

"No what?" A bewildered frown on his face, Wyatt dropped his hands and stepped back. "It's not beautiful storytelling and beautiful music?"

Nora whirled and strode away from the loud music and the crowd. To her relief, Wyatt trailed after her.

Tammy stood next to the bench where Brandon sat. She tapped her toe. Brandon simply stared at his boots.

"Could you please take me home, Brandon?"

He slapped his cowboy hat on his head, stood, and stalked toward the sidewalk that would begin the long trek back to the car.

Nora scurried to keep up. "I'm sorry. I had no intention of dancing with him."

"It's not your fault." Brandon didn't bother to keep his voice down. "He's like that."

"Like what?"

"Like the Pied Piper."

She knew the story. "I'm not easily led."

Yet he almost had her. Brandon chuckled, a dry humorless sound. "That's what they all say."

The drive back was quiet. No kissy noises emanated from the backseat. Brandon didn't even turn on the radio. Nor did he attempt to make conversation. His face set, jaw jutting, he insisted on walking her to the door. "It's the gentlemanly thing to do."

"You're a nice man."

"I try." He propped his hand on the door and towered over her. "Wyatt believes in what he does. It's just that sometimes he forgets that the end doesn't justify the means. He and Tammy both mean well. I try to remember that. You should too. Give them both an A for good intentions, forgive, and move on. It makes life easier."

"They put us both in a bad spot." *Do not look into those emerald eyes.* She studied her sneakers. "Sometimes you have to call a person on his bad behavior. I'm sorry I danced with him and not you."

"You didn't mean to do it, and you stopped. Most girls would've fallen into his arms. You're stronger than you know." Brandon held out his hand. Nora shook it. His hand swallowed hers. "It was nice meeting you, Nora Beachy. Have a good life."

She was trying. The fire, the house burning down, being separated from Levi, the attempts to convert her—the onslaught of life didn't make it easy.

"Nobody ever said life would be easy or fair." Her mother's voice echoed in the valley.

I miss you, Mudder.

She stood on the porch long after Brandon drove away, waiting for the ache under her breastbone to go away. *I'm sorry, Gott. It's confusing. I don't feel any different for having danced to a beautiful song on a beautiful evening, all Your making. Aren't these gifts of music, song, and dance from You?*

An owl hooted in the distance. Dogs barked.

God said nothing.

19

Forgive and forget. A Plain person didn't have a choice. A good Christian didn't have a choice. Nora had said her prayers before crawling under the covers the previous evening. Then she forgave Tammy for placing her in such an uncomfortable position. Yet her ire lingered as she studied the farmers' market setup on Ninth Street next to the Chamber of Commerce building. A few vendors trickled in from the parking lot at nearby Fireman's Park. Most dragged their feet as if they could use another cup of coffee. Caffeine would likely fuel Nora's irritation.

I'm only human, Gott.

God didn't deign to answer her this time. He surely had little patience for His children stating the obvious.

Nora tried humming as she added more jars of apple butter to the store's table next to baskets of fall produce. The baked goods, including breads, cinnamon rolls, muffins, and saucer-size cookies, should tempt even the most disciplined shopper. The thought didn't improve Nora's disposition. Not even "Amazing Grace" could erase her grumpiness this morning. Not even the smell of kettle corn, coffee, burgers, and street tacos drifting from other booths helped.

Brandon's face when he asked her if she played pool had surfaced in her dreams. Only she had said yes. She leaned over a pool table and knocked balls into every corner. Then she slow-danced with Wyatt. Mother said dreams didn't mean anything. Weird dreams were the result of eating before bed and indigestion.

Not the result of a guilty conscience. The memory of Wyatt's grin as he put his hands on her hips followed her, poking her in the side, as she arranged jars of jams and jellies.

Music wasn't bad. Who was she trying to convince? "Phooey." She growled and slapped away flies intent on attacking the baked goods. "You're not welcome here."

"I hope you're nicer to the shoppers." Lugging a large basket filled with broccoli, lettuce, tomatoes, and green beans, Aunt Roseanna ambled toward their table. She wore a scarf over her head, overalls, and a blue plaid flannel shirt like an English farmer's wife. "Why so grumpy this morning? You're usually such a sweet girl."

"I didn't sleep well."

"Could it have something to do with my oldest dochder?" Aunt Roseanna made room for the produce on the second table where a display of canned goods, including dill pickles, cherry jam, apple butter, rhubarb, and peach preserves, took up most of the space. "I heard her come in late last night, so I got up to talk to her." Her expression turned sour. "She didn't want to talk about where she'd been or who with. She just said she had a good time. She was tired and wanted to go to bed. When I woke her up to come here this morning, she said she had a headache and needed to sleep more."

"If she came in that late, she probably did have a headache."

"She lives in her parents' house. She should be more respectful. I worry when she doesn't come home."

Her inquiring tone suggested she expected Nora to share what she knew about Tammy's whereabouts. If she knew about Wyatt, how would she feel? "Mudder says it's hard when kinner get to a certain age—not quite adults but too old to take a switch to."

"Your mother is a wise woman."

Nora laid out the battery-operated calculator, a notebook where she would place all the stickers from the products they sold, pens, and a receipt book. Aunt Roseanna would handle credit card transactions. If Tammy had grown up in a truly Plain home, her life would be different. The rules, different. "How old were you when you moved from Kootenai to Libby?"

Aunt Roseanna scratched her nose and frowned. "Hmm, twenty, I guess. I was in a family way with Joe at the time."

"Do you ever miss it?"

"I miss my family." Her tone matter-of-fact, she laid out the plate that would be used for samples and arranged chunks of pumpkin bars on it. "I still see them, but it's not the same. They stare at me like I'm a lost soul. It's ironic because they're the lost souls."

Again? "But they're not. We're not." Blood pounding in her ears, Nora clasped her hands to keep them from flailing. "Do we have to worship the same way in order to reach the same end?"

"In Kootenai Ike wouldn't be allowed to preach unless he drew the lot. You've heard him preach. The Holy Spirit moves in him. He is meant to be a preacher."

How did a person know if the Holy Spirit moved in him? Nora batted the question away. She opened two folding chairs and slid them behind the table.

Aunt Roseanna didn't elaborate. They worked in silence for a few minutes. Finally, she stepped back and brushed her hands off. "Tell me what's really bothering you."

"I had a dream last night. About a man. A man who wasn't my special friend."

"Ach, it's just a dream. It probably doesn't mean anything. You probably had indigestion." Aunt Roseanna took a sip from her travel mug. Her eyes narrowed as she stared at Nora up one side and down the other. "Or it might mean you've got a thistle under your saddle and you can't get it out. It's like the princess with the pea under the mattress."

The first analogy made more sense to Nora than the second. How did a pea get under a mattress, and why wasn't it simply crushed? "I danced with him."

"Aha." Aunt Roseanna trumpeted the two syllables so loudly, the lady selling beads, necklace-making materials, and jewelry under the next canopy looked up and smiled. Aunt Roseanna smiled back and waved. "So you're wondering if you really want to dance with this guy. You know we consider music and dance gifts from God. I know you were taught something different, but you're not going to hell because you dreamed about dancing with a man. I promise."

"Gott decides, though, who goes to heaven and who goes to hell."

"True, but you don't sound convinced that dancing is wrong."

"I hate having all these seeds of doubt planted."

Aunt Roseanna bestowed a one-armed hug on Nora. "Better now than later."

"If there hadn't been a fire and I hadn't come here, there never would've been a later."

"Honey, there's always a later."

Aunt Roseanna was an elder, but her statement didn't make sense. If there had been no fire, Nora would never have left home. She and Levi would be that much closer to marriage. The house would still be there. The family that had been living there would have moved to Bonners Ferry by now.

If, if, if. Life was full of ifs.

The sound of a child screeching filled the air.

Jeannie, accompanied by Samantha and the little ones, strolled in the direction of the Farm-to-Market table. Missy had a caramel apple while Jason seemed intent on demolishing a chocolate chip muffin while singing a nonsensical song at the top of his lungs. They both had butterflies painted on their chubby cheeks. Samantha's children were nowhere in sight.

"Looks like you did some shopping." Aunt Roseanna gestured at Jeannie's bag. "I told you they have some great vendors here."

"I got Mammi a set of wooden bowls from the woodcrafter for her birthday." Jeannie unwrapped her package and showed them. The six small bowls were polished and stained hickory. "Do you think she'll like them?"

"Knowing Esther as I do, I'm sure she'll cherish them." Samantha made it sound like she and Grandma were best friends. "They'll make nice salad bowls."

"She'll love them." Aunt Roseanna smoothed her hand over the top one. "I'd love them."

"It's not your birthday." Jeannie pushed her hand away and turned to Nora. "I also bought Mudder some beeswax candles and some honeycomb."

"Are you trying to sweeten her up?"

"Nee, I just miss her."

"Me too."

"At a certain point we all have to leave our parents and cleave to our spouses." Samantha snatched a pumpkin bar sample from the plate, popped it in her mouth, and chewed. She smacked her lips. "Yum. I'll take a dozen of those. Putting our husbands first is the natural order of things. The Bible says so."

Levi wasn't Nora's husband. Not yet. Maybe he never would be. The thought of starting over with someone new or maybe never finding the right man hung over her like a shroud. "The Bible also says to honor our parents. One way we do that is by following the Ordnung and keeping our vows."

Aunt Roseanna and Samantha exchanged glances.

"Samantha's right. As women we go from following our parents' wishes to bowing to the desires of our manns." Jeannie finished cleaning Jason's hands. She tossed the wipe into the trash can. "Daryl listens to me, but then he makes up his own mind, and that's that."

She swiped her hands together as if brushing off the thought. Her chubby face filled with a strange expression—almost defiant with a touch of chagrin. "I've learned to save my breath."

"But you're happy, aren't you?" Nora placed the pumpkin bars in a white bakery bag and handed it to Samantha. Jeannie always seemed happy. She had everything a Plain woman could want. A hardworking, faithful husband and three children. "You're blessed."

Jeannie's expression lightened. "Of course I am. Gott is gut."

"I have to get back before my kinner tear up the house." Samantha handed a ten-dollar bill to Aunt Roseanna, who made change with practiced ease. "Do you want a ride, Jeannie?"

"Jah. Sadie will be screaming to eat if I don't hurry back." Jeannie smiled. "Mammi was sweet to give me a few hours of freedom."

"Freedom is a gut thing." Samantha scooped up Jason and stuck him on her hip. "If you know what to do with it."

Freedom. They talked often about freedom here.

The two women strolled away, the little ones trailing after them. Nora swiveled to study the people who swarmed the tables. Were they all free to do whatever they wanted?

No. They had to work, pay bills, take care of children, go to school, care for sick relatives, and adhere to the laws of the land. Plain folks did all that, but they put God's laws first. The bishop would argue there was freedom in that.

20

Aching shoulders and feet offered proof that Nora had worked hard three days in a row at the store, staying after it closed to clean, do inventory, and help with ordering product. Tammy hadn't shown her face once. Aunt Roseanna said she was "under the weather." More likely she was avoiding Nora's wrath over the so-called blind date.

Nora hung her jacket on the overstuffed rack next to the door in Grandpa's foyer. What a blessing to have a place to go each day. The work took her mind off the situation at home. Nothing could erase Levi from her thoughts, but keeping her hands busy passed the time.

Plus she'd met virtually everyone in the community and a good many Englishers from Libby. Such friendly people. Everyone expressed concern for Kootenai. They all wanted to help rebuild when the call came to return. Nora nudged one sneaker off with the other foot and plopped on the stool next to the rack so she could rub her feet. No one sat in the living room, which meant Jeannie and Daryl had turned in. If only Sadie would sleep through the night. A lot to ask of a three-month-old, but a person could hope.

Grandpa's deep voice penetrated the silence. He sounded perturbed. Nora eased from the stool and padded in her stocking feet toward the sound. He stood in the hallway, his back to her, talking on the phone.

"I know the call for them to go home could come any day, but we can't force-feed the Good Book to them." His shoulders hunched as he switched the receiver from one ear to the other. "They've been taught one way their entire lives. You can't change that in a few weeks' time."

Nora backstepped into the living room. A person shouldn't listen to a private phone call. On the other hand, Grandpa was talking about Nora, Jeannie, and Daryl. Didn't she have a right to know the contents of that conversation? Talking about people behind their backs amounted to gossip.

Eavesdropping didn't sit well either.

Grandpa's voice rose. "I'm as concerned for their well-being as you are, Suh."

Suh. It had to be Uncle Ike.

Nora's feet wouldn't move. Grandpa cared about her eternal well-being. So did Ike. So did Mother and Father. Such a great divide split the family. Nora's heart hurt. She might fall into that chasm. Who would catch her?

"What are you doing?"

Nora started. Grandma stood in the foyer in a nubby flannel housecoat gaping open to reveal a cotton nightgown. Nora's hands fluttered to her chest where her heart pumped double time. "N-Nothing. I just got home from the store. I stayed after closing to help out."

Grandma's eyebrows rose and fell. "I didn't mean to scare you." Her slate-gray hair cascaded to her waist. Even in old age, it was thick and healthy. "Why are you so sad?"

"What's going on out here?" Grandpa tromped into the foyer. His gaze went from Grandma to Nora and back. "I thought you were at the store, Nora. And what are you doing up, Fraa?"

"Indigestion. Insomnia. Old age." Grandma shrugged. "Take your pick."

Grandpa padded in man slippers to her side. "Go back to bed. I'll bring you a cup of ginger tea in a minute."

The look they exchanged made Nora smile. To still love after so many years and so much dissension would be a blessing. Grandma shook her finger at Grandpa. "Don't be filling her head with silliness, you hear me?"

"Me? Never!"

With a grunt she started up the stairs. Her progress was slow and measured. Nora glanced at Grandpa. His expression intent and concerned, he watched until Grandma made it to the top and disappeared. He turned to Nora. "I have something I want to give you."

A present? "You don't have to do that. It's not my birthday."

"You never know."

There was that language she didn't understand once again. She followed Grandpa into the living room, where he pulled a thick book from a stack in the magazine rack next to his recliner.

Not just any book. The title etched in gold on this leather-bound cover read *Holy Bible*. On the spine it read *New International Version*. He held it out. "I thought you should have your own copy."

Father had his English-German family Bible. He loaned it to her during her baptism class, but she'd never thought to ask for her own copy. It was so hard to understand the old Martin Luther German translation, and the King James Version in English wasn't much easier. "I couldn't—"

"You could and you should." His eyes narrowed over the rim of his glasses. "It's a gift. Not one you can turn down. You need it. Read it. Start with the Gospels. With Matthew. If you have questions, come to me or Ike. Don't ask Tammy. She means well, but she's not old enough or experienced enough to help a neophyte Christian."

A neophyte. More foreign language. More code. Nora accepted the Bible. It was heavy. Her own copy. To be read and studied. Was this the narrow path to salvation or the wide road taken by many who were deceived by their own wants and desires? She clasped it to her chest. "What about Wyatt?"

"Wyatt is a force of nature all his own." Grandpa's words were tinged with awe. "But he hasn't learned to harness that power yet. He will, with time and experience, if he doesn't do something stupid first."

Like drinking beer in a bar and kissing a girl in the backseat of a car? Those two acts alone didn't constitute a catastrophic fall from grace in his world. But in Nora's? "Danki."

"Make gut use of it."

"I'll try."

When Father and Mother sent their daughters to Libby, they couldn't have imagined this. Her father couldn't have imagined a concerted campaign to win his daughter over by his father.

Grandpa shuffled toward the kitchen. "Go to bed. Tomorrow is another day."

How could she sleep now? She had the answer to all her religious questions in her hands.

An hour later she lay in bed, staring into the dark. The Bible might be in modern English, but it didn't make it any easier to understand.

Ping-ping.

The insistent sound splintered the silence. Nora sat up in bed.

Ping-ping.

The window. Heart hammering in her chest, Nora tumbled from bed and hurried to pull back the curtain.

Sure enough. Tammy waved and hopped around like a crazy jumping bean.

Nora opened the window. "What are you doing here?" Caught between irritation and a sliver of laughter, Nora tried to keep her voice down. "You haven't talked to me in days, and now you wake me up in the middle of the night—"

"Shush. Come down." Tammy motioned with both hands. "Hurry. Please."

Curiosity overcame Nora's desire to dig in and nourish her anger at her cousin. "Fine."

"Hurry."

Nora changed into her clothes and dragged her hair into a ragged bun. She grabbed her sneakers and tiptoed down the stairs.

Tammy met her on the front porch.

"What is it? What's going on?"

"Do you still want to ride horses?"

"Now? Nee, I'm mad at you."

"Don't be mad. I'm sorry. Really I am."

Nora had no choice but to forgive. "What you and Wyatt did was wrong. It wasn't fair to me or to Brandon, but you already know that. I forgive you." She rubbed her gritty eyes and tried to focus her thoughts. "Just don't do it again."

"Okay. Gut. I'm glad we got that over with. I need your advice." Tammy grabbed Nora's arm and dragged her toward the barn. "You said you loved to ride. I need to blow off some steam."

Nora did love to ride. The idea of a night ride in the valley after being stuck in the store day after day would be perfect. "What happened to asking Daadi first?"

"He's asleep."

Maybe, but not for long. He didn't sleep much. Still, Tammy needed to talk. That was obvious. "What's this about?"

Tammy didn't answer. Together they saddled the roan and the butterscotch geldings. Sable wasn't in the barn. He would have to wait for another night.

Nora inhaled the crisp fall air and let the breeze wash away her confusion. The canter on a dark country road was perfect for what ailed her.

"Beat you to the highway." Tammy took off before Nora had a chance to respond.

Nora laughed and picked up her pace to a full-out gallop on the dirt road that wound its way from the house to the highway. Her hair flew behind her. Exhilaration ran through her. She and the horse were in sync. Nothing else in her life made sense, but in this moment the possibility existed that she would be happy again.

They could all be happy again.

The highway loomed in the distance with its semis, pickup trucks, and delivery vans. She slowed. Tammy waited until the last moment, but she, too, halted.

They both laughed. The sound rang out in the dark.

"That was fun." Nora clung to the saddle horn with one hand and patted her horse with the other. "It felt gut."

"Wyatt left town the morning after our double date. He just got back yesterday." Tammy turned her mount so she could ride alongside Nora. "I think I'm losing my mind."

"I would think you'd be thrilled that he's back."

"I am." She wrapped the reins around her hands and sank lower in the saddle. "I missed him so much. Being in love feels so gut, but it's scary too. Like, what if he doesn't like me as much as I like him? He's all I can think about. He got here early enough yesterday for us to take our walk like we always do. We always walk past the school and through the pasture and all the way to Sarah's. We hold hands and . . . do other stuff."

Having witnessed their "stuff" in the car, Nora kept her comments to herself. The dark hid Tammy's face, but her horse's pace quickened. "Her family's not home, so we can go into the barn and be alone. He lights a lantern. It is almost like candlelight. We snuggle in the hay and . . ." Her voice trailed away.

Nora urged her horse in a trot to keep up. The conversation would have been better in a place where she could see her cousin's expression. No, this was what Tammy wanted. To confess without having to see censure on Nora's face. "Tammy, you didn't . . . Tell me you didn't."

"He's so sweet. Sometimes I think I've died and gone to heaven."

"Ach, Tammy."

"The night we went out with you and Brandon was the first time."

Her fingers plucked at the saddle horn. "I couldn't leave the house the next day. I was sure people would take one look at my face and know what we'd done."

Dread lodged in Nora's stomach. What should she say? Hellfire and damnation? Plenty of Plain girls had done what Tammy had done. But mostly they aspired to do better. To follow Scripture. To follow God's plan for a man and a woman. Nora and Levi had been tempted, but they chose to wait, knowing this gift would be all the more precious because they had.

"It may be dark, but I can still see your face." Tammy sniffed. "I need a tissue."

"Sorry, I don't have one." Nora softened her tone. "I'm not sure what to say."

"Say you understand. Say you're happy for me."

"I can't do that. You know that Scripture is Gott-breathed. It is His Word. I'm not judging you, but I know I have to hold you accountable." These words could only come from God. Nora breathed a word of thanksgiving. She could never have said them on her own. "What you're doing is wrong. Repent, ask forgiveness, and don't do it again."

"We do know. We both do." Tammy's voice dropped to a whisper. "But it's like an avalanche. Once we start, there's no stopping."

"Then don't start." *They should marry, as soon as possible.* "Have you talked about getting married?"

"Nee. He hasn't asked me, and I can't be the one to bring it up." She sounded like a little girl denied the last piece of pie. "Can I? He hasn't even said he loves me."

"Did you talk at all about what's next?"

"You mean, like did we talk about where this is going?" Her voice trembled. Tammy eased back on the reins and brought her horse to a halt in the middle of the road. "Not exactly. But he always says, 'See you tomorrow,' and kisses me like crazy before I go in the house."

"That's not the same thing, and you know it."

"You don't think he feels the same way as I do?" Tammy took her hair tie from her long ponytail and retied it. "I think it's like you said. Men just have a harder time saying the words. They'd rather show you than talk about it. Wyatt is great at showing how he feels."

"You have to find the strength to stop. If he doesn't do the right thing, you must be the one."

"I'm so glad I have you to talk to."

Not that she'd helped much. "Me too. We better get back. If Sadie wakes up and I'm not there to pick her up, everyone will know I left the house. They'll be worried."

"You're supposed to say it will all work out. True love always works out."

Spoken like a girl truly in denial. Why hadn't Wyatt told Tammy he loved her? Why didn't he ask her to marry him?

Nora kept those questions to herself. The first time Levi had kissed her had changed everything, down to the color of the sky and the way air felt when she breathed.

Clouds had rolled in. Thunder boomed in the distance. They should've turned around, but they pulled off the road next to a small pond. The plop of big raindrops on the water and the smell of wet earth inundated Nora even as she tucked her hair into her kapp. Rain would forever remind her of Levi's lips on hers. The rough skin of his carpenter hands against her cheeks. The day-old dusting of prickly hair on his chin as he nuzzled her neck.

Would she still love him if he didn't want the closer walk with Jesus that the Libby Amish kept talking about?

Love should be able to withstand all obstacles.

If it didn't, was it really love?

"If it's part of Gott's plan, it will work out."

"That's not the same thing."

"I know." Speaking the truth wasn't much fun. "You better get home."

They made quick work of returning the horses to their stalls and unsaddling them.

Nora stood on the porch and waved. Tammy waved back. "See you tomorrow."

"See you tomorrow."

What would this turn of events look like in the bright light of morning? God said to be light in a dark world. Had she been light to Tammy?

It didn't feel like it.

21

Hey, wake up in there. Time to get up, sleepyhead."

Nora sat up in bed. Pounding accompanied the annoyingly cheerful sound of Tammy's voice. How could she be so lively after so little sleep? Morning light shone through the bedroom window. Why hadn't Jeannie awakened her? After her midnight adventure, Sadie had started crying before she could lie down again. At least Nora had time to put her nightgown back on. She and Jeannie had taken turns with the cranky baby. The little one had a tummy ache. Jeannie was no longer allowed to eat moose chili.

Nora rubbed her eyes. More pounding. "Jah, jah, I hear you. Come in, come in."

Tammy didn't need any more encouragement. She threw open the door so hard it knocked against the back wall. "Why are you still in bed? Mammi is making breakfast. Jeannie is feeding the bopli."

"Why didn't they wake me?"

"Jeannie said you were up half the night rocking Sadie. I take it she didn't know about you sneaking out of the house?"

"I didn't sneak out. I walked out." Nora slid from the bed and padded to the row of dresses hanging on hooks on the far wall. "But nee, she doesn't know."

"Whatever you say." Tammy sprawled across the bed. "Hurry. Daadi said to give you a message."

A message from Grandpa.

Driving. Today was the day she would drive a car. Nora shimmied from her nightgown and threw her dress over her head. "I have chores to do. Mammi said something about a frolic."

"Daadi thought you would be excited about this. What is it?"

"Daadi offered to give me a driving lesson, that's all."

"Whoop-de-do." Tammy giggled. "I already know how to drive. I just don't have a car, and Daed won't buy me one. He says I have to save up for it."

"I don't know how, and I'll never have a car. Daadi called it a get-out-of-jail-free card."

"By all means then, let's roll."

How did Grandpa plan to pull this off? What about Daryl? What about Jeannie? If Nora had to hide it, she shouldn't be doing it. She tried to ignore the clanging bell in her head. It was one lesson, nothing more. Scratch the itch and move on. "One time. That's it."

"Understood." Tammy jumped up, grabbed Nora's arm, and propelled her from the room. "Or maybe you'll change your mind and decide you want to drive. You'll decide to stay here with me."

"Nee, I promise you, that's not happening."

"Millions of people—even Christians—all across the world drive cars. It doesn't mean they'll go to hell. If they intentionally run over a guy and kill him, then maybe. But even then, if they repent and ask to be forgiven, they can still go to heaven."

"Those people aren't Amish. Let it go, Kossin."

Tammy kept making her argument as they ran down the stairs.

"Okay, okay, I get it." Nora tugged her arm free. "You make our Ordnung sound silly. It's not. I respect your beliefs. Do the same for me."

Jeannie looked up from the rocking chair where she sat feeding Sadie. "*Guder mariye,* sleepyhead."

"Guder mariye. Why didn't you wake me?"

"I owed you." She grimaced. "This little piggy eats like it's been days since she's been fed. I want to get ready to go to town."

"You're going into Libby?" Trying not to sound too interested, Nora took a plate from the cabinet and helped herself to two waffles from a stack next to the stove. "How are you getting there?"

"Samantha is picking me up. We're going shopping."

"As much as you can shop in Libby." Tammy scoffed. "It's not like there's a Walmart or a mall."

Nora scowled at her. *Don't discourage her.* Tammy grinned, snatched a waffle, and ate it with her fingers.

"What about Daryl? Where is he off to?"

"He's meeting Onkel Ike at the shop. He needs something to do. Sitting around doesn't suit him at all."

It didn't suit any of them. It bred boredom and discontent. "What about you, Mammi? What are you doing today?"

"Are you taking a survey of everyone's plans?" Mammi folded the newspaper she'd been reading and smiled. "I'm going to the Hostetlers. Remember, I told you about the frolic? We're making apple cider and working on Christmas quilts. You girls are welcome to come."

"Maybe later." Tammy jumped in. "I told Mudder we'd help at the store. One of her regulars is out sick today."

Nora kicked her cousin in the leg under the table. Tammy crossed her eyes and stuck out her tongue. She didn't act her age, certainly not old enough to be doing what she said she'd been doing. Lying for any reason was never good.

An hour later breakfast was done, dishes washed, and Jeannie left with the children in tow. They were being fitted for new shoes—a convenient reason for Nora not to offer to watch them while her sister went to town. As soon as they were out the door, Grandma left.

Nora scowled at Tammy. "You shouldn't have lied."

"I didn't. We'll go to the store as soon as you have your lesson." Tammy pushed her toward the door. "Come on, Daadi is waiting."

They flew out the door and around to the back side of the house. Grandpa stretched out in a lawn chair, legs crossed at his ankles, a pipe locked between his teeth. The sweet smell of cherry tobacco filled the air.

"I didn't know you smoked." Another habit upon which her parents would frown. "Why are you doing it back here?"

"Because my fraa gets the same irritated frown on her face when I do it as you have on yours right now." Grandpa sat up and dumped the pipe's contents into an ashtray on the rattan table next to him. "I like to have my small vice in peace. And watch the birds."

Two large bird feeders hung on a maple tree's bough not far from where he sat. Next time she needed to have five minutes to herself, Nora would visit Grandpa's quiet spot.

"Nora's ready for her driving lesson." Tammy opened the passenger door to his minivan. "Can I teach her? I'm a gut driver."

"Nee. You are a so-so driver." Grandpa shook a finger at her. "But you may go along—in the backseat."

"Are you sure this is a gut idea?" The minivan morphed into a humongous machine before Nora's eyes. "I have no clue how to drive. What if I wreck it?"

"You won't. I'll tell you exactly what to do and when to do it. There won't be any other cars around. One step at a time."

"He's a gut teacher. He taught me." Tammy slid into the backseat. "Come on. Don't be a wuss. Daadi is way better at this than Daed. He has more patience."

Patience would be needed. And prayers. Did people pray to God to make them good drivers? God had likely heard it all since the beginning of time.

An anxious pain poked her in the gut. Her stomach gurgled. *Don't be a wuss.* Sucking in a lungful of air, Nora marched around the minivan and got in. She ran her hands over the steering wheel. Her feet were too far from the gas and brake pedals.

"First thing first. Adjust the seat so you can easily reach the gas and the brake." Grandpa settled onto the seat next to her. He held out the key. "Put this in the ignition, but don't turn it on yet."

"Where's the ignition?"

Tammy screeched. "Ach, Daadi, you've got your work cut out for you."

"Hush." Grandpa smiled at Nora. "We'll start with the basics and work our way through everything on the dashboard."

Fifteen minutes passed before Grandpa allowed Nora to start the van. After she learned where the ignition was, she had to learn to adjust her seat and the mirrors. Then Grandpa explained the speedometer and all the other gizmos in front of her. Finally, she had to try to convince herself she knew what she was doing.

Maybe the engine wouldn't start. Then she could go back in the house and turn back into Nora the Plain girl. Her hands were slick on the wheel. Despite the brisk, cool fall breeze blowing through the open windows, sweat tickled her forehead.

"Nothing will happen unless you turn the key."

She turned the key in the ignition and blew out a breath. *You can do this. It's one time. Just one time and you'll never do it again.*

"Nora! My hair's turning white back here. We don't have all day." Tammy banged on the back of the seat. "We have to go to the store, remember? And Jeannie will be back from—"

"Just shush." Nora turned the key. The engine putted and began to hum. "There, I did it."

Her arms felt weak and her legs quivered. Her hands shook.

"You have to put the car in gear in order to move forward." Grandpa's voice held a hint of laughter. "Do you remember where the gear is?"

Of course she did. Nora sucked in air and moved the gearshift from Park to Drive. Easy-peasy, as Grandma liked to say. *Don't think about Grandma right now.*

"Now move your foot from the brake to the gas pedal."

She closed her eyes for a few seconds. *Gott, don't let me kill Grandpa and Tammy.*

"You can't drive with your eyes closed." Tammy leaned over the seat so her high voice screeched in Nora's ear. "We're all gonna die."

"No we're not." Grandpa sounded as cool as a midwife taking care of a soon-to-be, first-time mother. "Sit back or get out of the van."

Tammy sat back.

Here we go. Please don't let us die. Nora moved her foot to the gas pedal. Gingerly, she pressed down.

"A little harder. Not too hard."

Harder. Not too hard. Nora complied. The van jolted forward. They were moving, moving too fast. Nora grasped the steering wheel so hard her fingers hurt.

"Ease up, ease up."

She eased up. The van slowed, then stopped.

"Not that much."

"It sure is finicky." She stuck her foot on the brake pedal and put the car in Park. With a shaky breath she leaned her forehead on the wheel. "I almost ran into your wheelbarrow."

"But you didn't. Try again."

"Yeah, try again. This is fun." Tammy's voice bellowed in Nora's ear. "I'm definitely a better driver."

Because Tammy spent a lot more time in cars. That didn't mean a Plain girl—a true Plain girl—couldn't catch up. Chewing her lip, Nora put the van in Drive and gently tapped the gas pedal. This time they moved forward at a sedate pace that would make even the pickiest driving instructor happy.

A cat moseyed into the dirt driveway, stopped, studied the oncoming van, and sat down. Its tail flicked back and forth.

"A cat. A cat!" Nora swerved to the right. The van rocked. She slammed on the brakes.

Too late.

They ran smack into the pole that held up Grandma's clothesline. The van jerked to a halt.

Nora's head banged on the steering wheel. Grandpa groaned. Tammy stopped laughing.

Nora's driving adventure was over before it started.

22

Nora scratched driving a car off her list. It hadn't gone as she had imagined in her rumspringa days. Like riding a horse with her in charge. Instead, the car had driven her into a pole. She rubbed her neck and blinked away tears. Other people made it seem so easy.

Grandpa turned off the van's ignition. "That's one way of avoiding a cat. The other would've been to ease down on the brake and come to a stop on the driveway."

"Your van. I'm so sorry." Nora rubbed her forehead. Her chest ached from the seat belt that kept her locked in her seat. Otherwise, her body seemed no worse for wear. "I wrecked your van."

"You didn't even get onto the road." Tammy stuck her head over the seat again. "Are you okay?"

"I think so." Nora rolled her shoulders, tilted her head side to side, and rubbed her forehead. It felt bruised. "What about you, Daadi?"

"Ach, this is nothing. How do you think I lost the bumper to this old piece of junk?" He rubbed the back of his neck with both hands. "It's better to crash going twenty miles an hour than going fifty-five."

No way she'd ever drive fifty-five. Especially now.

"Do you have insurance?" Tammy offered the question matter-of-factly. "My daed says it's the law that you have to have car insurance to drive on the road."

"Just liability. In other words it covers the other guy." Grandpa's glum expression belied his earlier words. "This old rattletrap ain't worth insuring."

"What now?"

"We hide it from my fraa."

Grandpa was scared of Grandma. Nora joined Tammy in giggling. Nothing was funny about this situation, but laughing was better than crying.

A sharp rap on the window made Nora jump. She closed her eyes. Maybe if she couldn't see the person, he couldn't see her.

"It's Daryl." Grandpa sounded resigned now.

Of course it was. Nora opened her eyes and stared up at her brother-in-law. He knocked again. She rolled the window down. "You're back from the shop." Nothing like observing the obvious. "Didn't you like working on the kits?"

"What are you doing? What have you done?" His face looked like an overripe tomato about to explode all over her.

"I wanted to know what it was like—"

"So you crashed the van into a pole. You destroyed the van? You could've been hurt or worse."

"We were only going twenty miles an hour." Grandpa leaned forward so Daryl could see him. "No one was hurt."

"That's not the point. You know Harley and Wilma wouldn't want this for their dochder. You're ignoring their wishes and their beliefs. She's a young, naive girl. You're old enough to know better."

Not so young or naive. She was a full-grown woman. Now would not be the time to argue with her brother-in-law.

Grandpa growled. He sounded like Stinker when he went after a squirrel in the yard. On the hunt. "You're right. I am old. I'm your elder."

In other words, show some respect. Nora scrunched down in the seat, letting the fierce words fly over her head. It was her fault.

She shouldn't have given in to temptation. "I'm sorry, Daryl. I just wanted to try it once."

"You did and you're done." Daryl leaned over farther and stared into the backseat. "If I were a betting man—and I'm not—I'd bet you had something to do with this, Tammy. I'd ask you to respect our beliefs and try not to be a bad influence on your kossin."

"I'm not a bad influence—"

Daryl shook his finger at her. "I'm not sure what you learn about respecting your elders here, but in West Kootenai, girls don't talk back to their elders."

Especially to men. That's what he meant. Father had put him in charge of Nora. Neither she nor Tammy had a leg to stand on. Nora pushed on the handle and opened the door slowly, forcing Daryl to back up. Her legs felt like wet towels under her. She staggered a few steps and stopped. *Deep breaths.* "I really am sorry. It won't happen again."

"Nee, it won't. I have to call your daed. He'll want to know."

"Please don't do that. It will only worry him. He has so much on his mind right now."

Daryl crossed his arms and frowned at her. "I'll talk to your schweschder first."

That was something. Jeannie would be more concerned with someone being hurt than Nora breaking the rules. Her sister had a soft heart too. She never talked about her rumspringa, but it had been short. She and Daryl married at eighteen. Young for Plain couples, but they hadn't wanted to wait. Now that Nora was older, she understood why.

"Danki."

"Don't thank me. We're not done talking about this."

Nora turned to Grandpa, who'd gotten out of the van as well. He tottered around to the driver's side in a stiff-legged gait. Tammy followed him. "I'm really sorry, Daadi. Are you sure you're not hurt?"

"I'm a tough old buzzard. I'll recover. Like I said, it's only an old van." He grunted. "I'll see if it will start. If not I need you to help me push it away from the pole, Daryl."

Daryl harrumphed but didn't say no.

Nora slipped past him and started walking around the house. Tammy caught up with her a few steps later. "You didn't do anything wrong."

"You know I did." Nora's blood pulsed in her ears. Her heart raced. Her palms were sweaty. It wasn't just the accident. Guilt plagued her. "Since I've been here, I've worn English clothes, sang with musical instruments, received a lesson on a guitar, danced, and driven a car."

"You didn't drive the minivan, you crashed it." Tammy examined the back of one arm and rolled her shoulder as if in pain. "I hope that's not a sign Gott is angry that you're living it up."

Did crashing an old van qualify as living it up? A tortured giggle burbled up in Nora's throat. Hysteria. "If Daryl tells Daed, he'll make me go back to Eureka."

At least then she could see Levi. What would he say when she told him why she had to come back? "This has to stop."

"It's fine. Let's go to the store. Mudder loves having you there. You're an experienced worker."

Work would help. Work was good.

By the time they arrived at the Farm-to-Market Store next to the sawmill and log cabin–kit shop, Nora's nerves had calmed. No more adventures. No more breaking the rules.

"Let's get something to eat from the deli first. A car crash makes me hungry." Tammy led the way through the aisles crowded with bulk candies and nuts, Amish jellies and jams, and a huge display of Amish cookbooks. "They have gut banana cream pie."

"We just had breakfast."

"That was hours ago."

It only seemed that way.

Plain folks who dressed the way Nora did filled the three picnic tables in front of the deli. They were eating ice cream and chatting with Peter Bontrager. Nora had met him at church. He came to Libby from Indiana to help with teaching. He never returned home. Tammy waved. Peter waved back.

"Come meet my family!"

His family. What did they think of his orange T-shirt and baggy jeans? Tammy excused herself to go get ice cream. A banana split. Nora declined her offer to bring a second one for her.

"Sit, sit, with us." Peter scooted over and patted the spot next to him. He was a short, wiry man with the start of a dark beard on his chin. His eyes were huge and a warm amber color with flecks of gold and brown in them. "I'm glad you're spending time here. Do you think you'll stay?"

"What makes you think I would stay?"

"I came to teach for one year, and three years later I'm still here."

"Jah, we were very surprised when you didn't return to Indiana." One of the women, identified as his cousin, spoke up. "Your mudder still thinks you might come home."

"I won't. I love the mountains." He patted his T-shirt in the vicinity of his heart. "I love the freedom."

Another freedom lover.

"I'll go home when the evacuation notice is lifted in Kootenai." Nora studied her hands spread across the picnic table's rough wood. Here was someone who, like her, had been Amish most of his life—until he came to Libby. "Don't you miss being Amish? Were you baptized?"

"I was baptized in the faith. Amish is my cultural background, my history, my ancestors. It's the touchstone for my faith." Peter spoke with a kindness that lit his face. So much like Wyatt and the others when they touched on the topic of their faith. "But I've grown beyond it. I have the freedom to have a closer walk with Jesus."

Freedom. A closer walk. It was as if they had code words or a language only they understood. They all had a closer walk with Jesus. It must get mighty crowded on that road.

Nora turned to his cousin. "Do you understand what that means?"

"Nee, but I don't need to know." She shrugged and smiled. "He's still my kossin. We come to visit, and then we'll move on to St. Ignatius to go camping. We're not staying. It's his choice to be here and to worship the way they do. It's not for us to judge." The woman stood and picked up her Styrofoam bowl. "We don't try to sway him and he doesn't try to sway us."

Wyatt, Tammy, and Grandpa wanted to sway Nora. They didn't attempt to hide it either.

"You seem perturbed." Peter slid his bowl of strawberry ice cream with strawberries, whipped cream, and sprinkles toward her. "I can get you a clean spoon if you want."

"Nee, but danki." Her breakfast did cartwheels in her stomach. Her head pounded. "What does that mean to you, a closer walk with Jesus?"

"They think they know Jesus personally." Another man with golden blond curls peeking from under his straw hat chuckled. "They talk of conversations with Gott as if He comes down and sits on the front porch with them. I think they're touched in the head."

"Laugh if you will, Joshua." Peter's laugh was equally good-natured. "We study Gott's Word. We gather in our homes and go deeper into the Word. Your church is afraid you might go off on your own and no longer be hamstrung by rules handed down for generations that you don't even know why they were created in the first place."

"Tradition has strong, powerful arms that hold us together and apart from a world that is so fallen, its people are up to their hairlines in sin."

Peter tugged his bowl back from Nora and took a big bite. Spoon still in the air, he savored it, then waved the spoon at Joshua. "No one is perfect. All of us are sinners. Nothing you can do or say will change that."

"We can strive to do better. We strive not to fall into the stinky morass of sinful waste that sucks people in through TV, movies, the internet, trashy books and magazines, and churches where pastors preach a gospel not even closely resembling what Gott lays out for us in His Holy Word."

"On that we can agree." His face pensive, Peter stirred his ice cream into soft swirls. "We're not so far apart as you think, Bruder."

Joshua was his brother. They looked nothing alike and they lived nothing alike. Divisive theology split families. Nothing good came of it. "I better go help with stocking."

"Good talking to you, Nora." Peter waggled his fingers at her. "If you ever want to talk about that closer walk, feel free to come to me. I promise not to harangue or harass you but simply answer your questions. Don't ask Tammy. She's a silly girl."

"Am not." Tammy slung her leg over the bench and sat. The banana split was big enough for three people. "I'm a serious student of life. I have studied you. You are a nice man who needs a girlfriend, needs to get married, and needs to live happily ever after."

"Are you offering?"

They both guffawed and went back to their ice cream.

"It's all so confusing." Maybe ice cream *would* help. Nora picked up the extra spoon Tammy had kindly provided for her. "Your family doesn't seem nearly as upset about your decision to change the way you worship as mine does."

"Maybe it's because they live far away and they've never been to one of our services," Tammy speculated.

"Or they know we're right." Peter grinned. "Seriously, they know arguing about it won't change anything, so they don't waste their breath on it. Instead, I suspect they pray a lot."

Which was what Nora intended to do.

But first she would eat ice cream. Nothing could make the situation better, but ice cream wouldn't hurt.

23

Eureka, Montana

Tracking down a bishop determined to check on every Kootenai Gmay family scattered across a town of more than a thousand people proved to be more difficult than Levi expected. Noah had gone to visit families in Rexford and then his own relatives in St. Ignatius and Moore before he returned the previous day.

His lunch hour trickling away, Levi finally found him at the coffee shop on Dewey Avenue smack in the middle of downtown. Unfortunately, he wasn't alone. Noah shared his table and a pot of black coffee with Lucas Zimmerman, the minister, and Deacon Tobias Eicher. The three men made a formidable team. One Levi always avoided crossing as a teenager. As an adult, a baptized member of the Gmay, he need not feel trepidation in approaching them. Yet he did.

"You look like a man on a mission." Noah hailed Levi with a wave of his hand. In his day Noah had been an avid athlete who loved to play baseball and volleyball, hike, horseback ride, fish, and hunt. As a bishop and married father of four with another one on the way, he had set aside recreation for dedication to the tasks at hand. "Have a seat. Have some *kaffi*. It's hot and strong enough to melt the taste buds from your tongue."

"I don't want to barge in on a meeting." Levi put his hands on the back of an empty chair and surveyed the three men. They seemed tired and rumpled. Noah's face was haggard. "You must have serious matters to discuss."

"It's not an official meeting. We come here for kaffi most days to compare notes and talk about who needs what. Your family is on my list to visit later today. Did you come in search of kaffi, or did you need to talk to one of us?"

Levi shifted his feet. The nail gun scar on his middle finger was thick and white against his fading summer tan. More caffeine would be a mistake, but coffee made a good excuse for stopping by. "I like strong kaffi. Have you heard anything from Emmett?"

"Only that the evacuation continues. The firefighters on the line are doing their best to contain the fires, but there's no stopping them." Tobias poured a steady stream of sugar into his coffee without looking up. "They've had to evacuate families in northwest Libby. Emmett's included. They're stretched to the breaking point."

"Are the Eagle Valley folks in danger?" His legs suddenly weak, Levi sank into the chair. "Are they being evacuated?"

"Nee, the fire's on the north end. Eagle Valley's on the south. They're fine."

Levi grabbed a napkin and patted his damp face. "That's gut."

"I reckon that's your main concern, isn't it?" Noah signaled to the waitress to bring another coffee cup. His sharp gaze studied Levi. "Particularly folks from Kootenai who are staying in Libby."

Any words Levi uttered had the potential to boomerang and hit him smack in the nose. He edged into the conversation the same way he trod the narrow paths when he hiked in the Cabinet Mountains. Carefully, one foot at a time, testing the terrain. "The fires have caused such turmoil and upheaval. It's hard to know where to start."

"The Ordnung doesn't change depending on geography." Lucas spoke for the first time. He slid his rimless glasses up his nose and fixed Levi with an inquiring gaze. "Have you heard something that causes you concern? As members of the church it's our responsibility to hold each other accountable."

Levi should've waited. Noah liked to gather facts, take it all in, and then make a considered decision. His friend Lucas preferred to strike while the iron was hot. He chose to deal with malcontents and dissension front and center. Tobias served as the mediator between the two.

"The Eagle Valley community is different. Anytime we're together there's reason for concern. At the same time they're family." A logical argument would best serve Levi's purpose. "We can never stop praying for them to return to the fold. Isn't that true?"

Lucas tapped his fingers on the table in an annoying *rat-a-tat-tat*. "We also have to be vigilant that more of our number don't decide to join them in their heresy."

"It's not heresy. It's simply not our way," Noah intervened. "Let us be very careful not to judge. They, too, are our bruders and schweschders in Christ. They've chosen a different way to worship, as do many other Christians in this world."

Another voice of reason. Levi relaxed and accepted the cup from the waitress. Noah poured the coffee for him. The cup served as something to do with his hands. Levi busied himself doctoring the thick sludge with half-and-half and copious amounts of sugar. "So we don't find fault with their style of worship? The dancing, the musical instruments, the shouting and jumping?"

"It's not our way."

"But not a sin to join in?"

"What are you getting at?"

"Worshipping in a different way for a few Sundays doesn't break the rules, does it?"

Noah cocked his head. He wound his beard around his long fingers. "It doesn't matter where we go, we don't draw attention to ourselves. We don't play musical instruments, whether they're in someone's home or in a church. Visiting another church isn't a free pass. Our desire is not to stand out."

By not participating, they stood out.

By dressing differently, they stood out.

In their efforts to stay out of the limelight of a fallen world, they'd drawn attention to themselves. Tourists flocked to Plain communities to eat dinner in Amish homes, take buggy rides, and snap photos at every turn. People read Amish romances written by English authors. TV shows and movies had been made. Newspaper articles were written. They stood out. Saying any of this would only cause trouble for Nora and her family. What was more important? Her inevitable anger with Levi or her eternal salvation? "Have you talked to Harley?"

"Should we?"

Answering a question with a question should be against the Ordnung. "It's not my place to say."

"Maybe not, but your concern is written across your face and you've come this far. You sought us—or me—out." Noah's voice softened. "You spoke up despite obvious misgivings. That you care speaks well of you. This isn't a matter of tattling. We want to catch those who meander off the path before they're completely lost in the dense forest of a fallen world."

"We should all be concerned." How could he do this to Nora? *Gott, forgive me, because she may not.* "For the Beachys who've gone to stay with Jacob and Esther."

Noah leaned back in his chair. "Tobias will talk to Harley. If need be we'll all take a trip to the valley."

"They need to come home."

"Harley will do what is best for his family."

He would, but he also wouldn't appreciate Levi's meddling. "I know he will."

"Don't worry. You're doing the right thing."

Levi tried to contain himself, but the words burbled up. "Then why do I feel like a squished bug under someone's boot?"

"Doing the right thing isn't always easy."

"I better get back to work." Leaving his coffee untouched, Levi stood. "No one involved set out to do wrong. They've been pressured by others."

"They've given in to temptation." Lucas spit the words out. "Our faith must be stronger than that."

Noah turned his somber gaze toward Lucas. "Have you ever attended a service in Eagle Valley?"

His expression dour, Lucas shook his head. "Nee."

"Let's not judge until we've found our own faith tested."

"Go back to work. We have other fish to fry." Lucas's frown grew into a scowl. "A new baby at the Plank house. A visit to the Yoders. And a visit with the Beachys."

The chasm between Levi and Nora grew until the state of Montana could fit in it.

Seventy times seven. Scripture said followers of Christ had to forgive seventy times seven. Levi would count himself blessed if Nora saw fit to forgive him just once.

24

A chicken squawked. No, no, it was a baby crying. Sadie. Sadie was crying. Nora sat up in bed and rubbed her burning eyes. The red numbers on the alarm clock on the table next to the bed read two thirty. "Ach, Sadie." She threw her feet over the side of the bed and stood. The baby hadn't eaten since nine last night. She had to be hungry.

Waking up Jeannie was the worst part of being on night duty with Sadie. Jeannie didn't seem to be catching up on her sleep. She still had dark circles around her bloodshot eyes. If only they had one of those pumps, she could pump milk and Nora could feed the baby. Daryl would probably have something to say about that too.

Nora shuffled down the hallway to the children's bedroom. She had to get Sadie out of there before she woke up Jason and Missy. The baby fussed as she stared up at Nora with a red, tear-streaked face. "You're okay, I'm here, you're fine, little one. Hush before you wake up your schweschder and bruder."

Sadie cried more loudly.

"There, there, sweet pea, shush." Nora picked her up and hurried into the hallway. "You must be starving, bopli. Mudder's right here. Just be patient."

Only the spot in the bed where Jeannie normally lay was empty. The comforter was pulled up. No one lay on her side of the bed.

Nora usually tried not to look at Daryl. It seemed weird to peek at her brother-in-law while he slept. Far too personal.

But peek she must. Yep. Only Daryl slept in the bed.

Nora switched Sadie to her shoulder and patted as she tiptoed from the room. Where would Jeannie be at two thirty in the morning?

Bathroom.

Still patting the baby's back, she scurried down the hallway to the bathroom. The door was closed. She turned the handle. Locked. She knocked softly. "Jeannie? Are you in there?"

"Jah."

"Open the door. Sadie wants to eat."

A minute or two passed. Sadie's sobs ratcheted up. "Jeannie, she'll wake everyone up."

"Coming." The door opened. Dressed in her nightgown, hair loose, Jeannie looked like the sister who had shared a room with Nora all those years ago. Her cheeks were red to match her bloodshot eyes. "I was just, I mean, I had to—"

"I know what you do in the bathroom." Nora peered more closely. Jeannie appeared distinctly guilty. Both hands were behind her back. "What'cha got there?"

"Where?"

"Behind your back."

"Nothing."

"Jeannie, you're worse than the boys. It's clear as day you're hiding something. What is it?"

"All right. Come in."

Come in? Nora followed Jeannie into the bathroom. Her sister closed the door and locked it. When she turned around, she had a Bible in her hand.

Nora stared at it. Then she stared at her sister. Guilt billowed from every pore of Jeannie's face. The poor thing was about to have a cow. Nora couldn't contain her grin. She handed Sadie to her. "Wait here."

"What? Why? Where are you going?"

Without answering Nora raced down the hallway, grabbed her Bible from under her pillow, and raced back. With the door behind her securely locked, she held it up. "Ta-da. Me too. Grandpa?"

"You too?" Jeannie's dumbstruck expression made Nora giggle. Jeannie plopped on the toilet with Sadie on her lap. "Nee, not Grandpa. Samantha."

Samantha, the mother who'd offered friendship to a newcomer. Friend evangelism. That's what Tammy had called it. "When did that happen?"

Jeannie rearranged her clothing and helped Sadie latch on. Quiet, except for the excited *whap-whap* of the baby eating, reigned. "You have to promise me not to say anything."

"I'm already in trouble. Believe me, I'm not saying anything." Not yet. Not until she figured out what it all meant. For her. For Levi. For her family. Nora sat on the edge of the tub. She ran her hands over her Bible. "How did it happen for you?"

"Samantha and I didn't go shopping."

"You came back with new shoes for the kinner."

"I mean, we didn't just go shopping. We made another stop first."

"Where?"

Jeannie ducked her head. "I went with Samantha to her small group Bible study."

"Nee!" Nora put her hand to her mouth to keep from squealing and scaring the baby. A Bible study would be so much easier than reading the Bible on her own and trying to make sense of it. She kept falling asleep. Reading at the end of a long day of work didn't help. "What made you do that?"

"I don't know exactly. Samantha and I started talking after the service. She shared her thoughts on what Onkel Ike preached. She was so kind and sweet, and she didn't jump all over me about our style of worship. She just told me how she feels about theirs." Jeannie stroked Sadie's wispy hair. Despite her words she seemed sad. "She offered to take me to her small group. It's five or six women who get together once a week to study the Bible, do a devotional, and answer study questions."

"Ach, my, oh my." Nora couldn't help herself. She rocked back and forth. "Daryl will have a cow if he finds out. Or does he know?"

"He doesn't know." Tears trickled down Jeannie's face. "I'm afraid to tell him. But I think I have to tell him because I'm going again."

"It was gut, then? You liked it?" The shock sent a shiver through Nora. Her own sister had fallen into the chasm first. She tightened her grip on the Bible, lest it fall on Grandma's pristine bathroom floor. "What draws you to it?"

"They're studying Acts. They're talking about Pentecost, when the disciples were filled with the Holy Spirit. There was a mighty windstorm that filled the house where they were sitting. They started speaking in tongues."

"I know the story."

"It's not just a story. They live it. Samantha says it's a good example of how to worship. They were excited. They were pumped full of the Holy Spirit. It wasn't quiet or slow. They were so wound up the others thought they were drunk."

"You want to worship like they do."

"I think I want to know more. I want to feel that happy and excited. I want to be able to read the Word for myself and understand it. I want to feel it the way they do."

The sentiment was far too familiar. Nora clutched the Bible to her chest. "I keep thinking of what Tobias said in baptism class about Sunday schools and Bible studies—"

"He said it leads to people making their own interpretations of the Bible and acting like they're special because they say Gott spoke to them." Jeannie smoothed Sadie's plump cheek. "It's not like that. They're not trying to use the Bible to support their way of thinking. They're not saying they should do this or that because Jesus told them to instead of listening to what their church tells them to do. They just want a personal relationship with their Savior."

"It's not the idea of wearing pants and driving cars or having electricity in your house that attracts you?"

"I'm not that shallow." Jeannie's fierce scowl shot through Nora like an arrow to the heart. "Some of the women here still wear dresses and cover their hair. I'm not like you. I'd be afraid to drive. I'm more worried about what happens with Mudder and Daed."

The same fears that flailed at Nora every time she picked up her Bible. A person shouldn't have to give up everything for her faith.

The apostles did. The martyrs did.

Grandpa's voice grew loud in Nora's head. Christians around the world had sacrificed their lives in every century since Jesus' crucifixion and resurrection. To think of herself as special gave credence to the many warnings she'd received from Father and Mother over the years.

Gott, I love Levi. I love Mudder and Daed. I love my life. I vowed to live my life according to the Ordnung. Is it enough? Is Daadi right or is Daed right?

Confusion swirled around her. Nausea rocked her stomach. "Would you stay here?"

"I don't know. I haven't decided yet."

"Daryl will never let you stay." A worse scenario barreled its way past that thought. "Or would you stay and let him go home? What about the kinner? Does it mean so much to you that you would let him take them from you?"

Father had already lost his father, mother, brother, and his brother's family to this so-called closer walk. Just as her church predicted. These discussions led to dissension between brothers, sons and fathers, and now husbands and wives.

How would Levi react? The answer didn't take much imagination. He would be adamant. Devastated, but adamant.

"Daryl loves me. I know you don't understand him, but he feels deeply. He's a different man when we're alone." Two more tears rolled down Jeannie's face. She wiped at them with her sleeve. "He wants to do the right thing. He'll hear me out because it's me, his fraa, speaking."

"What about Mudder and Daed?"

"What about you?"

"It's too much. It's all too much." Nora laid the Bible on the sink. "I don't know what to believe. I don't want us to be banned from worship like Onkel Ike and Aenti Roseanna. I don't want to see your kinner only now and then. I don't want our family any more divided than it already is. I don't want to lose Levi."

"Maybe you can convince him to attend a service. Maybe he'll listen to you. If he loves you, he will try to understand."

"I think he would say that because he loves me, he can't do that. He'll want to save me just like Grandpa wants to do."

If she were a doll, they would tear her apart by the arms in their efforts to save her. All her stuffing would fall out.

No one would win.

Plain family members didn't often make declarations of love. It was understood in the working together, in the making of clothes, the making of meals, the teaching of how to put hair up under a kapp, in the teaching of prayer and the faith.

If words were ever needed, now was the time. "I don't want our souls to be in jeopardy because we make the wrong choice. Whatever we do, we both have to do it. You're my only schweschder."

"I love you too." Jeannie held out her free hand. Nora clasped it. They held on, gazes locked. "How can we ignore the longing?"

Nora closed her eyes and cocked her head. She listened for the sound of God's voice. For the sound of the Holy Spirit. Would He come to her in a tiny bathroom with her sister and a fussy baby? Or was He already there in the quiet, in the silent prayer, in the low, long songs, in Noah's voice when he gave the message, or in Father's voice when he spoke the Lord's Prayer?

Could there not be more than one road to the Savior? Noah's words pricked at Nora's conscience. Jesus Himself described a narrow path leading to eternal life. The other road was wide, but it was filled with people headed toward destruction because they embraced popular culture.

She opened her eyes.

"Please don't say anything to anyone until I talk to Daryl."

"When will that be?"

Jeannie smoothed Sadie's nightgown. The baby had ceased to eat and slumbered peacefully. "When I get up the nerve."

"Better sooner than later."

"Same for you and Levi."

"I don't even know where to start."

"Start with 'I love you and want to be with you for all eternity.'"

That was the truth. But sometimes the truth wasn't enough.

25

Eureka, Montana

Even when new information wasn't forthcoming, the information center at the church acted like a magnet. Levi couldn't stay away from it. He was too jittery to play checkers, read a Western, or sing to the little ones.

Singing only reminded him of Nora. She laughed every time he sang. Probably because he couldn't carry a tune in a bucket. Maybe Noah would be here and Levi could find out if he'd talked to Nora. Maybe they wouldn't need to go to Libby. Any minute word would come and they could all go home.

How could he be so upset with Nora and yet miss her so much?

Enough. Time would pass. All would return to normal. He trudged to the check-in table. Maybe Angie had some work he could do for her. He could lug some boxes of clothes or canned food in from the van that went around collecting them from Eureka's generous residents.

Harley shoved through the double doors just as Levi made it to the table. His scowl didn't bode well.

"What's going on?" Levi changed directions. "Is everything all right?"

Harley swerved toward Levi. "Jack said I'd find you here. You talked to Noah earlier today? He showed up at the RV with Tobias and Lucas. They said you sought them out."

"I needed answers to questions. It wasn't my intent—"

"To meddle in my family's business? That's exactly what you did. You had no right." Several people stared at Harley's gruff voice. He jerked his head toward the corner. "We'll not have this discussion in the middle of the room."

Levi followed him to a corner filled with pallets of bottled water. "I only have concern for your dochders, and I think you know that. I wanted spiritual guidance. I'm trying to understand the consequences. I thought maybe I overreacted."

"But you didn't."

"Nee. I didn't get into details. Noah—"

"You didn't have to. He's aware of the temptations."

"You're to bring them home, then?"

"Jah. I'm trying to track down Mel Tompkins. He's supposed to be here."

Mel Tompkins was one of the go-to drivers for Kootenai families. "I think I saw him talking to Jonas and Caleb earlier, but they're gone. Was his van outside?"

"Jah." Harley scrubbed his face with both hands. His beard was unusually unruly and his normal placid expression was tight with tension. "He has to be here."

Levi glanced around. "There. Talking to Tim and that smoke jumper. What's his name? Spencer?"

"Trouble on two legs, I reckon." Harley rarely said a bad word about anyone. Levi studied the man. One leg was in a medical boot up to his knee, and he was bruised around the face. Not much of a threat to anyone. Harley must know something he didn't. He headed for the knot of men. "I don't know why I said that. I don't even know the man."

Life had been turned topsy-turvy for everyone. Levi followed Harley, keeping pace with his long stride.

"It's not Nora's fault. From what she said, your bruder is a powerful preacher. And he brings to the table others who are even more persuasive." Not to mention a cousin who was Nora's age and whom Nora loved. An even more powerful presence—peer pressure. "I reminded her of her baptism and the vows she took."

"She knows better. She's a grown woman. She let temptation overcome her. I should never have let them go to Libby. They could've stayed in a motel farther south."

Motels cost money. "It's not too late."

"Daryl called. He said Daed convinced Nora to learn to drive—or Nora convinced him to let her drive. He didn't know. She wrecked the van. No one was hurt, but they could've been. I don't know which is worse—Daadi for encouraging her or Nora for giving in to temptation."

The words were like bullets tearing through Levi's skin, burning through muscle and sinew. "She wouldn't."

"He witnessed her in the driver's seat. Her forehead was scratched and her face red with guilt." Harley shook his head. "She's always been adventuresome. Climbing in the cliffs like a mountain goat, jumping into the lake from the highest rock, shooting her first elk when she was ten. You are the most reasonable thing she's ever done."

Was that a compliment? Was what they had reasonable? Safe? No adventure there? It didn't feel that way. When Levi held Nora in his arms, he felt ten feet tall and able to vanquish any evil that threatened her.

The Libby Amish were a threat. "Let me go. You're needed here."

"After what I saw the other night at the park, I'm not sure that's not opening the henhouse door to let the fox in."

"Mel will chaperone us."

"Your family doesn't need you?"

"There's twelve of us kinner. I think they can do without me for a few days."

Mother had said as much. She wanted him close, but she didn't need him close. There was a difference.

"A few days?"

"I want to get the lay of the land. Maybe Jeannie and Daryl should consider returning too. Jeannie is your dochder still."

"True." Harley's shoulders hunched. He mopped his face. "She's another man's fraa, yet I still concern myself with her well-being. Remember that. Once a daed, always a daed. Go, see what you can see, but don't stay long."

"You can count on me."

"You tell Nora she doesn't have a choice. Tell her if I have to come for her, it won't be pretty. Talk to Daryl. Find out how Jeannie's doing." His voice broke. "Bring them home."

"I will. Let's talk to Mel."

The driver spit his chew into a Styrofoam cup and agreed to take Levi to Libby as soon as he'd had his supper. "My wife is fixing a big batch of enchiladas. She'll have my hide if I don't show up." Mel scratched the red bulb on the end of his big honker. "Once I eat, she wants me out of her hair, which is perfect. I like to drive, and I can use the scratch."

Harley insisted on paying. Arguing over that took another ten minutes, but finally Levi was on his way back to the rental house to pack.

He would've paid and paid much more. He would see Nora tonight, and he had her father's blessing. In fact, Harley wanted Levi to see her.

No one seemed to notice his arrival at the house. Mom and the girls were in the kitchen cleaning up after supper. The boys were in the backyard playing on the trampoline. That left Jack in the living room, stretched out in a recliner reading the newspaper. Levi had to pass by him to get to the bedroom. His stepfather let the newspaper fall into his lap and stretched. "Any news at the church?"

"Nee, nothing new."

"That's why you didn't stay long, I guess. You look tired. Get some sleep."

Same old bossiness. Levi was a grown man. He would decide when he slept.

Mother's words banged against his hard head. *"You're more like Jack than you want to admit. Both of you are bossy. Maybe that's why he bothers you so much."*

Not only were they bossy, they were stubborn and hardheaded. His own father had been a thoughtful peacemaker. "I am tired, but I'm headed to Libby."

"To see about Nora? That's gut." Jack's head bobbed. "Your mudder told me about your quandary. You should talk to Harley, though, before you stick your nose in his family's problems."

He couldn't help but tell Levi what to do. *"Because he cares about you."* "I did. He was at the church. He knows I'm going. He wants me to bring both his dochders home."

"See to it that you do."

Talk about sticking his nose in another man's family. Levi laughed.

"What's so funny?"

"Mudder says we're a lot alike. We're both bossy. I never realized it before."

"Jah. She said something similar to me." Jack cracked a smile. "I guess that's why we bump heads so often."

"I don't mean to be a troublemaker. I know you have your hands full taking care of this family."

"You're not a troublemaker. You're a suh who misses his daed and is faithful to his memory. I remind myself of that every day."

Jack's hand went to his heart. "Don't stay in Libby too long. Your mudder doesn't say it aloud, but it gives her peace of mind. You'll be a parent someday. Then you'll understand."

"I understand I've made this harder for you, and I'm sorry."

"I'll always be bossy. You can't teach an old hund new tricks."

For Nora's sake, Levi would do better. He wasn't an old dog yet. He simply acted like one. "I'm trying to do better. I will do better."

"You go get your girl, Suh. She needs you."

She might need him, but would she want him after she found out what he'd done? There was only one way to find out. Levi packed his duffel bag and went to find her.

26

Libby, Montana

The breeze that filtered through the windows in Grandpa's living room had a nip to it. Night sounds serenaded them as Nora played checkers with Grandma while Jeannie went upstairs to try to get Sadie down for the night. Grandpa pretended to read *The Budget* newspaper, but his glasses were on the end table and his snoring gave him away. Daryl had followed the little ones to bed early, citing a full day at the shop.

"How'd you get that cut on your forehead?" Grandma hopped over two of Nora's red pieces and landed in the last row. "King me."

Grandma's age and failing eyesight had not affected her checker-playing abilities. Nora did as she was told. "I'm thinking you already know."

"I heard Daryl telling Jeannie about it."

"Did you already chew out Daadi?"

"Why would I? Waste of breath. The old man does what he wants to. He always has and he always will."

"Mammi!"

"He's asleep, and you know I'm right. The question is what does it mean?"

"What does driving the van mean to me? Nothing, really. Like an itch that had to be scratched. I'm sorry about Daadi's van. Do you think he'll replace it?"

"I'm sure he will. Ike has another car he and Tucker have been working on. They've turned into mechanics. They buy old clunkers and fix them. At least they haven't lost their frugalness. The cars are paid for and the insurance is cheap. They've embraced the world's love of cars without the need for the latest, greatest, biggest, and fastest. I can be thankful for that. But that doesn't mean you can change the subject on me. If you hadn't crashed the van, would you want to drive again?"

"Nee. I don't know. Maybe." The feel of the wheel in her hands, the rumble of the engine, being in control—if only for a minute—every part of driving had tickled her fancy. Until she wrecked it. "Probably, but Daadi will never trust me again."

"Don't count on that. He sees it as a means to an end." Grandma shoved her spotless wire-rimmed glasses up her nose, but they didn't relieve her squint. "Surely you see that."

"Surely I don't. A means to what end?"

"The more you experience what he calls freedom, the more it will call to you in other ways. You see how Tammy dresses. You see her and Tucker playing instruments. You think about being able to talk on the phone with your special friend. It's like water dripping on a stone, wearing it away until it's changed."

"Is that a bad thing?"

"Use your noggin, girl. What have you been taught your whole life?"

To hold herself apart from the world. Not to be influenced by the world. "I see what you're saying."

"I'm not sure you do." Grandma triple-jumped across the board and hooted as she picked up Nora's vanquished pieces. "It's not just about how you live, but what you believe."

Nora let her words soak in as she studied the checkerboard. In

Kootenai, life had seemed simple with clear-cut rules. "You don't stand up during the sermon. You don't clap or yell or even say anything. Don't you agree with Onkel Ike?"

"I believe what I've always believed. I don't see any need to act foolish about it." Grandmother's hand hovered over the checkerboard, but she didn't move a piece. Instead, she withdrew it and removed her glasses. Her eyes were misty. "Even after all these years, this is foreign to me. I miss the services we had at home. But the jumping and hopping and hollering like you're drunk are only symptoms of a more deadly disease."

They did seem feverish, but sick people usually lacked the energy to act like jumping beans. "What disease, Mammi?"

"They think they have the corner on the market when it comes to religion." Grandma's gaze drifted to where Grandpa lay, head back, snoring. Her voice dropped to a whisper. "That theirs is the only way to Gott. They have their own special way of speaking to Him. They're too big for their britches. Their heads are so swollen, they can't think straight."

"Wouldn't it be wunderbarr to be able to talk to Gott and get an answer? Right then and there. Aloud. They did in the Bible. Job did. Abraham did. Moses did."

"Ach, girl, you sound like them. If Gott wants to talk to us, He will. That's for Him to say, not us."

"Daed says we shouldn't judge them."

"He's right. I try every day not to judge." Mammi sniffed and stuck the glasses back on her skinny nose. "But I won't sit by and not speak up now. Not when you and Jeannie are here. I had no chance with Ike's kinner. With you there's still time."

A single rap on the door kept Nora from answering. Her mind still reeling from Grandma's burst of honesty, Nora pushed back from the table. "I'll get it."

Wyatt stood on the porch.

"What are you doing here?"

"What kind of welcome is that?"

The only kind Nora could give him, considering the circumstances. "I assumed you would be with Tammy. Or getting ready for the revival."

"I saw Tammy. And then I helped with the prep. The tent's up. The chairs are in place. The Holy Spirit will do the rest."

"Who is it, Nora?" Grandma called. "We have a game to finish before I get too tired to beat you."

"It's Wyatt."

"Don't just stand there, invite him in."

If Grandma knew what Wyatt and Tammy had done, she would shut the door in his face.

"Danki, Mammi." Wyatt responded before Nora could. "Can I borrow Nora for a little while?"

"You're welcome to come in." Grandma stood and trotted to the front door. "We'll finish our checker game another night. Or maybe you'd like to play Nora."

Wyatt didn't seem like the checkers-playing type.

"Could we sit on the front porch for a bit?" Add mind reading to Wyatt's list of talents. "I promise not to keep her too long."

Grandma frowned. Then she snatched a sweater from the hook next to the door and handed it to Nora. "It's cooling off out there. I'll be up for a while doing some mending if you need anything. There's cherry pie if you get a hankering for sweets."

Nora accepted the sweater. Grandma held on for a second longer than necessary. Her scowl deepened the wrinkles that lined her face. "Remember, child, free will comes at a cost."

"I'll be right back, I promise."

Nora stepped out on the porch and waited for Grandma to close the door. Giving herself time, she slipped on the sweater and buttoned it. Finally, she faced Wyatt. "You've got everyone hoodwinked, don't you?"

"Why such hostility, my friend?"

This was the man who'd taken a special gift from her cousin and refused to acknowledge the value of what he'd taken. "Tammy's my cousin and my friend."

"This isn't courting. It's a visit."

Parsing words. "Whatever you have to say, say it and move on down the road."

His puppy dog eyes professed his hurt, but Wyatt waved his arm in an *after-you* fashion. Nora took a seat in a hickory rocker.

He chose the other rocker and settled in. "You've had some time here in Eagle Valley. You've been to a few services. What do you think?"

He wanted to talk about religion when all Nora wanted to do was smack him upside his head. Chalk up another sin next to her name. "I haven't had time to figure all this out."

"I see your face at the services, and I know you're questioning. Maybe I can answer some of those questions." Wyatt's tone deepened to the one he used when he shared a message at the service. "Maybe I can help."

"You think you can answer my questions?" Nora stared at the sky. The clouds parted like drapes revealing the distant mountains. How could he be concerned with her eternal future when he didn't live by God's Word? How did he keep these parts of his life separated? "You're not Amish."

"I've spent a lot of time in Amish communities. They're part of our mission."

"Amish communities like this one, you mean? They're not really Amish. I think you know that."

"It's as close as we can get. And when we touch their lives, we touch the lives of people like you and your family. Seeds are planted. At least, that's our hope."

"There are all those unchurched people out there who don't know Jesus, so why pick on us?"

"Is that how it seems? We're not picking on you. Your faith is based in rote tradition. It's as if you're trying to earn your way into heaven by following rules. That's what the Pharisees did. They believed in a strict observance of the traditional written law."

Who were these Pharisees? Nora rubbed her eyes. Nothing became clearer. "Why are you here talking to me tonight?"

"Because you're smart and you're questioning." Wyatt leaned forward and put his elbows on his knees, his hands clasped. He was so earnest. It seemed as if there were two Wyatts. The one who spirited Tammy into a barn and lay on the hay with her. Then the one whose face became luminescent every time he said the words *Jesus Christ our Lord and Savior.*

"If it weren't for the fire, I wouldn't be here. I wouldn't be hearing your messages. I'd be at home with my family, getting ready to marry my special friend."

"But you are here. God has a plan for you. You are exactly where He intends for you to be. Don't you believe that?"

All her life she'd been taught that God had a plan for her. She would not be here now if it didn't fit with His plan. "I do."

"Then how can your attending Eagle Valley's church not be part of that plan? How can shedding the chains of your Amish ancestors not be part of that plan? How can your sitting in that chair right now talking to me be anything other than God's plan?"

Blood pulsed in Nora's ears. The pounding made it hard to think. Her hands were sweaty. "Wasn't it Gott's plan for me to be born into a Plain family?"

"Absolutely, but now He's given you the opportunity to grow closer to Him, to delve into His Word, to be on fire with the Holy

Spirit." Wyatt's face shone with sheer joy. His smile lit up the porch as his dimples deepened. "He gives us free will, but He wants us to be His children. He wants us to choose Him."

"I did when I was baptized. I took vows to live my life according to His will."

"This is His will for you, Nora." Wyatt sprang from his rocker and knelt in front of her. He took her hand and stared into her face. His blue eyes shone in the porch light. "Can I pray for you?"

Nora was frozen, mesmerized. She wanted to jerk her hands from his, but she couldn't. This was what Brandon meant by the Pied Piper. This was how he drew Tammy into that barn. Before Nora could answer, he bowed his head and began to pray aloud.

"Heavenly Father, I lift up to You my sister in Christ Nora. She needs You to take her right hand and help her find the path that leads to a closer walk with You. She is bound by rules that keep her from that closer walk. Help her to have the strength, the faith, the will, to break those chains. It will come at a cost, Lord, I know that. She knows that. To walk away from a way of life that keeps her from truly being Your child means leaving her family. I pray You will give her the strength to leave behind those family members who cannot be convinced to change their ways as well. Give her peace, give her strength, give her discernment, but most of all, give her joy."

The words stopped, but his hands didn't leave hers. His head remained bowed. His eyes were closed. Breathless, Nora waited. She couldn't imagine leaving her family. Mother. Father. Her brothers. Her home. Until now.

Levi. *Gott, it's too much to ask. Must I lose him too?*

Faith, family, community. The bishop always emphasized the three most important things in a Plain person's life—in that order. Faith before family.

Gott, do You expect me to believe this man who drinks beer and takes advantage of Tammy's love for him? He's no angel. He's a sinner.

So are you.

Three words, a mere three syllables. They fell, first like awkward, misshapen musical notes, then with the weight of an avalanche on her head, her shoulders, and her face.

So are you.

Wyatt opened his eyes. His smile reached into her heart. It brushed against her soul like the gentle touch of a dove's fluttering wing.

"I know what you're thinking." He squeezed her hands and let go. With a sigh he returned to his rocker. "I'm only a man, Nora. I'm flawed. We all are. We don't have to be perfect. Our sins are forgiven."

"Shouldn't you aspire to do better?" Her voice quivered. She sucked in a breath. How could she even begin to judge him? To criticize him? He'd done nothing but try to win over her soul. He wasn't asking for her body, only her very essence. "I know it's just as wrong for me to judge you. What you're doing with Tammy is wrong. You know it, but you don't stop. You say one thing, but your actions show you to be someone else."

"Don't apologize for holding me accountable for my actions. We're called to do that for our sisters and brothers in Christ. I do aspire to do better, so much better. God knows I do."

"How do you know?"

"I pray to Him all the time. When I'm walking, when I'm eating, when I'm playing music, when I lie in bed at night." His pale cheeks deepened to a delicate pink hue. "It's good to know I can make mistakes and still be loved."

Wyatt had given her permission to hold him accountable. It seemed a great gift of trust and one of expectation. She had to do her part, just as he did for her. "You can't keep making the same mistakes over and over and still expect God to forgive you. It doesn't work that way. Repent of your sins, be forgiven. Then go and sin no more."

"He will always welcome back the prodigal son, one of the many things I love about my gracious God."

"He won't keep forgiving the same sin over and over again."

"The spirit is willing but the body is weak."

"Try harder."

"You're a gut woman. That's how I know you want a true relationship with your Lord Jesus Christ."

God knew everything. Which meant He knew how her heart banged in her chest at the sound of "How Great Thou Art" and "Just a Closer Walk with Thee." His will would prevail. "When the fire is out and the evacuation order ends, I'm going home with my family and my friend Levi."

"We'll see."

Indeed they would. "I like Levi the way you like Tammy. Would you give her and your family up so you could worship differently?"

His smile slipped. The pink on his cheeks turned a ruddy red. "I like Tammy, but my faith will always come first."

Technically he had his priorities right. Plain people put faith first too. But his cavalier dismissal of Tammy's love made anger pulse through Nora again. Heat burned her face. She shucked off her sweater. "You like her? She's given you her heart, her everything."

She couldn't have this conversation with a man.

"Tammy is sweet. She's beautiful." His easy certainty fell away like sheets from a clothesline on a blustery day on the mountain. "So yes, I like her. She's a firecracker. She lights up the night, but I don't think I know what love is. Not yet."

Nora forced back a barrage of fierce words that wanted to rain hellfire on this man. "You should talk to Tammy."

"I will." Consternation plain on his face, he chewed his lower lip and studied his sneakers. “It’s too late to do it now. And tomorrow is the revival. But we’ll talk. Soon.”

“It’s chilly.” Nora stood. “I have Daadi and Mammi to help me if I have questions.”

As she tried to slip past him, his hand shot out and grabbed her wrist. “I will keep praying for you.”

Nora tugged her arm free. “You should pray for yourself. And for Tammy and for the pain you’ll cause her when she realizes you took something from her and you have no intention of giving her something of equal value. What you’ve done is inexcusable because you claim to be a believer. You know what Gott expects of you, but you allowed pleasure to come before your faith. Go, and don’t come back.”

Rejecting his prayers served only to make her feel guilty. Everyone needed prayer. She and Levi needed prayers that they would find a way to be together with God in the center of their relationship. Only then could they be bound together by vows that would make them one body in Christ.

An engine revved in the distance. Nora turned toward the long gravel drive that led to Grandpa’s patch of land. Wyatt rose and stood next to her, one hand propped on the porch column. A van careened up the drive and halted behind Joe’s car.

The passenger door slid open.

Levi hopped out, all 180 pounds of muscle and calluses. He slapped his straw hat on his head of thick, curly, brown hair. His faded blue shirt tightened across his thick chest. The desire to run to him battled with the inescapable knowledge that she stood on the porch with an English man.

No doubt it appeared as if she and Wyatt were courting. Nothing could be further from the truth.

Levi’s gaze locked with hers. No smile. No hello. No welcoming hug or kiss would be forthcoming, no matter how much her body ached to be held by the man who had professed his love for her. Unlike Wyatt, Levi threw himself heart and soul into loving her while still respecting the godly boundaries of their faith.

A second that might have been an hour passed. Nora breathed. "Hi, Levi. What are you doing here?"

27

On the ride from Eureka to Libby, Levi had imagined all sorts of reactions to his unexpected arrival. But not this one. After a few seconds in which her feet appeared cemented to the porch floor, Nora shot down the steps and met him in the middle of the sidewalk. She glanced over her shoulder at the man who'd been standing next to her. He didn't move. He was a dainty thing, slender, like he'd never done a day's work in his life. Levi dragged his gaze back to Nora. She looked no different—except for the guilty expression written all over her pretty face.

She should look guilty. She'd allowed herself to be led astray in a multitude of ways in the last month. As if traveling a few miles from home meant the rules suddenly didn't apply. What if he had waited and let Noah and Tobias get to her first? They would've found her sitting on the porch in the dark with an English man.

Standing on the porch together after dark with no others present might lead a person to think Nora was courting.

Hurt fought with anger. Which would prevail? One fueled the other.

"I came to see you." Levi backstepped toward the van. Mel was waiting for him to talk to Jacob about inviting himself to stay in the older man's home. If Jacob didn't have room, Levi would have to check at the motels in town or maybe stay with another family here in the district. "It seems as if you're *busy*, though."

Sarcasm did no good in this or any other situation, but that's what happened when hurt mingled with anger.

"I'm not busy." Emotions dashed pell-mell across her plump face, each vying for control. "I'm . . . this is . . . I'm happy to see you."

The stuttering words didn't bear testament to their truth.

"You must be Levi. I'm Wyatt Brubacher." The man finally straightened. He was wearing English clothes, but around here that meant nothing. "I preach with my dad. We do Christian revivals across the country."

More than Levi needed to know. An English preacher courting his girl. The man looked young. Like a teenager. But self-possessed. Eager to engage. Levi introduced himself. "Nice to meet you."

Wyatt had peculiarly pale-blue eyes fringed by even paler eyelashes. His complexion suggested that he needed to stay out of the sun. He had a weak chin. His blond hair curled around his ears, onto the collar of his jean jacket, and across his high forehead.

"He was just leaving." Nora backed away. "Wyatt, I reckon you have to get up early tomorrow to head to the revival. Don't you have to greet people?"

"I do. People from all over this region come to our revivals." Wyatt directed this unsolicited explanation at Levi. "They especially come in times of travail, when they're worried and anxious like they are right now because of the fires. I hope you'll come with Nora."

"We won't be here that long."

If he had his way.

"We won't?" Understanding registered in Nora's face, followed by trepidation. "Daed sent you?"

Now was not the time to mention that Levi had been the one to talk to her bishop about her transgressions. It had been for her own good, but she surely would not see it that way. "Jah."

"That's a shame." Wyatt's deep bass didn't match his looks. His earnest tone made him sound like a preacher. "We have so much to talk about. Consider staying for a visit. I know Ike and the others would love to have you attend a service."

He held out his hand again. Levi had no choice but to take it, but he ended the shake as quickly as it had begun. Wyatt smiled and half saluted. "God bless you."

God had already blessed Levi. With a beautiful, kind, hard-working girl who kissed with a joyful exuberance that left Levi dreaming of the day they would become one and nothing could separate them—especially not a salesman peddling Christianity like it was a big-box-store discount item for what ailed a man.

Levi waited, not moving, until Wyatt drove away. Then he tore his gaze from the receding taillights and focused on Nora. She ducked her head. Levi swallowed his anger. He worked to keep his tone neutral. "What was that all about?"

"Come, sit with me." Nora gestured toward the porch. "I have so much to tell you."

"Starting with how you came to be standing on the porch with an Englisch man tonight?"

"That's part of the story." She took his hand. Her fingers were those of a woman who worked hard. No softness there. Levi shivered in the night air. He struggled to harness his emotions. A man couldn't simply let such things go, no matter how much he longed to kiss her instead of talking about a man who claimed to be a Christian. Or her other transgressions.

"I need to talk to your groossdaadi about a room for the night." He gestured toward the van. Mel appeared half asleep, his head back against the headrest. "Mel is waiting to take me into town if there's no room for me here."

"There's two free bedrooms. Daadi's house is huge, and all his kinner are out on their own."

"I can't just invite myself."

"I'll invite you."

"Not your house—"

"What's going on out here?" Jacob Beachy pushed open the screen door and stuck out his hatless bald head. "You're making such a racket I can't nap in my chair. The windows are open, in case you haven't noticed."

He hadn't. "Sorry, Jacob. It's me, Levi."

Jacob squinted against the porch light. "I wondered when you'd show up. The bed's made up in the back room here on the first floor. See that you stay downstairs at night." He eased the screen door shut. "I must be losing my mind. I thought I heard that boy Wyatt out here. He sounds just like his daed when he talks."

"He left." Levi beat Nora to the response. "Danki for letting me stay."

"Not a problem. I like to keep things interesting."

Before Levi could ask what that meant, Jacob closed the door.

Levi bid Mel good night and thanked him for his services. With Mel's help a Libby driver was on call for when Levi was ready to return with Nora and the rest of her family, if Daryl decided it was time to go home as well. So much depended on the baby. The wildfire still raged in the forest, and the smoke still drifted across the countryside.

He took a long breath and turned back around. Nora had moved to the swing. If she thought he would plop down next to her, she was sadly mistaken. He tromped up the steps and chose a rocker instead. Her expression didn't change.

"What is going on with you? You've changed so much—"

"I know what you're thinking, and it's not true." She twisted the fabric of her apron in knots. "Wyatt is Tammy's special friend. At least, that's what she thinks. Wyatt seems to be set on breaking her heart."

"Something we agree on. It seemed more like he was here courting you."

"It's only been a month since we kissed and said goodbye. Less than that since we talked on the phone." Her scowl didn't make her look any less pretty. "Do you really think my feelings change that quickly? That I'm that fickle?"

Focus. She'd been sitting on the porch with Wyatt this evening. Much more than that had led up to this moment. "The girl who left Kootenai said she wouldn't drive a car. Yet she did." His anger bubbled to the surface. He paused and worked to collect himself. "You sang with a band that used a sound system. You played a musical instrument. You violated the Ordnung."

"Daadi offered me the chance to try something I've always wanted to do." The red blotches on her face and neck deepened. A sure sign of anxious guilt. "Just once. Not to change my whole life. Driving isn't what this is about."

"What is it about?"

"Have you ever heard the phrase 'a closer walk with Jesus'?"

Understanding dawned. She was right. Driving was a relatively minor infraction. In this case it represented so much. These people had their claws in deep. They had her questioning her faith. "I've heard talk like it. From people who think worship is about them. It's not. You know that. Worship is humble adoration of our Lord. Don't make it about you."

"I'm not. The thought that He would care for each one of us so deeply that He would speak to us individually is overwhelming, but it also makes my heart fill with joy." She raised her hands in the air and then let them drop into her lap. "I understand why they jump and hop and dance at their services. They are joyful with a kind of joy I admire. That I want. I'm drawn to the idea that Gott speaks to us all."

"What took your mudder and daed twenty years to build collapsed in less than a month." He should've come after that first phone call. He should never have let her come here in the first place.

"How is that possible? You took vows when you were baptized. You chose to become Plain in that moment. It was no longer an accident of birth. It was a choice."

"So were Onkel Ike, Aenti Roseanna, Daadi, and many others who live here." She lifted her chin. "I'm not weak, no matter what you think. This hasn't been easy. I know what's at stake. I may be only a woman, but I have a brain in my head and a heart in my chest. It hurts. Everything about it hurts. I love you. I want you to belong to Gott. I want to be Gott's. Don't believe for a second that I just let it happen. I fought. I asked questions. I backed away. And yet my heart kept asking for more. This is a matter of the heart, not the brain."

She'd never spoken like this to Levi. She wasn't the same woman who kissed him that night in the RV park. He leaned forward and bowed his head so he wouldn't have to look at her. "I don't know what to say." Something much worse than her father feared had taken place here. Anxiety used a crowbar on Levi's heart. All the fear and aching sense of loss climbed out and scattered. He'd given his heart to this woman. He could lose everything.

"Are you saying you plan to stay here? Are you leaving your family? Are you leaving me?"

"There's been much to think about." Her quandary showed in her face. Her voice quivered. "Even Jeannie . . ."

The lump in his throat grew. He struggled to swallow. "What about Jeannie?"

"Nothing. She's got her hands full, that's all." Wincing, Nora pressed her fingers to her lips, then let them drop. "They put us in a position to have to justify our beliefs, our way of life, and we've never had to do that before. We weren't given the words to do that."

"You don't have to do it. You simply nod and move on."

"Easy for you to say. You weren't there. You didn't see all these people who call themselves Amish jumping and hopping and dancing during a service with musical instruments that made the songs more beautiful."

That music would be a tool—a weapon—for getting to Nora should've occurred to Levi and to Harley. She loved music and singing. Her pleasing voice made him smile at the singings before they started courting. One of the many ways he admired her in those days. She'd never been in the position of having to defend her way of life. Despite being a grown woman, she was still naive. "I'm sorry. We should've seen this coming. Your daed should never have sent you here."

"And the sermon was about how we can be closer to Jesus. We can have a real relationship with Him, a closer walk with Him." Nora went on as if she hadn't heard him speak. "I've gone to church my whole life, and I don't know what that means. Do you?"

"It means building a relationship with you in the center instead of Gott. It's all about you and your wants and your needs." Levi cleared his throat and groped for words to make her understand. *Gott, give me the words. I'm no preacher. I'm not even that smart.* "That's not the way we think. We put Gott first, then family, then the community. We have a living hope of salvation. We show our faith by quiet example. What's so hard about that?"

"I wonder sometimes . . ." She stopped. Her hands moved from her apron to her kapp. "Why can't we do that and have a car or wear jeans? What does one have to do with the other?"

"I reckon having a car takes us farther into the world, away from faith and family. It's a mess in the world." It seemed a simple enough idea to grasp. "Those Englisch clothes draw attention to the person wearing them. That's not what we want."

"You don't think people gawk at us because of the way we dress?"

His exact thought when he spoke with Noah. Levi heaved a sigh. He didn't have all the answers. He didn't need them. Faith was believing even when a person didn't understand. "That's on them, not us. We go about our business. This is why I didn't want you coming here."

Her face crumpled. "But it wasn't up to you."

"Nee, it wasn't." If they'd been married, things would be different. They'd chosen to wait, and because of circumstances, a sinkhole had appeared in the road they traveled together. "Have your feelings for me changed?"

"Nee, not at all. I only want you to give them a chance. Not because I want to drive a car or wear a T-shirt." Tears made her eyes luminous in the stark porch light. "Because of what they believe. That we can have a personal relationship with Jesus. That Gott will talk to us if we listen. That we can read the Bible for ourselves and study it with others. Doesn't that sound wunderbarr?"

It sounded as if Beelzebub had grown from a serpent to a pale-faced man with an angelic face, blond curls, and soft hands. "It sounds like you've forgotten the Ordnung. It sounds as if you've developed a case of spiritual amnesia." The knot in his throat grew and throbbed. It plummeted into his chest. His heart ached. He needed to regroup and figure out how to lead her out of this morass. He would not give up on her soul. Whether he could trust her to be his soul mate after this remained to be seen. Harley was depending on him. Nora's future depended on how he handled this.

He gritted his teeth and stood. "It's late and I'm tired."

She rose and came to him. "Please don't be mad. Let's talk about this. Hear me out and then make a decision."

"It's hard to believe how much you've changed in such a short time."

"For the better. You'll see. I'm letting you know how I feel. That's what I should do. You know you're bossy. We talked about it." Nora stood so close he could smell her scent of soap and see the tiny scar on her forehead left by the measles. "I know that a woman's place is to do that, to bow to her mann's wishes. But this is so important.

I'm only asking you to give it a few days. Let's go to the tent revival together. Daadi and Mammi will be there. My onkel and aenti. These folks are my family too. If we're to be married, you should know them."

She was right about his tendency to run roughshod over her opinions. To tell her what to do. Just as Jack did with him. Levi's intention to change his ways stared him in the face. He wanted to share decision-making with her. But not on this. On this issue of faith he was right. She was wrong.

Before he could tell her so, Nora ran her hands up his chest. Her slender fingers stroked his face. The entreaty in her face called to Levi. He leaned forward until his lips brushed hers. Despite the brevity of the kiss, her touch lit a fire in his gut. This was his weakness. She knew that. To never have this again, he couldn't bear the thought. *Please, Gott, don't let this happen.*

He threw his arms around her and tugged her tight against his chest so he could kiss her cheeks and neck. "I don't want to lose you," he whispered in her ear. "I couldn't bear it. You seem so far away."

"I'm right here." She leaned her head against his chest and closed her eyes. "I want us to be together. I want us to make the right choices."

Us. As if his choices were in question. Nora really believed that. His faith would never change. If she chose to embrace the way of life and worship of her kinfolk here, he would have no choice but to let her go.

The wildfire had done more than destroy the house that would've been theirs—it had destroyed his trust in a woman he loved. His heart threatened to implode. He wanted her and he needed her more than he dared admit. For the sake of love he would give in to her desire to spend a few days experiencing what she had experienced. He would attend a service before closing the door completely.

He knew how this would end, but he also knew he had to walk a few steps in her shoes.

Levi leaned back so he could see her face. *Gott, don't let me make the wrong decision either.* "We'll stay until Monday. My prayer is that we'll be able to go back to Kootenai then. That you'll leave all this behind so we can be together the way we've planned. Things can go back to the way they were before the fire."

She would have to admit her sins to the elders and receive counseling. Would she be willing to do that? He needed time to show her the error of her ways. If she refused, she would be shunned.

Please Gott, I need time.

"Danki," Nora whispered. "I want us to be together, whether it's in Kootenai or here."

"It won't be here." Even if his heart ended up another pile of ashes, it couldn't be here. He forced himself to let his hands drop from her waist. He backed away. "I can promise you that, Nora. It won't be here."

She didn't speak. She didn't move.

He didn't dare fill the space. The slightest move and he would give in.

Let me be strong in my beliefs, Gott. Let me do what's right, even if it means the end.

The pain in her eyes spoke for her. "I should go in. If Sadie cries, I get up with her." She stood and edged past him toward the door. Once she had the screen door open, she turned back. "I have a baby monitor so I can hear her. It has a little screen on it so I can even see her. It's battery-operated. Do you object to that?"

"It's not for me to object to anything." Levi kept a tight grip on emotions that wanted free rein to gallop across the countryside. "You should see the truth for yourself."

"I do. That's what I keep trying to tell you."

"Not my truth. This will never be my truth."

28

Levi stared up into the darkness. The bed frame squeaked every time he moved, which was every other second. The guest bed mattress was plumper than the one he slept on at home. Almost too soft. The scent of lilac and rose wafted in the air from sachets tucked under the pillow. It tickled his nose. The sheets were fresh and soft. None of these things kept him from sleeping.

The thought that Nora lay in a bedroom above his pestered him worse than a swarm of hornets.

He should march up those stairs and convince her that Ike and the others had sold her a bill of goods. He should remind her of her baptismal vows. He could convince her before she had to face Noah and the other elders.

Or he could simply kiss her until she forgot everything she'd heard in the Eagle Valley church. She wouldn't need a guitar and a piano or a band and its sound system. She would forget about driving cars and passing time alone with an English man. She would only think of his lips and his hands.

Gott, forgive me.

What had gotten into him?

On the other hand, were his thoughts any worse than hers?

How could he see the splinter in her eye with the plank in his?

He was judgmental and self-righteous. Or doing his job as a brother in Christ by holding her accountable.

He sat up. The moon, a half crescent, cast pale light across the bed, the dresser, and the closet. It might as well be day. He lay down and rolled over on his side with his back to the light. What if he was wrong? What if the Eagle Valley Amish were right?

A closer walk with Jesus. How could that be bad?

He sat up again. Where had that thought come from? Doubts chose nighttime and silence to creep in with their buddy temptation.

Levi slipped from the bed and knelt. The quilt felt soft and worn under his restless fingers. *Lord, help to me cling to my baptismal vows no matter what comes. Please do the same for Nora and Jeannie and the others. Amen.*

God expected him to do his part. Not only hold himself and others accountable but gently and without judgment.

He could do that. But first he had to confess that he had spoken to the bishop about her transgressions.

Levi dressed and went to the door before he could change his mind. With great care he turned the knob and opened it.

Jacob stood in the hallway. "Going somewhere?"

"Nee, nee, I mean, nee." He hadn't stuttered since kindergarten. "I just wanted to . . . I needed to . . . I needed a drink of water."

"I know what you needed." Jacob, still fully dressed in black pants and a blue shirt, crossed his arms. "Just to clarify, we may have rejected much of the old Amish ways, but we still don't allow any hanky-panky in our house."

Hanky-panky? "I'm a Plain man who takes his faith seriously." Levi drew himself up straight and tall. "I only wanted to talk to her. I have something I need to tell her."

"Uh-huh." Jacob pursed his lips and studied Levi in an unnerving silence for several seconds. Finally, he turned. "A cup of hot chocolate might settle you down."

It seemed doubtful. His heart still rattling around in his chest,

Levi followed the other man into the kitchen. "I don't mean to keep you from your sleep."

"Old men like me don't sleep much." Jacob proceeded to put sugar, salt, and cocoa in a saucepan, to which he added milk. He turned on the gas burner and stirred the concoction. "Don't tell my fraa I know how to make this. I always let her do it. She's happier that way."

"I'll never tell." Levi dropped into a chair. "I just wanted to talk to Nora."

"A gut many men have said something similar. Better to avoid temptation—especially in my house."

Considering his thoughts earlier about kissing her into submission, Levi couldn't help but agree. "Temptation isn't always physical."

Jacob stopped stirring. After a second he swiveled, allowing Levi to see his whiskered, wrinkled face. "If that's your roundabout way of saying we're tempting her spiritually, you're wrong. We're offering her a faith unchained from all the rigmarole the old-fashioned Amish love to cling to even when it means building concrete barriers between you and Gott."

"There are no walls between us and Gott."

"You're wrong, but you're so brainwashed you can't see it."

Tammy and her friends were using gentle tactics that lulled Nora into changing her way of life to match theirs. This, on the other hand, was a full-out verbal assault. Levi stood. "I don't need hot chocolate. I need sleep. Gut nacht."

"You can't even take the time to listen? Maybe that's why Nora has been touched by our community. She takes the time to listen. She's thoughtful. She always has been, since she was a little bitty girl."

"She's also naive."

"And you've spent so much time out in the world that you can say for certain how all people should pray and worship and live their lives?" Jacob poured the steaming hot chocolate into matching stoneware mugs. He tossed in a handful of marshmallows. "You're much more fortunate than I am. I'm old and I still can't be sure what is right. Only Gott knows for sure. One day He'll answer all our questions."

Despite his intention to march back to the bedroom, Levi stood rooted to the floor by his irritation and unquenchable desire to give Nora's grandpa a piece of his mind. Except that Jacob had a good point. "I don't know anything for sure either. But I do know Nora and I took the same baptismal vows two years ago. She vowed to keep to our faith. And to follow the Ordnung. Planting seeds of doubt and egging her on in breaking those rules could lead to punishment, even Meidung. Is that what you want for your granddaughter?"

"I want her eternal salvation." Jacob set one of the mugs in front of Levi. "I want to greet her in heaven when she steps through those pearly gates."

"I want the same thing, but neither you nor I can guarantee that. Only Gott. With us she has the living hope of salvation."

"With us she need only repent of her sins and ask Christ into her heart." Jacob sipped and smacked his lips. "She is saved."

"You're so arrogant as to think you know what Gott will decide about Nora's salvation or mine or yours?"

"Not arrogance, Suh. It's right there in the Scripture. We know because we read it, we study it, we discuss it, we live it. Through Gott's mercy and grace, we are saved."

"Gut nacht, Jacob." How could Levi spar with someone so versed in Scripture? Jacob was right about one thing. His Plain Gmay did not engage in the activities he described. But they still believed with all their hearts, their minds, and their souls. His feet dragging, heart heavy, Levi trudged toward the hallway.

"I'll be here dozing on the couch if you want to talk."

Talk or hurl sharp word-arrows at Levi. "I won't."

◆ ◆ ◆

What Grandma had said about the princess and the pea under the mattress sprang to mind. Nora ripped the twisted nightgown and sheets from her clammy body and heaved herself around to face the opposite direction. Until tonight her bed had been pleasant. The mattress plump, the sheets cool and soft. Now, every time she moved, which was every few seconds, the bed frame squeaked. "Grrrr." She sat up and threw her legs over the side of the bed. Her bare feet touched cool pine wood. What now?

She had her Bible. Maybe Jeannie was in the bathroom studying again. Maybe they could find answers to their questions—and Levi's questions—in there. She didn't even know where to begin searching. Maybe Jeannie had learned enough in her Bible study group to know.

It didn't seem right with Levi sleeping downstairs.

In a bedroom right below hers.

Levi.

"Grrrrrrr." She crawled back under the covers and stuck a pillow over her head.

Gott, I'm listening!

If God knew what she was thinking and doing, why did she need to tell Him?

Another good question. Nora threw the pillow aside and breathed night-cooled air. "Instead of talking, I'm listening, Gott."

She must be losing her mind, talking out loud to a God who had millions upon millions of people He shepherded every single day.

Nothing.

What do I do about Levi? How can I make him understand, Gott? Is he right? Am I right? Can we both be right?

Nothing.

The audacity of her prayers must boggle God's mind.

She needed to talk to Mercy and Christine. She needed to talk to Levi.

Gott, I feel so alone. Help me.

Nothing.

Levi slept one floor down. He'd come all this way to take her home. He cared. Not all was lost between them.

She flung the sheets aside yet again. Three minutes later she'd exchanged a nightgown for a dress and knotted her hair in a bun under her wrinkled kapp.

Sucking in a long breath, she opened the door.

"Where do you think you're going?" Grandma stood in the hall. Nora backtracked into her room. Arms flapping like an angry brood hen, Grandma followed. "Nee, nee, back to bed."

Nora sank onto the bed. Her toes curled up in shame. Only pride kept her from covering her hot face. "How did you know?"

"I have ears." Breathless sounding, Grandma fanned her face with both hands. "I can hear Jacob and Levi downstairs jawing like the earth is about to end. They don't seem to know people are trying to sleep up here."

"I only wanted to talk to him."

"This is not the right time or place for that. You know better."

Despite all these years attending church in the Eagle Valley Amish Ministry, Grandma had not given in to their arguments, their spiel, or the way they kindly, sweetly wormed their way under a person's skin. "How do you do it?"

Grandma eased onto the bed next to Nora. She yawned so widely her jaws popped. "I am who I am. Just like the great I Am. Nothing they say will change my mind. Jacob says I'm just stubborn that way."

"Are you right or are they right?"

"I cling to my beliefs."

Nora shook her finger at Grandma. "That's not an answer."

"You have enough folks whispering in your ears." Grandma

didn't sound the least apologetic. "You have to decide and then stick to your decision."

"Levi came to take me home."

"You should go."

"So they can't sway me anymore?"

"To try on those new beliefs in your own home." Grandma patted Nora's hand. She sighed. "If they still fit, you don't belong there."

"Then what?"

"You come home to this home."

She loved her family in Libby, but her heart was in Kootenai. "I can't imagine my life without Levi."

"Gott asked the disciples to leave their families and everything they knew to follow Him."

"You're not helping."

Grandma's dry chuckle didn't help either. "That's not my job. Not allowing my granddaughter and a man who may or may not be her special friend to congregate under my mann's roof—that's my job."

"I only wanted to talk."

"That's not what your face said when you opened that door." Grandma rose. "You'll see him at breakfast. The revival starts early in the morning. Sleep."

"I can't. I tried. I even prayed." Nora swallowed a wail. She couldn't admit to her own grandmother that she was right. Her desire to roar down the stairs to find Levi had little to do with theology. Mostly she wanted to shake him and demand he stop splitting hairs and start kissing her. "I'll write letters to Christine and Mercy. They'll know what to do."

"Fine, but I doubt that." Grandmother trotted to the door. "But if it keeps you from doing something that breaks the rules, by all means, write letters." She closed the door, leaving Nora in silence.

Grandma was right. Mercy and Christine couldn't give her

advice. They'd never experienced such a rift in their family and their beliefs.

As far as she knew. What if their time away from Kootenai had been equally eye-opening?

It wasn't possible.

Footsteps sounded outside her door. They paused in front of it.

Levi? She rushed to the door and put her hand on the knob. Her heart pounded in her chest so hard her ears rang.

The footsteps resumed, headed down the hallway.

Grandma.

Nora fought the urge to bang her head against the door.

Instead, she leaned her forehead on the wood and counted to one hundred.

"Gut nacht, Levi."

29

Like children to the Pied Piper, they came. Or was it lambs to the slaughter? Neither image gave Nora comfort. A cool, wily autumn wind lifted her skirt. She wrapped her fingers in the cotton fabric and held it down while using her other hand to make sure her kapp didn't take flight. Her small cluster of family joined the steady stream of folks entering the enormous blue-and-white-striped tent that rose from the grassy plain, like a bright intentional eyesore in the midst of so much natural beauty.

She didn't look back. She didn't have to. Levi's dour countenance followed her wherever she went. Through breakfast, through the van ride to the fairgrounds, and now as they walked to the tent. He said nothing, but everything about the set of his shoulders and the disbelieving frown on his face scolded her.

He was only doing this to make her happy. Then they would go home and forget about it—to his way of thinking.

If that's Your will, Gott, so be it. Send me a sign, Lord. Please, send me a clear sign.

She put one foot in front of the other. She didn't know what else to do.

Inside the tent Uncle Ike worked with men Nora didn't recognize to raise and tie back flaps so the breeze could enter. The hum of enormous fans mingled with the muted murmurs of a crowd that swelled and filled row after row of metal folding chairs that were hard and unforgiving. She picked a row in the middle and moved that direction. Jeannie caught her arm. Nora turned. Daryl shook his head and led them into a row farther back.

As if distance would inoculate them against the ideas that would spread like a plague through the sound-system speakers. Daryl hadn't wanted to come any more than Levi did. The scowl on his face and the rigid set of his shoulders made that clear. What words had been exchanged between husband and wife that propelled him into the tent had not been shared. Nora fell in line behind Jeannie, who carried Sadie, and Grandma Esther, who had Jason and Missy firmly in tow. Levi came next. Under his Sunday best black hat, his forehead furrowed. Still, he said nothing. His eyebrows rose and fell.

"We sit together, men and women." For a man accustomed to an orderly men-on-one-side, women-on-the-other world of worship, this would be a strange, even uncomfortable, arrangement. Nora tried for a reassuring smile. This experience would only get more uncomfortable. "Families sit together. It's nice."

"I'll take the seat next to Nora." His expression stern, Grandpa squeezed past Levi and Nora. He plopped into the closest chair. "Go on, sit. You're giving me a crick in my neck."

Levi's face turned a peculiar shade of pinkish red. He sat. His conversation at breakfast had been limited to answering Grandpa's questions about his job at the furniture store and his family with short but polite responses. He said nothing to Nora, even when she sat a towering plate of Grandma's flapjacks topped with a melting square of butter and warm maple syrup in front of him.

Now his sidelong glance seemed to scream, *What are we doing here?*

"People from all around Libby come to these prayer meetings," Nora offered. That's what Uncle Ike called it. They would pray for the people affected by the fires, for the firefighters on the front line, for law enforcement officers, and for rain. "We all pray to the same God."

Without a word Levi leaned back in his chair.

Nora glanced at Grandpa. He shrugged.

Her relationship with Levi might not survive this day. Why did it have to be this way? God's plan? As if the fire and the destruction of Chet's house weren't enough. If they had God at the center of their marriage, how could they go wrong? Did where they sit in the tent or whether they met in a church building instead of someone's house matter?

How could it? Suddenly tired beyond all measure, Nora closed her eyes. *I don't have any answers, Gott. You have them all. Are You planning to share them with me? Or show me the way?*

Her prayer teetered on sacrilegious. God was God. He didn't have to share anything with her.

Patience, My child.

Nora's heart thumped. The sound of rushing blood filled her ears. She peeked toward the tent's ceiling. No wisdom-filled angel gazed down upon her. Only a dingy canvas and the metal skeleton that held it up.

What?

Patience, My unruly child.

The voice echoed in her ears. Nora straightened and peered up and down the aisle. Daryl frowned. Jeannie rocked Sadie. Jason and Missy took turns tying and untying Grandma's kapp strings. No one seemed perturbed by a voice that rang as loudly as the school bell that had demanded she leave her beloved swings and enter the schoolhouse after recess all those years ago.

God spoke to her in her confusion and consternation. He spoke to a sinner who slipped each day farther from the beliefs her family and community had impressed upon her since birth.

"What man of you, having an hundred sheep, if he lose one of them,

doth not leave the ninety and nine in the wilderness, and go after that which is lost, until he find it?"

Have I gone astray?

Breathless, she strained to hear over the chatter about weather, the fire, new babies, funerals, and the details that filled up the well of life.

"Hey, you're here! Earth to Nora. What are you thinking about?" Tammy sashayed through the row in front of Nora's and stopped. She stuck one knee on a chair and leaned forward, both hands on the back of the chair. "Why didn't you call me to tell me Levi showed up in all his deliciousness?"

Embarrassment streaked through Nora, faster and hotter than the Caribou Fire. Any connection to a great and glorious God dissipated. "Tammy!"

"Sorry." Her expression unrepentant, Tammy stuck her hand out to Levi. "It's good to see you again. You might not remember me. I'm the kossin Tammy."

Levi's face went from pinkish-red to scarlet. The handshake lasted two seconds. "I remember you."

Tammy was unforgettable. She didn't realize the impact she had on people with her unbridled enthusiasm and desire for the next fun thing. Her life would never be boring.

Undeterred, she sank sideways in her chair between Tucker and her older brother, Joe. Aunt Roseanna and half a dozen other family members filled the rest of the seats. That didn't stop Tammy from ogling Levi. "Tell me all. How long are you staying? You have to go to our church on Sunday. And come to our house for supper. Do you like music? We have a band. This is my brother, Tucker. He plays guitar and banjo. I play violin and my boy—a friend is teaching me to play piano—"

The unmistakable first notes of "Just a Closer Walk with Thee" sounded. Nora dragged her gaze from the one-sided exchange to the front of the tent where a makeshift platform had been built. Wyatt played an old-fashioned upright piano. A hush ripe with anticipation settled over the crowd.

Gripping her hands in her lap, Nora breathed and forced all other thought from her mind. Only Jesus. A closer walk with Jesus. Uncle Ike, Tammy, and Wyatt himself said such a walk was possible. The elders of her Gmay said such folderol reeked of arrogance and pride.

Which is it, Lord, which is it?

Wyatt began to sing softly, his exquisite baritone soaring over rapt faces—some who knew him well, like Tammy, and many who had never before seen or heard him. They were held captive by his voice and his hands on the yellowed ivory keys of the old piano. The notes carried on the air as sweet as any roses Nora had ever held to her nose.

His immense voice deepened. It rose and filled the space. The words bore down on Nora. They knocked on locked doors. Padlocks came undone. Doors swung open in welcome.

Here I am, Lord.

"You know the words, folks. Join me." Wyatt's fingers never stopped moving as he leaned into the microphone. "Let our voices be a sweet, sweet sound in our Lord and Savior's ears."

His audience needed no encouragement. Their voices rose and mingled, some mangling the words, others flatter than an old much-used rug. All intent on praising the Lord in such a joyful noise that tears flowed. Women sniffed into hankies. Men ducked their heads and sneaked a swipe at their faces. The tight fist in Nora's chest unclenched. Her voice joined the others, note for note, united in joy.

A woman on the second row stood. A man a few seats down joined her. One by one, then groups of three and four arose. "Sweet Jesus," a man shouted.

"Amen," another responded.

Some raised their faces to the unseen sky and then their hands.

The desire to stand with them struggled to break from its bonds, bound by a lifetime of teaching. God saw. He knew. Nora didn't have to draw attention to herself. Singing the words was enough.

Her lungs hurt. Her throat ached. Her fingernails dug into her palms, the pain barely discernible in the fight to stay seated. She bit her lip and concentrated on the discomfort.

Grandma's hand clamped on Nora's arm. Her grip tightened. Nora sought Grandma's face. She shook her head ever so slightly. Chastisement without a single word. So like Mother when the boys got out of hand during a service. A simple, fierce frown did its work.

Nora would honor her parents. She would honor Grandma Beachy. Scripture said she should do that. God would see and know her heart.

She peeked beyond Grandma to Jeannie. Tears rolled down her sister's face. She rummaged through her canvas bag and produced a hankie. Sadie fussed, but Jeannie didn't seem to notice.

The song ended. Wyatt's face glistened with sweat. Or tears. His hands remained on the keys for a few seconds. He closed his eyes and bowed his head. The crowd quieted.

"Heavenly Father, prepare our hearts and minds for the message. Let us seek You with all our hearts. Remove any barriers to our complete and utter surrender to You. Whatever chains bind us, let them fall away. Let all who are hurting, weak, weary, angry, bewildered, unsure, unworthy, surrender themselves to You today. No holding back. These things I pray in the precious and holy name of Your Son, Jesus Christ."

Wyatt slipped from the platform. Uncle Ike took the stage. For it was a stage as much as an altar. He urged the crowd to join him in prayer. Nora lost track of time. So many concerns lifted up. Uncle Ike implored. He cajoled. He begged.

Then he was done. "And all God's people said, 'Amen.'"

And so they did.

He hopped from the platform and settled into a front-row seat.

Silence descended and stretched.

A man who looked much like Wyatt, only thicker in the middle, broader through the shoulders, blond curls shot through with silver, ascended to the microphone in the center of the platform. He adjusted the height but said nothing. Everything about his demeanor suggested a calm patience. He studied the crowd.

"Jesus is here with us now. Do you feel Him?" Despite a distinctly backwoods Southern drawl, George Brubacher had a polish that could only come from having said these words many times in many places over many years. "I asked you a question. Do you feel His presence?"

"Yes, yes, yes," A man shouted from the back of the room. "Praise the Lord, He is here."

Reverend Brubacher picked up a Bible from a wooden stand next to the microphone. He held it up with both hands. "Lord, have mercy on us. Hear our prayers. Accept the confession of our sins. We have fallen short in every way, but we crave Your goodness and Your mercy. There are those among us who are nonbelievers and doubters, but every one of us is a sinner."

A strangled sob followed by a strange hiccup emanated from close by. Nora opened her eyes and peeked. Tammy sniffed and wiped her nose on the short sleeve of her brilliant blue shirt. A tissue in her hand, Jeannie leaned forward and nudged Tammy from behind. With a muttered thanks Tammy took it. A noisy honk followed.

Even Tammy, who grew up believing she could speak directly to Jesus, could be overcome by Pastor Brubacher's words. That said a lot.

Or did a chorus of sins heckle her? The sin of fornication surely weighed like an albatross around her neck. Nora reached toward her. Grandma's hand touched Nora's. Again with the shake of her head, this time fiercer.

Nora subsided once again.

"And all God's people said, 'Amen.'"

Again a chorus of "amens" rolled through the tent and out the openings created by tied-back flaps. Reverend Brubacher laid the Bible on the pulpit and thumbed through the pages. The seconds ticked by. He stared at the pages.

"Jesus answered, 'Very truly I tell you, no one can enter the kingdom of God unless they are born of water and the Spirit. Flesh gives birth to flesh, but the Spirit gives birth to spirit. You should not be surprised at my saying, "You must be born again." The wind blows wherever it pleases. You hear its sound, but you cannot tell where it comes from or where it is going. So it is with everyone born of the Spirit.' John 3:5–8."

With a flick of his wrist, Reverend Brubacher snapped the Bible shut. He stared out at the crowd, his gaze seeming to devour those closest to him before roving farther afield. The desire to sink down into her chair, then to the ground to be covered by earth overcame Nora. He would seek her out. He would know from her face that she didn't understand.

"Most of you think you understand Jesus' words, but you don't." The reverend's tone went soft with forgiveness. "He understands. He knows. He sees you. He hears you. The Word tells us so. This morning He uses me as a conduit to unpack this Scripture so you can understand. That closer walk is yours for the taking. I'll walk you through it. Jesus will be waiting at the other end. All you have to do is meet Him halfway. Be reborn in Him."

More "amens" and "hallelujahs" punctuated his words. Daryl snorted. Jeannie's face turned beet red.

Nora peeked at Levi. He stared straight ahead, arms crossed, consternation written across his features.

Keep an open mind, please keep an open mind. Please, Gott, let Levi keep an open mind.

Bible in hand, Reverend Brubacher paced the platform. He jabbed the air with his other hand. Sweat poured down his face. Wet spots dotted his white shirt. His voice grew hoarse, but he didn't stop talking. In fact, the words poured out faster and faster. "You hear that wind blowing, don't you? You hear it, but you can't see it. It doesn't matter, because Hebrews 11:1 tells us 'Now faith is confidence in what we hope for and assurance about what we do not see.'

"Jesus, I know You are here with us today. Holy Spirit, roar through this tent. Fill us up. Rise up, people, rise up."

Across the tent, people stood. Men and women shouted. They hopped. They raised their hands and cried out for Jesus.

Perspiration trickled down Nora's temples. Her clothes felt hot and heavy. Her throat burned for a drink of water. Her lips were dry. Swallowing became painful. Sweat from her armpits soaked her dress. Grandma looked as cool as a tall glass of iced tea. Grandpa's face creased in a smile that kept growing with each "amen" or "hallelujah." If Levi smiled, his face would crack. His whole body would crumple to the ground in a pile of utter rejection of every word.

"There are those of you who long for salvation. You ache for the unconditional love of Jesus Christ. It's yours for the taking. All you have to do to be reborn is come forth, repent of your sins, and ask Jesus into your heart." Reverend Brubacher's voice broke. "It's as simple as that. Who among you needs Christ in your life today? Don't delay. Come now. Join me here at this altar built especially for each one of you. Give your life to him today. You will be born again."

An ache blossomed in Nora's chest and spread until her entire body shook. Pain spiraled through her. *Gott? Gott?*

Did He hear her? Did her measly prayers reach Him? Did He know how she longed for His presence? *I don't know what to do, Gott. I'm cut in half, split in two. They're all my family, but no one more than You.*

The desire to stand burned in her belly. The need to seek her Lord and Savior worked her arms and legs like a puppeteer working his magic on a wooden puppet. Her feet moved.

Nee, nee. I can't.

You can.

Gott?

A middle-aged woman in capris and a sleeveless cotton shirt stumbled toward the front. A young man dressed in jeans and a Jason Aldean T-shirt tromped behind her. More followed. A trickle became a steady stream. Those who didn't go forward stood and clapped, a steady, pulsing rhythm that pounded inside Nora's head.

Reverend Brubacher's thundering, unceasing words surrounded her like a life jacket on a rough, stormy Lake Koocanusa. Her muscles tensed. Her arms reached for the safety of the boat. Jesus stood in that boat and calmed the seas.

He beckoned to her. *Get in the boat with Me. You'll be safe here.*

Her legs belonged to someone else. Someone who wanted to leap from her chair and race down the middle aisle, shouting, "Here I am, Lord. I'm Yours, Lord."

Eyes closed, Nora clutched at her seat with both hands. *Nee, stay. Stay.*

Gott, what do I do? Do I need to be born again? I've been baptized. I took vows. I live my life according to the Ordnung. Must I do more?

The decision is yours, child.

I'm sorry, Mudder. I'm sorry, Daed.

She stood.

Grandma reached for her. Nora ducked away. Grandma's hand grappled with air.

Grandpa stood to let her by. "Go, child, be free."

"Nee." Levi rose and blocked the aisle. "Don't do it."

His body, so sturdy, so familiar, stood in the way of her escape. Nora ducked her head and plowed past him. Surprise marred his sweet face as he gave way to her mighty shove and sat.

A single man couldn't stand in the way of God's plan.

"Nora, please!"

She didn't dare turn back. Instead, she focused on Reverend Brubacher waiting for her at the altar. Dozens of other people knelt before him, faces glowing, hands raised. Reverend Brubacher stalked up and down the wooden platform, Bible in hand, his expression fierce with joy. "Come all ye heavy laden, come to Jesus. Come now."

Nora sank to her knees before him. She bowed her head. The reverend's words flowed over her in a river that rose and rose until she couldn't breathe. She drowned in them. His sonorous voice pinned her to the river bottom.

Breathe. Breathe. Gott, I can't breathe.

The crowd's shouts faded. A strange, ominous silence pressed on her so hard, her body was flattened. Other noises, other voices, voices she recognized, filled her ears.

Noah's deep voice inviting her, Levi, and the others to kneel. The hard wood bit into her knees through her cotton dress. The barn smelled of manure and hay.

The words had flooded her that day too, only two years earlier. Noah's deep bass rang in her ears. She shook her head. *Nee, this is different.*

The bishop's stern yet kind face stared down at her. No histrionics. No shouting. No pacing. No cries from the crowd. He simply asked the questions. In a soft but assured voice, she answered. She and Levi and their friends. People she'd known all her life in front of family and friends. Her community.

"Do you confess that Jesus Christ is the Son of God?"

"Yes, I believe that Jesus is the Son of God."

"Do you also recognize this to be a Christian order, church, and fellowship under which you now submit yourselves?"

"Yes."

"Do you renounce the world, the devil with all his subtle ways, as well as your own flesh and blood, and deserve to serve Jesus Christ alone, who died on the cross for you?"

"*Yes.*"

"*Do you also promise before God and His church that you will support these teachers and the Ordnung with the Lord's help, faithfully attend the services of this church, help to counsel and work in it, and not to forsake it, whether it leads you to life or to death?*"

"*Yes.*"

Water had flowed over her then. Not a river of fiery words. The water of holy baptism. Noah's wife gave her the holy kiss on her cheek and shook her hand. They hugged.

In that moment Nora had been set free in the promise of a living hope.

"*Do you renounce the world, the devil with all his subtle ways?*"

"What is your name?" Reverend Brubacher bent over her. His sweaty hand brushed her cheek. His eyes were the same pale, ethereal blue as Wyatt's. "Do you wish to renounce the ways of the world and embrace Jesus as the Lord's only begotten Son?"

"Yes . . . no . . . I mean I already have." At least two hundred sets of eyes watched. Most of them strangers. They weren't her community. They didn't know her. "I've been baptized."

"Often we go through rituals by rote. We don't truly receive Jesus into our hearts." He knelt and put both hands on her shoulders. His breath reeked of coffee. "Do you want Jesus in your heart? Let me help you find that which you seek."

What am I doing?

"No, I can't." Nora crawled back on her hands and knees. She knocked into the chubby, sobbing woman in a green sweat suit who knelt behind her. "Sorry, I'm sorry."

She stumbled to her feet, turned, and fled down the aisle. Tears raked her face. *Gott, forgive me.* She dodged the stragglers who'd made up their minds to do that which she had already done on the day of her baptism.

She raced past Levi, who now stood in the aisle. Past Grandpa, who stared wide-eyed, and Grandma, who tucked a child under each arm and followed.

Nora picked up speed as if the devil himself chased her.

Maybe he did.

She burst into the sunlit morning and gulped fresh air. Her legs crumpled. She collapsed on the ground. *Forgive me, Gott, forgive me.*

"What has gotten into you?" Levi's voice followed her. Once the voice of reason . . . now the voice of censure. "You're acting crazy. Addled."

His face crimson, he towered over her.

"Don't. Just don't." She cradled her head in her hands. "Leave me be."

She wanted to run far away, but her legs wouldn't hold her. Her body sagged to the ground like a rag doll that had lost all its stuffing.

"Leave you be? Are you saying you don't want anything to do with me anymore? That's fine." His voice hoarse, Levi knelt next to her. His hands reached for her, then dropped. "You can be done with me, but I'm not leaving you here. Not when they've done this to you. I don't even know you anymore. But I told your father I'd bring you home, and that's what I intend to do."

Nora stared at his face, once so familiar, now a stranger's. "Why are you so angry? I didn't do it. I saw what was happening to me and I stopped. I wasn't overcome by temptation."

"I saw the look on your face. You wanted it more than you've ever wanted anything. Even me. You didn't even look like that when you were baptized."

"I was scared that day."

"This snake oil show didn't scare you?" His face bewildered, Levi shook his head. "It scares me. People buy into it. They don't see the devil in sheep's clothing."

"Their way is different than ours. It doesn't make it wrong."

"So why did you stop?"

"Because I took vows, that's why."

"Thanks be to Gott you remembered those vows. Better late than never." There was anger in his face and disappointment and resolve. But no love. The Levi who kissed her and nuzzled her neck had disappeared. "Get up. You'll wait in the van for me."

He rose. His voice compelled her to do the same. He took off across the parking lot. She struggled to keep up. "Why? What are you going to do?"

"I'll get Tammy's brother to drive us into town to find someone to take us to Eureka. But first I need to get Daryl." Levi slung open the Farm-to-Market van's door. "He'll want to take Jeannie and the kinner too. Go on, get in."

He didn't know Daryl had his own fight on his hands. Jeannie didn't want to go. She wanted that closer walk. Nora leaned her head against the van and closed her eyes. She would get in when she was good and ready.

The sound of a child shrieking filled the air. "Mudder, Mudder."

Jason. Nora forced her eyes open and turned. Grandma had the little ones by the hands, marching them into the grassy field. No Daryl and no Jeannie.

Maybe Jeannie had gone forward. Maybe she hadn't been able to resist. A boulder sat where Nora's heart had once been. Her family torn to pieces once again.

"Stay here." Levi took off running toward the tent. "Don't move."

"She's my schweschder."

If he heard, he didn't respond.

He didn't know. He couldn't understand. Jeannie needed someone who did understand to help her do the right thing—whatever that was.

Nora bolted toward the tent. Levi picked up speed. He had long legs on his side.

Nora had a sister's love on hers.

30

This must be what it felt like to be run over by a tractor-trailer rig. Levi darted into the tent two strides behind Nora. The sheer number of impressions, thoughts, and ideas sparring in his head provoked dizziness. The picture in his head of Nora kneeling in front of that viper flashed again and again. A vise squeezed his temples. Blood pounded in his ears. No wonder Nora was confused. A snake in a suit had wheedled his way into the lives of these people. Even Levi had felt the pull of this preacher's magnetic words and powerful delivery.

"To each their own, Suh." That's what his father would have said. Right after he grabbed his children and whisked them away from whatever and whoever would lead them astray.

That Nora didn't wait for him at the van didn't surprise Levi. Nor did the fact that she beat him back to the tent. She had a mind of her own. She was past doing as she was told. She didn't understand that his anger was born of fear. Fear of losing her forever. Watching her stand on the precipice, certain she would jump or be pushed.

In a flash he had to say goodbye to cherished dreams. Nora feeding their baby in a rocker by the fireplace. Nora making gingerbread men with their daughters at Christmas. Nora brushing her long hair and then climbing into their shared bed every night. He'd been sure of those dreams, of their destiny, until that moment when reality pierced his dreams like a pin in a balloon.

He didn't dare let them come flooding back. Not yet. Not when his legs still shook and his heart still hammered against his rib cage.

He halted inside the tent within arm's reach of Nora. She stood stock-still, hands out. He followed her gaze. Jeannie rose with the others at the altar. Together they stood and turned to face the audience. Cheers bounced from the canvas ceiling. Wyatt played a song Levi didn't recognize. The lyrics said something about a good, good Father.

"Go to Daryl." Nora lifted her voice over the noisy exuberance of the crowd. "I'll try to get to Jeannie."

Now they were a team? Not to do as she said would be prideful. Levi dug his way past Grandpa, who seemed engrossed in the song, to Daryl, who held Sadie.

"What happened?" Levi leaned in and lifted his voice to be heard. "You couldn't stop her?"

"I should've seen this coming. I thought Nora would be the one, not my fraa." Disbelief warred with anger in Daryl's hoarse voice. "Nora's the one who plays with fire, not Jeannie, not my fraa."

Tears dripped from his chin. They darkened the collar of his Sunday best shirt. He didn't seem to notice. "I told Harley I'd watch over them. I failed her. I failed him. I failed my kinner." His voice broke.

"It's not too late. We'll take them home. Harley and Wilma will talk some sense into them both."

"I can't have her like this. She's broken her vows." His Adam's apple bobbed. "She'll have to go before the Gmay. She could be excommunicated."

The same was true of Nora, even though she hadn't gone through with Brubacher's terrible charade. She'd played musical instruments, sang with a band, driven a car, and those were just the infractions

Levi knew about. She'd taken vows to uphold the Ordnung and failed miserably, like a girl just starting out on her rumspringa.

"We have to try. If Jeannie admits her failings, she'll be forgiven."

Which meant Daryl would have to forgive her and go on as if nothing had happened.

Levi would have to do the same with Nora. Noah would say he had no choice. Levi wanted to forgive. He loved her. She'd violated the Ordnung, but at the last moment she'd stepped back from the worst infraction of all. That should count for something. "First things first. Let's get out of here."

Daryl shifted Sadie from his chest to the crook of his arm as he watched Nora talking to Jeannie. The two sisters had their heads together. Her hands moving, face crimson, Nora obviously wanted to convince Jeannie to leave.

Jeannie smiled and allowed herself to be led from the tent. Levi caught Nora's gaze as she stayed close to her sister in the crowded aisle. She jerked her head toward the door.

"We need to follow them." Daryl didn't move. Levi raised his voice over the excited chatter of the crowd. "Come, Daryl, let's go to your fraa."

"Jah, jah, we must go." Daryl hugged Sadie to his chest and allowed Levi to lead him outside.

Nora stood in front of Jeannie at a picnic table next to a concession stand where workers prepared hot dogs and hamburgers for the hungry worshippers. The smell, normally so inviting, turned Levi's stomach.

Daryl rushed ahead of him. He held out Sadie to his wife, who took her. "Your bopli, in case you've forgotten her."

"I've forgotten nothing."

"Only your vows, both baptismal and marriage."

"Accusations won't help," Nora intervened. She took Sadie from Jeannie. "I'll take the bopli so you two can talk." She brushed past

Levi and trudged toward the field where Jason and Missy picked weeds under Grandma's watchful eye.

"What did she say? Did you talk her into leaving?"

"Nee, she's sure they're right. Grandpa and the others have convinced her she must leave her old ways of worship behind. She's being ripped to pieces." Nora's voice cracked. "I know exactly how she feels. I'm not sure she didn't make the right choice. I'm not sure she's not braver than I am."

"Maybe you did the brave thing." Levi softened his tone. His anger had turned to ashes. It didn't help. It would only drive the wedge deeper. "Daryl blames you for her decision. He thinks you convinced her to do this and then chickened out yourself."

"I knew how she felt. I felt it too." Her voice quivered. "Her friend Samantha gave her a Bible. Jeannie's been attending Bible study with her. I don't know why I couldn't go through with it when she did."

"You didn't say anything to Daryl when you found out what she was doing?"

"She said she would tell him."

"Like you told me."

"It hasn't been easy. I've been trying to understand why our rules are so important." Nora rubbed Sadie's back in a soothing circular motion. How good that must feel. She probably had no idea she was doing it. "Onkel Ike, Aenti Roseanna, Tammy, and the others are Christians. They believe Jesus is the Son of God. That's not different from what we believe."

"They're Christian but not Plain." Levi picked his words with care. She teetered on the edge. With the slightest provocation she would plunge into the crater with Jeannie. "Our traditions are rooted in our history. Those from around here who have strayed from their roots expect us to do the same—or try to influence us."

Her forehead wrinkled, eyes worried, Nora's pace quickened. "I never questioned. I always felt safe and secure in our way of worship.

And then the fire happened and we came here. We always say God has a plan for us. What if this was His plan?"

Dangerous territory. They couldn't claim to know God's plan. "As long as we stick to Scripture we can't go wrong."

"Preacher Brubacher would tell you he sticks to Scripture."

"He puts on a show. He riles up people's emotions. Then he moves his circus to another town and leaves them to flop around on the ground like fish out of water. It's a flash in the pan, not something that lasts, not something built on a strong, steady foundation. Faith is something you live day after day, year after year, not something that magically appears because of a dog and pony show."

"I agree."

Did she just say that? "You do?"

"About the preacher, jah. But not about the desire for more. Many of these folks are already Christians. They're seeking a closer walk with Jesus, like the song says." With each word her voice gained strength. "Don't you ever feel a void in your life? Don't you ever want more?"

"More of what? I want to be a humble and obedient servant of God. I want to do His will." Levi summoned a patience he didn't feel. "I also want to be with you. Do you still want to be with me?"

She ducked her head. Her hand smoothed Sadie's hair. "I do, but we also learned to put faith first, then family. What if we no longer believe the same thing?"

A knot ballooned in Levi's throat. Because of this slimy serpent and his legion of followers, Levi's relationship with Nora would forever be fractured. The pain pulsed through him head to toe. His legs wanted to stop walking so his body could sink to the ground.

No. He had a job to do. Get her home to her family. Let them repair the damage that had been done. Nothing was more important than that. Not even his fractured heart.

He cleared his throat. "Let me take you to Eureka. We can talk to Noah." Getting her away from these influences had to be the priority. The emotions would fade. True faith would prevail. "We can work through this."

"What about Jeannie? I can't leave her and the kinner. I came here to help her. I knew she was going deeper and deeper into their ways, but I didn't say anything."

"That's on her mann, not on you."

"She's my schweschder."

If only he had an answer to the question wrapped around her plaintive statement. What would happen to Jeannie?

"I'm taking you home, one way or another. Your daed sent me to get you." The words didn't want to come. He had to tell her. She needed to know the consequences. She needed to understand why he had to tell the bishop. "If I don't, Noah and the others will come, and that will be much worse."

"They know?"

"Jah, they know."

"How?"

"I went to Noah for counsel. I didn't know what else to do—"

"You betrayed my confidence?" Anger warred with hurt on her face. Hurt won. It drew lines around her wide eyes and trembling lips. "How could you?"

"I needed his advice. He said I was right to tell him so we could get to you before it was too late. As it is, I barely made it."

"You're so sure you're right. How can you be so sure?"

By now they were only a few feet from Nora's grandmother and the children. "Esther, can you take the bopli?"

Her wrinkled face creased with sadness. "You're leaving?"

"Jah."

"And Jeannie?"

"I don't know."

Esther held out her arms. Nora didn't move. Her grandmother made a *tsk-tsk* sound. "Come, child, give her to me. All is not lost."

"How could this be Gott's plan? On top of everything else?"

"Who are you to know Gott's plan?" Her voice firm, Esther took the baby. "Young people think they know it all. You do not. Go home. Listen more, talk less."

Good advice for them all.

"Say goodbye to the little ones and go."

Nora went to Missy first. The little girl offered her a thistle. "Aenti, here's a flower for you."

"I have pretty rocks." Not to be outdone, Jason toddled over to Nora and dumped a small pile of pebbles in her hand. "Pick one, Aenti, pick one."

Her back to Levi, Nora prattled with her niece and nephew as if she hadn't a care in the world. Then she turned. Her eyes were bright with unshed tears. She lifted her chin. "We better go before it's too late to get a driver."

Silence so thick it would take an ax to cut it swelled between them as they walked back toward Daryl and Jeannie. The anger on Daryl's face was matched only by the stubborn insistence on his wife's. Music billowed from the tent. Wyatt Brubacher's voice carried with it. "What a Friend We Have in Jesus."

Jeannie whirled and marched into the tent. Daryl stalked away from it. Levi stepped into his path. "I'm taking Nora home. Are you coming?"

Daryl's gaze darted from Nora to the tent and then to Levi. "I'll not leave the kinner. I can't take them from their mudder. Especially the bopli. She's still nursing."

"Only until you can come back with the bishop and her daed."

"I never dreamed I'd have to make such a choice. A month ago I had a life. All was well." Daryl's voice broke. He hunched his shoulders and looked around as if seeking escape. "Take Nora home. Don't wait. Go. Now."

"I told Harley I would bring both his daughters home."

"Jeannie is my fraa. It's up to me. She has said she won't go. If I leave her now, the battle is lost. So I'll not go." He whirled and stumbled away.

Levi let him go. A man needed privacy to pull himself together in such a time as this.

✦✦✦

To leave without Jeannie and the kinner was unfathomable. Nora shook her head. "I'm not going without her."

"You're not the one to help Jeannie. That's obvious. You heard Daryl. He'll do whatever is necessary." Despite the sharp assuredness of his tone, Levi's gaze darted to the tent. He wanted to help Daryl, but he didn't trust Nora. That was obvious too. "Your daed and the bishop can come here to talk to her. This isn't over."

He'd gone to the bishop about her. He would do the same about Jeannie. The thought was like a caustic acid burning her skin. Levi claimed to love her, yet he had thrown her to the wolves and would do the same to her sister.

Accountability was more important to him. Even if it meant they couldn't marry. He couldn't marry a woman who was banned, could he?

"There you are, Nora!" Tammy's shrill voice carried over the crowd's excited chatter as picnic baskets came out and a concession stand opened. "Over here. You too, Levi."

Levi didn't turn around. His face tightened. "Nee. Don't go to her."

In moments like this his bossiness was understandable. Everything about his face, his stance, and his tone said he cared for Nora. His decision to tell the bishop about her sins still rankled. He didn't trust her, and she didn't trust him. "She's my kossin."

"She's poisoning you. She's making you doubt everything your parents taught you, everything you learned from attending services from the time you were a bopli." Levi edged closer, standing as a physical barrier between Nora and the walking temptation he saw in Tammy. "I'm telling you, if you love your family back home, don't go to her."

The agony molded his face into that of a much older man. It seeped into Nora. Pain held her captive. That he didn't mention their love was not lost on her. He believed he was doing the right thing, the best thing for her.

Levi took her hand. She jerked it back. His eyes smoldered with pain and grief. "Let's go home. Now. Right now."

No matter what happened between them, she had to go. She would not lose her family too. Her knees creaked when she stood. Spiritual conflict didn't simply bruise the soul, it aged the body. "Fine. I'll go."

"Nora! Where are you going?"

Nora couldn't help herself. She turned.

Her hair mussed, cheeks bright pink, eyes brilliant, Tammy had the same glowing countenance as Jeannie. Alive with the Holy Spirit.

Nora slowed.

Levi stepped into her path a second time. "Nee, you must not go back."

Why? Would she turn into a pillar of salt like Lot's wife? Why did the wives always get the short end of the stick? "I need to explain."

"Get in the van. I'll talk to her."

He didn't trust Nora to do it. She bowed her head. *Gott give me the strength to be the woman I should be.* The familiar words of Scripture learned in baptism class came to her. "*Wives, submit yourselves unto your own husbands, as unto the Lord. For the husband is the head of the wife, even as Christ is the head of the church: and he is the saviour of the body.*"

To Tobias's credit, he also read to them the verses that followed regarding the duty of a husband. *"Husbands, love your wives, even as Christ also loved the church, and gave himself for it."* And the other part that stuck in her mind. *"So ought men to love their wives as their own bodies. He that loveth his wife loveth himself."*

Words to live by. Levi had come for her. He didn't just love her passionately. He loved her soul. He might not be able to put words to those feelings, but his actions shouted love.

Even someone as inexperienced in love as she was could hear his unspoken words. In order to love him back, she would have to forgive him.

Gott, he means well. I know that. But his actions hurt. Help me to forgive him. Please. "Tell her I'll talk to her when they come to Kootenai to help rebuild. It won't be long."

He jerked his head in assent. "I'll get Joe. Wait in the van. Don't get out."

31

The air around the tent reeked of sweat, hot dogs from the concession stand, and holier-than-thou attitude. Levi needed a stick to draw a line in the proverbial sand. Instead, he simply approached Tammy and her cluster of friends with a smile firmly fixed on his face. Tammy's forehead furrowed, but she smiled back.

"What's going on? I wanted to buy you and Nora hot dogs. We're headed back to the church for band practice." Her head bobbing, she plucked an imaginary guitar. "You should hear Nora play the guitar. She's a natural. One lesson and she could play 'This Little Light of Mine' by ear."

"We're going home."

"Don't be that way." Tammy reached as if to touch his arm. Levi backed away. Her hand dropped. Her smile faded. "At least let us talk about what happened in the tent. It was probably overload for you because you didn't go to our services first, but give us a chance to talk about it. Come to church with us Sunday. You'll see."

"We don't need to talk. I don't need to see. We were baptized in the faith. We're gut. We don't need your help." His sarcasm burbled up above the surface on that last word.

"At least let me say goodbye."

"You'll see her again when your families come to Kootenai to help with the rebuild. It should be any day now."

Tammy's smile faded. She looked around. Tucker and the others were busy stuffing their faces. She stepped into his space. "I need to talk to her."

Entreaty mixed with something close to tears. This was more than Tammy not getting what she wanted. No doubt existed that she usually got what she wanted. But this was different. Levi shook his head. "I'm sorry. Don't you see it only makes it harder for her? Jeannie is staying. The kinner are staying. Nora only wants to do what is right. You make that hard."

Tammy chewed her lower lip. Her green eyes were liquid with tears. She fingered the hem of her blouse. "I understand."

Nobody really understood. Least of all Levi. He was no scholar. "I'm sorry."

"Don't be." She tossed her tangled hair over her shoulder and smiled. "Like the reverend says all the time, we plant seeds." Her voice quivered. "We're not always around to see them sprout."

"Could I bother your brother Joe to give us a ride to the house?" Levi didn't want to be mean. This felt mean. He cleared his throat. "He can bring the van back. We'll call a driver to take us home."

"Right this minute?"

"Right this minute." Right this second. "I'm sorry, Tammy."

"We're not contagious, you know."

He begged to differ, but he wouldn't argue. It wasn't the Plain way. "We'll wait at the van."

"Whatever."

Not whatever. Family ties were at stake. Souls were at stake.

✦✦✦

Nora slid into the van's middle seat and leaned her head back. From there she could see Grandma and the children. They danced around in a circle, holding hands and singing. Ring-around-the-rosy. With squeals of laughter they fell to the ground. Jeannie stood nearby, holding Sadie, laughing. As if nothing in the world bothered her.

That must be what it was like to believe Reverend Brubacher's words. To follow him to the far reaches. Even if they fell, they would go down laughing, unaware of the danger.

Tears pricked Nora's eyes. She gritted her teeth and swallowed. This wasn't over. Father and Mother would know what to do. Noah, Lucas, and Tobias would know what to do.

This wasn't goodbye forever.

She couldn't leave without trying one more time. Levi wasn't the boss of her. Not anymore. She jumped from the van and ran across the field.

Her smile blissful, Jeannie grabbed Sadie's hand and made her wave as Nora approached. "You're back. I thought Levi had taken you away."

Her sister was unrecognizable in her newfound happiness. Had Jeannie been unhappy before? Or had ignorance kept her from fulfillment?

"I wanted to talk to you again. I couldn't understand you before, when we came out of the tent. You were babbling."

"It was so amazing. You should've stayed. You wanted to stay. I could see it in your face. Were you afraid?" Jeannie spewed the words like an enthusiastic geyser. "Were you afraid of what Levi would say? It's worth it, Schweschder—"

"How do you know it's worth it?" Nora attempted to stanch the flow with reasoned logic. That's what Mother would do. Unlike Father, who would simply slam the door to the conversation. "What about Daryl? What about the kinner? Do you not want to live in Kootenai again? Is it worth giving up seeing your family regularly?"

Jeannie's glow didn't fade. She twirled Sadie around and dipped her. Sadie gurgled and crowed. "My sweet bopli is dancing with me." She dropped kisses on the baby's forehead. "Daryl will come around.

He loves me and the kinner. He wants what's best for them. He'll see that I'm right. You'll see."

"What if you're wrong?"

"You know I'm right. I can see it on your face." Jeannie's euphoria made her skin pink and her eyes sparkle. It made a plain woman pretty. "You're just afraid of what Daed will say. You're afraid of change, but you know what Pastor Brubacher said is Gott's truth. You know it in your heart."

"Jah, I thought about it, but then I thought about my baptism and the vows I made. I thought about the Gmay and how I promised to follow the rules—"

"You've broken many of the rules here. You drove a car. You played a musical instrument—"

"Don't throw that in my face. You've been attending Bible study." Nora drew a long breath. Noah said this would happen. They would cease to be a community when they all struck out on their own paths. Critiquing the Bible led to factions and caused discord. "Don't you see what this is doing to us? We're schweschders, we're family, we're part of a community. Are we so weak in our faith that we'll let this rip us apart?"

"Stop." Levi marched toward them. "I told you to wait in the van, Nora. Stop trying to convert her, Jeannie."

"She's my schweschder." Jeannie stood her ground. The old Jeannie would never have talked to a man that way. "I want what's best for her."

"Nee, you're being selfish. You've chosen your path. You want to take as many people with you as you can." Levi didn't raise his voice. He didn't rush his words. He reminded Nora of her dad. Steady and firm as a ponderosa pine. "You're a fraa and a mudder. Shame on you for dragging them into your folly."

"You've forgotten a basic tenet of our faith. You're not to judge." Jeannie nodded at Nora. "See you back at the house."

With great dignity she stalked toward her other children.

"She's right." Nora tested the waters. Could Levi find even a smidgen of good in this situation? "They say they're not judging or criticizing our ways. They only want everyone to be as close to Gott as they feel."

"I'm not judging her." Levi seemed entranced by Jeannie's progress. Missy and Jason ran to show her the treasures they'd collected. She oohed and aahed over them. Pain flittered across Levi's face. "I'm holding her accountable for the vows she took when she was baptized and when she was married. Someone needs to, and right now Daryl's not able to see clearly. He's been blindsided by this. He needs us to stand with him."

"Even though Jeannie is my schweschder."

"Jah, and even though you could barely contain yourself in there today."

He'd read her face, no doubt. "But I did."

"I'm thankful to Gott for that."

Keys jangling in his hands, Joe strode toward them. "Headed to Grandpa's then?"

"Nee, to find a driver who can take us to Eureka." Levi spoke first. "We'll pick up Nora's things another time."

Nora climbed into the van and scooted into the farthest corner of the seat. "Don't worry, they won't try to kidnap me. I won't run away. We can pick up my clothes."

"I just want to get on the road." His face crimson, he slid into the front seat next to Joe. "Your parents are anxious to get you back home. I don't want to keep them waiting."

He was right. Her dad would never pace the floor or show his angst. He would be Mother's rock. Even so, he would be just as worried about his daughters' standing in the Gmay as she was. "Let's go."

Dad had trusted Levi to bring her home. He'd done everything for her good. So why did it feel like betrayal?

32

Eureka, Montana

Sadness mingled with anger hung like low-lying storm clouds in the RV's humid interior. Nora fought the urge to list the reasons why she hadn't been able to convince Jeannie to come home. She almost hadn't come herself. Father stared through an open window, but his thoughts took him elsewhere, that was obvious. His face etched with pain and uncertainty, Levi sat at the tiny table. The trip home had been long and exceedingly quiet. She didn't dare speak, or hurt would've spilled out everywhere. Nora had trusted him, and he'd blabbed not only to her father but to Noah and the others. She needed time to figure things out, and he chose to cut that time short.

Because of him she sat here trying to find a way to make her parents understand what happened to Jeannie and almost happened to Nora. The boys had been glad to see her, but they couldn't hide their curiosity over what had occurred in Libby. They'd been allowed to go fishing in order to clear the room for this discussion.

Her eyes red, Mother busied herself making coffee and placing chocolate chip cookies on a plate.

Somebody say something.

No one did, leaving it up to Nora to find the right words. "I'm sorry, Daed. I tried to talk Jeannie into coming home, but we ended up arguing." She squeezed into the banquette as far from Levi as she could get in these cramped quarters. "I had my own quandary, it's true, but I chose my faith. I chose my family."

"She did, Harley. I saw how much pressure there was in that tent." Levi gave Nora a beseeching glance, then directed his gaze to her father. "The preacher was a serpent in a suit. Nora teetered, but she didn't fall. I'm thankful for that."

Father turned from the window and leaned against the kitchenette's narrow counter. "I'm thankful for that. I truly am." His eyes hard, he rubbed at his whiskered cheeks with both hands. "If Jeannie's own mann couldn't convince her, I don't know how you could be expected to. Daryl didn't notice his own fraa falling into their trap until it was too late. Then he didn't insist they all come home. He stayed. He never struck me as a person with much backbone."

"Harley!" Mother set mugs of steaming coffee in front of Levi and Nora. She added a miniature pitcher of milk and a bowl of sugar. "Be kind. Daryl is a hard worker. He is faithful. We couldn't ask for more."

"I've watched him for these six years. He is who he is." Father accepted his cup of coffee already fixed the way he liked it—a bit of milk and three heaping teaspoons of sugar. "I can't change who he is or who Jeannie married. I do know what I would do if it was my fraa."

Father and Mother exchanged glances. The air between them shimmered with heat and unspoken words. Mother smiled and ducked her head. Father needn't worry. In twenty-seven years of marriage, Nora's mother had learned how to bring him around to her way of thinking so deftly he rarely saw it coming.

"The question is, what do we do now?" Mother squeezed into the padded bench on the other side of the table and pushed a plate loaded with cookies toward Levi. "Word will spread. We'll have to meet with Noah, Lucas, and Tobias."

"There'll be talk of Meidung." Father spit the word out like it tasted bad. "The kinner will no longer be Plain. We'll see them on special occasions."

"What about Nora?" Levi posed the question foremost in Nora's mind. "She came back, but she also broke several rules while in Libby."

"I don't know." Father's expression held a mixture of bewilderment and pain. His gaze fell on Nora. "It's likely you'll have to meet with Noah. He may want you to make a confession. He certainly will want to counsel you."

"I know how it seems." Nora closed her eyes and opened them. "I love my family and my life here. I was confused. I still am. Jeannie's confused. There's still time to convince her. We could go with Noah to Libby to talk to her."

"You'll not go back to Libby." Father infused the words with deep certainty. "They've done enough damage to my kinner."

When would she see her nieces and nephew again? "I'm sorry, Daed. I meant no harm."

"I know you are, Dochder. I'm thankful you made the right choice. Noah will be too. But the fact remains that you violated the Ordnung." The lines on his face cut deep around his eyes and mouth. His shoulders slumped. He looked like Grandpa. "I'll talk to Noah tomorrow. I'll go with him to Libby. We'll do our best to bring them home."

Banging on the door drowned out Mother's response.

"Coming, coming." Father tromped to the front of the RV. "Hold your horses."

Father opened the door. Deputy Tim Trudeau stuck his head in. "Hey, everybody. We're spreading the good news. You can go home first thing tomorrow."

Quiet reigned for a few seconds. His face a big question mark, Tim lifted his cowboy hat and resettled it. "I know it's late and you're tired, but I expected a little more celebration. Did you hear what I said?"

"We did." Father clapped the other man on the shoulder. "It's really good news. Like you said, we're tired. And we were jawing about another problem that came up. But thanks for letting us know. We'll pack it up tomorrow and head home."

Home, sweet home. Hallelujah. Nora sucked in air and let it out. It felt like her first breath in a month.

They were blessed to have a home to which they could go. *Danki, Gott. Praise You.*

Was God still listening to her? Was he disappointed in her? She'd resisted the final temptation, but that didn't erase her earlier transgressions or her inability to reach Jeannie.

"Would you like to come in for some kaffi?" Mother rose and picked up the glass carafe that came with the RV's fancy electric coffeemaker. "It's fresh. So are the cookies."

"Thanks, ma'am, but I need to get home. You're my last stop." Dark circles around his eyes told Tim's story. The sheriff's deputies were all working double time during this fire season, plus they had their own families to worry about. "I don't want to fall asleep on the road between here and Libby."

"All the more reason to take some coffee."

"Yes, ma'am."

Mother bustled around the kitchen, likely relieved to have something to do. She produced a travel mug and poured the rest of the steaming coffee into it. The mug and cookies wrapped in a napkin went to Father, who handed them to Tim. He thanked them, and with a wave he disappeared again.

"I should get home, too, and let you folks get some sleep." Levi stood and edged his way down the narrow aisle to the door. "Tomorrow is a big day. Will you go to Kootenai first, or do you still want to go to Libby?"

His expression glum, Father tossed his straw hat on the miniature couch. He ran both hands through his flattened hair so it stood on end. "Kootenai first. We owe it to the others to be there to plan the rebuilding. I can take the news to Libby when I go."

"Do you want company?"

"Nee. You did what you could." Father's face smoothed. "I appreciate you trying."

"I'd better get going then." Levi stood. Joe had dropped him off at the Rabers' rental house so Levi could get his horse and buggy. He would be home in a matter of minutes. "It's a relief to know tomorrow we'll be in our own homes."

"Those of us who have homes to go to." Father's statement summed up what they all thought.

Levi paused at the door. He shoved his hat back on his head. "Gut nacht, then."

Mother and Father responded. Nora opened her mouth, but no words came out. She couldn't act as if nothing had happened. Levi had simply chosen sides. Knowing the consequences, he made a beeline for those who could bring her missteps to the entire Gmay.

For her own good.

He deserved to be forgiven.

Ignoring her father's testy grunt, Nora picked up her coffee cup and went to the sink to wash it. Her back to her parents, she gripped the counter with both hands. If only she could wash the sour taste from her mouth. Of one thing she was sure—she didn't want to live in this new world without Levi. He had done what he thought was best. So had she. Learning to compromise came with marriage. With time they would learn.

A lonely silence assailed Nora.

"You must be tired, Dochder." Mother bustled to the counter. "It's been a long day. The boys put up your tent. Why don't you get some sleep? There will be much to do tomorrow."

It would be nice to get away from her thoughts. She'd probably dream about Libby. "I don't think I can sleep."

"I'll make you some hot chocolate. Sit at the picnic table and read a book. It'll help you relax."

"You know your mudder." Father plopped onto the couch and stretched out his legs. "She thinks food and drink can fix everything. I wish it were so."

"I'll make you some hot chocolate, too, Mann." Mother made a shooing motion. "Go on, Nora, I'll bring it to you. Tomorrow will be a gut day. You'll both see."

"Danki, Mudder."

Mother patted her shoulder. "Everyone makes mistakes."

A hard lesson—one Nora seemed to have to learn over and over.

33

Even a good book couldn't make it better. Nora inhaled the scent of hot chocolate and buttoned her coat. The kerosene lamp on the picnic table cast plenty of light for reading the novel by Elizabeth Byler Younts that Christine had given her for her birthday in August. Still, she didn't open it. An escape into a story would be nice. A relief. Instead, she stared into the darkness, trying to discern a future where Jeannie and Daryl joined the ranks of family members not allowed to worship with her. And those sweet babies. They would grow up in another world, even though Libby was only an hour away.

Almost two hours had passed since Levi's retreat. The boys were asleep in their tent, oblivious to the night noises in Eureka's largest RV park. Nora should sleep too. Instead, competing problems clashed in her brain. Problem number one: Jeannie's decision to embrace the Eagle Valley Ministry's way of life and Daryl's decision to allow her to do it. Problem number two: her pending discussion with Noah and Tobias. What could she tell them that wouldn't make her situation worse? She couldn't truly say she was sorry for the things she'd done. It would be a lie. She was sorry for the hurt and shame her actions had caused her parents. Problem number three: Levi's decision to tell Noah about her behavior after she'd asked him not to.

She laid the book aside and picked up her mug of hot chocolate. Mother had added lots of marshmallows to Nora's. No matter how upset they were, her parents forgave. Pure and simple.

Life had been so simple before the fire and before Libby. Nora wanted that life back. She'd been ignorant of life outside her tiny world. Grandpa would say innocent, not ignorant. Why couldn't Levi see that? There was something to be said for the wisdom that came with age. Levi needed to acquire some wisdom quickly, or it would be too late for them. To be fair, so did Nora.

A car engine rumbled in the distance. Gradually it grew louder. It sounded so familiar, but it couldn't be. That car should be parked at Ike Beachy's house outside Libby. Besides, no one usually gallivanted about at night in Eureka. The residents were early to bed and early to rise because they worked and their children went to school.

Nora scooted around on the bench so she could see the road that intersected the RV park. The car came into view. Against all odds, Joe Beachy's silver four-door sedan had come to Eureka. Did Wyatt still have it on loan?

Wyatt would not come to visit her. He'd moved on to the next prayer service, the next tent revival, the next person in need of saving.

The car slowed. It stopped. The passenger window rolled down. Tammy's face appeared. "Is that you, Nora?"

"Tammy?"

"Oh, thank You, Jesus." Tammy's voice quivered. "I had no idea how I would find you in an RV park in the dark."

"What are you doing here?"

The window rolled up. Tammy pulled the car into a slot off the road. The engine died. She emerged a few seconds later, trudged to the picnic table, and collapsed on the bench across from Nora. "You have no idea how happy I am to see you."

Nora leaned to her right so she could take another peek at the car. "You came by yourself?"

"I did. I drove all the way from Libby by myself." Pride mingled with surprise on her flushed face. "Is that hot chocolate? Can I have a sip?"

Nora pushed the mug in her cousin's direction. Tammy sipped. She sighed. Her hands clasped the mug as if they were cold.

Still, Nora waited for an explanation.

"Do you remember when we went camping that time and we roasted marshmallows over the campfire?" She dabbed at a miniature marshmallow with the long fingernail on her index finger. It bobbed in the hot chocolate. "I ate too many of them and threw up all over my sleeping bag."

"*My* sleeping bag, you mean." Nora smiled at the memory. "We always made s'mores when we went camping, but that time you ate almost a whole bag of the big marshmallows."

"I miss being a kid." Tammy moved the mug to one corner of the table. She laid her head on the rough, weathered wood. "I want to go back. Can we just go back?"

However nice, it was impossible. Tammy's words echoed Nora's thoughts from only moments ago. Like homesickness. They weren't kids camping. She couldn't go back, and neither could Tammy. "We had some gut times, didn't we? But now you can drive. You can work in the store. You can court with Wyatt. You can do grown-up things."

"That's the problem." Tammy straightened. Tears on her cheeks glistened in the lamplight. "Wyatt and I did something we shouldn't have. There's no taking it back, and now I'm going to pay for it."

"Did something else happen?"

"I'm pregnant," she whispered. "I'm pregnant with Wyatt's baby."

Not possible. Simply not possible. Life could twist and turn around until a person couldn't recognize it. Nora's hands smoothed the book's cover while her mind scrambled to rearrange the pieces so they resembled something understandable. Tammy and Wyatt, two people who professed to love Jesus and to have this close walk with Him, had given in to temptation. Now every decision they contemplated must take into account this small life they'd created.

Nora's mind groped for wise words and found the cupboard bare. Tammy stared at her with big eyes red from crying. Her lips were dry and cracked. Strands of her tangled honey-blonde hair hung in her face, escapees from a drooping ponytail.

Tammy was waiting for a life raft to descend into stormy waters. Nora had none. Not that Plain girls didn't find themselves in this situation. They did, but no one talked openly about it. A quick, quiet wedding ensued. Old ladies whispered to one another at quilt or canning frolics. They counted on their fingers.

Imagining herself in this situation, Nora ignored the wave of nausea that swept over her. A few times she and Levi had come close, but they never crossed the line. Whether it had been her restraint or Levi's that walked them back, she couldn't say. Or God simply knew about another wildfire that would tear them apart and stepped between them. "Have you told Wyatt? What does he say?"

"He's gone with his father to Wyoming. I used Grandpa's phone to call his cell, but I got his voice mail. I told him I needed to talk to him. I don't know when he's coming back. He didn't say." Tears meandered down Tammy's cheeks and dripped on her shirt. "I'm so scared."

"How do you know for sure?"

"I waited until Mudder went to the store, and I did a home pregnancy test."

Home pregnancy tests were foreign territory. Nora nodded and tried to look sage. "So you know for sure, that's gut."

"Nee, it's not," Tammy wailed. "What am I going to do?"

"Have a bopli." As if there were another choice. None existed in Nora's world. It didn't seem likely that a professed Christian like her cousin had any other choice either. "Boplin are gifts from Gott, no matter how they come to be or when or where."

"I know." Tammy dug a crumpled tissue from her jeans pocket and blew her nose. "I never thought this would happen to me. I know better. Daed and Mudder taught me better."

"It's hard." The memory of Levi's hands on her waist and his lips on hers sent a volley of shivers through Nora. She would never judge her cousin. "You love each other. You'll get married. Wyatt is a gut man. You'll be happy together."

The wailing turned into sobs.

"Ach, I'm no gut at this." Nora whipped around to Tammy's side and slid onto the bench. She hugged her cousin's shaking body close. "It'll be fine. You'll be fine."

"Nee. I told Wyatt I loved him. He never said it back." Tammy hiccuped a sob. "What if he doesn't want to marry me? He likes traveling all over the country. What kind of life would it be for a fraa and a bopli to live on a bus?"

"You do what you have to do." Easy for Nora to say. She'd never been farther than Missoula in her entire life. "I reckon your daed knows when they're coming back. Ask him."

"He'll take one gander at my face and he'll know."

"You'll have to tell him sooner or later."

"Not until I see Wyatt's reaction. I have to know where he stands on this first."

She wouldn't be able to wait too long. "Do they know you're here?"

"Nee. I borrowed Joe's car while they were at Daadi's house. They went to talk to Jeannie and Daryl."

The ache under Nora's breastbone returned fivefold. "How are they?"

"Jeannie is happy and sad and scared and lonely and sure she's doing the right thing. Daryl mopes around like he's trying to figure out what hit him."

"I miss her and the kinner already."

"What about Levi? Is he still mad?"

Mad, hurt, bewildered, aggravated. All of the above. "He says we need time to think."

"So what do you think?"

"He told the bishop about my transgressions after I begged him not to. I'm mad and hurt and confused. Just like he is."

Tammy leaned her head on Nora' shoulder. "Now you know why I wish I could be a kid again."

She'd done womanly things. No going back.

The RV door squeaked. Tammy shot upright. "What was that?"

"Is that you, Nora?" Mudder peered at them. She looked younger without her glasses. "Who are you talking to?"

"It's me, Aenti Wilma. Tammy."

"What are you doing here?" Mother padded down the steps in moccasin slippers. "It's the middle of the night."

Ten o'clock, but close enough. "Tammy needed to talk to me."

"Is everything all right? Is Jeannie okay? The kinner?"

"All asleep by now, snug as bugs at Mammi's house." Tammy dabbed at her face with the tissue. "You don't have to worry about them. The whole community will embrace them."

Mother's scowl deepened. "Does your mudder know you're here?"

"I left her a note."

"You're too old to run away from home." Mother utilized the same tone with Tammy that she did with her own children. "Better get some sleep, Nora. We'll head to Kootenai come first light."

Whether that included Tammy remained to be seen. Mother disappeared inside. The door shut with another squeak.

"I guess that was the wrong thing to say." Tammy huddled close to Nora. "It's all such a mess. Shouldn't she be glad Jeannie gave her life to Jesus today?"

"She did that a long time ago when she was baptized."

"I'm too tired to argue." Tammy laid her head on Nora's shoulder. "Can I stay here tonight?"

"Of course you can. Tomorrow's another day."

For both of them.

34

A new day, a new start. The truth of that cliché depended on a person's perspective. Nora didn't dare complain. Today she would return to her home while the Yoders and the Knowleses, Caleb, Andy, and others would return to a pile of ashes and debris where their homes once stood.

Careful not to wake Tammy, who still snored softly under Nora's favorite Chain of Fools quilt, she slipped into the RV. Mother would want to feed everyone before they headed to West Kootenai. The boys could disassemble the tents while Nora and Mother made breakfast.

Mother stood at the counter making coffee. "Gut, you're up." She whispered even though Father wasn't in the nearby bed, which meant he was in the bathroom. "Why is Tammy here? The real reason."

No morning greeting, no lighthearted chatter—straight to the nitty-gritty.

The tight quarters didn't give Nora much room to dodge the question. She would never lie to her mother. Yet it didn't seem right for Mother to know before Wyatt and before Tammy's own parents. "She needed advice."

"Is she thinking of leaving that church?"

Such a question would tickle Tammy. Mother had no way of

knowing that. Nora scrambled for a way to explain without revealing too much. "Nee. She's in a bad situation."

"Tell me she's not in a family way."

Did all mothers have this ability to ferret out the truth and unlock secrets? "How did you know?"

"I've seen that look of desperation on more than one girl's face over the years." Mother poured steaming coffee into three mugs. "Does Ike know?"

"No one knows but Tammy and me."

"Not even the father? She has to tell him."

"It's a hard situation."

"He's not from the community?" Mother's soft *tsk-tsk* didn't hold judgment, rather dismay at what her niece now faced. "My heart would be broken."

Ike and Roseanna would surely be heartbroken at their daughter's sinful ways, but whether they objected to Wyatt not being Amish wasn't clear. At least not to Nora. They opened their church doors to everyone. Wyatt was the son of a good friend. A man they admired. "Tammy's scared."

"I can imagine."

"She wants to stay, at least for today."

"Who's staying?" Father squeezed through the narrow bathroom door and shut it behind him. "Did we hear something from Jeannie or Daryl?"

"Nee. Your kaffi is ready." Mother edged past Nora to place the mug on the table. "Tammy is visiting."

"Our dochder is in Libby, and Ike's dochder is here with us?" Father mussed his already wild bed hair with both hands. "What is going on? Does she have news of them, then?"

"She says they're doing fine. She's spending the day. She'll help us move back in." Mother held up a skillet. "How do you want your eggs?"

"Like I always want them, Fraa. Over easy." He dumped more sugar in his coffee and stirred. "What's going on here? What are you two trying to hide?"

Father already thought of Tammy as a bad influence. This would be the final straw. Nora sought her mother's gaze. Mother lifted one finger and shook it. "Nora, go make sure the boys are up. Tell them to take down the tents. I'll bring out breakfast when it's ready."

Relief nearly bowled Nora over. She didn't need to be told twice. She grabbed her coffee and hustled to the door. Mother's words carried over the squeak of the door. ". . . in a family way."

Her face pale in the first light of dawn, Tammy stood outside the tent. She wrapped her arms around her middle. "You told them, didn't you?"

"I had to. I can't lie to Mudder."

"Do I have to leave?"

"They're your aenti and onkel. They won't judge you."

The door opened and Mother flew down the steps. "Tammy, your mudder will be beside herself if you don't get home." She held out a paper sack. "I made you a scrambled egg and toast sandwich. Eat it before you start driving. Be careful on the road. So many of the tourists don't know where they're going. They'll run right over you."

"Mudder—"

"Daed doesn't feel it's right for us to keep Tammy here." Mother lifted her hand to her face to shield it from the rising sun. "Her parents need to know what's going on. It's best to get these things out in the open quickly and deal with them."

"I'll tell them." Tammy swallowed hard. Her hands went to her stomach. "I don't think I can eat eggs, but danki, Aenti."

"Eat some saltine crackers with Sprite. Stop at the gas station on 93 before you head out." Mother hugged Tammy hard. "You'll be okay. Gott forgives and so must we. But you have to go home and face them. Running away only makes it worse."

"I needed to think." Tammy didn't budge from Mother's arms. "I needed Nora to help me think."

"Sometimes a person can think too much. Now that you've thought, go home, tell your parents, and tell the bopli's father."

To her credit, Mother didn't seem even mildly curious to know who he was.

"I'm sorry. I shouldn't have come." Tammy hugged Nora. "I didn't mean to make trouble for you."

"You didn't." Nora hugged her back and whispered, "You'll be back to help with the Libby crew that comes to help rebuild. We'll talk then. Mercy and Christine and Juliette will be there. We'll have an ASAP meeting."

"If Daed doesn't make me stay in my room for the rest of my life."

"It'll be okay. Talk to Jeannie. She'll be kind. I know she will."

So would Grandma Esther. She wouldn't approve, but she loved Tammy and she would love the baby the same way she loved all of her grandchildren.

Her face wet with tears, Tammy stumbled to her car. She opened the door and tossed the paper sack on the seat. "Talk to you soon."

"Be careful." Nora trailed after her. Nothing she wanted to say could be uttered in front of Mother. They would see each other soon, God willing. And if Father was willing. And Uncle Ike. So many obstacles. They were family and yet divided by faith. Her throat clogged with tears. Hands gripped behind her back, Nora swallowed. "No speeding, and be sure to stop at every stop—"

"This from the girl who wrecked Grandpa's van." Tammy attempted a hoot, but it came out in a fizzle. "See you soon."

If only they had cell phones. Sixty miles seemed like six hundred. Not knowing how Wyatt would respond might make Nora crazy. "Write me a letter. A long letter."

Tammy waved and slid into the car. The engine turned over the second time, and she pulled away.

"It's time to put the tents away."

Mother hadn't moved from the steps.

"How can you send her away like that?" Nora fought to keep her tone one that a daughter should use for her mother. "She's really hurting."

"Imagine how her parents would feel if we didn't send her home." Mother tugged her ragged green sweater tighter across her ample belly, as if the early morning wind chilled her. Or maybe it was the thought of how she would respond if it were her daughter. "Ike and Roseanna need to know what their daughter is doing. And with whom."

Again, perspective was everything. Nora went to work on the tent.

"I know you're hurting too." Mother moved to the picnic bench and sat. "You were thrown into a situation you weren't prepared for. We didn't teach you to defend your faith. That is our failing."

"So you forgive me for what I did in Libby?"

"I do. Ultimately you did the right thing. You chose your faith and your family, despite the pressure brought to bear by people you care about. That shows strength of character."

"Daed doesn't think so."

"He's upset. He's worried about what Noah will say. He's worried about Jeannie and the boplin. When he calms down he'll recognize that you did something courageous by leaving. You're stronger than your big schweschder."

"I don't feel strong."

"You are. Because you are strong, you need to be the first to apologize. You need to tell Levi you're sorry for what you put him through. Assure him that you will be the fraa he wants."

"I'm not sure that it's possible anymore." Not so long ago, being Levi's wife was all she wanted in life. To be the wife he wanted now seemed a tall order. "He tattled on me to Noah and Tobias."

"Tattled? You're not a child, Nora. You're a grown woman who broke more than one rule you vowed to hold sacred." Mother didn't raise her voice. Somehow that made her words sting even more. "Levi did what he's supposed to do. He held you accountable for your own gut. He didn't want to lose you to that church. And neither do I."

"So much of what Tammy and Wyatt said made sense." The censure in her mother's voice sliced through Nora like a finely honed carving knife. "Have you ever talked to Daadi or Onkel Ike about what they believe?"

"Of course, your daed did. He had many conversations with them both. He tried with all his heart to change their minds. He spoke with the bishop at that time and with the other elders." Mother rose and paced between the table and the tents. "They talked and talked and talked until everyone was sick of it. Do you think you know more than they do? Are you smarter or wiser?"

"Nee, nee. I didn't mean that." Nora clutched the tent canvas to her chest. "I listened and I tried to make sense of it. I only wanted to be closer to Gott. Is that wrong?"

"Nee, it's not wrong as long as you don't put yourself on the throne in Gott's place. He's on the throne. Not you."

"You don't believe we can have a closer walk with Gott?"

"I don't know what that means."

Exactly Nora's thought the first time she heard the phrase. "But it sounds wunderbarr, doesn't it?"

Mother's face crumpled. She patted her face with her apron. "It sounds like a wolf in sheep's clothing came very close to taking both of my dochders."

"But I came home. I chose my faith. Levi didn't trust me to do that. He told Noah about me when I asked him not to."

"So you learn from your mistakes—both of you. You turn to each other in hard times. Marriage takes work. Your daed and I didn't always have the marriage we have now. We went through a long season of loss, grief, turmoil, and hurt. We couldn't understand why it was happening to us. Sometimes we blamed each other. Sometimes we stopped talking. Or we argued. But in the end we stayed the course."

A pole in her hand, Nora stared at her mother. She never spoke of baby Amelia or of her feelings. "You're talking about Amelia?"

"It started before that. Before you were born. I had two miscarriages between Jeannie and you." Mudder's gaze grew distant. The fine wrinkles on her face deepened. "Then you came along, and we were sure we'd weathered the storm. You were a toddler when we lost two more. We thought we were done with this torment, but no. When you were six, I carried Amelia to term, only to have her die in my arms."

"I know. I remember."

"I couldn't bear the thought of going through it again. Nor could your daed." The pain marred her face as if it were brand-new. "I had you and Jeannie. I tried to convince myself that was enough, but I knew your daed longed for boys, and I longed to give him the desire of his heart."

"I don't remember you ever arguing or even seeming sad. Daed told funny stories by the fireplace and played checkers and Animal Farm with us. He joked at the supper table and tickled us. He gave me horseback rides and taught us songs."

"Gott's will be done."

The words of a faithful woman who'd clawed her way through a dense forest of agony, loss, grief, and despair.

"Then came James."

"Two years went by, and then came James. I prayed and prayed day after day, night after night. I worked so hard not to get too excited. I worked so hard not to worry. To trust, no matter what happened. When I held his plump, rosy body in my arms and he bellowed to be fed, it felt like I breathed for the first time in nine months."

"You were giddy. You kept giggling. Daed had a silly grin that lasted for days."

"Now you know why."

"Why have you never talked about it?"

"No sense in it. Until now." Mudder drew a long breath. "I never wanted to dwell on that time. It was a dark cloud that followed us around for years, but we never gave up on each other or Gott. We became seamless, each cleaving to the other, hands clasped, finding our way together. That's what marriage vows are about. That's what you and Levi must be about. I don't know who the father of Tammy's bopli is, and I don't want to know. A bopli is a gift from Gott. No matter what happens next, she has been given a gift."

"She knows."

"She also needs a gut friend."

"I know."

Mother rose and trotted to the RV. "It's a big day. I'll get breakfast going. Finish with the tents and come help me."

The talk was over. She closed the door with a firm snap.

Atlee's head popped through the flaps of the tent he shared with James and Menno. "Hey, what's all the jawing about?"

"Nothing. It's time to get up."

"It's too early in the morning for so much talking."

No, it was just the right time. Nora ignored her brother and went back to breaking down tents. She had thinking to do and then more talking. With Levi.

35

West Kootenai, Montana

The house still stood, but it hadn't come through the fire unscathed. Nora shoved open one window after another to let the wind blow through the one-story sprawling cabin. It didn't help much. The stench of destruction permeated everything. Curtains, bedding, and any clothing left in the house would have to be washed. Father and the boys would repaint all the walls. The drive through Kootenai had made clear one thing for sure. They were blessed to still have a house. Heaps of ashes and mangled rubble were all that were left of Mercy's and Juliette's houses, along with many others. Rebuilding the community would take time.

Buildings could be rebuilt, but could relationships scarred by the events of the last month also be restored? Nora carried a pile of curtains to the laundry room. The sound of the boys calling to each other outside floated through the window. She stopped to stare at the mountains. For her entire life she'd stared out that window at the endless forest of Douglas firs, ponderosa pines, and larches that crept up the mountains toward the heavens. God's art. She'd taken it for granted. Now grotesque swaths of blackened earth scarred the landscape. Trees were reduced to blackened rows of sticks.

Daed said they weren't dead. They would come back. In the

spring, green tendrils would pop out from the ground and the cycle would begin again.

Could the same be true for families torn apart by the flames of religious oration?

Could relationships sprout from the ruins?

Or had the flames of dissension scorched them beyond recognition so that no one would ever be the same?

She closed her eyes and bowed her head.

"What are you doing?"

They'd come full circle. A month ago Mother had stood in the bedroom door and asked that same question. Now she stood in the kitchen doorway, a box in her arms, her expression quizzical.

"Praying."

Mother hoisted the box onto her hip. "Are you done?"

"I'm done."

"Gut, gut. Here's a box of cleaning supplies." She settled the enormous produce box on the table with a thump. "The buckets should still be in the laundry room. Start a load of towels first before you start cleaning. The curtains can wait. It's so gut to be home. I can't wait to get every room cleaned and everything back in its place."

"Me too. I can't wait to sleep in my own bed in my own room."

"It won't be the same knowing that Jeannie and the boplin aren't going to pop in for supper or invite us over to visit." Her chin quivered, but she sniffed and raised her head higher. "Gott's will be done."

"No one is giving up on them coming home. Jeannie knows she will have a choice." Nora pulled a big sponge from the box. "If they don't come back right away, we'll still see them from time to time, just like we do Onkel Ike and the rest of them."

It wouldn't be the same. Nothing would ever be the same.

"It's the kinner's faith that worries me the most." Mother handed Nora a huge bottle of clothes soap. "Even though I know worrying is wrong. My faith is weak."

"You and Daed have the strongest faith I know. Daryl will keep working to bring them home."

The back door opened and Father tromped through. Following behind him were Noah and Tobias.

Nora's moment of truth had arrived.

"I figured we best get this over with so we can focus on rebuilding." Noah spoke first. He had his bishop face on. His lips pursed and his eyebrows lifted. His church voice rumbled from deep in his chest. "We don't want to let these transgressions simmer too long. They tend to grow like weeds and spread."

That he referred to her behavior seemed almost surreal. Her mouth suddenly dry, Nora swallowed hard and nodded.

"Have a seat, have a seat." Noah acted as if they were in his house. He waved at the chairs around the kitchen table. "Harley, Wilma, you should go about your business. Nora is a grown woman. She must answer for herself."

Mother cast one last anxious glance at Nora. She tried to convey a reassuring smile in return, but her mouth refused to work. Mother's hands fluttered. "I could get you some coffee and cookies first—"

"Nee, Fraa. Let's go." Father took Mother's arm and led her from the kitchen. She kept glancing back, but he didn't let go.

"Do you understand why you're here?" Noah dove in. "Why we're concerned?"

"Jah. I broke the rules." Nora refused to lower her gaze. "I'm expected to make a free will confession for my *fehlas*."

"You're expected to, or you want to?' Tobias leaned back in his chair and crossed his arms. "A free will confession means exactly that."

"I'm still working my way through what happened and why." Nora drew a long breath and tried to calm the quaking that threatened to shake her from her chair. "I still have many questions, but I came back because I stand by my baptismal vows. I put my faith and my family first."

"That's a gut start. We praise Gott that you made the right decision." Noah studied her with a gaze so piercing, Nora was certain he drew blood. "Tell us what your failures were."

Shame sparred with a rebellious spirit. Nora silently shushed them both. "I drove and crashed my daadi's car. I played a musical instrument. I tried on Englisch clothes. I danced. I considered changing my way of worshipping to one at odds with the one I chose when I was baptized."

The litany of infractions spoken aloud sounded so much worse with her district elders as an audience. Neither spoke for several seconds, as if allowing her to hoist with her own petard.

"It's true technically that these are your fehlas," Tobias said finally. "But this is a listing of your actions, not the intent behind them. You have a rebellious spirit. You questioned our faith and the way we practice it. You think maybe it's not so bad to drive a car or play an instrument. What's the big deal, right? That's much more concerning."

Nora clasped her hands in her lap and allowed her nails to dig into her skin. He was right. The actions themselves meant less than her attitude toward them. "I found their arguments very persuasive, it's true, but I stopped short. I came home."

"Why?"

Why indeed? Because she didn't want to hurt her parents. Because she couldn't imagine her life without her family. Because of Levi.

Those weren't the reasons Noah wanted to hear.

Nora picked at a ragged cuticle. She cleared her throat. Still she couldn't find the words.

"Nora?" Noah spoke her name with a gentleness that caused tears to clog her throat. He laid both his hands on the table as if reaching out to her. "We don't want you to tell us what you think we want to hear. We're asking you to search your heart. We're asking you to cling to the values and beliefs that you vowed to keep when you were baptized. Can you do that? Or had they convinced you that theirs is a better way before you ever attended one of their services?"

"Nee, and I won't."

Noah raised his hand to his beard and smoothed it, but his gaze said he wasn't aware of the action. "It's best to avoid temptation. I choose not to engage in a tussle with your onkel Ike and the others. Better men than I did to no avail when they left the Gmay. I don't judge how they worship. I'm only asking that they give us the same respect. We're no less faithful than they are."

"They say we're chained by our rules and rituals. That they have a closer, more personal walk with Jesus. It sounds so gut, so special, when they explain it."

"Yet when you approached that altar and fell to your knees, you knew something wasn't right. You didn't just walk away. You ran."

"How do you know that?"

"Levi came to see me last night."

"Levi's the one who told you about my transgressions."

"Jah, but this time he came to tell me of your faithfulness. How did you think we found out you were back? He saw how deeply troubled you were and what a temptation it was to give in. But you didn't. You resisted. He wanted me to know that you showed great strength in walking away from this temptation."

Levi had spoken up on her behalf. Tears demanded release. Nora fended them off. "I know there's room for more than one way to worship. I choose our way. I choose a living hope of salvation. I choose humility and obedience. I know it's not about me."

"I'm glad to hear that." Noah smiled for the first time. "Our faith is honed by testing. Scripture tells us so. I'm thankful you chose to come home. Your family loves you. Your community cares for you. Never forget that."

"I know, and I am blessed," Nora whispered. "Truly blessed."

"These last few weeks have been trying for everyone. Our world has been turned upside down." Tobias's tone softened. "People older, wiser, and more experienced in these things have been shaken by their circumstances. We recognize this and pray for Gott's forgiveness for all of us."

His conciliatory words eased the pain in Nora's chest. "I pray that Gott's will be done."

"We all do. We will have counseling sessions in the coming weeks. I don't see any necessity of public confession, as you have made a free will confession to us." Noah pushed back his chair and stood. "Tell your daed that we'll go to Libby next week to speak to Daryl and Jeannie. We'll get back to him on the day and time."

After they left, Nora remained seated. She needed a drink of water, but she was afraid her legs would give out if she stood. They had been kind. It could have been so much worse. She'd been given a pass. They had shown compassion she didn't deserve. Censure tempered by love and caring.

She closed her eyes and let the quiet wash over her. Levi had spoken to Noah a second time, this time on her behalf. Because of him, they would give her another chance. He truly wanted what was best for her.

"They're gone then." A broom in one hand and a mop in the other, Mother hustled into the room. "Is everything all right?"

Nora recapped the conversation, ending with Noah's promise to go to Libby in the coming week. The worry drained from Mother's face, leaving it pale and tired. "Praise Gott. Now if only they can get through to Jeannie. I would go myself, but your daed won't let me." Mother leaned on the broom as if it were a crutch. "I wake up in the morning, and just for a second I think I'll run over to their house so I can hold the bopli and sing to Missy and teach Jason how to write his name. Then I remember." Her voice cracked.

"I'm so sorry, Mudder. I wish we'd never gone to Libby."

"The house won't clean itself." Mother's no-nonsense voice was back. "We'd better get busy."

"After I get the laundry going, I need to run an errand, if that's all right." An errand that couldn't wait. "It'll only take a few minutes. I'll be right back."

"I'd rather you didn't go far. It's a mess out there." Mother grabbed a bucket from under the sink and filled it with water. "The store's not open. The school's closed. Everyone is still regrouping."

"I just need to see something for myself. It's nearby."

"The house? The one you planned to buy?" Mother's tone was kind, but she shook her head. "It's better not to wallow in what can't be helped."

"I'm not wallowing. I need to meditate on the error of my ways."

"Gut for you." Despite red eyes and tear streaks on her cheeks, Mother managed a smile. "You'll see it's not forever, only postponed."

Mother's optimism buoyed Nora. They could all use an extra dose of optimism on a day that had been spent tallying losses and beginning to pick up the pieces. This was another step on the road to forgiving and being forgiven.

Nora filled the wringer washing machine, added soap, and used a hose to fill it with water. The familiar back-and-forth *chug-a-chug-a-chug-a-chug* soothed her nerves. Drying her hands on her apron, she trotted outside and climbed into the buggy Father had left by the front door after a quick trip to talk to the Knowleses about their construction timetable. Juliette's family was first up on the rebuild schedule.

The *clip-clop* of Checkers's hooves on the hard-packed dirt road only served to remind her of all the buggy rides she and Levi had taken together. Which led to all the times he'd parked in the shade and kissed her so thoroughly she couldn't remember what day it was. She would've been hard-pressed to remember her name.

Nora wanted more of those moments. She also wanted to hike

the mountain trails with him, fish, and pick berries. Pain wrapped itself around her chest and squeezed. She couldn't breathe.

She pulled into the cement driveway that no longer led to a two-car garage. A blackened pile of ashes and curled metal lay in the middle of the seared plot of land. Her roomy two-story, four-bedroom, two-bath Craftsman-style house no longer existed. She'd known that, yet it didn't seem possible. This must be how Juliette and Mercy felt right now. Only their houses had truly been homes. Someone else hung the festive red and blue curtains in this house. Someone else enjoyed the breeze from the Adirondack chairs on the front porch. For them, the pile of rubble represented years upon years of memories. For Nora, dreams of memories not yet made filled that pile of rubble.

She had a hole in her soul that only Levi could fill. Fierce pain engulfed her. She doubled over and gasped. "Gott? Gott!"

I am here.

Tears running down her face, Nora climbed down and let the reins drop. She knelt at the edge of the blackened earth, clasped her hands in her lap, lowered her head, and closed her eyes.

Gott, it's not my place to ask why. Your ways are mysterious. I only need to know that in all things You work for my gut. But I humbly ask for Your forgiveness and Your help. I'm lost. I'm so lost. I don't know how I got so lost. It's only sixty miles to Libby, but it's a world away. How do I get back to where I belong? Is this where I belong? Should I have stayed at the altar? Should I have stayed in Libby? Who is right? I'm so confused. Could you please soften my heart toward Levi? Help me to be a better person. Please help me. Please help Tammy too. Make Wyatt a better man than I think he is. I'm sorry to have bothered You, but they said I could talk to You anytime. Anywhere. Danki. Amen.

Nora inhaled the scent of loss and exhaled grief. Both would always be in her nose, on her clothes, and in her dreams. That didn't mean joy and new beginnings weren't just beyond the horizon.

Ignore the pain. Just breathe. Listen.

The quiet washed over her. A waterfall of memories, each one more bittersweet than the next, came with it. Life would go on. Soon snow would blanket the scarred landscape and hide the ugly remnants of a fire long gone. Ice would sparkle in the sunlight. The mountains would glisten. Mother would make hot chocolate with extra marshmallows. They would sit by the fireplace and mend socks while Father read *The Budget* aloud to them.

Life would be good again.

Gott?

Life will be good again.

Gott?

Just breathe.

A hand clamped down on Nora's shoulder. She jumped, threw out her arm, and flung herself backward.

Her screech likely scared the elk on the next mountain range. Levi loomed over her. "It's just me. Levi."

Heart racing, Nora scrambled to her feet. "You shouldn't scare a person like that."

"Sorry. I thought maybe you'd fallen asleep. I only wanted to make sure you were okay."

"What are you doing here?"

"The same thing you are, I reckon." His broad shoulders slumped. His chocolate eyes were damp. "I guess I was hoping maybe you would be here."

Just breathe.

How did that help?

Meet in the middle.

God's voice?

Maybe Levi had forgotten how to breathe too. Maybe every inhale and exhale hurt him too. "I guess I hoped you would be here too."

The wind lifted ashes into the air. They swirled and floated to the ground again. "It makes me sad."

"I'm not sad." Levi kicked a dirt clod with his dusty boot. "Okay, I'm sad, but we're made of the hardiest stock. We'll rebuild even better than before. That's what we do."

"Gott is gut. He has a plan."

"Is that what you were thinking about when I scared you?"

"I wasn't thinking. I was praying."

"Ah." He squatted and scooped up a handful of dirt. It crumbled and slipped between his long fingers. "It's hard to know what to pray for sometimes."

"All the time, lately." Nora's fingers ached to touch his hand. She scooted back. "Is it wrong to pray for discernment?"

"I don't know anymore."

The simple, unadorned truth.

"Me neither."

He rose. The pause grew long and awkward. Did he expect her to bring it up? Fine. She was no coward. "I've been thinking as well as praying."

He ducked his head and stared at his boots. "Me too." His gaze came up and mingled with hers. "Are you still mad at me?"

"Noah and Tobias came to see me today. Noah told me you spoke to him last night."

"I did."

Nothing more. No explanation. "Danki for doing that."

"He needed to know what I saw. After what I told him the first time, I wanted him to know that you made the right choice. You were tempted, but you chose your faith. You were strong in the face of enormous pressure."

"I understand why you did what you did."

"I talked to Noah about your transgressions because I love you." He chewed his lower lip, his eyes full of emotion. "I had to care about your eternal salvation more than about how disregarding your wishes would affect me. It was the hardest thing I've ever done.

When I had the chance to tell him about your strength, I had to do it because he needed to know how you chose to be faithful. If it benefited me, so be it."

The desire to hug his middle and kiss his face rushed through Nora. He was a special man. She inched closer. "You did what was right even though you knew it would cost you. I see that now. I'm sorry I didn't see it before."

"We're both growing up. Gott knew we needed to do that, I reckon."

"Do you think we're there yet?"

He shook his head. "I don't know, but I'm still trying."

Nora did her best to smile. "Gut. I'm still trying too."

Levi offered her his own smile, a beautiful sight to see. "When we stop trying, then it's over. Not before."

Relief made her muscles turn to mush. "I'm glad you feel that way."

"I have to go by the Yoders'." He didn't move. "Jonah is the lead on the construction project. We start day after tomorrow."

She didn't want him to leave. "If you hear anything from Chet, will you let me know?"

Levi nodded and tipped his straw hat at her. "Keep praying. I don't think we can ever go wrong by praying."

Nora nodded, but she couldn't speak. Not without bursting into tears.

"I have to go."

"So go."

He trudged out to the street, climbed into the buggy, and left.

Determined not to cry, Nora swallowed against the lump in her throat and waved.

He still wanted this house.

He still wanted her.

36

Hard work kept a man's mind occupied. Levi laid his hammer on the picnic table and rubbed his neck. His muscles ached, but it felt good. His boss and the other employees from Montana Furniture worked alongside Plain and English folks from Kootenai, Rexford, Eureka, Libby, St. Ignatius, and beyond. Two days of work and they already had all the debris removed from the Knowleses' property. Several dumpsters had been filled and hauled off. The cement basement now stood exposed. The new home would be even better than the one destroyed by fire.

Hard work also kept his mind off Nora. He could pretend she didn't stand on the other side of the construction site chattering with Juliette and her mother. They needed to talk soon, but not where everyone could see them. Since their talk at the Sutton house, they hadn't spoken again. They both needed time to regroup. The talk had been the start of rebuilding, but they still had a ways to go.

He grabbed a paper plate and started down the line. Ham, chicken, roast beef, and peanut butter spread sandwiches on homemade bread. Bushel baskets of apples, oranges, plums, and peaches. Pasta salads, green salads, gelatin salads, pickles, green tomato relish, potato chips, cookies, cakes, pies. The women treated every day like they needed to prepare food for a large wedding. His mother and sisters stood in a serving line that stretched along three picnic tables. They hustled back and forth between coolers and boxes behind the tables, replenishing food as the workers, at least seventy-five of them, took turns filling their plates.

The weather cooperated by offering a gorgeous October day. Temperatures that morning began at a crisp forty-five degrees. The sun warmed their faces and offered a soft breeze of encouragement.

"It's a beautiful day." A work belt around his waist and a coffee travel mug in one hand, Jack strolled toward Levi. "A man couldn't ask for a better way to spend his time."

The man could read minds.

"Jah."

Jack smiled. "You have grown into a man of few words, Suh."

For once the word *son* didn't sting. It was a term of affection. One Levi could appreciate. "No point in beating a dead horse."

"I would never do that." Jack sipped his coffee and smacked his lips. "I've been hearing about your trip to Libby. Are you all right?"

That Noah had spoken with Jack didn't surprise Levi. The bishop wanted to make sure every family in the Gmay sorted out its problems before they got out of hand. "I will be."

"Your mudder is glad you're home." Jack stuck his dirty boot on the picnic table's bench and leaned his elbow on his knee. He had a smudge of dirt on his nose. "We—she—worried you might get drawn into the cult in Libby."

Levi was an adult, but then Mother had made it clear parents never stopped seeing their children as their responsibility. Jack worried about him. It was a revelation Levi still needed time to digest. "I had no intention of doing that, but cult is a strong word. They're gut people who worship differently than we do."

"Yet call themselves Amish." Jack wrinkled his nose. "I don't see even a speck of it in them."

"We're not to worry about what others do. Or judge." Levi kept his voice neutral. He'd had enough discussion of the Libby folks to last him a lifetime. "Only pray."

"You're right. That should be a given. You're a wise man." Jack let his foot drop. He smacked Levi on the shoulder. "You don't just say the words, you live them. You set a gut example for the rest of us."

The words of praise caught Levi off balance. So did the lump that grew in his throat. Plain folks didn't believe in heaping praise for doing the right thing. A person simply did it. Jack's efforts to encourage Levi meant even more for that reason. He didn't have to say anything, but he chose to do it anyway.

"I made my share of mistakes in this mess." Levi had no experience in responding to a compliment of this magnitude. He took a big swig of water and swallowed. "I'm surprised Noah didn't mention that."

"You got Nora to come back home. Even Noah himself couldn't get Jeannie to do that."

Harley, Noah, and Tobias had traveled to Libby earlier in the week to speak with Daryl and Nora's sister. To no avail. Wilma took it particularly hard. She missed her grandbabies. "Nora made up her own mind. I'm thankful for that."

"I'd better get back to work." Jack tossed his coffee dregs into the grass and set the travel mug on the table. "Just know there's always a way to make more room at the house if you decide not to wait for Chet to rebuild. Bea and I were talking about adding on a couple of rooms. Your mudder likes having her kinner where she can see them. So do I."

Mending his relationship with Nora might take as long as the rebuilding of Chet's house. That didn't change the kindness of Jack's offer. Or the sentiment. "Gut to know."

"Like I said, a man of few words." Jack grinned and stalked away. "Are you coming?"

"I'll grab some lunch first," Levi called after him. "I'm right behind you."

To his surprise his stomach rumbled. His appetite had been missing since his return from Libby. The gray fog of depression might be lifting. How would Nora feel about living with Levi's parents? If it meant marrying sooner rather than later, Levi was for it. At least until they could get their own place. It no longer seemed onerous to live under his stepfather's roof.

The fire had taken much, but it also honed each of them in ways they were only beginning to understand.

One thing at a time. Nora was working on forgiving. So was he. They didn't need to rush.

He surveyed the offerings. Tammy Beachy stood behind the serving table. The jumping bean girl he'd met previously was gone, replaced by someone who seemed to be sleepwalking. She held out a plate of individually wrapped sandwiches on white bread. Labels stuck to the front indicated the contents. "Ham or roast beef or both?"

Levi helped himself to one of each. "How are you? I didn't realize you were here." He glanced around. Did that mean the others had come? Jeannie, Daryl, Jacob, and Esther? Another opportunity might present itself to convince them to come home—for good.

"Okay." She didn't sound okay. She didn't sound like the same happy-to-be-alive woman he'd met several times before. Her fair complexion had turned sallow and her eyes red. She'd shed a few pounds on an already skinny frame. "Do you want some spinach salad or pasta salad? There's an apple and whipped cream salad that Mudder made. It's tasty."

"Spinach salad would be fine, and the apple stuff. I could eat a barn with no butter. So did Jeannie come too?"

"Jeannie didn't come. Daryl's here. I don't know if he's staying, though." She used tongs to lower a generous portion of salad onto his plate. "I saw Jeannie the day before I left. She was crying."

"It's a hard situation."

Tammy stared at the tongs without returning them to the salad. "You think it's my fault, don't you?"

"Nee, why would I?"

"I tried to convince Nora to stay."

"Fortunately, she has a mind of her own."

"You should forgive her." Tammy added a package of Doritos to his plate. "The desserts are on the other table. I made the—"

"Tammy!"

Tammy cringed and ducked her head.

Roseanna slid another platter of sandwiches on the table. "Remember what I told you." She grabbed the empty platters and stomped away. "Just serve the food."

Tammy hunched her shoulders and held out plastic silverware wrapped in a paper napkin. "I'm not supposed to talk to anyone. Work and stay out of trouble."

"Why?" Levi accepted her offering. "What kind of trouble could you get in here? You're among family and friends."

"You don't want to know." Her eyes widening with fear, she put her hand to her mouth and coughed. The cough turned into a gagging sound.

Levi glanced around, seeking a trash can. "Are you all right?"

Her hand dropped. She nodded and cleared her throat. "I'm fine. Just something in my throat. Anyway, have some of the cherry crisp. I made it."

If she was sick, she shouldn't be cooking or serving food. "I will if I'm not too stuffed."

He moved down the line, but something in her tone made him glance back. Tammy scrubbed the plastic checkered tablecloth with more force than necessary. A sadness so like grief marred her pretty face.

◆ ◆ ◆

A few dozen yards seemed like a million miles. Nora turned so she couldn't stare at Levi. He'd lingered forever, talking to Tammy. Poor woman, her face was green. Levi looked good, as always. They couldn't have a conversation in the swarm of every district family working on the house. Better to keep busy. She grappled with two empty coolers that needed to go back to her family's buggy.

The sound of Daryl's voice stopped her in her tracks. Nora peered over her shoulder. His face scarlet, her brother-in-law stood talking to Father, who seemed equally unhappy. Nora hadn't seen Daryl since leaving Libby. She left the coolers and marched over to the men. "Where's Jeannie and the kinner?"

Daryl's gaze swept toward her. "She didn't want to come. She said it would be too hard. It was too soon."

"And you didn't insist?" Father broke in. "What kind of mann are you?"

"The kind who is trying to do what's best for his family." Ire, confusion, and sadness married in Daryl's face. "I considered bringing the kinner and leaving her there—until she comes to her senses."

"Why didn't you?" Father's scowl grew. "If I could, I would. You're their daed. Do you want them brought up by people who've forsaken their Plain faith?"

"Nee, but I want them to have a daed and a mudder. She's my fraa. I'm her mann. Nothing changes that. We are forever linked." To his credit Daryl didn't back down. He looked weathered but not beaten. "I have the bigger say in how they are raised as long as I stay with them. I won't rip a nursing bopli from my fraa's arms."

Daryl was right, as difficult as the choice was. Nora tried for an understanding smile and a placating tone. "It's a horrible situation for everyone, but especially you."

His Adam's apple bobbed. "Jeannie said to tell you she wishes you would come back."

"Tell her I'll write her."

"She sent your things. They're in the buggy."

"I'll get them."

"I'm not giving up on her." Father's tone was more conciliatory. "I'm not giving up on the kinner."

"Me neither. As long as I'm breathing, I'll keep trying to talk sense into her. You and me will go back to Libby together after this build." Daryl picked up a hammer. "Which we'll never finish if we stand around jawing all day."

The two men strode away side by side.

Nora returned to her coolers. She'd take them to her family's buggy and pick up her clothes at the same time.

"Honey, get one of the guys to cart those for you. It's one of the things they're good for." Juliette's voice carried over the chatter, the banging of hammers, and the rumble of a backhoe. "You'll hurt your back."

Nora eased the coolers onto the picnic table and found herself enveloped in a warm hug. Since their return to Kootenai, her friend had been like that. Anxious for a hug at every turn. The hugs were like medicine for weary souls. Juliette had been changed by circumstances. Like a precious stone polished until its sparkle lit up the room. "Your face says it all. You're happy."

"I know, it's crazy that I should feel so good with everything that's happened, but life is good." Juliette cocked her head toward Tim Trudeau, who was raking rubble from what had been the garage. He filled out his faded jeans and Colorado Rockies T-shirt nicely—if a Plain woman was allowed to notice such a thing. Juliette sighed and grinned. "I'm good."

"I'm so glad." Nora couldn't help but smile. She might not get her dream, but Juliette was closing in on hers. Whatever her problems had been, she'd leaned into them and come out on the other side. "You and Tim are made for each other. Have you come to an agreement about your beliefs?"

"I'm working on it. Be sure to come to the community church service this weekend."

That sounded promising. "I'm so happy for you, Juliette, for both of you."

Tim was a sweet, kind, hardworking man who wore his love for Juliette like a warm coat. And he was probably the only man alive who could handle her.

"You and Levi are made for each other too." Juliette grabbed the coolers. "Walk with me to your buggy."

"I can carry those."

"I'm working on my muscles. I've been taking a self-defense class. You should see my kicks."

Feeling like she'd been tricked into being a sluggard, Nora trailed after her friend. "Have you talked to Mercy or Christine? I've barely seen either one since they got here."

"Mercy's here. She and her smoke jumper talked, and he left."

"Her smoke jumper?"

"It's a long story. I don't know exactly what happened to Christine, but she got into big trouble hanging out with a Native American man she met at her uncle's store in St. Ignatius. Caleb was super jealous. I'm not sure if they'll work it out."

Because of the wildfire, she and her friends had been thrust into new situations. All of them had been changed by their circumstances. "I can understand that. It's hard to believe how much we changed in such a short time out there in the world."

"What exactly happened in Libby?"

Nora ran through the highlights as they walked out to the line of buggies, cars, and trucks on the dirt road. Juliette slid the coolers into the buggy and dusted off her hands. "Seriously? You both believe that the Lord Jesus Christ is your Savior. You're both Amish. You love each other. Get over yourselves already. Life is short."

"It's not that easy. I violated the Ordnung, something I vowed not to do when I was baptized. I almost joined another church. I backed off at the last minute, but I can see how that would give Levi pause. I like the idea of a closer walk with Jesus. I like the idea of Bible study."

"You were trying to figure out what you believe. I have some experience with that. Some people, like Tim, take the direct route. Others, like me, have to take the longest, winding, rockiest, pothole-filled road in order to get to where we think we see a little speck of faith in the distance." Juliette flung her hands in the air in her newfound enthusiasm for religion.

"You and Levi are somewhere in the middle. I'll tell you what my pastor told me. He said an untested faith is a puny faith. It's easy to believe when everything goes your way. The crud that happens to us in this world that rips us up and leaves us like a pile of trash in the dump helps us develop true faith."

A lot of words about faith from a woman who had avoided the topic for years. Something big had changed Juliette—for the better. "I'm sorry for whatever you went through, friend. I've never had to explain or defend the way I worship. I thought maybe they were right. I did feel closer to God. It's not about what I believe. It's about how I act on it."

"You and your folks have always been an example for me of Christian faith. Don't let anyone tell you differently, sugar." Juliette tugged the hair band from her thick blonde curls and redid her long ponytail. "I've wasted a lot of time denying my faith and shaking my fist at the sky. Don't do it. Life's too short. God's too sweet. You can talk to God anywhere, anytime, anyway you want to. Just do it."

"So you've finally admitted you're a believer. That's so wunderbarr!" Nora hugged Juliette hard. The other woman returned the favor.

"Pssst. Pssst."

Nora broke away from her friend to see where the sound came from.

Wyatt peeked around the pickup truck parked across the road from the Beachy buggy. "Nora, over here."

The fallen angel had returned.

37

Sic Stinker on him, kick him in the shins, or do the Christian thing and hear Wyatt out? Nora couldn't decide which she should do. All of the above in that order?

"Do you know this guy?" Juliette stepped in front of Nora. She planted her feet and fisted both hands. "I know karate. I carry Mace. Plus, one shout and my friend Deputy Sheriff Tim Trudeau will come running. He carries his weapon even when he's off duty, by the way."

"It's okay, it's Wyatt." Nora put her hand on Juliette's shoulder. "This is the man I told you about from the tent revival."

Juliette let her hands drop. "So, Wyatt, the baby daddy fallen angel, why are you skulking around behind dumpsters, freaking out women?"

"I need Nora's help. I don't want to cause any trouble, I promise." Still he squatted next to the pickup, casting anxious glances at the beehive of workers on the construction site. "Just talk to me for a minute, Nora, please."

He'd never been an angel, fallen or otherwise. He was simply a man who sinned. Wyatt was no different from Nora or Levi or any other human being. That he hurt Tammy made Nora mad, but she'd hurt Levi, so they were in the same boat. "It's fine, Juliette. I'll be back in a second. Take some pie to Tim. You know how much he loves apple pie."

"I'll be watching you." Juliette pointed to her eyes with two fingers and then at Wyatt. "This woman is a good friend of mine. Mess with her and you're messing with me. Understand?"

Wyatt's face flushed a deeper red. "I understand."

Juliette shot him one last withering look and stalked away.

"Why are you hiding out here?" Wanting nothing more than to turn and walk away, Nora forced herself to cross the road. She couldn't be gone long or Mother would notice. She'd been stuck to Nora like a burr since Tammy's first visit. She would be horrified to see Nora talking to Wyatt. No Plain woman wanted to talk about love, lust, and out-of-wedlock babies with a man, Plain or English. It couldn't matter. For Tammy, Nora would have this conversation. "What are you doing here at all? I thought you didn't want anything to do with us—with Tammy."

"That's not true." Wyatt straightened, but he stayed well behind the truck. "I never said that. I never got the chance to say anything."

"Tammy called you. You didn't call her back. Your daed talked to her daed. At least that's what I heard." Nora hadn't been able to spend much time with Tammy since she and her family arrived in West Kootenai to help rebuild. Aunt Roseanna insisted Tammy stay at the campgrounds in Rexford when they weren't working. Mother called it closing the corral gate after the cattle had already escaped. "Tammy's heartbroken, and you're skipping from one tent revival to the next like it was nothing. Like she's nothing."

"First of all, I don't skip anywhere." Wyatt huffed and glared at Nora. "It's true I freaked out when Ike told my dad—"

"If you'd returned her call, you could've heard the news about the baby directly from Tammy."

"I didn't know that's why she was calling. She didn't say. I was busy. Dad let me start preaching." His shoulders hunched, he stuck fisted hands in his pockets. "I got the podium. I got to do the altar call. It was powerful. I couldn't wait to tell her."

"You were too full of yourself to think of anything else, in other words."

"No, before I could call her back, Ike called Dad, and then the world exploded." Wyatt's chin, with its sparse, pale hairs barely in need of shaving, quivered. "The worst thing is, Dad didn't get mad. He was so disappointed, he cried. I cried with him. The only other time I ever saw him do that was when my mom died, and that was years ago."

Disappointment would be harder to bear than anger. On that they could agree. Nora caught her anger in a tight grip. "Did he tell you that you couldn't talk to Tammy?"

"He said to take some time and think about my calling and my responsibilities. Not to rush into anything. Being on the road with a wife and a baby would be hard. People need us at all hours of the day and night." Wyatt's voice broke. He hiccuped a sob. "I know we did wrong. I know we sinned. I want to do what's right. I'll marry her. We'll raise that baby. I know my responsibility."

Not a word about loving Tammy and wanting her for his wife. Would a marriage built on these shifting sands survive? Her parents and the bishop would say they'd made their bed and must lie in it. Getting in that bed early hadn't worked out so well for them. Was marriage always the right choice in these situations? Nora's church said yes. "So why are you hiding out? Go talk to her."

"I tried to find them at the campgrounds. I ran into Joe. For an Amish guy he's definitely capable of taking my head off. He told me I should stay away. That he and the family would take care of Tammy. He told me to go home and not come back."

The Eagle Valley Amish weren't really Amish. Yet again, their response was different. Or maybe Joe spoke out of turn. An angry brother might do that. "Is that what you want?" Wyatt would be off the hook, free to roam the country, preaching, winning the lost, and making disciples. When he himself continued to be lost. "Do you love her?"

"I've never known anyone like her. She's sweet, she's funny, she's smart." Wyatt's Adam's apple bobbed. "She has a beautiful voice and she's a good musician—really good."

He made a grocery list of all Tammy's qualities as if trying to assure himself of her desirability.

"She's also a hard worker, and she can cook, bake, clean, and mop." Nora fought to keep sarcasm from her voice. Sarcasm, contrary to Juliette's assertion, was not one of the fruit of the Spirit. "That means she'll be a good fraa. That doesn't mean you should marry her."

"I love her, but I'm not good enough for her. Tammy is—was—a devout Christian. I led her astray." Wyatt cleared his throat. "What kind of husband would I be? What kind of father?"

"Tammy isn't a sheep you led to the slaughter. She had free will." Just as Nora did. She had no right to be judgmental or self-righteous. Her sin wasn't any less just because she hadn't crossed the line with Levi. "We all do. If you believe you and Tammy belong together, you should tell her."

"I just know I need to talk to Tammy." Wyatt edged closer to Nora. "Can you please help me?" He held out a cell phone. "Give her this. It's a prepaid disposable phone. My number is programmed in it. Tell her to call me as soon as she can."

"I don't want to get her in more trouble. Her daed didn't want her to have a phone before. He won't want her to have one now."

"I need to talk to her." Wyatt grabbed Nora's hand and stuck the phone on her palm. "Her dad won't listen."

"You don't know that." Nora tugged her hand free. The phone fell to the ground. "Do the right thing. For Tammy's sake. Don't take the cowardly way."

Wyatt scooped the phone up. "I thought you loved your cousin. Don't you want her to be happy?" Once again he took a swipe at Nora's hand. "Give me a chance to make this right. I do love her. Let me prove that I'm worthy of her."

He wanted to make it right. Like she wanted to make it right with Levi. He deserved a second chance. They all did. "I'll tell Tammy you're here, but you need to stop being a coward. Talk to her. Talk to her daed. Be a man who's going to become a father." Nora pivoted. She marched toward the Knowleses' property.

A dozen women, including her mother, stared in her direction. She lifted her chin and kept walking.

Her mother met her at the edge of the cluster of picnic tables. "Is everything all right?"

"Nee, but that's the way it is." Nora brushed past her. "A gut friend once told me faith that hasn't been tested is puny."

Hers should be able to carry the weight of the world on its back. And then some.

38

A messenger bearing news—of the good or bad variety as yet undetermined—should get the job done quickly and efficiently. Nora slipped behind the serving tables and went in search of Tammy, who no longer stood at the sandwich and salad station. A quick survey of the desserts and fruit showed no sign of her cousin. There she was, waiting for an open Porta Potty. Nora dodged between two women debating the best recipe for chocolate pudding upside-down cake and raced to the other side of the construction site.

"Tammy!"

"If I have to wait another minute, I'll hurl all over my shoes." Tammy leaned over and hugged her stomach. "I'm not kidding."

Nora grabbed her arm and guided her to a trash can behind the first row of Porta Potties.

Tammy was as good as her word. The gagging and the stench combined to make Nora's stomach rock. She pinched her nose and studied the peaks of the Purcell Mountains. *I will not throw up. I will not throw up.* Even with five younger brothers, she still couldn't handle other people's vomit. "It's okay. Get it all out. You'll feel better."

"Nee, I won't." Tammy managed a mangled giggle. "But nice try."

She wiped her face on her jacket sleeve and stalked away from the trash can. Only too happy to distance herself from the foul smell of both the can and the Porta Potties, Nora followed. "You poor thing. I'm sorry you're going through this."

"Mudder says I get what I deserve."

"She's angry."

"You think?" Tammy stumbled over a rock and cursed under her breath. "I've never seen either of them more horrified, angry, hurt, and disappointed. I feel like such a bad dochder—the worst on the planet, the worst ever."

"You're not. You're not the first to do this."

"You can't tell from the way Mudder and Daed are acting."

"It's the first time it's happened to them. Like it or not, your daed is a minister in your church. He's a leader in your community." PK. Preacher's kid. That's what Brandon had called her. Higher expectations were unfair but no doubt existed.

Nora slid her arm around her cousin's shoulders and squeezed. "I reckon he's expected to set an example. He probably feels like a failure. I'm sure it bothers him that people are talking and pointing fingers. You didn't live up to their expectations."

"I can't help what other people think. And it's not happening to my parents. It's happening to me."

"You know that's not true. Your actions affect them. Are you doing a kneeling confession?" The thought made Nora's stomach heave. She had come so close. She had no right to judge. "Do they do that in your church?"

"Nee, we don't. That is barbaric and the height of judgment, according to Mudder. They'd like to see a quick wedding, but I don't see that happening." Tammy heaved a dramatic sigh. "Wyatt never returned my call. Mudder says I shouldn't want to marry a man who doesn't want to marry me. It's not the foundation of a gut, lasting marriage. Even if it would shut people's mouths. She says they'll help me raise my bopli."

"See, she is kind and she is thinking about you. She's not pushing you to marry a man who might not love you."

"I thought he did love me. I love him." Tammy burst into tears. "I would never have done what I did if I didn't love him."

The line between love and lust was paper thin. Nora's experience was equally thin, but she knew that much. Tammy needed to know Wyatt really did care. Love? He'd come this far. "Maybe you should try talking to Wyatt again."

"If he wanted to talk to me—"

"He does. He's out on the road, waiting for you."

"He's here?"

"He is." Nora handed Tammy a napkin. "Wipe your nose. Talk to him. You'll feel better. I think you can work things out."

Tammy ran her fingers through the hair in her tangled ponytail. "I'm a hot mess and I smell."

"He won't care, I promise. Go."

"You have to go with me."

"What? Nee. This is between you and him."

"Come with me. Please. Be my wingwoman." She blew her nose with a hard honk. "I would do it for you. You know I would."

"This is private."

"Please, please, please." Her voice rose. "If we go together, no one will wonder what we're doing. If anyone asks, we're getting more supplies from the wagon. Otherwise I'm not to leave the serving line."

She was right. If Tammy left on her own, her mother would be hot on her trail within seconds. "Let's go."

Holding her breath, Nora guided her away from the construction site and toward the road. Tammy stumbled and meandered a bit, but no one stopped them.

Wyatt popped from behind a truck as soon as they crossed the road. "You came. I'm so glad," he bellowed. "And I don't care who knows it."

Her hands on her cheeks, Tammy wailed.

"Hush, both of you. This is a conversation between the two of you." Nora glanced over her shoulder. No one had followed them. If Tammy kept caterwauling, someone would hear and come running. "You don't need company." She edged toward the road to give them the space they needed.

"I mean it. I'm sorry I didn't call you back." Wyatt lowered his voice, but the emotion still bled through. "I'm an idiot."

With that Nora could agree.

Tammy and Wyatt eyed each other like wounded animals.

"You *are* an idiot." Tammy finally spoke. She straightened. Her chin came up. The quiver in her voice and the tears disappeared. "I gave you something special, something I can't get back, and you dumped on me."

"I was scared."

"I am scared, and I need you."

They were a man and a woman gathered at a fork in the road. They could choose to go forward together, or they could part ways. Years of spiritual training, years of guidance from family and church spun around them, influencing their decision. Yet only their hearts mattered in this moment.

The most private of conversations played out like a strange dream.

Wyatt dropped to one knee. He held out a small felt-covered box. "This is my mother's wedding ring. I don't know what size it is. I don't even know what size you wear." He flipped the lid and pulled from the box a sparkling diamond on a silver band. "I'd be honored if you would marry me."

This wouldn't be the time to announce that Plain folks didn't wear wedding rings, would it? That this would be a marriage made of mixed values, histories, and faiths was obvious.

"I don't hear a question in that." Tammy took two steps toward him, then two more. "Are you asking me something or telling me?"

Wyatt held the ring up to the sky like an offering. "Will you marry me?"

A proposal that would go down in the annals of history as one of the most romantic ever, in Nora's book. She held her breath.

"Jah, the answer is yes." Tammy rushed to meet Wyatt halfway.

He scrambled to his feet and did the same. She slammed to a halt. Wyatt opened his arms wide. She jumped into them and wrapped her arms around his neck. Wyatt lowered his head and covered their faces with his baseball cap. Both honored and embarrassed to witness such a joyous reunion, Nora swallowed back tears.

Maybe this union began on rocky ground, but it would proceed with declared love and a proper marriage. She glanced back. No one was coming—yet. She waited. The kiss didn't seem to be ending. "Tammy, we have to go before your mudder notices you're gone."

Tammy gave Wyatt another smacking kiss and unwound herself from his hug. "She's right, Wyatt. Come to the RV park tonight. We'll talk to Mudder and Daed together." She slipped the ring from her finger and stuck it in her jeans pocket. "We'll do this the right way from here on out."

Wyatt nodded. "I'll be there. I won't let you down again. I promise."

Still grinning, Tammy walked backward for several yards, blowing him kisses. Nora had to tug her along toward the work site. She'd served as her cousin's wingwoman. Time to get her own business in order.

She surveyed the work site. No Levi. He'd been there only a few minutes earlier. Where had he gone? His sister stood at the dessert table, helping one of her eleven siblings fix a plate.

Nora moved so quickly it seemed her feet skimmed across the charred grass, barely touching it. "Where's Levi?"

Her eyebrows lifted, Diane settled a cherry pie on the table and wiped her hands. "He left. He didn't say where he was going."

"He left before the work is done?"

"He's been out of sorts since the fire." Diane's smile was sly. "You probably know more about that than I do. Maybe you can ferret out the problem and get him back to his old self."

Nora returned the girl's smile. She would do her best.

She sought out her father next. His expression pensive, he stood near a stack of Sheetrock, watching Daryl work from a distance.

"Wanting to keep his family together is understandable." Nora offered the words as comfort, but her father would only see how it took the children away from their conservative Amish faith. "We'll still be able to see them now and again. You know Grandpa will bring the kinner for visits like he did our kossins."

"Gott's will be done." Father bent over a set of blueprints on top of the Sheetrock. Like Mother he turned to work when big emotions threatened to overwhelm. He and Mother would accept this new development, just as they did the loss of their own babies. They would carry on.

Nora would too. With Levi by her side. "I'm taking the buggy for a bit, Daed."

He raised his head and frowned. "You are?"

"If it's all right."

His gaze raked her face. "I'd rather not have to ask forgiveness for more worrying."

"I promise you have nothing to worry about from me. I'm here to stay. Permanently."

His weathered hands rubbed his grizzled face. He nodded. "Be back before dark."

Nora picked up her skirt and ran.

39

Showing up at a man's house in broad daylight and asking for him would be a huge break in tradition. Plain women simply didn't do that. Nora tugged at the reins and halted the buggy on the edge of Jack Moser's property. If Levi had thinking to do, he wouldn't return to the house. A man with eleven siblings had no privacy and expected none. The older ones and Jack were still at the build, but Beatrice had stayed home with the younger ones, who had the flu. Maybe Nora had fled the construction site on a fool's errand.

"Where to now, Checkers?"

The horse nickered and dipped her head.

"You're no help."

"Who are you talking to?"

Nora jumped and dropped the reins. Charlie, who was her brother Seth's age, climbed into the buggy without so much as an invitation. He wore a straw bag on a strap around his neck. "This is Dodger, my puppy." He pulled a fluffy, wiggling, brown puppy from the bag. "I have a bunch of puppies. Daed says I have to take care of him or he'll give him away. Do you want a puppy? We're looking for homes for the others, but no one wants a puppy right now. I want to keep them, but Daed says nee."

The child did love to talk, but he was sweeter than a piece of fudge. "Seth might, but we already have Stinker, so my daed might say nee too."

"Who were you talking to?"

"Our horse, Checkers."

"I talk to animals all the time. Mudder says I'm daft."

"I know how that feels. As long as they don't answer, we're fine."

"Why don't you go up to the house?"

"I want to talk to Levi."

Charlie giggled behind his hand. His cheeks turned pink. "Are you Levi's special friend?"

"Maybe." She wasn't sure. "I hope so."

His chubby face scrunched up in a puzzled frown. "Is that how it works?"

"Not usually."

"I don't like girls."

"You will someday. But not too soon, Gott willing. Do you know where Levi is?"

"Not home."

"Okay."

"He went to the build, but then he came back." Charlie's elaborate shrug and puzzled tone made him look like a miniature adult. "I reckon he left to go to his other house."

"He has another house?"

"The one that burned."

"How do you know about that?"

"Sometimes I hide in the back of the buggy so I can ride along."

"He doesn't know you're there?"

"He always hears me. He says he knows I'm there all along, but I don't believe him."

"You can't go this time."

"Why not? Dodger wants to go for a ride."

"Dodger will have to wait."

"Kinner and hunds always have to wait for everything." Charlie's shoulders drooped. He sighed. "It's not fair. I can't wait to be grown up and have my own buggy and my own house. With no big bruders and schweschders to tell me what to do all the time."

With so many older siblings that probably did sound good, but grown-up life was harder than it looked. "Don't be in a hurry to grow up. Sometimes it's easier to have someone to tell you what to do. Then you don't have to figure it out for yourself."

"I'm gut at figuring stuff out." He stuck Dodger back in the bag and climbed down from the buggy. He turned and stuck his hand on his forehead to shield his eyes from the sun. "So is Levi. He doesn't talk to me like I'm too little to understand stuff. He says I'm smart. If you have a problem, he can figure it out for you."

From the mouths of babes. Suddenly cheered up by a five-year-old, Nora scooped up the reins and waved at Charlie. "Levi's right. You are smart, Charlie. Next time—if there is a next time—I'll take you with me. You can help rebuild the house."

Such a big if, but Nora longed to take this one on faith.

"That would be fun. I like hammers. And saws." Charlie waved back. "Maybe you and Levi can take one of Gussy's puppies to live with you when you move into your house."

He kept waving until she turned the buggy around. The thought of Charlie with a saw sent Nora's heartbeat soaring. She smiled. A person couldn't help but be optimistic around a guy like Charlie. Now, if only she could patch things up with his brother.

It took about twenty minutes to drive to Chet's property. Sure enough, Levi's horse and buggy were parked in front. Levi sat cross-legged like a child on the spot where cement met crispy fried grass. Nora parked and hopped down. She joined him on the cement.

Neither spoke. The sun warmed the autumn air and their faces. No wind rustled leaves in the trees. They no longer existed. No birds chattered, having no trees in which to plant themselves. No crickets sang.

A big silence in which a conversation war waged.

The seconds ticked by, donging like an enormous English church bell.

Finally, Levi sighed. He tossed a burnt bit of grass aside and wiped his hands on his pants. "How did you know I would be here?"

"Charlie told me."

"Charlie has a big mouth."

"Charlie's smart."

"Smarter than most grown-ups." Levi studied the scorched mountains in the distance. "He gets some of that from Jack."

"That almost sounded like you're complimenting Jack."

"He's not so bad."

"When did you figure that out?"

"Since the fire he's been trying so hard to reach out to me. Which made me realize I haven't tried hard ever. I acted like a brat. I never thought about my mudder's feelings. Or his." His expression wistful, Levi glanced sideways at her, then back at the debris that once was a home. "He even suggested we could make room for one more person at the house. He said something about building more rooms."

A possibility all shiny and new presented itself. If Levi was considering marrying her and living with his family, anything was possible. "You did the right thing—talking to Noah. I've always known that. I was just too stubborn to admit it. I hope you'll forgive me for blaming you for what I did. I'm to blame for my situation, and I know it. I'm sorry for what this has done to us. I can't say I'm sorry I went to Libby, though. Crazy as it sounds, I think it was gut for me to have to wrestle with my faith."

"It was gut for us to be apart, I reckon." Levi moved so he faced her. "I needed to realize how bossy I was. I'm sorry I didn't listen to you more. I promise to do better, but you have to promise to speak up. Tell me when I do it. Right now, I need you to tell me about wrestling with your faith. What does that mean?"

"I promise." Nora savored his sweet, earnest tone. He wanted this to work. "Starting with my faith. I am an obedient follower of Christ and a member of this Gmay. My prayer life and how I study my Bible alone in my room will never interfere with my baptismal or marriage vows." Nora walked a line so thin she felt the urge to throw out her arms to balance herself. "I can follow Gott and be a gut Plain wife at the same time."

His face lit up with that smile that always warmed her. "You're smart enough to walk a high wire, honoring family and faith at the same time."

"I hope so."

"I know so. You understood that the Libby Amish have something we don't. You sought a way to deepen your faith, even though it was painful for you and for the people you love." Levi raised his face to the sky. The uncertainty in his gaze drained away. "I don't like it, but I respect it. You chose to cling to your Amish faith and family despite your misgivings. That's a hard choice."

"Danki for understanding."

"Some things are between you and Gott."

"Do you think He understands why I chose to come home?"

"I think Noah would say Gott extends grace to believers who seek to follow Him."

Such a comforting thought. To know Levi extended grace to her, as well, sent hope welling up in Nora. "Where does that leave us exactly?"

"Chet says insurance will pay to rebuild. Because he doesn't live in the house, he's low on the list of builds. Families in need of shelter are first." His expression somber, Levi scooped up a few pebbles and tossed them into the seared grass. "He's decided to use some of the money to bring in an outside construction company. He loses more money by waiting. He calls it better business sense."

"Either way, we still have time to find our way."

Levi swiveled to look directly at Nora. "Do you want time?"

"Do you?"

His chuckle accompanied an eye roll worthy of Nora's teenage brothers. "You'll never make it easy, will you?"

"Nothing is easy about life, but I just watched Wyatt propose to Tammy. She accepted. She's in a family way. It's taken them a while to figure out what to do, but now they're committed to working it out so their bopli will have a mudder and daed who love each other."

"So that's why she looked so awful this morning."

"Jah. Because of the bopli and because she knew what a mess they made of things. She's been miserable, but she knows she has a chance for what she really wants. A mann who loves her for who she is."

"What do you want?"

"I plan to love, honor, and respect my mann."

"Gut to know." Levi rose to his feet and held out his hand to help her up. "You better get back. I reckon your daed wants you home before dark."

"He did say that."

She took his hand. He pulled her into his arms, a sweet, familiar, solid place she could call home. He tipped her chin up and kissed her gently on the lips. Smiling, he drew back. "I plan to love, honor, and respect my fraa."

Peace like the valley at dawn on a cool spring morning swept over Nora. Tiny, precise stitches worked their way across the wound that separated her from the man she loved. They still had work to do, but this season of change promised a sweet reward in return.

She stood on her tiptoes and sealed the promise with another kiss. His lips were soft and warm and familiar, yet they held a new heady sensation of love refined by the fire.

40

West Kootenai

Two months later

Not even a snowy December could stand in the way of progress. Determination propelled Levi from bed before dawn. It didn't matter that two feet of new icy stuff blanketed the landscape. He buttoned the top button on his heavy wool coat, tugged on his gloves, and drove to Chet's place. Chet's truck wasn't in the driveway, so he hadn't made the trek in from Rexford yet. If he could at all. Sometimes four-wheel drive and tire chains weren't enough. The crew would do their best to make it. They worked six-day weeks to try to frame in the house before winter. With his job at the furniture store, Levi couldn't help as much as he would like.

So much to do and so little time to think. Mercy and Caleb were married. Juliette and Tim were engaged. Tammy and Wyatt had married. Tammy was adjusting to life on the road with her traveling preacher husband. Christine and Andy's banns had been announced. The simple invitation postcard that set the date for next week had arrived yesterday.

That left Nora. The last of the four horsewomen who loved to camp, hunt, fish, and canoe together at Lake Koocanusa.

Mercy and Caleb's wedding had been a good starting point.

Levi sat across from Nora. Her Sunday shoe kept touching his boot. Accidental or on purpose. They sang and played games far into the evening and helped with the cleanup the next day. Not one word was spoken about her time in Libby or the absence of Jeannie and Daryl from the festivities.

Every time he saw her they moved a little bit closer to a new kind of friendship, far from the one they'd enjoyed before the wildfire. They would never be that couple again, so sure of everything. A couple who let the sparks fly and land where they may. They spoke less and listened more. They went ice-skating. They hunted. They sipped hot chocolate at the kitchen table after everyone was asleep, talking deep into the night.

They kept a tight lid on their passion.

But that didn't mean they couldn't crown each evening with kisses that heralded a future filled with sweet, passionate embraces.

The clatter of boots on the boards that served as a makeshift sidewalk from the cement driveway to the half-finished building warned Levi of impending company. The crew had arrived. He dropped Chet's blueprints over a sawhorse and went to shove aside the Sheetrock that served as a door of sorts.

Nora greeted him from the other side. Her cheeks were rosy with cold. A black wool bonnet covered her kapp, and a gray coat hung past her knees. She held out a huge thermos. "I brought you hot kaffi and warm cinnamon rolls." Her gaze traveled past him. "Enough for the workers, if they're interested."

"No one is here yet. I reckon the roads are icy and still need to be cleared of snow." He took her offering and moved aside. "Come in. It's not much warmer in here than it is out there, but at least there's no wind."

"You're making gut progress." She pulled off her gloves. "It's starting to take shape inside. Is this where the living room will be?"

"Jah, and the kitchen over here and the bedrooms to the back."

After much discussion, they'd agreed to a one-story house this time. The footprint took up more land, but Chet preferred it, and he was the homeowner. "Four bedrooms, but more can be added if needed." His whole body warmed before he even opened the thermos. "I didn't mean to suggest—"

"It sounds wunderbarr." Nora's smile widened. "One story means no carrying clothes from the upstairs to the downstairs laundry room."

A woman would think of that. "He's installing electrical wiring."

She shrugged. "He can't always be sure he'll have Plain tenants."

"Nee, he can't."

"When do you think it'll be ready?"

Levi surveyed the piles of Sheetrock. "Not until after Christmas. Probably end of January or early February, I reckon."

Silence descended for a few seconds. Christmas would be hard this year. Jeannie and Daryl had settled into their new life in Libby. It seemed unlikely that they would come for the holidays. Too much raw hurt stood in the way. Maybe next year.

"Will there be a porch?" Nora pulled her gloves back on. Was she leaving already? "It needs a porch where the family can sit in the early summer evening and enjoy the breeze and the flower garden. I can see it now. It's so pretty."

"Who do you see sitting out there?"

"You and me and our kinner. A bunch of them. They're drawing pictures with chalk on the sidewalk and playing hopscotch. I think we're having a barbecue. Mercy and Caleb, Tim and Juliette, and Christine and Andy, and all their kinner are there."

"The four horsewomen and their manns. You have quite the imagination."

"Can't you see it?"

"I can." He took her hands in his. "I sometimes dream that dream when I sleep."

"Me too."

The room grew warm. The wind whistling through the cracks became a sweet ballad. Levi couldn't tear his gaze from the woman he loved. She was so beautiful, so sweet, and so smart. Everything he'd ever wanted. "I love you, Nora." He tugged her closer. She smiled and leaned into him. "These past few months since you came back have been sweet."

"I love you too. Things have been better than ever."

"Iron sharpening iron?"

"It seems that way." She stood on her tiptoes and kissed his cheek. "My heart is full, knowing you have learned to trust me again."

"My heart is full, knowing you chose family and faith." He edged closer. "You chose me despite my bossiness. Any regrets? No plans to hike back to Libby?"

"None. I love my Libby family, but I'm where I belong. And Gott is with me wherever I go. He hears me and sees me right here." She touched Levi's chest with one finger. "He knows my heart. He knows what's best for me. I'm at peace with my decision."

Levi touched her cheek. She raised her head. He kissed her, softly at first, but harder as he fell into that sweet place where the world receded and they were united in their love for each other. His Nora, sweet, sweet Nora had returned.

He drew away and memorized the way her face welcomed him into a place open only to him.

No holding back. No turning back. This time she tugged him down to her and sought his lips. His need for her burned through Levi. He caught her up in his arms and swung her around, kissing her cheeks, her forehead, and her neck. "Marry me, Nora. Marry me."

"I will. I will."

Laughing, breathless, they twirled around the rough, half-formed space that would one day be their living room.

The Sheetrock door tumbled down. In walked the construction

crew led by a guy the others called Two-Ton Tony. He paused and stuck out his arm to block the others. "I think we came to the wrong party, boys."

"No, you're fine." Laughing, Levi planted Nora on her feet. Still giggling, she grabbed his arm to steady herself. "This is my . . . my future fraa, Nora Beachy."

"Congratulations." All six men marched into the house with rousing cheers, even though they hardly knew Levi and didn't know Nora at all. "You're a lucky man, Levi."

"We have cinnamon rolls," Nora said as each man came by to pump her hand and offer his personal congratulations. "They're in the buggy."

"Sounds great, but you two should go celebrate." Two-Ton Tony grinned. "Just leave the cinnamon rolls for us. We'll take care of the rest."

"How did you know this house was for us?"

"Levi has been on top of every detail from the beginning. No one does that unless they have a personal stake in it. Go on, go find a warm place to roost together."

Levi grabbed Nora's hand. Together they moved to the door, where they turned to watch the crew work.

"I love it already," Nora whispered.

"I love you."

"I love you more."

"I love *you* even more."

Her head cocked toward Two-Ton Tony and his deft work with an electric saw, and Nora threaded her arms around Levi's waist. "I think I'd rather stay right here and help build our house."

She was indeed a smart woman. Levi dropped a quick kiss on her kapp. "You get the cinnamon rolls. I'll get started."

Their new lives together, forged by the fire, had begun.

A Note from the Author

Every novel I write is a journey of learning, but *Peace in the Valley* particularly stretched my understanding of what I believe and why. My research led me to a charismatic Amish district in Libby, Montana. If you're interested in learning more about them, check out the videos on YouTube by searching for Eagle Valley Amish Ministries. They also have a website. My husband and I were blessed to visit the community during my research trip before starting the Amish of Big Sky Country series. We parked next to the school, and my husband was taking photos when a young man on a bicycle stopped to ask if he could help us. We don't know his name, but he confirmed what I'd learned through my research. The folks are Amish, but they wear "regular" clothes, have a church building, drive cars, etc. They don't mind photos, either. As it happened, the man, who came to Libby as a teacher, had family visiting from Ohio and they were at the general store. He invited us to stop by and meet them. His family members were conservative Amish. It had to be a God-thing. I felt so blessed to have that opportunity to talk to them, and they seemed equally interested to talk to a writer of Amish romances. I say all this to underline that *Peace in the Valley* is the result of hands-on research. It is certainly a work of fiction, but the starting point is real. The theological questions raised are difficult ones I still wrestle with.

As always, I want to thank my HarperCollins Christian Publishing team, in particular my editor Becky Monds, who helped me work my way through the sticky theological questions posed by the juxtaposition of these two Amish branches. Her help in making sure Levi and Nora's happily-ever-after didn't get lost in the shuffle was critical. Thanks once again to line editor Julee Schwarzburg for her attention to detail and her patience.

This final book in the Amish of Big Sky Country series wouldn't have been possible if I didn't feel strongly grounded in what I believe as a Christian and why. For that I want to thank my church family at Northwest Hills United Methodist Church. Y'all are a blessing!

Hugs and kisses to my husband for his patience and support throughout the research and writing of this series. You're the best!

Last but never least, thank you, readers, for sticking with me. You make it possible for me to live my life's dream as a full-time novelist. Godspeed!

Discussion Questions

1. Amish couples follow biblical principals regarding husbands and wives. Nora knows that when she marries Levi, she will be required to submit to his wishes. At the beginning of *Peace in the Valley,* she finds him bossy and wonders if she'll be able to be a good wife. This is very different from what mainstream culture tells men and women today. How do you feel about the verse that says "wives submit to your husbands"? Do you think it still applies to marriage today?
2. Nora stays with family members in Libby who are Amish but wear English clothes. The women don't cover their heads. Nora questions why God would care what clothes she wears as long as she believes in Him and obeys His laws. How would you answer her question? Do our clothes send a message to others about our beliefs?
3. Bishop Noah Duncan tells Levi the Amish chose to dress the way they do in order to not stand out. They don't want to call attention to themselves by wearing bright colors, immodest clothes, etc. Levi thinks they've called attention to themselves by dressing differently, that the rest of the world notices them because they are different. Do you agree with Levi? Does the way they dress have an impact on their faith?
4. The Amish don't play musical instruments because they

believe it makes that person stand out from others. They don't use them in their worship services. Their songs are slow and everyone sings them together. Do you agree with their assertion that the purpose of singing in church is to worship God and not to draw attention to individuals? What about Tammy's point that people in the Bible play musical instruments, sing, and dance for joy? Can both be right? Why or why not?

5. The Libby Amish are charismatic. They worship with great enthusiasm, dancing, shouting, and hopping up and down during their services. This is the antithesis of how Nora's Amish district worships. It's very emotional and she finds it powerful. Is there room for both kinds of worship? Is one "better" than the other? Why or why not?
6. The conservative Amish believe in a "living hope" of salvation. They believe it is arrogant to assume they know what God will decide about their eternal lives. The Libby Amish consider their more conservative counterparts as "lost" and in need of salvation. Do you agree? Why or why not?
7. Levi is so worried about Nora's behavior in Libby he feels compelled to talk with the church elders about it, even though she asked him not to. He sees it as his duty to hold her accountable. He believes he must be more concerned about her eternal salvation than whether he'll lose her. Do you feel he betrayed her trust, or did he make the right decision? Why or why not?
8. Much of the strife between the Kootenai and the Libby Amish districts portrayed in *Peace in the Valley* centers around the belief that it is possible to have a personal relationship with Jesus. The Libby Amish referred to it as a "closer walk." The Kootenai Amish felt it was egotistical and contrary to their

communal spirituality. Is there room for both approaches? Why or why not?

9. First Peter 3:7 says husbands must treat their wives with respect "as the weaker partner" and "heir to the gift of life." Levi and Nora seek a middle ground where they hope to approach marriage as a joint endeavor in which decisions will be made together. Ultimately Levi will be the head of the household, but he will respect and honor Nora. How is this different from the world's view of marriage today? Is it possible to find that middle ground? How would you approach it?

About the Author

Photo by Tim Irvin

Kelly Irvin is the bestselling author of the Every Amish Season and Amish of Bee County series. *The Beekeeper's Son* received a starred review from *Publishers Weekly,* who called it a "beautifully woven masterpiece." The two-time Carol Award finalist is a former newspaper reporter and retired public relations professional. Kelly lives in Texas with her husband, photographer Tim Irvin. They have two children, three grandchildren, and two cats. In her spare time, she likes to read books by her favorite authors.

✦ ✦ ✦

Visit her online at KellyIrvin.com
Instagram: @kelly_irvin
Facebook: @Kelly.Irvin.Author
Twitter: @Kelly_S_Irvin